BLACK
RIVER

BLACK

RIVER

STEPHEN HARRIS

BLACK RIVER

9 8 7 6 5 4 3 2 1

First Edition

Printed in the United States of America.

Book cover and interior design by Jonathan Sainsbury
Front cover image source: ©Shutterstock

978-1-68524-470-5 Paperback
978-1-68524-482-8 Ebook Epub
978-1-68524-483-5 Ebook Mobi

DEDICATION

For my wife. Without her I never would have pursued this crazy dream. All of my love for you, my angel.

CHAPTER I

Megan Prince slipped on the soaked swamp mud as she ran for her life. The rain and the wind made it hard enough for her to tell where she was going, but the deepening black mud beneath her bare feet made it seem hopeless that she would ever get there. She cried as she ran forward; her feet sinking into the dark mass of mud and decaying plant matter every step of the way. The rain beat against her naked body, making her feel like a thousand needles were piercing her flesh every few seconds. The sound of the howling wind and the creaking cypress trees were reassuring to her frightened mind.

This wasn't supposed to be how things worked out. Just two short months ago she was home. Now she couldn't figure out why she had ever decided to listen to her friends and to leave Rochester, her hometown in New York, for a trip to Myrtle Beach. If only she had listened.

She worked hard in school and she earned good grades, but the pressures of being young, cute, and full of life in high school had gotten to her by the time she turned sixteen. It started with an invite to a party that only the most popular people at her school were invited to attend. Soon, it was a couple of weekends a month that she told her mom that she was going over to her best friend Lena's house to study; only to attend another party with all the right people.

It was at one of these parties that things started to change for her. She couldn't remember the guy's name but she could remember that he was a strong Italian-looking-type from Brockport. She was so drunk that night that she had trouble saying the word bathroom, and he said all of the right things to her. The jello shots, however, couldn't erase the memory of what happened in the empty bedroom on the second floor of that house.

She couldn't move. She could only feel his weight on top of her, pinning her to the floor. She could feel the pressure and the pain that came with every single thrust of himself into her virgin body. Tears ran down her face and smeared her mascara as he crashed into her over and over. She thought the pain would never end, but eventually she felt his body tense and heard him screech in release.

He got off her, pulled his jeans on, and said something about it being great before telling her that he would go and get her a drink. He disappeared and left Megan there on the floor.

She bolted to the bathroom as soon as the door shut behind him. She thought she had lost control of her bladder, but once she inspected herself she discovered the wetness on her body was a disgusting mixture of semen, vaginal fluid, and blood. She cleaned herself up and read dozens of articles from her phone's google search before she realized this was a relatively normal part of sex for the first time.

She felt dirty, ashamed, and unwanted. Her friends assured her that the first time was always confusing, and she gradually buried the memories and continued to have fun through her junior year. They were right to an extent. Sex with her three successive boyfriends was much better. Still, she couldn't shake the idea that the whole experience she had with tall, dark, and Italian had taken something precious from her that she would never get back.

She went wild. Her schooling didn't suffer, but she began to take greater risks. She and her friends began regularly traveling to Buffalo, Syracuse, and even Cleveland a time or two to attend parties. Her mom was always placated by a plausible story and misplaced trust in her daughter and her daughter's friends. The thrill of getting away with being bad was better than the liquor, dancing, or sex.

When Lena texted her about taking a road trip to Myrtle Beach for an amazing spring break, Megan couldn't resist. Her head filled with images of palm trees, cold drinks, and dancing in paradise. All of that paled in comparison to the thrill of slipping away; her mom trusted that her little girl was being responsible.

Megan fixed her mom her favorite dinner, baked ziti and Caesar salad, and brought up being invited to spend spring break with Lena's family in the Adirondacks. All it took was a nice gesture on her part, assurances that Lena's parents would be there the entire time, and Megan had permission to go. The rush that she felt was indescribable as she hugged her mom, did the dishes, and rushed to her room to pack for the trip. Finally, she was treating herself for all of her hard work at school, and her mom didn't suspect a thing.

The beach was unlike anything Megan had ever seen and completely different than her expectations. Sure, there were palm trees—lots of them, in fact—but there also were tons of people and trashy little buildings along the shore.

That part was disappointing, but the parties, sun, and all of the excuses to break out that sexy little green romper made up for it.

They had been having more fun than she had ever dreamed of for their first two days on the beach. Then, as she was reapplying suntan oil to her copper legs, she saw him walking up to her.

He was the most gorgeous thing that Megan had ever seen. His tall frame, tanned skin, washboard abs, shaggy blond hair, and green eyes made Megan weak in the knees. Even his accent was sexy when he introduced himself. She was putty in his hand from the word, "Hey." When he asked her, and not her friends, to go with him to a house party in North Myrtle that night, she couldn't say no.

She took her time to make sure her long blond hair, red lips, and lime green dress were perfect before he picked her up at the hotel the girls were staying in. Lena wasn't sure about her going off by herself with a guy that she had just met in a place that she didn't know. Megan understood where she was coming from, but she assured her that she had nothing to worry about. When he texted her that he was out in front, she hugged Lena and said that if everything went well, she wouldn't see her until tomorrow, but she would definitely text her and let her know that everything was okay.

The house was up on stilts, which Megan thought was kind of odd. The party inside the house was beyond crazy. They were blaring hip-hop and party country songs so loud that it sounded like they were about to go into a concert venue instead of a house party. Megan was a little nervous, but when Jake slipped his large hand over hers, she melted and went inside with him. He introduced her to some of his friends, and she was relieved to see that two of them were girls. He grabbed her a beer in a plastic cup, and the two of them danced and drank for what felt like hours.

She was having the time of her life. Then things got even better as he kissed her in the middle of a living room dance floor. He led her to a room in the back of the house and Megan pounced on him. She locked her legs around his back as he drove into her, sending wave after wave of pleasure through her brain. It was the best sex that she had ever had, and she was pleasantly surprised when she felt herself tense, the pleasure reach its peak, and her body shudder as the release overwhelmed her senses.

She kissed him deeply as he pulled himself out of her and pulled his light blue shorts up over his hips. He told her to wait there, that he would get her a drink, and her heart sank as she thought back to tall, dark, and Italian. She waited for an eternity that only proved to be around six minutes before the door opened and Jake's perfect body stood in the doorway. She was relieved and pulled him back to the bed for another round of lovemaking.

Jake smiled and told her he would need a few more minutes to be ready to go again and handed her a red plastic cup with what looked and smelled like rum and coke.

She took a long swig of the sweet liquid. She felt her buzz deepen as she drank more while the two of them talked. She learned he was in college not far from the beach and was studying to be a physical therapist. She learned he was on the intramural rugby team and that they had made it to the final round of a tournament before losing to a squad from Georgia. She learned he enjoyed playing guitar and knew how to play some of the songs she listened to when nobody was around and she could dream of what it must be like to be loved like those songs described.

The more he talked, the sleepier she got. She pulled him towards her and kissed him but afterwards she had trouble reaching her arms toward him. Jake laughed and said she may have had one too many as she laid back on the bed. She could remember trying to tell him that she was ready for round two before the blackness at the edges of her vision overtook her.

The next thing she knew was that she couldn't move. The bed had been replaced by a hard surface that she guessed was made of metal, and her feet were bound and her hands were tied behind her back. She was still very foggy from the drinks she had but was alert enough to tell that she was in the bed of a vehicle, too small to be a truck, and that the vehicle was moving over a bumpy road. She couldn't see anything, and after a minute of panic, thinking she was blind, she discovered that she had a cloth bag over her head. She tried to scream for help but no sound escaped the duct tape over her mouth and whatever they had shoved inside of it.

Terror gripped her, and her mind began running dozens of possible scenarios in seconds. Was this some sort of elaborate prank? Had she been arrested last night? Had she been kidnapped? Ice water ran through her veins and she knew the last scenario was the most likely. Where were they taking her? Was she about to be raped or worse? In the midst of her terror, another emotion pushed its way to the surface of her consciousness: regret.

She wished she had stayed in Rochester with her mom. She chastised herself for being so stupid, thankful that nothing bad could happen to her. She wished she hadn't blown Lena off about Jake. She wished she was still in the hotel room with her friends who were probably worried sick about her.

That last thought brought a glimmer of hope. She had told Lena she would text her and let her know that everything was okay. She had been drunk, but she knew for a fact she hadn't responded to her texts in hours. The heat of the sun on her skin was proof of that, and she was certain that as soon as she didn't return to the hotel this morning, Lena would have gone to the police. Lena wouldn't let her get into trouble; she would make sure that she was safe, no matter what. Her spirit rose and she steeled herself with the knowledge that no matter what they were going to do with her, the cops would find her and she would eventually go home. The full stop of the vehicle jolted her back to reality.

She was fully alert as the sound of boots on gravel, the feeling of strong hands gripping her arms, and the sounds of cicadas and songbirds assaulted her senses. The darkness she had been enveloped in disappeared into a blinding white light. Megan shut her eyes against the shock and squinted her eyes. She was deep in a swampy forest. All around her were towering pines and cypress trees weighed down with heaps of ghostly Spanish moss. She saw there was a spot of open land that was sheltered from the sky by a canopy of trees that reminded her of a documentary she had watched in biology about the Amazon rainforest.

The strong hands that still gripped her arms began to drag her forward. The one on the left was a lanky white guy. His face was pockmarked with acne scars and he hadn't shaved in a good five or six days. He wore a dirty black t-shirt emblazoned with a stock car and the driver's number. He also had a badly done tattoo on the inside of his left forearm. She tried to make out what it was but he was swinging his arm too quickly with each step for her to get a good look.

The captor on her right was black and built like a truck. His face was obscured by a thick black beard, but the dirty white tank top he wore revealed massive arms that were marked by dozens of faded tattoos. She looked ahead and saw they were taking her to a large building that looked like a cross between a barn and one of the empty warehouses she had seen by the docks on Lake Ontario as a kid. The walls of the building were made of weathered old wood and covered in brown sheet metal that also covered the roof.

The plots of dozens of horror films flashed through her consciousness and her hope began to falter. She struggled against the two men, desperate not to enter the building ahead of her. The man on her right tightened his grip and jerked her arm forward so hard that she was afraid he would dislocate her shoulder.

"Keep fucking playing like that you little bitch and see what you gon' get," he said.

The sound of his voice, the voice of a man who wouldn't hesitate to follow through on his threat, chilled her to the bone and twisted her stomach into a fisherman's knot. She sobbed as they reached a metal door. The door opened and a man in a checkered button-down shirt and jeans stepped outside and addressed the two men who held her captive.

"She's gonna be a high dollar asset so see that she doesn't get any marks on her," the man said.

"Yes, sir," they replied.

They dragged her through the door, tears dropping from her eyes like rain. She blinked some of them away and saw that the floor was finished hardwood. She heard the sound of male voices and what sounded like a baseball game being broadcast over a television. Her captors dragged her for what seemed a mile before they opened a door to their right, pulled her inside of the room, and released her onto the floor. Rather than clattering to hard concrete, or even to the hardwood that her bare feet had slid against on the way to the room, she came to rest on soft carpet. She craned her neck and saw a fully made bed, a plush chair in the corner, and a television mounted on the wall across from the bed.

Her puzzlement melted away in an instant as she saw the white captor open a large pocket knife and step towards her. The rush wasn't from a thrill this time. This time it came from the need to fight for her survival. She thrashed wildly on the floor, her screams and curses muffled by the duct tape and gag.

"Quit yer wigglin'. Neither you nor me wants to cut your purty skin," the white captor said.

He took hold of her legs and she began to kick them as wildly as she could manage.

"I said to fuckin' quit it," he shouted. She continued fighting.

"You gonna give me a hand or are you gonna stand over there with your thumb up your black ass?" he asked the black captor.

Megan fought for all she was worth. She heard a metallic click-clack. She froze and her bladder released. She turned her head and saw the black captor pointing a pistol directly at her face. Urine began cascading down her thighs and her body began to tremble involuntarily. Her white captor took full advantage of the brief pause in the struggle.

"Took you long enough," he said as he cut the zip ties that bound her feet together. He dropped her legs, flipped her over on her belly, and repeated the procedure with her hands.

Once Megan was free, she retreated into the far corner of the small room. She hugged her knees against her chest and tried to make herself as small as she could.

"Now see, it wasn't so bad. You just try and relax. Somebody'll be by in a little while to explain exactly how this place is gonna work," the white captor said.

He closed the door and left her in silence. In a little while, a woman came to her and explained her situation.

Her hope sank, and for the next two months, her life became a living hell. The television in her room and the movies her owners continually broadcast onto it were her only escape. A week and three clients later, she came to the realization that she would never see her mom again. Lena had abandoned her.

She was forced to accept the reality that she would be used and brutalized until either she outlived her usefulness or she succumbed to one of the fantasies of her owner's clientele. She knew she could never escape, she would never be found, and they would never let her go. The regret for all she had done was inescapable and merciless.

She tried not to dwell on her regret as the days went by, but she couldn't escape thinking of the ways she had taken her mom for granted. Her mom had done the best she could for her. Being a single-parent in a world where the income of two parents was a necessity to raise a child was hard enough, but being the single-parent of a teenage girl had to be even more difficult. She now realized all of the times her mom had done without so she could have the best. Her mom hadn't even splurged to buy herself new clothes, but Megan always had the latest fashions in her closet, even to the point where she had run out of closet space. Megan had never taken the time to notice. She was too busy lying to the one person who had given everything for her. None of the thrills were worth what she had done to her mom. She wished she had told her how much she appreciated her. She wished that she could tell her she loved her one last time. She wished she had been a better daughter to her.

It had been on a day where she was filled with melancholy that she had left her room. They were allotted staggered shower times, and she had gone to the large shower room at the end of the hallway. She started her shower, hearing the thunder and the howling of the wind outside of the room's very small windows. She started rinsing the shampoo from her hair when an earth-shattering crash shook the building. She dropped to the floor of the shower and curled into a ball. She felt her body being pummeled with pine needles, sand, and other bits of debris as she lay on the floor of the shower room.

It took a second for her mind to process what was happening, and she chanced a glance at the direction of the loud noise. She saw that a massive oak tree had fallen, destroying the roof and one of the walls of the shower room. The rain was falling in sheets through a small opening between the trunk of the tree and what was left of the wall. The violent swaying of other trees behind the building cast ghastly shadows when the lightning flashed across the sky as the storm raged. This was her chance.

She picked herself up off of the floor and ran, naked, as fast as she could through the hole made by the oak. Her brain was so flooded with adrenaline that she didn't notice the small shards of glass, wood splinters, and bits of gravel that embedded themselves into the soles of her feet as she burst through the opening.

All she could think of was running. As she bolted into the forest, the wind and rain's assault on her naked skin relented; the canopy provided some cover from the storm. She tripped over the roots of a massive live oak tree, shredding the delicate skin on her toes, but still she got to her feet and ran onward. She had no idea where she was, nor did she know what direction she was running, but all she could think was, "Run! Freedom is out there!"

She had been running for at least five minutes before she heard the sound of an engine accelerating in the distance behind her. Her step quickened, her stomach knotted, and tears stung her eyes. She sobbed and ran, pleading that God would allow her to escape. Her feet sank ankle deep into the muck, slowing her pace. Her pleas to God now became frantic as she sloughed through the mud at half of the speed she was going before. The sound of multiple engines were now considerably closer. She summoned all of her will and plowed forward; her feet sinking knee deep with every stride.

The water-level abruptly rose from ankle to knee deep. A few seconds later, she was struggling through waist-deep muddy water that seemed to be moving through the swamp. The sound of moving water and the sights of branches being swept through the forest fortified her soul. If I can just make it to the river, she thought, I can let the current take me away.

She took four more steps, the black water was up just beneath her chest, and the cypress swamp revealed a wide river before her. Strangely, she remembered learning that most towns were built close to rivers when she was in grade school, and her prayers for help became prayers of thanks. This river would be her ticket to safety.

She took a step forward and felt like she was hit with a sledgehammer in the middle of her back. She lost the feeling in her legs and she fell forward into the water. The echo of a rifle rang out just before the current swept her under. She willed her legs to move, but her brain's commands went ignored. The current of the river swept her up and began moving her downstream. Her lungs burned and she tried to flip onto her back using her arms. The pain in her chest was nearly unbearable. She summoned what strength she still had and her head broke the surface.

She gasped for breath as the current swept her farther and farther downstream. She tried to paddle her arms but felt her body weakening. The most bone-shattering cold she had ever felt set in and it was all she could do to stay awake. Sleep would take her soon, she knew, and she no longer cared. Her thoughts drifted to her mother once more, and she silently hoped she knew how much she loved her. The blood that had been pouring from her gunshot wound persisted, and in a few seconds, Megan Prince's young life slipped away in that dark South Carolina river.

Chapter 2

Sheriff Raleigh Myers cruised down US Highway 52. The sheriff was on his way back to the Craven County Sheriff's Office after spending most of the morning tied up with a criminal trial in the city of Florence. He had been summoned to testify in the case of a Florence County man who had been charged with distributing OxyContin, fentanyl, and other drugs in Florence and the surrounding counties, among other crimes. The man in question, Tyrone Weeks, had been on the radar of the Craven County Sheriff's Department for some time, but none of the local junkies would ever give up exactly where he could be found. The same story had been true for Nelson Earle, the sheriff of Clarendon County, as he and his department had been chasing this ghost for years. His capture, however, had proven to be somewhat anticlimactic as Tyrone was arrested, stoned on his own product, during a raid of a luxury condo where he was hiding out in Myrtle Beach.

Raleigh, or Ray as he preferred to be called, had been

familiar with Weeks and his drug operation that had been running in northeastern South Carolina since he joined the department four years prior. For three of those four years, he watched as Sheriff Percy Killen had stood by, tacitly allowing the operation to continue unabated. Ray had thought that it was odd, but he also understood that the old man may have lacked the strength to stand up to those who thought that Weeks was "not a priority for the department." Either way, it technically was not Ray's job to say one way or the other which criminals got pursued and which were ignored.

Ray had been brought aboard to lead the department's fledgling special operations division. Ray's extensive experience in the US Army, along with his reputation around the county, made him the perfect man for the job. For three years he trained his small group of five tactical deputies and observed the political theater of the department. The constant positioning, alliance-building, and posturing of the heads of the various divisions was tiresome at best and disturbing at worst. It seemed that only Ray and his friend Captain Garrett McFadden, of the investigative division, were the only divisional heads without any designs on the department other than bringing offenders to justice. None of the posturing seemed to matter though. Sheriff Killen had been in charge for decades, and it didn't look like the old man was ready to throw in the towel any time soon.

That all changed five months ago. Sheriff Killen announced he would be retiring, triggering a special election for sheriff. Surprisingly, he urged Ray to run for the office in the special election. Ray had no interest in politics, but the more the old man talked, the more he convinced Ray that somebody who wasn't a politician needed to steer the department forward. The old man convinced him to throw his hat into the ring, but he didn't seem to have much of a chance against his challenger. Kelvin Matthews had been with the department for ten years and was very well connected with all of the right organizations in the county. Not only that, but his father was Thomas Matthews, the patriarch of one of the wealthiest and most powerful families in Craven County, not to mention all of South Carolina. The prospects of coming out of the special election with a win looked grim at best.

Ray had gone into election day not expecting to win but rather to simply fulfill his word that he would run. He had none of the advantages of his challenger. His father had managed to turn the struggling cattle ranch and pig farm his family had owned for generations around in the previous ten years, and his partnership with the owners of a regional barbecue restaurant chain, Lawson and Underhill's Whole Hog, even brought a smaller location to the economically struggling Queen's Bridge downtown. His mother was the principal of Queen's Bridge Senior High School and beloved by both the white and the black communities for the work she did for their children. Ray's military service was also an asset to his campaign, but it came nowhere close to matching the fortunes and the clout of the Craven County blue bloods: the Matthews', Burgesses, Magruders, Spates', Browns, and Manigaults.

The historic power of the county elites, in place since the time of the American Revolution, was unmatched and insurmountable. His quixotic campaign was doomed from the start, and the machine kept on spinning into the future. Election day rolled around, and as the votes were tallied, he was shocked. He had defeated Kelvin Matthews by a forty percent margin in the special election. The gears of the county machine seized up, and the first electoral change in centuries had occurred.

Ever since that day, Ray dedicated himself to serving the people of Craven County and protecting them from criminals like Tyrone Weeks and his crew. Ray had shaken the bushes in Craven County by raiding every crackhouse, juke joint, honky tonk, and even a couple of bait shops. In the process, he and his deputies managed to systematically dismantle all of Tyrone Weeks' operations in Craven County. For the first time in decades, the sheriff's department was serving a purpose beyond ticket writing, domestic dispute mediator, and incubator for future political careers. The change had not come without cost or friction.

His actions had ruffled some very powerful feathers in the county. There were murmurs, the same murmurs common to all Southern towns, that Sheriff Myers was taking too hard a stand on crime and that he would unwittingly incite violence in their little town if he kept it up. "Just look at the so-called war on crime they had declared in big cities like Chicago, New Orleans, and Los Angeles, and the violence that these flawed efforts had created," he had heard one of the town leaders remark at one of the town's exclusive garden parties.

Ray ignored their remarks and pushed forward. He even began to coordinate his efforts with the sheriff's departments of the surrounding counties to form a regional task force on drugs. It was through this effort of cooperation and the sharing of information that it was ascertained that Weeks was hiding in a Myrtle Beach condo. As a part of their task force, deputies from each of the five counties took part in the raid, and the heads of each county's sheriff's department were required to testify at Weeks' trial at the Florence Circuit Court.

Ray's testimony had lasted a mere twenty minutes, during which he was grilled by Weeks' attorney and glared at by Weeks himself. Weeks' defense was based upon the idea that the entire prosecution was driven by racism and a personal vendetta on the part of Clarendon County sheriff, who allegedly had disliked Weeks since the time when they were both classmates at East Clarendon High School. The jury didn't buy this tale, and they found Weeks guilty on charges ranging from racketeering to capital murder. Sentencing wouldn't be for a couple of weeks, but given the reputation of Judge McCrea and the South Carolina Department of Justice, Weeks getting a needle in his arm was a very real possibility.

Ray had intended to celebrate his first major victory as sheriff by chasing snapper off the Georgetown coast. The crackling of the police band changed all of that.

Now, as he turned off of Highway 52 and onto an old dirt service road that snaked for miles to the banks of the

Black River, the call he heard over the radio still rattled around in his head, "10-105, Black River at Morgan Swamp. 10-105, Black River at Morgan Swamp, requesting all available units, paramedics, and the coroner."

"10-105" was the signal code for "deceased person." He prayed that one of the local kids hadn't drowned out here while fishing or partying. It was common for kids in Craven County, especially boys and girls who leaned more to the redneck side of life, to spend virtually all of their free time out on the river. Just last week, one of his deputies caught two local boys as they were dropping a flat-bottomed boat into the water with all the tackle they would need, minus their fishing licenses but plus eight beers they stashed in a cooler in the boat.

Most of the time, the mischief that took place out here on the river climaxed with some broken bones or an unwanted pregnancy. Last summer, Malik Iverson, a thirteen-year-old from Queen's Bridge, had disappeared out here. Ray and others had taken part in a frantic search to find him, and after two days of searching, his body was found washed up on the bank near the Georgetown County line. That death had shocked the community to the core.

Vigils were held at the middle school and at several area churches for close to a month. The sheriff's department held talks at the area schools focused on water-safety. But just like with anything else, the community moved on and gradually the shock of his death faded from public memory. Ray was hoping the short memory of the community hadn't led to the loss of yet another young person before their life had truly gotten started.

He parked his truck on the side of the dirt road, right behind an ambulance that had shut the lights off, grabbed an olive-drab baseball cap with the letters "CCSD" embroidered across the front and got out of the vehicle. He had come directly from the courthouse so he was still dressed in his uniform, but he took a few extra minutes, grabbed the duffel bag he kept in the backseat, and quickly changed into a grey sheriff's department t-shirt and a pair of chest-high waders.

He shut the door to the vehicle, slid his holster and weapon on, and began trudging into the jungle of trees, vines, and mud before him. He could see the footprints that his colleagues left in the mud before him so it didn't take too much to figure out which direction the scene lay. The way to get there was tough-going though. Several times his feet sank deep into the black mud, and each time it took considerable effort for him to pull his feet free of the muck. It wasn't the worst terrain he had trudged through in his life, that crown belonged to Venezuela, but it was still difficult for even a seasoned outdoorsman like him to navigate. After a few hundred yards of trudging through the muck, battling mosquitoes, and suffering through the humidity, Ray spotted several people milling about near the water's edge.

As he approached, the mud he walked through gave way to shallow, dark water that seemed to swallow his feet with every step. The towering cypress trees that stood all around nearly blocked out the sun, soaking the area in dungeon-like gloom. Places like this always played havoc with the animal side of Ray's brain. The smell of rotting vegetation and stagnant water only seemed to heighten his sense of awareness and dread as he approached the scene.

"Good of you to show up, buddy," shouted Captain Garrett McFadden.

"At least I did. What've we got, Gary?" Ray asked.

Gary stepped aside to reveal the pale skin of a young woman, the left half of her body protruding from the shallow swamp water. He was relieved to see that he didn't recognize her face but he was horrified to see that where two eyes should have been staring back at him, masses of maggots shifted back and forth. She had been wedged inside of the massive root system of one the cypress trees, which made it difficult to see where the tree ended and where she began. Her flesh was swollen, cuts and scratches covering every inch of her body, and sections of her flesh that were underneath direct sunlight appeared to be more leather than skin. Her left leg was a mangled mess of flesh, meat, and bone. The visceral pale white, pink, dark red, and yellow of the wound contrasting with the dark water around her. Did she get run over by a boat?

Ray Myers had seen horrors like this before, but that was in another life. A life where you could stare into the darkness and laugh as it stared back at you. But here in the middle of this South Carolina swamp, it seemed as though that darkness that he once stared into is now laughing back at him.

"Not too good I'm afraid," Gary replied. "She's a Jane Doe. No ID, no clothes, no nothing."

"So, she isn't local then?"

"I ain't never seen her around here before. That don't mean anything in this day and age though," Gary replied. "Could be from out in Sandy Bay. Hell, she could even be from Florence for all we know. I figure she's probably somewhere between fifteen and twenty."

Just a kid. "She get torn up by a motor?" Ray asked.

"You ain't gonna believe this, but these two boys that found her," he pointed at two young boys being questioned by another of Ray's deputies off to the side. "They said when they saw her, a gator was going to town on her leg. Big one too. Shit, it had to be to have torn her up so bad."

"How'd they get it to run off?"

"They were carrying this old .22 rifle. The smaller boy shot at it about four times before it turned her loose and booked it back to the river."

"Shit," Ray said as he shook his head. "It's a thousand wonders that it didn't drag her out from under the roots. We got any idea about cause or time of death?"

"Lavion said he'd know more once he got her back to the funeral home."

Lavion McCutcheon was the owner of McCutcheon Funeral Home and Reception Center in downtown Queen's Bridge. The business had been in his family for generations, but it was only after desegregation and the bankruptcy of George Yancey who owned the white funeral home that their business, which traditionally catered to Craven County's black population, became the only place to have a funeral service done in the county. There were plenty of people in Craven County who weren't happy to leave their loved ones in the hands of "a bunch of niggers," and some of them had taken their dearly departed loved ones to funeral parlors in Florence, but most bit their tongues and trusted Lavion and his kids to do right by their loved ones. He had also been elected to the office of Craven County coroner ever since the office went up for election in 1976.

Ray nodded at this new information; his gaze still fixed on the gruesome state of the dead woman in front of him. "Alright, we find any physical evidence?"

"Nah, I'm afraid not. We looked around in about a five-hundred-yard radius, but the only thing outta place here is her and a few empty Coke bottles here and there. Besides, it's pretty certain that the water's washed away any kind of trace evidence we could hope to find either."

"Did the boys that found her say they noticed anything odd, like footprints or anything?"

"They were pretty well focused on her, buddy. I got here before the EMTs did, and I can tell you there weren't any footprints or any other kind of evidence that people were out here before us. I think she died somewhere upstream. We had that storm a couple of days ago. That'd explain how she got jammed up underneath these roots."

"Yeah, I think you're probably right. I seriously doubt she was out here in this swamp and somehow drowned, especially naked like she is. Even if this is a homicide, I doubt the killer would've killed her here and then gone to all of the trouble of pulling her up into those roots like that. They'd have just dumped by a road somewhere."

Ray crouched and took one last look at the corpse before shaking his head and saying, "Reckon that you've got a pretty good handle on things here. I'm gonna head back to the office and get started looking for any girls reported missing in the last couple of days. Take a picture of any notes you've made and text 'em to me too if you please, dude. Oh, and tell Lavion that as soon as he knows something to give me a call, please."

Gary nodded, "You got it, buddy. How'd it go with Weeks?"

Ray grinned, "Guilty on all charges. Son of a bitch is going away for life if I had to guess. Unless the judge decides to put a needle in his arm first."

Gary grinned, "It don't much matter either way. He ain't gonna be slinging any more dope or shooting any more rivals. That's what counts. You done good, buddy."

"I appreciate it Gary, but I couldn't have done it without you. I'm gonna head on back to the office. Lemme know if anything changes."

"Rest assured."

CHAPTER 3

Ray spent four hours searching and cross-referencing any missing persons that matched the description of the Jane Doe. Gary texted him pictures of his notes, and the description he had written down had been useful in narrowing his search, but there were still thousands of white women between the ages of fifteen and twenty with blonde hair who had been reported missing just in the previous month. It was like trying to find a needle in a stack of needles.

Just as he had pushed his chair back from his desk for a five-minute break, his cell phone began vibrating in his pocket. He finally got it out of his jeans pocket and saw that the name of the caller was Lavion McCutcheon. Lavion had found some more information about the Jane Doe. Ray offered to walk the city-block distance to the funeral home, but Lavion told Ray he'd be in his office in five minutes.

Five minutes later, a stocky man with skin the color of dark coffee walked into the office. Lavion was sixty-three years old, and his ever-widening midsection betrayed his tendency to over-indulge on Perlo, a local dish with striking similarities to Louisiana's jambalaya. His hair was almost completely silver, as was his small mustache, and his glasses had thickened, but the dark brown eyes behind them were as sharp as they had ever been.

"Somebody needs to get after those EMTs for wanting to just jerk her out the roots. If it wasn't for me and Gary, them boys would've tore her all up worse than she already is. I don't know what they in such a hurry for. Ain't like they're run out of hamburgers at the Hardee's before they get there," Lavion said as he sat down across from Ray's desk.

"I'll see what I can do. Y'all managed to get her outta there okay, right?"

"Yeah, we finally got Trent to come down with a little chainsaw so we could get her out of there. Be glad you weren't out there then. That alligator wasn't the only thing trying to make a meal off of her. The fish had been gnawing at her something awful underneath the water too. She's in bad shape."

"That might make identifying her a little tougher than it already is. What else you got to tell me?" Ray asked.

"You old enough to remember Rodrick McFall? Used to teach up at the high school when ya mama was still teaching English up there?" Lavion asked.

"Can't say it rings a bell."

"No matter, he's been gone close to thirty years. Moved on down to Orangeburg and got himself a doctorate in entomology. These days he teaches a class on it up at NC State as it relates to forensics. I took some pictures of the maggots that was crawling in her eye sockets and sent them on to Rodrick so you can establish a timeline. He said that with the amount of development they had, it means that she's been dead at least two days. So that would put time of death either on or immediately after that storm we had a couple of days ago."

"Okay, that's good to know," Ray added.

"Well, it don't stop there. I also think I have the cause

of death."

"She didn't drown, did she?"

"She might have, but if she did it wasn't on account of her being a bad swimmer, I'm betting. girl's been shot too," Lavion said.

"How do you know that for a fact?"

"I been in the funeral home business since before your daddy and mama started dating. I know entrance and exit wounds when I see 'em."

"How many has she got?" Ray asked.

"She got an exit wound above her left breast about the size of a quarter that matched with a tiny little entrance wound on her back. There's another entrance wound on her back too, but I didn't see where it exited. Probably still in her unless it finagled its way out the exit."

"I doubt that happened. Quarter-sized exit wound; entry point about the size of a pen?" Ray asked.

"That's about the long and short of it."

"That's probably from a .222 or a .223 then."

"The entry wounds look about like my deer rifle's on the target when I take it out there to the range," Lavion said.

"Could be a deer rifle or an AR. Won't really know until the pathologist comes down here. Either way, I reckon we've got a murder on our hands," Ray said.

Lavion shook his head, "There ain't been a murder around here since 2009 when that Cromartie boy got mad at his brother and shot him at the family reunion."

"I know. Mom told me about it when I was in Afghanistan. Do me a favor and keep this to yourself," Ray said.

"Boy, you know you ain't gotta worry about me running news around town," Lavion replied.

"I know I don't, but I'm just letting you know how serious this is. I'm not kiddin'. Don't say anything to your kids. Don't even say anything to Loretta. If any of them ask, say that you could only pronounce her dead. Nothing else, okay?"

"Say no more. But answer me this. How come you so worried about word of this getting out? On account of it being an active investigation?"Lavion asked.

"Yeah, partly because it's an active investigation. It's partly because I don't want there to be any rumors around town until we know for sure what we're dealing with. You know as well as me that once that rumor mill starts turning, everybody in the county will be clued into what we've got going on. Then whoever shot her has gotten a head's up to cover their tracks or to skip town."

Lavion nodded, "Don't you worry none. I'll keep it all locked down."

"Thank you, Lavion. I appreciate you. I'm sure that whoever this girl is, she's probably got people who love her, and they'll appreciate what you've done for her too."

Ray clasped Lavion's hand, "I just hope you find whoever did that to her. A girl so young, with her whole life ahead of her, left out in an ol' swamp to be ate. Ain't no sense in it at all," Lavion said.

"Gary and I will see to it that they spend the rest of their life at Lee Correctional. You can bet on that," Ray replied.

Lavion gave a grim smile. "I got faith in you. I'll call you in the morning and let you know when the pathologist gets here."

"I'd appreciate that."

"Oh, I almost forgot to ask you something. I'm hosting the McCutcheon family reunion this coming Saturday, and I'd appreciate it if you could ask your daddy to give me a call sometime this evening so he could give me some prices on a whole hog for the party."

CHAPTER 4

Gary McFadden had knocked off a little early that afternoon and headed home. There wouldn't be any new information about who the girl they had found in the swamp was until the next day anyway. Ray agreed and told his friend and colleague to go and get some rest. Gary was afraid he was about to need all the rest that he could get.

It was two o'clock in the afternoon when Gary walked out of the sheriff's office and hopped into his truck. He drove the seven miles to his double-wide in relative silence. Only the sounds from the country radio station in Charleston were to be heard as he zipped past newly plowed cotton fields, ancient gas stations with attached barbecue restaurants, and the seemingly endless miles of forests and swamps that dominated the South Carolina coastal plains.

He knew he should be trying to quit. He knew how much his kids hated it, never mind Nora's consistent disapproval. But he couldn't keep himself from smoking two

Camels from the pack he had bought, along with a plate of grits and sausage, this morning at Cooper's Gas and Grub on Highway 521. The action of fishing a cigarette from the pack, the striking of the butane lighter from his shirt pocket, and the euphoric calm feeling from the first draw he took of the cigarette were all necessary today.

He turned off the highway and into Craven Estates, the small trailer park that he lived in along the Clarendon/Craven county line. He pulled up to his double wide, which he had meticulously maintained with new paint, a gravel drive, and two lush flower beds that flanked the red wood deck to the back door. After he watered his hydrangeas and his palmetto trees, smoking a third cigarette as he did so, he ambled up the steps to the deck, mashed out the cigarette in a metal bucket beside the door, and stepped inside.

He kicked off his boots on the linoleum floor of the kitchen and padded into the laundry/mudroom immediately to the left of the back door. He tried everything that he could to keep himself busy, but the image of the dead girl wouldn't go away. Every time he blinked, he could see her sun-cooked flesh entangled in the roots of that old cypress tree. It was like a scene from one of the old David Cronenberg horror movies he had seen as a high school kid in the late eighties.

He tried to exorcise the images from his head as he stripped off his clothes and tossed them into the wash. It had clawed its way back as he started the machine and walked his naked body down the hallway and into the bedroom. He started the shower, thinking that the physical act of washing his body might have the effect of washing his mind clean of the horror of the day. For three minutes his mind was free before the specter reemerged to torment him once more.

How in the hell did she wind up way out there? How come she was naked? Dear God, I hope that she was long dead before that alligator got to her. He turned off the water and stepped over to the sink. Maybe shaving would do the trick.

He looked at himself in the mirror, thinking for the first time in a while about how much his hair and his face was beginning to show all of his forty-three years. He couldn't remember how so much of his black hair had been streaked with grey, and he hadn't noticed that all of the stubble that poked through his chin and cheeks was now silver instead of black. He was still in great shape for a man his age, though his midsection betrayed the fact that he liked to enjoy a beer or two every now and again.

He hadn't really noticed until now just how much he was showing his age. He had never felt old, despite the grey in his hair. That was until he had seen that girl. Seeing something like that made you old in the blink of an eye. Just like having kids had made him a man. Then the thought that his subconscious was suppressing broke through his defenses. Callie Anne is about that girl's age, and she even looks a whole lot like her.

He wrapped the towel around his waist, grabbed his personal cell phone, and walked to the kitchen. An irrational feeling of dread seized his stomach as he opened the contacts on his phone. He found Callie Anne in the contacts, along with all of the emojis she had put next to her name, and he almost hit the call button. He stopped, thinking that she may be busy and that kids these days preferred texting to talking anyway.

"Hey honey, this is dad. Just was thinking about you and wanted to make sure you are okay. I love you."

He hit send and heard the zip noise the phone made whenever a text had been sent. He reached into the fridge, and though he knew he probably shouldn't since he would have to be back at work bright and early in the morning, he grabbed a bottle of his favorite beer. He had just taken a long gulp of the cold liquid when his phone pinged. He breathed easy when he saw that it was a text from his little girl.

"Hey Daddy! I'm okay. Just hanging out with Marion and some friends at the mall in Pineville. Why you ask?? You doing good too, old man?? lol, I love you too!!"

She was okay. Thank God she was okay.

"Good to hear, honey. Just got off work a little early and-" He stopped typing. What was he going to do? Was he going to tell her that he wanted to make sure she was okay because he had been called to a scene where a girl who was about her age had been found naked, tangled in cypress roots, and had been partially eaten by an alligator? He resumed typing.

"Just got off work early and I was just thinking about you is all. You have fun with your friends, okay? Love you honey." He hit send and took his phone and his beer to the couch in the adjoining den. His phone pinged again as he sat down:

"Will do! Love you Daddy! Have a great afternoon off!" she replied. He smiled when he saw the kiss emoji that she added at the end of her text message. It was the same thing Nora did whenever she texted him goodnight.

As he took another long swig of his beer, he couldn't shake the feeling he needed to talk to someone about what his day was like. That was against his nature. He would much rather keep his thoughts and feelings bottled up rather than talk to anyone about what was troubling him. It was that bottle inside that had ended his marriage to Lisa ten years ago.

She left on a Tuesday and filed the divorce papers the previous Monday. She didn't clean him out. She didn't threaten him with never letting him see his kids again. She just told him when he got home from work on that Tuesday night that it wasn't fair to the kids, to her, and to him to keep everything locked inside of his head; whiskey being the lock that kept it there. He was angry with her, for sure, but over the course of the months that followed and the finalization of their divorce, he finally realized that she had done it not because she didn't love him, but because she did love him. That hurt the most.

Lisa and the kids moved to Charlotte after he and Lisa had both agreed that them staying in Queen's Bridge was not the best for them. Divorce was more common these days, but kids could be cruel in a small town. A fresh start somewhere new could nip that in the bud. She had remarried, to a doctor of all people, and Gary and he had immediately hit it off. He was happy for her and the kids and the world of good that the move and Lisa marrying Robert had done for them.

Gary had dated a few women here and there over the years, but none had ever proven to be the right kind to stick around. Gary worked on himself through it all; becoming a better person with each passing day and with each relationship. He had even learned to talk about what was going on inside of his head and stopped using alcohol as a crutch to make it through. Still, women came and went. That was until he met Nora.

He finished his beer and he got up to grab another one. The relief of talking to his daughter had not allowed him to shake the profound feeling of dread. He knew he wouldn't be able to sleep that night if he didn't get it off of his chest. He needed to hear her voice.

She lived in Charleston, nearly two hours away, and she had told him how to video call not long after they had started dating. Now, he used it to talk to and see her at least twice a week. If I can just see her and tell her about it, maybe I'll be okay.

The call rang several times. The front-facing camera of his phone reminded him that he had not yet dressed from his shower. The call ended with a message telling him that she was unavailable. He took a swig of his beer and got up to finish getting dressed when his phone pinged. The text was from Nora.

"Hey lover. It's early and I don't have my face on yet. Everything okay??"

"You don't have to go to any trouble for me." He took a deep breath. "I just have had a pretty rough day and wanted to talk to you about it," he replied.

In a few seconds, three bubbles appeared at the bottom of the screen telling him that she was typing a response.

"Of course I am going to take the time to get all girly for you! You've never seen me like I am during the day, baby," she replied and sent another text.

"I'm so sorry that you've had a rough day. Is there anything that I could do to help you forget about it?" she replied with the wink emoji.

He was pulling on his gym shorts and a t-shirt as he answered. "Just would like to see you and talk to you about it is all, honey."

"Tell ya what, lover. I'm gonna cancel my morning appointments tomorrow, rush home, and get myself all dolled up. Then I'll be at your place and you can tell me all about while I help you. . .forget." She ended the text with the purple devil emoji.

This woman was unlike any that Gary had ever known. "Sounds good to me. I'll get started figuring out dinner. Be safe, babe. Love you." he replied.

"Can't wait to see you too, big guy. Love you," she replied with the kiss emoji.

She still managed to amaze him. He was apprehensive when he had first met her. He had never thought about what it would be like to love a woman like her, but he had still fallen hard and fast for her. Now, he couldn't understand why he was so apprehensive to be with her in the first place.

He got up and pushed the darkness that clouded his mind away as best as he could as he busied himself with preparing for the incredible night he was sure to have coming his way.

CHAPTER 5

FRIDAY, 7:33 AM
CRAVEN COUNTY SHERIFF'S OFFICE
QUEEN'S BRIDGE, SOUTH CAROLINA

Ray hunkered down and sifted through the thousands of missing persons fitting the description of the girl lying in the funeral home a few hundred yards from his office. By 11:00 pm, he managed to narrow the pool of possible matches from somewhere in excess of seven thousand to somewhere around one hundred and twenty. All reported missing were from thirty-seven states and four Canadian provinces. He decided that he had done just about everything he could for the day and trudged out to his truck and made the twenty-minute drive to his home out past the rural community of Hebron. Once inside the renovated farmhouse he called home, he peeled off his clothes, jumped into the shower, and collapsed onto his bed sometime after midnight.

At 4:00 am he got up, pulled on his sneakers, and ran his daily four miles before breakfast. The morning run was often his favorite part of the day. He didn't listen to music while he ran; instead he preferred to enjoy the music of the crickets, frogs, and cicadas as he ran down those old backroads he grew up on. The run did little to clear his head this time.

Who were you and where did you come from? What were you doing out there in that swamp all by yourself like that? Was it a boyfriend that shot you or was it somebody that took you out there to rape you?

The questions stayed with him throughout his run, shower, and drive to the sheriff's department. Where were you when they shot you? The thought stuck in his mind like an old song on the radio. He turned the thought over and under, backward and forward, as he sat behind his desk, sifting through missing persons reports. At 6:30 am, Captain Gary McFadden knocked on the door to Ray's office.

"Mornin', buddy."

"Morning, Gary. What's going on?"

"Just was gonna stop in and tell you that I've got the official statements of the two boys. Their story is pretty much the same as yesterday. They were going out there to do a little fishing. They were trying to figure out the best place to stake their claim when they saw and heard that gator thrashing this way and that. They said at first they thought it had a hold of a dead deer, but they figured out it was a person pretty quick. Had that little .22 to shoot snakes and managed to scare the gator off with that, and the other boy called 911 on his cell phone. It's a good thing them boys did what they did too, 'cause that gator would've torn that girl apart."

Ray nodded his head. "They say that they saw anybody else out there? Or really anything out of the ordinary?"

"Nah, just the body and a few pieces of trash out there the storm blew down river. I went over the whole area with a fine-tooth comb and I didn't find shit," Gary said.

"Hopefully the pathologist finds something we can go on. You hanging in there okay?" Ray asked.

"Hanging in there like a bad tooth. I talked to Carrie Anne a little last night. That seemed to help some."

"What grade is she in now?"

"She's getting ready to start her senior year. It's getting real, buddy. I'm officially old," Gary said.

"That ain't true. You ain't even hit your prime yet. Besides, that girlfriend you got down in Charleston is keeping you young, I bet," Ray replied.

"She does what she can. Still, don't stop the creaking in my joints or the pictures in my head, though."

"I know all about that, unfortunately. That Jane Doe didn't make it any better, either. I tell ya, Gary. Seeing that girl like that was one of the most awful things I've seen in years," Ray said.

"You mean more awful than watching Clemson win the national championship?" Gary quipped with a smile.

Ray grinned. "Yeah, including seeing Clemson win the national title."

Gary chuckled, "Well speak for yourself, 'cause seeing them hoist that trophy in the air was about the most awful thing I've seen in my life to date."

"I had cut it off before the trophy ceremony. I saw plenty of shit in the army I didn't want to, and I was gonna be good and damned before I chose to sit and watch that," Ray replied.

"Seeing that kid yesterday took me back to some dark places, dude. Reminded me of some things I'd rather forget or at least tell myself only happened overseas. I can't hardly imagine some of that shit I saw popping up around here. I have to keep telling myself this isn't combat and I can't go shoot the guy who killed her. I've got rules to follow," Ray said.

"I'd like to hunt 'em down too, buddy. But you've gotta take some solace knowing that one way or the other, we're gonna see that they're punished," Gary replied.

Talk of punishment triggered the memory. Images of blood and body parts appeared behind his eyelids, the metallic smell of coagulating blood mixed with cordite whiffed through his nostrils, and the sounds of chopping, sizzling, gunshots, and bone-chilling screams echoed in his ears. He squinted his eyes shut and took several deep breaths until the assault on his senses slowly faded into the darkness of his subconscious.

"You good, buddy?" Gary asked.

"Yeah," Ray lied. "Just had a random attack of nausea. Think the milk I put into the eggs this morning may have turned. Anyway, all I'm saying is that I can't get her outta my head like I kinda could over there. I need to get justice for her."

"I understand what you're saying, buddy. And believe you me, I want justice for her too. You had any luck trying to identify her?"

"Not really. I've narrowed it down to a little over one hundred possibles. You'd be doing me a huge favor if you'd give me a hand trying to eliminate some of these missing girls from our search."

"Absolutely. Whatever you need, buddy."

"Thanks, dude. I emailed half of them to you."

"I'm already on it."

Gary got up from his chair and ambled out to his desk, closing the door to Ray's office as he did so. Ray started sorting through the missing person files once again, but his mind was occupied by the sudden attack of memory he experienced moments earlier. He hadn't thought about that night in years. It had been even longer since the memory of it had assaulted him so suddenly and violently. He closed his eyes, mumbled a stream of unintelligible words under his breath, and forced his mind to focus on the task at hand.

CHAPTER 6

Ray had cut his list of sixty possible persons down to twenty when he heard a knock at the door to his office. He had closed the blinds on his floor-to-ceiling windows but assumed that it was just Gary telling him that he had sorted through all of the missing person reports.

"It's open." He said, never taking his eyes from his computer screen.

He heard the door open and then footsteps. "Good morning, Sheriff Myers. I hope we aren't interrupting anything important?"

He looked up from his computer screen and was surprised to see Reginald Manigault, the Craven County manager sporting a televangelist smile alongside Queen's Bridge Mayor Elrod Tisdale. Ray was surprised to see Manigault, but to be accompanied by the mayor, who spent most of his time promoting the business climate of Queen's Bridge on social media and the rest of his time fucking around with one of the waitresses down at the

Huddle House behind his wife's back, was an even bigger surprise to Ray.

"Gentlemen," Ray began. "To what do I owe the pleasure?"

"Elrod and I just wanted to drop by and see how things are going for you. I personally wanted to congratulate you for working so hard to take drugs off of our streets these past months. You've done this community and, if you ask me, the state, a huge service by spearheading that takedown," Manigault said as he and Elrod each took a seat in front of Ray's desk.

Reginald Manigault was a tall, lanky man of around six-and-a-half feet, a full four inches taller than Ray, with silver hair, a finely manicured mustache, and wore a tailored three-piece suit. He was the patriarch of one of Craven County's oldest families, the Manigaults, who had moved to the area from Charleston sometime between the Revolution and the War of 1812. The Manigaults, like the other blue-blooded families who ruled the county and the surrounding area like the oligarchs of ancient Greece, the barons of Medieval Europe, or the Cosa Nostra of twentieth century Sicily, came from old money.

They almost never discussed how they had made their fortune. After all, the façade of humility was an admirable quality in the Deep South. Though anybody who dared to brave the collections at either the University of South Carolina, University of North Carolina, or University of Georgia could eventually discover that they had made their fortune back when cotton was king and black folks were under the lash. These days that sort of thing wasn't politically convenient, so Reginald and his sons had embarked on a rebranding campaign for their family some years ago.

They used a small portion of their fortune to construct a new rec facility for young people in the black section of town, and they also spearheaded the effort to get Lee Avenue, one of Queen's Bridge's main roads was named for Confederate General Robert E. Lee, changed to Martin Luther King Jr. Boulevard.

Reginald and his boys touted this effort as a win for

STEPHEN HARRIS

progressive values and a step towards healing the racial wounds of Craven County. Many people, however, saw it for what it was. It wasn't about healing racial wounds or progressivism. Hell, the rec facility wasn't even about helping young black kids have a safe place to hang out after school. All of it was a big production aimed at securing the political support and sympathy of Craven County's black voters to solidify the Manigaults' place of power in the county government.

The sad thing was that the Manigaults weren't the only ones tearing communities apart by removing names, monuments, and flags and declaring them victories for a new progressive America that was as fake as their outward concern about social justice. The same thing was happening across the south from Tulsa to Orlando and Richmond to Houston. Even Thurman Spates, the former governor, now senator, of South Carolina, who also happened to be a Queen's Bridge native, a few years prior, had ordered the removal of monuments to the Confederacy and the renaming of streets in the name of what he had termed "a better world." That had endeared him to all the coastal elites, Hollywood crowd, and the media.

Of course, the real irony of it all was the fact the same people in power who pushed for these changes were often the same people whose current power and fortunes were provided by their families' support or profited off of either slavery, segregation, or both. Those sorts of conversations were off limits, and anyone seriously discussing it was ridiculed at the county level or discredited. Even the schools seemed more concerned with telling people what to think instead of showing them how to think for themselves. If only ignorance and under-education were not also implicitly encouraged by these people in power. Then some real healing could occur.

Some would say that was starting to change in Craven County. Ray's election to the office of sheriff was a shock to the status quo of the county. It represented the possibility of a challenge to the political détente that had held sway ever since the years immediately following the

Revolution. If the people were prepared to support an outside candidate for sheriff, maybe they would do the same in other county or state offices. Some had even said that Ray, provided he was successful as county sheriff, might be destined for higher offices.

Ray, however, knew better than to think that. He didn't intend to pursue politics any further than the office of sheriff. Being an officer in the US Army for fifteen years had shaped how much he hated politics. His bucking of politically expedient but practically redundant guidelines had endeared him to his guys. Conversely, it had also made him a liability in the eyes of some of his superiors who took pleasure in locking him into the purgatory of the rank of major. Sheriff was his only stop on the political ladder and he was fine with that. He did, however, hope that his improbable victory inspired others to aspire for political office in Craven County.

Elrod, on the other hand, was something of a contrast to the refined southern gentleman that Manigault was. Elrod was short, pear-shaped, and the son of a poor black sharecropper out in Rehobeth. He was one of the first black men, other than Lavion McCutcheon, to open a business in Craven County; an old juke joint out on Highway 521 on the Craven/Georgetown line near Andrews. He never admitted to it, and why would he, but illegal liquor and gambling allowed him to amass a small fortune that he used to endear himself to the black community. Sponsoring pig pickin' events, setting up a college fund, and shoveling a fair amount of blame on the law enforcement community did the rest.

Still, that influence alone wasn't enough to win him the prestigious, if powerless, office of mayor. His bootlicking of the Manigaults and the Burgesses had ultimately secured him the support he needed to win the mayoral election. His continued loyalty and service to his patrons had meant that for the last twenty years he had served as mayor.

Neither of these men had been supporters of Ray's populist campaign for sheriff, and neither of them had been particularly helpful since he had been in office. Those facts made this visit particularly strange.

"Well, I appreciate that, fellas. I really do. But as far as everything else goes, I think I've got a pretty good handle on things. Unless there was something else y'all need to discuss? I doubt y'all would personally come down here just to congratulate me and to check and see if I have everything I need to do my job. Y'all could've done that with a phone call," Ray replied.

"Well, Sheriff. Of course we'd come down here to personally congratulate you on removing a dangerous criminal from our county, but now that you mention it, there is something else we'd like to talk about with you," Manigault admitted. "We understand that a body was discovered by some kids yesterday out in Morgan Swamp."

"Yeah, a couple of boys were going to do some shore fishing out there, and they found a body stuck up in the roots of a cypress trees. It was a young white female. Signs are that she had been out there for at least a couple of days. We don't know who she is or how she died yet, but Detective McFadden and I are working multiple leads on missing persons, and we've got the pathologist coming down today from Florence to do the autopsy. We should know something by the end of the day, hopefully."

Ray held back the information that Lavion had given him about the gunshot wounds. No need to show them all the cards he was holding just yet.

"That's just tragic. Wouldn't you agree, Elrod?" Manigault said in his refined drawl.

"Oh yes, I sure would. It's always a terrible tragedy when a young person dies," Elrod replied.

"Yes, a terrible tragedy," Manigault continued. "But it's that tragedy we wanted to discuss with you. As you know, Sheriff Myers—"

"You can call me, Ray. That's fine."

"Thank you, Ray. As I was saying, you know that this month is pretty big for business for Craven County. We've got pig pickin,' the bass fishing tournament on Lake Murray, and the mac and cheese festival all taking place over the next three weekends."

Manigault paused and looked directly at Ray. "Yes, I am fully aware of these events. I'm just a little confused as to what it has to do with the dead woman we found yesterday."

"Well, Ray, it is related in a couple of ways. First, you know that we are expecting large crowds of people from all over to be in town, so we're gonna need most of your deputies to help with security for the festivals."

"I'm aware of that."

"Which brings me to my second point. I'm not sure what good it's going to do for the local economy if we are publicly investigating the death of a young woman in our county. You know as well as I do how people's imaginations start running wild whenever a tragedy like this takes place, and the last thing we want is for people to not feel safe coming into town."

Ray had to work to control what words he chose. "I understand what you're saying, Mr. Manigault, but–"

"Reginald, please."

"Reginald. I understand what you're saying, but the Scotchman station on 52 is reason enough not to feel safe coming into town. And that's not even mentioning the condemned restaurant across the street from it. I don't see how investigating the death of this young woman is going to affect the festivals in any way. It's not like I'm gonna be having a press conference about it."

"Think about it, Ray. You know how these rumors get started. It starts with somebody telling someone else that she drowned, then they tell someone else that she was drowned, who then goes on to tell someone else that she was drowned, just like that boy from last year, and that we've got some kind of a killer roaming the county. You see what I'm saying?" Manigault asked.

"Sure, but the boy last year was an accidental drowning. And we still don't know what happened to this girl. Even if there was some killer out there, the fact they were of different races and genders pretty much guarantees they were separate instances. So, I don't see how anybody can seriously draw any conclusions or connections between the two, and I definitely don't see how it can negatively affect the festivals."

Ray was working overtime controlling his tone and volume. All he could think of, as they were practically asking him to let this case go, or at the very least put it on the backburner for a while, was the question of how they would pursue justice if that girl was the daughter of either one of those men. Of course, they would demand that Ray and his department tirelessly investigate her death, and Ray would do so relentlessly. Asking him to back off for the sake of making a little extra money for the county seemed inhuman.

"And I'm not sure that you've considered the racial implications that the timing of your investigation will have for the community," Elrod said.

"What racial implications are you talking about?" Ray asked.

"The fact that this is a young white woman. The black community will see you and your department as giving special attention to cases involving white victims over African-Americans. Let's face it, Sheriff. If you give the full court press to this, then people in the African-American community will start wondering if you'd do the same sort of thing if the victim was a young black girl."

Ray gripped the arm of his chair so hard that his knuckles turned white and his fingertips ached against the hard wooden surface. He was done being nice.

"And who do you think would give them such a crazy idea, Mayor Tisdale?" Ray asked.

Elrod blinked and readjusted his mouth. "Nobody will have to give them that idea, Sheriff. They'll see it for what it is. You pulling deputies from keeping black people safe at the festivals in favor of a white girl who, though it is a tragedy that it happened, is dead. It's as clear as day that our county's top cop isn't all that worried about black people. I don't think I have to tell you how poorly my people view the police given all of the police shootings all over America. You keep pushing this dead white girl and you're running the risk of bringing that kind of righteous anger to our town. And I'm not so sure it wouldn't be warranted, Sheriff."

Ray was about to respond to the soulless race hustler when Manigault spoke up.

"Gentlemen. I understand that this is a sensitive topic for everyone, and believe me when I say that both Elrod and I want justice for the poor girl just as much as you do. All we are asking is that you think about the needs of the town as you move forward. No need to sacrifice the opinions of the many for one individual. I believe you have a bright future here, Ray, and I don't want to see you pursue anything that might jeopardize that future."

Ray seethed at Manigault's threat. Still, he sat in silence.

"The fact of the matter is people disappear and turn up like this girl did all over America every day. It's tragic but it happens. I just hope that you don't allow it to hurt the community."

Manigault stood and buttoned his coat. Elrod, seeing that his master had risen, followed suit. "If there's anything that either I or Elrod can do to assist you, please let us know. I trust you to do what is best for our community, Ray."

And with that, Manigault and Elrod slipped out of Ray's office, waving and speaking to deputies they passed on their way out of the small building. Gary watched them leave and made a beeline to Ray's office. He closed the door and looked at Ray, still gripping his chair. Gary furrowed his brow and spoke, "What the fuck was that all about?"

Ray took a sharp breath through his nostrils and exhaled, "We've just been asked to fucking let this go."

"What? Why?"

"Apparently, this dead girl has the potential to wreck our economy and to stir up a hornet's nest of fake racial bullshit because I'm white and she's white, so I clearly only care about white people."

"That doesn't make any fucking sense though. Don't those assholes know that you won the election by winning the black vote? Hell, you told the news that the driving force behind stopping Tyrone Weeks was because he was leading young black men into lives of crime."

"I know, and so do they. It's just political bullshit. They're still pissed that I won the election, and they know their empire isn't as strong as it used to be. So, they're doing some major dick swinging."

"Still doesn't make it any less bullshit, though."

"I know. Honestly, I hope that's all it is."

"What do you mean by that?"

"Nothing," Ray said after a pause. "Just talking to hear myself talk, I guess."

"Well, I wouldn't get too worked up about it. I was gonna let you know that Lavion called and said the pathologist had gotten here from Florence. Then I saw those two fuckers walking in. Figured I'd better wait till they left. I figure the autopsy will be about done after you and I go over to the Waffle House. You could use some fresh air and some grits after that, buddy. C'mon. I'll drive."

Ray smiled as he got up from his chair, re-tucked his shirt into his Carhartt pants, and followed Gary out of his office. The nerve those two had to come into his office and try to leverage the town, economy, and delicate racial peace they enjoyed against him in order to back off the case of the girl lying over at the coroner's office was unsettling. They could be right. She could just be a runaway or a vagrant who had tragically met her end. There were thousands more just like her all across America who turned up dead every day. That much Manigault was right about.

But Ray couldn't shake her from his mind. At the end of the day, that girl was a person with a family who loved her and definitely missed her. The least Ray could do for them is to figure out who she was, find out who the people who loved her were, and bring her home to them. He also owed it to her family to figure out who put two bullets into her back before she wound up on the river bank.

CHAPTER 7

Gary was right. Grits definitely seemed to take some of the edge off of the outrage that still simmered in Ray's soul. He had ordered a western omelet smothered, covered, capped, and chunked with a side of crispy bacon and grits. Gary, on the other hand, ordered three waffles, link sausage, and hashbrowns scattered, smothered, and covered. As they sat there enjoying their breakfast, Ray sat mostly silent as he listened to Gary regale him with stories of fishing expeditions, epic bar crawls, and female conquests.

Gary was a good dude. At forty-three, he was seven years older than Ray and had been a part of the Craven County Sheriff's Department for the past twenty-one years. He was a tall enough man, standing right around six feet tall, but he was built like a freightliner. His presence alone was enough to intimidate nearly anybody, but his laid-back personality couldn't be further from the image he projected.

He had been married once but it hadn't lasted. That

was seven years before Ray returned to town three years ago, and his kids were in their mid- to late teens now. He saw them every other weekend. It's only three hours from Queen's Bridge to Charlotte, but as they got older, the more they wanted to do their own thing.

Gary had gotten sober two years ago and started seeing a woman who lived and worked down in Charleston. Ray had never met her, nor seen any pictures of her, but he knew that Gary wouldn't have mentioned he could see himself possibly marrying her if he wasn't crazy about her. Ray would believe it when he saw it. He was sure that Gary McFadden liked the idea of marrying her, but Ray also knew that he liked being able to spend the weekends with her and then have the week all to himself. He swore up and down that he would retire in four years, and if he was still hooked up with her, then Ray figured that would be when marriage would happen.

Ray sipped his coffee as Gary finished the last few bites of his waffles along with a story about how he went on a deep sea fishing trip off of Hilton Head with a female captain. The meat of the story was that he had the fight of his life reeling in a five-hundred-pound marlin that day and had the ride of his life with the female captain that night in her bungalow. After laughing heartily at his own story, and paying the bill as promised, he and Ray headed over to the funeral home.

"Well, Ray, what do you think is gonna be the COD?" Gary asked.

COD was the acronym for cause of death, and Ray was almost certain it was going to be related to those two gunshot wounds.

"I think they're gonna tell us that she died as a result of those two gunshot wounds Lavion told me about. I think we've probably got a murder on our hands here, dude."

"Sheeit. Been a good little while since we had one of those."

"Yeah, it has been, and with Manigault and Elrod breathing down my neck, it doesn't look to be getting any easier to solve it."

CHAPTER 8

Gary turned his unmarked Charger onto Chicora Street and whipped into one of the curbside parking spaces in front of the McCutcheon Family Funeral Home. The county had been discussing building a real morgue and coroner's office since before Ray was born, but it seemed like every time they brought it up, it was back off the table almost as quickly as it was put there in the first place. Ray didn't care either way. He liked how it added to the small quirks that made him love the county he grew up in.

"Yeah, but it doesn't really matter if it turns out to be murder. They can get pissed and give us shit all they want, but a murder definitely warrants priority for the department," Gary said as they got out of the vehicle.

"I know," Ray replied. "I just don't want to keep biting my tongue every time they come up to my office and give me grief. And I'm willing to bet you that just as soon as they find out it's a murder, they're gonna be all over us like never before."

Gary opened the door to the building and they both strode into an entryway that was festooned with paintings of Jesus and his disciples, angels carrying people toward heaven, and the empty tomb with the stone rolled away as Ray concluded, "Get ready for a tough job to become nearly impossible."

They stepped off of a laminate landing and onto the deep green carpet that Ray could remember from when Uncle Clem was lying in state when he was twelve. The sound of softly playing hymns and the smell of carnations brought the memory of it all rushing back. Uncle Clem was the only sibling that his mother had in the world. He started out by building souped-up cars when he was in high school, and by the time he graduated, he won dirt track races from Queen's Bridge all the way to Spartanburg. It didn't take too much longer for his reputation to earn him a shot on the NASCAR circuit, and it didn't take much longer after that for him to rack up the wins just like he did on those old red dirt tracks.

It had all gone well for a few years until, for what seemed like no particular reason at all, he decided to see just how fast his new Mustang would go on an old backroad near Kannapolis, North Carolina. The highway patrol said that it looked like he hit an oak tree head on at over one hundred miles an hour. He had hit it so hard that he and the Mustang became one as the metal entwined with his flesh and bone upon impact.

Ray could still remember the sound of his mother's quiet sobs, the hushed conversations of those paying their respects, and the platitudes that rang as hollow to the metallic casket sitting at the head of the parlor. It had struck Ray that how many of those people, many he had not seen in years, knew for a fact liked to talk about his family among their own little cliques, said words like, "If you need anything just let us know," or "We're praying for y'all during this."

He wondered how many of them had actually meant it rather than just living up to the expectations of good southern etiquette. He wondered what would have happened if he actually told them he needed something or sat with them at supper and joined hands to say the blessing before eating. Would they have said, "Now Lord, please be with Kerri Myers and her family as they try to make it through losing Clem so young and so suddenly," or would it have just been a quick word to say thank you for the meal before asking someone to pass them the black-eyed peas? In a way, maybe that was what had pushed Clem to drive his Mustang into that tree. Finally seeing life for the empty husk that it was and deciding to get off the train on his own terms.

He pushed those thoughts aside as he and Gary walked through the door to the mortuary that was tucked away behind the gold velvet curtains and vibrant flower displays.

His eyes immediately focused on the slab before him, and to his relief, he saw that the young woman they pulled from the swamp the day before was covered with a white sheet.

"You're just in time. Dr. Poston just finished up the autopsy," Lavion explained.

"Good timing on our part I guess," Ray said as he extended his hand to Dr. Leonard Poston.

"Good seeing you again, Ray. How's your daddy these days?" Dr. Poston asked, his voice as southern as shrimp and grits, deep as the Mississippi, and smooth as a bottle of Kentucky bourbon.

"He's doing pretty good these days. He's got a bunch of kids from the FFA that come and help him with the hogs and the fields, but he's still getting out there every morning at 4:45, running that Kubota all over the place. I keep telling him that he ain't twenty-five no more, but he don't listen. Just keeps doing his thing," Ray replied.

Dr. Poston chuckled. "Knowing Sam, I wouldn't expect any different. You tell him I said hey."

"I'll tell him."

Dr. Poston waved his gloved hand in front of his face like his train of thought was a gnat that needed swatting. "Anyway, lemme tell you what we've got going on with this young lady over here."

Dr. Poston gently pulled the sheet down to reveal the face of the young woman. Ray was both relieved that her eyes were no longer writhing swarms of hungry maggots. Lavion did masterful work with sewing them shut. She looked like she was sleeping.

"I took samples of the maggots and some pictures first, and went ahead and told Lavion he could close her eyes. Figured we could at least give the girl some dignity."

"As long as we have photos of her before, and all the evidence collected, I think we're fine giving her a little dignity," Ray replied.

Dr. Poston gave a grim nod before continuing. "I conducted a full autopsy, examined every inch of the body carefully, and took samples of all the bodily fluids, mucous membranes, skin, hair, and fly larvae. I'm gonna take it all back to the lab in Florence with me today and get started on the tests this afternoon. Your estimate that she was between fifteen and twenty-five was pretty good, but I narrowed it down further to sixteen to nineteen. Once I was able to get all of the maggots and mud off her and got her skin clean, I found a small tattoo on the inner right wrist."

He lifted the girl's right arm and turned the hand over to reveal a small tattoo of the word "Hope" but with a heart in place of the o.

"I took photos of it. There's also what looks like a scar from an appendectomy on her abdomen. Took photos of that as well. This should help you identify her at least."

"That'll be a huge help."

Dr. Poston respectfully covered her chest with the white sheet before he raised the sheet that covered her lower body. "She's also got a bite mark on her leg."

"Yeah, when she was found there was a pretty big alligator trying to make a meal off of her leg," Ray said.

"I knew that. Even found a tooth embedded in her knee," and motioned toward an evidence bag. Inside of the small plastic bag was an alligator tooth that looked to be about three inches long and definitely from an animal that was at least fourteen feet long.

"I was talking about a human bite mark on her inner left thigh, just above where the alligator got to her." Dr. Poston pointed a gloved finger at two faint, pink crescent-shaped marks. "Right there."

Ray couldn't believe his eyes, nor could he believe how fortunate they were that the alligator or fish hadn't completely destroyed the evidence.

"My God."

"Particularly savage if you ask me," Dr. Poston said. "I also made this discovery."

Dr. Poston turned and grabbed a small, sealed plastic evidence cup and held it up to where Ray could see it. Inside it, suspended in a solution to preserve it, was a small object that looked something like a giant tadpole that had grown its legs. Before he could ask about what this piece of evidence was, Dr. Poston explained, "This is her baby. She was six weeks pregnant, give or take a day or two."

Ray was stunned.

"Her baby wasn't too far past the embryo stage, but it could help us determine who the father is."

Ray stood there and stared at the tiny person robbed of a chance at life. He could feel the darkness he had learned to suppress begin to claw its way up his spine and into his consciousness. He shut his eyes tightly for a moment and recited the words in his mind that had served him in subduing his dark passenger for years. He took a deep breath and opened his eyes to see Dr. Poston standing there, his mouth a thin strip.

"It's good that we are reminded of our humanity while witnessing the utter lack of humanity displayed by others," Dr. Poston said as he gently set the tiny container that held the remains of the tiniest person that Ray had ever seen back onto the counter. The grim silence continued for a few seconds as Dr. Poston covered her lower body before uncovering her upper body once more.

"Cause of death was exsanguination resulting from two gunshot wounds. The one furthest to the left," he pointed to the exit wound above her left breast, "nicked her aorta. She would've bled to death in a matter of seconds. The other bullet though," he grabbed a sealed evidence bag that held a small deformed bullet, "severed her spinal cord and was lodged in between two of her vertebrae. You're likely looking at a homicide."

Ray nodded and glanced at Gary. "That's what I was thinking we had. Did you find any other physical evidence that could be helpful in catching her killer?"

"Unfortunately," he began, "all trace evidence would have been washed away by the water. I did find several pieces of glass, a couple of nails, and several large slivers of wood embedded in the soles of her feet and in her ankles. I collected it all and bagged it up. You never know if that sort of thing will be useful or not. I didn't find anything else, but there was one more thing."

He solemnly covered the girl back up with the sheet entirely. "I found evidence that this girl had been raped both vaginally and anally."

Ray's mouth went dry. "What?"

Dr. Poston pressed his lips flat against themselves. "I discovered some extensive vaginal scarring and relatively fresh vaginal injuries. I examined her anus and found similar scarring and fresh injuries there. It all points to this girl being raped and sodomized repeatedly over an extended period of time. I've never seen anything quite this awful, and I've been doing this since before you were born."

"In your opinion," Ray asked, "do you think there is a possibility that her rapist was the father of her child?"

"It's a very real possibility."

Silence settled onto the mortuary as Dr. Poston removed his gloves and dumped them into a garbage can labeled for biohazardous waste. He sanitized his hands before he turned around to face the silent figures of Ray Myers, Gary McFadden, and Lavion McCutcheon.

"This," he paused as if he was searching for the right word, "horror is unimaginable. I have been in this business for forty-two years, and not once have I seen a murder as savage as this. And understand me, fellas. I was here when Pee Wee Gaskins was still running loose. This is right up there with that."

The fact that Dr. Poston had compared the girl's murder to that of Pee Wee Gaskins, a local psychopath who raped, tortured, and killed men and women from the 1960s to the early 1980s as a part of what he termed his "coastal kills" chilled Ray to the bone.

"Somebody brutalized this girl over and over. Her injuries and the location where she was found have every indication that she was hunted down and killed like an animal."

His eyes burned with intensity as he met Ray's gaze. "We have another Pee Wee on our hands here, boys. And he may just be getting started."

CHAPTER 9

The two men didn't speak until they were both behind the closed door of Ray's office with the blinds shut for an extra sense of privacy.

"What's our next move, boss?" Gary asked.

"Same thing as before. Figure out who she is, let her family know, and catch the sick bastard who did this to her."

"What about Manigault and Elrod?"

Ray didn't hesitate in his response. "They can kiss our asses. We're pursuing this with all of our energy. I don't give a damn if it costs me another term or if they brand me a racist. There's somebody in our community who has raped and murdered a woman, and I'm gonna make sure that he can't do that to anybody else. You got my back?"

"One hundred percent."

"Alright. Call Knight, Campbell, and Johnson in here."

Gary stepped to the door of the office and called out the names of all three of the deputies. Gary closed the door behind them.

"Alright," Ray began. "We just got confirmation from the pathologist. We're dealing with a homicide. Not only was the woman shot twice, but there is forensic evidence that she was raped repeatedly. She was also pregnant, so we are going to be asking the DA to upgrade it to a double homicide. First step is going to be identifying the victim. Hopefully the scar and the tattoo that Dr. Poston found will help us figure out who she was.

"There was a little bit of physical evidence recovered, but nothing that is gonna be of use immediately, so it's up to us to get out there and shake the bushes and see if anybody knows anything. We don't have the official ballistics report right now, but I can tell you that we're gonna be looking for a .222 rifle."

The deputies all suspected they knew how he knew the caliber of the weapon, but none of them were brave enough to ask. Better to just take him at his word rather than risk making him relive a time when he had seen those types of wounds.

"Knight," Gary said. "I'm gonna need you to start over on the black side of town. See if anybody will tell if they heard any word on the street about somebody holding a young woman against her will, or if anybody saw anything while they've been out in the woods over on that side of town. Campbell, you're gonna do the same thing with the rural white communities. As many boys as there are out on the river, somebody is bound to have noticed something odd. Johnson, I want you to start calling all of the gas stations in the county and the ones in Clarendon, Florence, Georgetown, and Horry counties. The sheriffs out there won't mind you making some calls and trying to figure out if our girl was seen by anybody."

"It's important that you don't say anything about this case to anybody, and I mean anybody. It's an active investigation, and we don't need the integrity of the case we're building threatened because one of y'all didn't see any harm in telling your mom, wife, or boyfriend about what's going on and what we know. We also don't want a media circus on our hands. The last thing I want is to get a call from WPDE or WCSC about a murdering rapist." He gave a sideways glance at Gary as he spoke the next words like he was swallowing gasoline, "We have the town and the festival circuit to think about too. So, for God's sake, keep it to yourself and between the five of us. Is that clear?"

"Yes, sir." they replied.

"Also," Ray continued. "I'm gonna assume that it's gotten around the department that the girl was murdered. That a fair assumption?"

"Yes, sir," Knight replied. "Lowell hooks up with one of the EMTs that responded to the scene, and she told him that she thought she saw a couple of gunshot wounds on her back as they helped put her in a body bag. So, Lowell kinda spread that around. You know how he's a talker, sir."

"I do, and I'll make sure he sees things my way. Nothing that a week of taking calls can't fix. Anyway, nothing we can do about it now but just stop it from spreading. Make sure that y'all spread it that if anybody keeps repeating this rumor, they'll have to deal with me. Anybody have any questions about their jobs?"

"No, sir," they replied.

Ray nodded. "Okay, I'll expect status reports every day at 10 am. Any overtime you work, I'll approve. If there's nothing else, go on and get started. Let me or Captain McFadden know if there's anything ya'll need to get the job done. Let's get this guy off the street."

"Actually, sir, there is one more thing," Knight said. "Captain McFadden texted me a list of the identifying marks that the pathologist found. I used them in the search for missing persons and we got a hit."

Chapter 10

Jarrod Knight handed Ray a manila folder that he had been holding behind his back. Ray opened it and scanned a missing person printout, complete with a photo that, if you were to imagine the corpse still had eyes, was an exact match of the girl over at the morgue. Her name was Megan Prince and was just a couple weeks shy of her eighteenth birthday. She was missing from Rochester, New York, and her mother, there was no father listed, had reported that she had travelled to Myrtle Beach, South Carolina, with some friends without her knowledge.

The wheels began turning in Ray's head when he saw that she had travelled to Myrtle Beach. For most northern tourists, it was viewed as a paradise of seafood, arcades, and palm trees. It was actually a place that anyone from any southern state could tell you was more of a haven for drugs, prostitution, and other illegal activity. Anything could have happened to her there that would have led to her winding up dead in Morgan Swamp. As he continued to read her physical description, he mentally checked off all of the characteristics that matched the girl they found. His heart simultaneously sunk and swelled as he read that Megan Prince had her appendix removed when she was fifteen and that she had gotten a tattoo on her inner wrist of the word hope with a heart standing in for the o. Ray was certain this was the identity of the girl they found.

He looked up at the deputies who still stood, patiently waiting to hear if Knight had identified the young woman. "This is her. Run her prints against the autopsy scan just make sure, but this is her. Good work, Knight."

"Johnson," Ray said. "Once we have fingerprint confirmation, I need you to call up to Rochester and tell them we've identified a dead body that we believe to be Megan. We're gonna need to get confirmation from the parent, and we'll need to video-conference with her and the friends she traveled down here with. Tell them if they have any questions to call my cell number and that I'll be in the field personally conducting the investigation."

"I'm on it," she replied before she rushed outside with the others.

Gary stayed behind and propped himself against the support to one of the glass walls that surrounded Ray's office. "How long you figure till we've got a positive ID on those prints?"

"Shit, probably less than twenty minutes. Poston scanned her hands and uploaded them to the system today. All they've gotta do is search for possible matches to Megan Prince and they'll match up, guarantee it," Ray replied

"That's good. With all that, I figure we should get that conference with the mother and the girls she was down here with by tomorrow morning."

"Oh no, I'm pretty sure that's gonna happen this afternoon at the latest. Betcha we get to talk to the people she came down here with this afternoon too."

"How you figure on that?" Gary asked.

"You've got a daughter. If she went missing for a while and the cops said they thought they'd found her, would you waste any time or would you come right down to the station?"

"You're right," Gary nodded. "But why do you think the same thing about the girls?"

"When the cops call their parents and say they need them to come down for questioning immediately, I guarantee their parents will rush them down there to get it all cleared up too. No need to take your time and let accusations fly."

Ray glanced out at Johnson's desk. Her computer monitor scrolled through fingerprints faster than the naked eye could tell.

"Just a matter of getting that positive ID now," Ray continued. "This case is gonna speed up now."

Gary nodded. "I'm gonna go and smoke me a cigarette or two. I'll bring you a Coke, and don't tell me not to worry about it."

Once Gary was out of his office, Ray began to type an email to different organizations: police departments, county sheriff's departments, and hospitals. He listed general details about the girl's description and requested that they send any information they may have to his department email and his personal cell phone. He had just finished typing in the different email addresses and hit send when his door flew open. He looked up to see Johnson. "Positive ID. It's Megan Prince."

CHAPTER II

It was exhausting being a family man at times, but Wade wouldn't have it any other way. He'd been a father for two years shy of a decade now and was impressed that he hadn't managed to screw it up in some shape or form. While he'd never admit it to his wife, he thought he might have this father thing all figured out. His three girls loved him, and they were always clamoring to do everything with Daaaddy, and he loved every bit of that. That's not to say that he didn't miss what life was like before: drinking beer every weekend with the guys, taking the wife on spontaneous little adventures, and making love to her anywhere and anytime that the mood struck. He missed that from time to time, but there was just something about those little girls and the way they seemed to worship the ground that he walked on that seemed to make him forget all about what he thought he missed.

One of the things he definitely did not like about being a family man was the task of packing all of the endless luggage necessary for four females and one male to make it through a long weekend in the mountains into the back of the family Expedition. He had been at it for a good twenty minutes so far, and despite the muffled commotion that he heard through the floorboards above where he stood in the garage, he had not been pulled away once to referee, comfort, or get anybody into gear.

He had just placed the last piece of luggage, a leather box filled with all of his wife's makeup, in its place among the carefully stacked and balanced bags, when he heard the door that led from inside of the house into the garage open. He glanced around the edge of the SUV once he had closed the back hatch and saw his wife walking towards him. He knew right away by the taut expression on her face and the tight crossing of her arms that he was about to be pulled into fatherhood, whether he liked it or not.

"Come on now, Peaches," he said. "Don't tell me that you decided that we had better take the rest of the girls clothes with us, just in case."

His joke went nowhere with her.

"I'm gonna need you to go upstairs and tell your daughter that she needs to get her little butt moving," she said.

"What do you mean, sugar? You trying to tell me that only one of them is mine and the rest of them come from the mailman?"

He smiled but could see that she was still not having any of it. "What are you talking about?"

"I mean you did just say 'your daughter,' if I'm not mistaken. So that must mean that the other two come from the mailman. Which one is mine, Peaches? Is it Hailey-Brooke? Naw, it couldn't be; she's got a temper, and Lord knows I ain't got one of those."

He could see her trying to suppress a smile. "Is it Chandler? Naw, couldn't be her either 'cause she definitely don't have my charm."

Her face now broke into a wide smile. "So that must mean that it's Caroline. But she's so daggum stubborn, just like her mama."

She laughed as she pulled him into a kiss. "I dunno, partner. You just made a good case that ain't a one of them mine either 'cause they sure do act like you when they're mad, being stubborn, and acting as charming as an old possum," she said.

He kissed her again, this time with a little more passion. "Funny you say that, 'cause it just so happens that I was in a hospital room with you on three separate occasions, and on each of those occasions, I witnessed each of those little girls pop right on outta you."

She laughed as she kissed him again with passion building. "I suppose they're ours after all. But that still doesn't change the fact that Caroline is sitting up in her room saying that she ain't leaving this house without four stuffed animals."

She traced her index finger down the front of his button-down shirt. "Sure would be nice if her daddy would go get her to pick one out so that we can make it to Gatlinburg before midnight." Her finger trailed down to the front of his jeans. "I might be inclined to reward him for that once we've had a glass of wine or two out in the hot tub tonight." She rested her palm on the front of his jeans and slowly began moving it back and forth. "What do you say?"

"I say that I'll go tell our little angel that she's only carrying one of them things to Tennessee," he replied.

She kissed him. "My hero." She gave his swelling manhood a gentle squeeze before walking back towards the door to the house. "I'll go make sure the other two are ready. Meet you in the truck in five minutes."

"Me and Caroline are gonna be sitting in the truck ready to go in three," he called after her once she was inside of the house.

He had just begun following her into the house when he heard the trilling sound coming from the phone in his back pocket. He stopped altogether and answered the call on the encrypted phone.

"Did you determine if that was her?" he asked.

"I did," the man on the other end of the call said. "She fit the description and the tattoo matched up to what you told me."

"Was there any evidence linking her to the enterprise

or any of the clients?"

"Possibly. She was pregnant and she had a bite mark on her inner thigh. Other than that, you're free and clear."

Wade felt relief wash over him. "What can we do about that evidence?"

"It's pretty simple. I can find a scapegoat to pin it all on, so long as you and the boys can ensure he is so overcome with guilt that he decides to end his own suffering."

Wade nodded as he replied. "We can do that. Give me a target seventy-two hours from now and I'll make sure he eases his own pain. You make sure that the evidence lines up whenever the law tries to verify it."

"I'll take care of that, don't you worry," the man on the phone replied. "Sure was a shame for you to lose her, though. She was a pretty little thing. Not my taste, but I can see that she was for many of your clients."

Wade shook his head. "No, I know what pretty little things you like. Tell you what, I'll give you a double bonus. An extra five and give you pick of the litter once I get fresh stock in. How's that sound?"

Wade could hear the delight in the man's voice as he spoke. "That sounds more than generous. I'll have all this taken care of on my end, rest assured."

Wade walked into the house and began climbing the stairs towards his youngest daughter's bedroom. "I'm sure you will. I'll check in on Monday to make sure that we have everything taken care of."

Chapter 12

"All I know is that my back hurts. I think it'll be alright in a couple of days, but I'll need the pills to help me deal with the pain until it gets better," the quivering man said.

Dr. Erin McKee had been watching him since she entered the small exam room in the ER wing of the hospital. He looked more like a walking skeleton than a man. His grey skin clung loosely to the bones in his arms and legs to give his sunken face an almost corpse-like appearance. His chart said that he was thirty-six years old, but had she only looked at him, she would have guessed that he was somewhere closer to sixty-six. His poorly designed and faded tattoos, dingy jean shorts, and sweat-stained ribbed tank top told her that years of hard living and poor choices had taken its toll on him.

It was 98 degrees in Florence on this summer day, and he sat there on the paper-lined examination table shivering like it was 32 degrees outside. The sweat that soaked his already stained tank top, the tears that were streaming down his face, and his complaints of stomach cramps only confirmed what she suspected.

"I understand what you're saying, Mr. McGee. The facts of the matter are that all of our tests have come back and show you have a perfectly normal back. So, there's no way that I can prescribe you any Vicodin for pain for an injury that doesn't exist," she replied.

He blinked tears away and wiped his eyes with his hands. "I know, that's what they told me a couple of months ago when I seen Dr. Patel. He just didn't know what to make of it."

"I know, I see on your chart," she clicked a tab on the wall-mounted computer monitor, "that Dr. Patel could find no evidence of injury, nor could he come to a diagnosis of any disorder, so he gave you the pills and sent you on your way."

He clapped his hands together and smiled. "See, that's what I'm saying right there. Y'all are having a hard time figuring out what's going on with my back, but y'all know the pills help me get through the pain."

She wheeled her stool away from the small computer station mounted to the wall of the small room and met his gaze. "I don't agree, Mr. McGee. I think that you don't need the pills at all."

"What're you talking about? Why do you think I'm asking for them, then?" he asked.

"I think that you are addicted to opioids. I think that you got hooked on them after the surgery you had to repair your hernia five years ago, and you've been using aches, pains, and injuries to get more ever since," she replied.

He was incredulous and shook his head as he gestured with his hands. "That's some theory you got there doctor, but it simply ain't true. I ain't addicted to nothing."

"It's not a theory, Mr. McGee. It's a fact. I assure you of that. I can't prescribe you any painkillers of any type. I am going to suggest that you enter into one of the rehab programs we have here at the hospital. It's not too late to get clean and to get your life back on track, Mr. McGee."

He shook his head. "No, I ain't going to no rehab, 'cause

there ain't nothing I'm addicted to, and that's the truth. And I think that it's downright cruel for you to be accusing me of things and for you to keep me in all this unnecessary pain I'm in."

Erin stood up from the stool. "I'm sure you're in pain, Mr. McGee. But that pain is not because of an injury; that pain is from withdrawals. Please, Mr. McGee. Let me get you into our rehab program. You're only thirty-six, and if you keep going like this, you're not going to stand much of a chance of seeing forty-six. Help is here. All you have to do is say yes."

He whipped his head around and glared at Erin through a rippling jaw. "I guess I see how it is around here. You don't help nobody. You just accuse them of being a junkie and let them go on suffering so that you ain't gotta do your job. Well, that's fine by me Doctor McKee. I'm just gonna go on down to Carolinas and see if they'll help me and not humiliate me."

Erin pressed her lips tightly together as all of her energy rushed from her soul like air from a balloon. She filled her palm with hand sanitizer from the station bolted to the wall and opened the door to the exam room. "That's certainly an option, sir. I'll get the nurses started on your discharge papers. The offer for help is open any time you choose to take it, Mr. McGee. I just hope you choose to let us help you before it is too late for you. Have a great day."

As the door eased shut behind her, Rodney McGee fired a parting shot at her. "Uppity bitch."

She took a deep breath and retrieved her hospital-issued smartphone from the pocket of her white coat and scanned the screen for messages or alerts. She saw that she had ten new emails in her inbox and slipped the phone back into the pocket. The emails were just one of the many things that seemed to make her time on duty tedious at best and arduous at worst.

Rodney McGee was one of many patients she had encountered over the course of her career that had turned out to be a junkie looking to score some opioid prescriptions. It was a problem that had only gotten worse as time marched forward. During her residency in Miami, she encountered opioid junkies in about ten percent of her cases. Now, that number was closer to sixty percent of the time. It was a true public health crisis. Worst of all, it was only getting worse.

Politicians on both sides of the aisle would occasionally declare that the opioid crisis was a serious problem that local, state, and federal levels of government needed to address. They were right, of course, and Erin, along with countless other healthcare professionals across America, cheered for the awareness that the crisis was finally garnering in the public discourse. But every single time it seemed that the media and other opportunistic politicians would shout and scream over what was termed "the true threats to society."

Threats like controversies over a fast-food restaurant's founder being an evangelical Christian who personally disapproved of homosexuality. The restaurant still served homosexuals, hired them, and treated them with the same dignity and kindness as everyone else they served, to be sure. But the views of the founder were too egregious to not be used as cudgel for political and cultural gain. These non-issues, in Erin's mind, were what were always trumpeted as the most important threats to American lives and its society. Never mind the fact that over 70,000 Americans died as a result of opioid abuse in the last year. Actual death, suffering, and human misery was not what was important in the minds of the media and the politically opportunistic. All that mattered were the feelings of some and the polling data and ratings generated from it.

It was disgusting. And, unlike all of the talking heads and politicians who screamed that this policy or that would "kill thousands of Americans," their inaction on bringing greater public and governmental awareness to the opioid crisis actually did result in the deaths of tens of thousands of Americans annually. Gay, straight, male, female, transgender, cisgender, white or non-white, the opioid crisis was killing all in equal fashion. The talking heads and politicians didn't care though. People like Rodney Mc-

Gee couldn't get them the emotional voters and viewers they wanted.

She ran her fingers through her long brown hair and began to reorient her thinking. She walked to the nurses' station down the hall; the odd quiet making the thuds of her green pumps sound as loud as hammer strikes. Once she rounded the corner to the nurses' station, she saw Lacey Robinson seated behind the high counter of the station, rhythmically typing away at the computer behind the counter.

Erin sauntered up to the station counter and caught Lacey's attention as she took a sip from her teal and pink insulated tumbler with the letters "LSR" stenciled on the side in an elaborate font.

"Give you five bucks if you can guess what that case was all about," Erin said.

Lacey looked up and gave a crooked smile. "Make it $7.50 so I can buy myself a drink at Marion Tavern tonight."

Erin let out a chuckle. She needed that chuckle after the week she was having. "Deal."

Lacey rested her forefinger on her chin and rolled her brown eyes towards the ceiling like she was deep in thought. "Hmmm. . ..I'm gonna say. . .." She met Erin's gaze with a playful grin. "Another junkie looking for Vicodin."

Erin nodded. "You're right on the money, girl." She reached into the back pocket of her mustard skinny slacks and slapped a ten on the counter.

"Keep the change. Why don't you just do what I used to do, though?" Erin asked.

"And what did you used to do?"

"I'd put on something short and a little low cut and hang out near the bar. Guaranteed at least one free drink and maybe a decent conversation if I was lucky. Keep the ten for lunch tomorrow or something," Erin said.

"Oh, trust me. I did the same thing." Lacey tapped her engagement ring against the side of her tumbler with a metallic clang, "But Jonathan might not be too happy with me batting my eyes at random dudes while I'm out with my girls."

"That's right. We definitely don't want him to feel like you've been running around town or anything like that. I got the save the date a couple of days ago, by the way, and consider this my RSVP," Erin replied.

"Wait a couple of months before I get you locked in. You might have a plus one by then; never can tell," Lacey said with the raise of an eyebrow.

"No, ma'am. It's just gonna be me. Warren made me swear off men for a while."

"A while? It's been what, seven months? Surely you'll be back out there before next February."

"Nope, I'm not getting back there until the right time," Erin said.

"When's that gonna be though?"

"I'll know it when I see him," Erin replied with a grin of her own. "Anyway, Mr. McGee is refusing to enter rehab, so let's cut him loose. He said he was gonna try his luck over at Carolinas," Erin explained.

"I'll get on it right now."

"You're the best, Lace." Erin checked the time on her smart watch. "While it's quiet, I'm gonna head to my office and eat some lunch and maybe catch up on some emails. I'll be back in a half hour unless there's an emergency. Okay with you?"

"Okay with me. See you in a half hour. I'll hold down the fort," Lacey replied.

Erin took two steps toward her office at the end of the hall that was opposite the supply closet when Lacey got her attention. "Hey, Erin. Sorry, I forgot to tell you this morning. I saw your friend Ashanti on my last shift."

Erin stopped walking and turned on her heel toward Lacey. "Really? When? Didn't you and Jonathan go to Garden City all last week?"

"Yeah, we were at the beach last week. I saw her the Friday night before we went down. You had already left for the day, and I just now remembered it for some reason," Lacey said.

"Well how was she? Had she gotten beat up again?"

"No, no. Nothing like that. She said she had come in to

talk to you about something; said it was an emergency," Lacey explained.

She had Erin's full attention. "What kind of an emergency?"

"She was kinda ranting and raving a little bit. Said she needed to talk to you about something to do with the woods."

CHAPTER 13

Erin's blood ran cold.

"Did she say anything else?" Erin asked.

"Just going on and on about the woods. She was hysterical. She seemed like she was really scared and in some trouble. She said for me to tell you that she was gonna try to take a Greyhound to Nashville, I think? Anyway, she ran out of the front doors once I said I could call you."

"Why didn't you call me, though? I would've been up here in ten minutes," Erin said.

"I was about to, but literally right after she stormed out, we had six people brought in by ambulance from that bad wreck that happened on 501. We got busy for the rest of my shift, and I guess I just forgot. I'm sorry," Lacey said.

"No, you don't have anything to be sorry about. It happens. I know. Thanks for telling me. I might try to see if I can get a hold of her right now. You're still the best in my book, Lace," Erin said with a smile.

Lacey returned the smile as Erin strode down the long empty hallway to her lonely office. Her mind filled with questions and conclusions that only seemed to make the knot of anxiety in her stomach worse. Had that bastard finally tried to make good on those threats he kept making against her? Did she get away clean and is laying low? Was she dead in a ditch somewhere like so many others tended to end up around there? The anxiety was too much for her to handle so she retrieved her personal phone from her back pocket.

She tapped in the passcode and opened her contacts. Ashanti was the third contact on her list and she tapped the call button. An automated voice announced that the wireless customer she was calling had disconnected their service. Her brow furrowed with a new round of questions with no answers that had invaded her mind. She quickly put a lid on the pot inside her mind that was rapidly boiling over and instead opted to use self-talk to get herself back under good emotional control.

She reached her office and closed the door behind her as she shed her white coat and promptly hung it on the coat rack beside her door. She ran both of her hands through her long hair and took a deep breath in a semi-successful attempt at decompressing from the morning excitement. She kicked off her green suede pumps and padded across the tile floor of her office, grabbed the small kale salad she had stowed in her mini-fridge, and sat down at her desk.

She didn't have much of an appetite, but the doctor in her forced her to eat so that she could be as sharp as a tack for the rest of the day. As she picked through the salad and stabbed at cucumbers, cherry tomatoes, and mandarin orange slices, she couldn't help but think of the chilling words that Ashanti had said to Lacey over a week earlier. The story had seemed far-fetched when she was told it. But then again, Ashanti had never lied to her in all the years that she had known her.

They had first met when they were sophomores in high school. Erin was a late bloomer and reached her current height of 5'6" and filled out into a young woman once she was nearly sixteen. It was the spring before her junior year that she decided to test her new body out by trying out for the girl's track team.

She was far from sure of herself as she had developed womanly hips and a well-developed bust over the course of the previous summer and fall. Most of the other girls on the track team at West Florence High School were skinny as rails and sinewy as a piece of cord wood. Erin was just as lithe in all of the right places, but her figure set her apart from the rest of the crowd on the team. Everyone except for Ashanti Livingston.

Ashanti was blessed with the same body-type as Erin, and seeing how fast she could run gave Erin all of the confidence in her body image that she needed to not only try out, but also make the team. She always used to say that Erin was "the only white girl in Florence who was fast on the track but not in the sack." She also gave Erin a friendship that withstood the test of high school drama and an unspoken racial divide within the culture of the school.

It was sort of understood that black kids hung out mostly with black kids, white kids with mostly white kids, and the few hispanic kids with other hispanic kids. The friendship between Erin and Ashanti broke that understanding wide open. They were always with one another, whether that was on the track, at lunch, sporting events, and outside of school. Pretty soon, others started to forge bonds across the imagined color lines and the whole school was a better place.

Their friendship was one that could change things. It was not one that could stand the challenges of life after school. After graduation, they both went to different schools. Erin earned a full ride to the University of North Carolina at Chapel Hill to run and to study biology, and Ashanti decided to stay close to home and to attend Francis Marion University in Florence despite the scholarships that she had earned at South Carolina State and North Carolina A&T.

They kept in touch for most of the year through texts and phone calls. That started to change when Erin accepted an opportunity to work for the summer at the UNC Medical Center in Chapel Hill. Her summer of work became paid internships every other summer, and eventually the two drifted apart.

By the time that Erin had graduated with a degree in

biology and a national championship ring on her hand, Ashanti had dropped out of school altogether. Erin went on to attend medical school at the University of Florida in Gainesville, and Ashanti began living the fast life. Erin would see Ashanti's posts pop up on social media every now and then. Judging from the language of the posts, the content of the pictures, and the drastic way that Ashanti had changed her looks, it was clear she had fallen into the same cycle of bad decisions that so many people fell into.

Once she finished her residency in Miami, Erin decided to move back to Florence to be closer to her father. Her mother had died when she was very young, and she wanted to decide where to plant her roots. Three years later and Erin had slipped into the routine of an ER doctor; never giving anything but thought to the idea of moving on to something better.

Erin was working a night shift on an unusually cold December night. The hospital foyer was decked out with Christmas decorations, and the nurses had tried to spread a little Christmas cheer by decorating a fake tree behind the counter of the nurses station. Erin walked into exam room four, and there sitting on the paper-covered exam table was Ashanti Livingston. The years had not been kind to her. Her hair was a mess, several poorly done tattoos ran up her arms and on the sides of her neck, and her left eye was purple and swollen to the size of a grapefruit.

Both of them hugged one another and cried, and they spent some time catching up. Erin learned that the shiner on Ashanti's eye came from her "boyfriend." He wasn't so much her boyfriend as he was her pimp and he was the latest in a line of bad luck that went back to her sophomore year in college.

She dropped out because her boyfriend at the time had gotten her pregnant, and against Ashanti's will, he had driven her to an abortion clinic in Columbia where he forced her to end the life of her child. The remorse over that act, combined with the knowledge that the doctor who performed the abortion had botched it and left Ashanti barren, had sent her into a downward spiral. She began drinking heavily and using drugs regularly. She contracted herpes and Hepatitis C from using dirty needles. She lost a few teeth to crack and a few teeth to beatings.

By the time Erin began her residency in Miami, Ashanti worked as a prostitute from Wilmington, North Carolina, down to Savannah, Georgia. It was a miracle that the worst she had contracted was herpes and gonorrhea. It was a miracle that she wasn't dead.

Erin had urged her to go to the police, but Ashanti was emphatic in her refusal. She kept saying she would be alright and that it wasn't her boyfriend's fault really. If only she could keep from sassing him so much, she wouldn't hurt his feelings to the point that he hit her. Erin at least managed to convince her to stay a few nights in the Colonial Motel, just down from the hospital on the corner of Pine and Irby. Erin gave Ashanti her phone number and told her that she would drop by to check in on her for the next couple of days.

Eventually, Ashanti managed to begin piecing her life back together. She had left her old life behind and was slowly putting all the pieces back into place. She got herself a steady job at the Dollar General in Effingham, and she had managed to save enough money to fix her teeth and begin the process of removing the tattoos she had accumulated over the years. Within six months, she was waiting tables at two different restaurants in Florence, attending church with Erin, and taking online classes at Florence-Darlington Technical College with the hope of finally finishing that nursing degree. Everything was falling into place until three months ago.

Ashanti asked Erin to meet her for lunch at La Vaca Loca, Florence's newest taco bar. Erin showed up to find Ashanti distressed. She said that she needed to tell her something in case something happened to her. Erin thought she was just being dramatic, but the fear in her friend's eyes told her otherwise. She listened as Ashanti told her about working with women and girls who were trying to get out of prostitution. At first, it had made Erin proud that her friend was doing so much good in the world, but then the story took a dark turn.

Ashanti told her about a place known to her and some of the women that she worked with as "The Woods." The story both chilled her to the bone and filled her head with skepticism. It was sort of like watching one of those reality shows where people hunt ghosts. At first that sudden sound or movement sends a chill down your spine. Then, you are immediately skeptical that it was anything other than a natural occurrence at all. She had left that lunch feeling both unsettled and puzzled as to why her friend, a smart and rational woman, had bought such a story hook, line, and sinker. At least, she had been until today.

She busied herself by checking her emails. She clicked through several from different pharmaceutical reps, and one from a medical journal calling for papers, before she clicked on an email that the hospital had forwarded to all of its employees from the Craven County Sheriff. What she read curdled her blood. She immediately lost interest in her picked over salad as she read the description of the girl they had found and her injuries. Rationally, she knew that there was no way that this could be related to the crazy story Ashanti had told her. But Ashanti was missing and her gut told her otherwise.

She unlocked her personal phone, typed in the personal number that Sheriff Raleigh Myers had attached in the email, and began tapping out a message.

CHAPTER 14

"To tell you the truth, Anna, I think that it is reprehensible and inhuman. There is simply no excuse for allowing discrimination like has been shown by Mrs. Flores to a couple whose only desire is to have a nice arrangement for their wedding," Representative Brian Sparrow said to the reporter on the other end of the telephone conversation

Brian was in his fourth term as the Congressional representative from Colorado's second district, and his hard work was finally paying off. He had been appointed the chairman of the House Rules Committee and was in a position to influence the types of legislation that would be debated and voted on as a congressional body. Even his chances at reelection in his home district, which wouldn't happen for a little over one year, were solidly in his favor for a fifth term. He had paid his dues and used every bit of his considerable appeal on social media and in the mainstream media to push the agenda set by the party.

It was finally going to be his time. He had finally

backed the winning horse. He was prepared to endorse the right candidate for the presidential election following the announcement of their campaign next year. Nelson Yancey, the Speaker of the House and an eight-term congressman from Memphis, Tennessee, had promised Brian that he would ascend to his office once the incoming president, whom they both were beholden to endorse, had appointed him the new Secretary of State. It had been a long road from being a Boulder city councilman, to serving Coloradoans in Congress, and now become the next Speaker of the House. The better world that he and many others in Washington were committed to building, under the guiding hand of their shared mentor, was finally within their grasp.

The very thought of the new era they were about to usher into existence filled Brian's soul with joy. He had always viewed politics as something like a sacred calling placed upon a chosen few in society. For Brian, it was much deeper than that. To him, politics and the government to which he pledged to help guide, was his religion. His mentor, who in a few short months would be sworn in as the next and final president of the United States, was his Messiah to whom he owed everything. It was his mentor, teacher, and king who encouraged him to get out of Washington for the weekend and invited him down to a sacred place in his mentor's backyard to celebrate the success that he and the world were about to experience.

"You see, Anne, there is nothing more un-American or disturbing than people hiding behind their religion to marginalize a group of people, just because they love who they love. And I, for one, think that we ought to hold those people accountable as a nation anytime and anywhere they see it. So, I was happy to see that the new human rights committee that we set up in Colorado was able to step up and make sure that people like Gabriela Flores are held to account for the pain and suffering they have caused people like the Jacobsens," Brian said.

The case of Gabriela Flores and her declining to make a floral arrangement for the wedding ceremony of Jeremy and Peter Jacobsen had thrust itself into the national spotlight after the couple had filed a complaint with the Colorado Human Rights Committee. They had alleged their civil rights were violated by the Gunnison florist, and the commission ruled that Flores had violated the state's anti-discrimination law. The Jacobsens then filed a lawsuit against Gabriela Flores, which they subsequently won.

The ruling held that though Flores declined to make a custom arrangement explicitly for their wedding due to her Catholic faith and instead offered to sell them pre-arranged or individual flowers, she was guilty of discrimination. The commission ordered her to make the arrangements of their choice, change her small business's policies, attend 200 hours of committee-mandated sensitivity training, and provide documentation quarterly to the commission to demonstrate her compliance with the order. The case had been appealed and now was being heard by the Supreme Court.

For Brian to have such a potent social controversy sprout in his home state of Colorado made him an instant authority on this case. Every time it was presented to him, he hawkishly took the side of the Jacobsens and he decried the inherent immorality of Flores's beliefs. There was no place in a modern and diverse society for such hurtful and archaic beliefs that had historically led to a dark age of ignorance, shame, and violence. Brian, and he believed a majority of the American people, held true to the belief that all people should be compelled to act within the bounds of what he often referred to as "common decency," regardless of how it conflicted with beliefs that had no business in the public sphere or within a modern society at all.

He glanced at the time on his smart watch as the driver of his Suburban informed him they were two minutes out from their destination. "Listen, Anne. I'm actually on my way out for a couple days of vacation. Could we pick this up when I get back to DC the day after tomorrow? Great. I'll see you in my office at 10 am then. Thanks again, Anne. Talk to you soon."

He ended the call as the SUV turned off the forest-lined

highway and onto a winding gravel road. Brian was surprised at how the canopy of the forest, some twenty feet
above the roof of the vehicle, had made it seem that the
sun had just sunk below the horizon. The forest that created a green tunnel of sorts along the gravel road stretched
out for miles in either direction. To Brian's eye, it was more
of a jungle than a forest, to tell the truth.

Brian strained to see the mixed forest of loblolly pines,
oaks, sweet gums, and bald cypress trees stretching out
endlessly into a seemingly impenetrable swamp. He shuddered for a moment when he thought that the shallow
stagnant waters hidden beyond his field of view were
surely crawling with snakes, alligators, and all manner of
creatures uniquely designed to kill and feast on flesh. That
last thought had stirred something within him.

He put the feeling back in check as the SUV rounded
another curve in the winding gravel road and emerged in
front of a large building after what seemed like ten minutes. The building was truly a sight to see. It was a large
hybrid Federal and Greek Revival-style plantation home
with a roof and second floor portico supported by six columns. The entire house was surrounded by a towering cypress canopy, and the front of the mansion was flanked by
twin sprawling live oaks. The curtains of moss that hung
from the oaks and the canopy of cypress trees above gave
the entire property an otherworldly feel that chilled and
delighted the moonstruck Brian Sparrow.

As Brian stepped out of the back seat of the SUV
parked in front of the ancient brick steps of the front
porch, he couldn't help but feel that he had stepped back
in time to the idealized image of moonlight and magnolias that he had seen in Gone With the Wind in college. The
smell of the purple wisteria that blanketed the trellis on
the left end of the house, combined with the warbling song
of cicadas in the trees, only seemed to enhance the feeling
of stepping into a different time. He could hardly keep his
mind focused.

The twin black doors at the top of the stairs swung
open and the sight of a man dressed in jeans, a checkered

shirt, and khaki sport coat who walked through the doors caught his attention. The sound of the man's brown cowboy boots' rhythmic smacks against the wooden planks of the porch and on the steps to the porch only served to complete the image of southern genteelness exuded by the house, grounds, and the man coming out to meet them.

The man reached the bottom of the steps, the heels of his boots sinking slightly into the sand of the drive, and extended his hand to Brian. "Welcome to Oakmoor Hall. I trust you had a comfortable trip down, Mr. Sparrow?"

Brian shook the man's hand with a politician's smile that came as natural as breathing to him. "Absolutely. You guys have made every part of the trip down as comfortable as possible, Mister?"

"Call me Jimmy," he said as he nodded his head. "And I'm delighted to hear it was comfortable; we certainly aim to please." Jimmy motioned for him to follow him up the stairs. "I hope you understand why we have our plane land at the airfield up across the state line in Robeson County before we drive you the rest of the way by car. I know that it can be an annoyance having to ride for a couple of hours along North and South Carolina country roads, but we've always made a point to err on the side of discretion over expediency."

"I understand completely, Jimmy. Believe me when I say that your discretion and the lengths that you and your people have gone to protect the privacy of my visit are very much appreciated." Brian said as he stepped through the doorway and into the foyer of the plantation home. It was absolutely breathtaking. The twin staircases gracefully twisted along the walls of the foyer up to the second floor. They were absolute works of art. The rich hunter green of the walls, decorated with paintings that depicted scenes from nineteenth century European battlefields to varied nature scenes of the American South was as beautiful as anything he had seen in Washington. But the most amazing sight was standing in the middle of the rotunda beyond the grand hall in front of the doorway. There stood a twenty-five-foot Bald Cypress tree, perfectly preserved, as if it had uprooted itself and decided to rest its gnarled roots there. At the base of the tree was a large wooden base upon which sand, part of a fallen log, and a few strategically placed aquatic plants stood perfectly rigid as if they were still under the surface of the swamps outside. The most magnificent parts of the already incredible display were the perfectly taxidermy alligators, captured in a pose to show them swimming around the base of the tree and toward two largemouth bass, one of which the alligator on the left already had its massive jaws ready to strike.

"Oh, wow." Brian said.

"Yes, sir. They sure are magnificent. Your benefactor took the one on the left, and his oldest boy took the one on the right," Jimmy explained as they strolled down the fifty-foot grand hall entrance.

"Were they killed here?" Brian asked.

"No, sir. The one on the left was taken during a hunting trip in Louisiana, and the one on the right came out of a catfish pond he owns. Said he couldn't figure out for the life of him why ducks never stuck around it, and why he could stock the pond with catfish and not catch a damn thing. One morning we took a drive out there to see if there was some way the fish were getting out of the pond and into the swamp a few yards away, and we saw this big thing pulling itself outta the water."

"They sure are magnificent," Brian said, still in awe.

"We could organize a hunt for you during your stay with us, if you'd like. You'd be completely safe, of course," Jimmy said.

Brian shook his head. "Not this trip. Maybe next time."

"Of course, Mr. Sparrow. Shall we step into the parlor where we can talk about business comfortably?"

"That'd be great," Brian said. He followed Jimmy through a doorway off to the left of the great hall and into a luxurious parlor decorated with plush leather couches, two fireplaces, and taxidermy heads of whitetail bucks, wild boar, and mountain lions interspersed among more tasteful paintings. Jimmy invited him to make himself comfortable wherever he liked.

"Would you like a drink or cigar?" Jimmy asked.

"I'll take a martini if you've got it," Brian replied.

Jimmy smiled. "Vodka or gin?"

"Gin, please."

Jimmy walked over to a desk on the far side of the double parlor, pushed an intercom button on the telephone on the desk, and ordered a gin martini and a bourbon neat to be sent into the parlor as soon as possible. Brian took a seat on one of the leather couches arranged in a horseshoe between the columns in the middle of the double parlor and took in the sights of the elaborate room.

So far, the experience was top notch. While it was a little inconvenient to be shuttled away from his Georgetown townhome under the cover of darkness to a small airfield in the middle of nowhere West Virginia, only to fly from there to a small airfield in Robeson County, North Carolina, and then travel in the backseat of a car for the remaining two hours, the need for discretion was of the utmost importance. Besides, the private jet was stocked with everything needed to make a good drink, and the backseat of the Suburban was far from uncomfortable. The only source of discomfort was Brian's own anticipation.

The anticipation had begun the moment he was told that he had been invited to this place the week before. The recognition of hard work on behalf of the man he knew was his ticket to success and who would be the architect of the future.

His heart had leapt when he was told to be ready, and his knees went weak when he was assured that he could pursue his passion to its fullest while only paying half of the usual fee.

Now, sitting on this rich leather couch in this palatial home and having his every need attended to, it was as if his wildest dreams had indeed come true. He was giddy with anticipation of what the next day would bring. And he was nervous about what would happen when the time came.

Jimmy ambled over to have a seat on the couch opposite Brian, crossed one leg over the other, and restied one arm on the armrest and the other along the top of the couch as he sat.

"She'll be along in just a moment. In the meantime, let's discuss what services we'll be providing you," Jimmy said.

"Sure thing. Fire away," Brian replied.

The two men discussed the services that would be provided and the accommodations for his stay until the door to the room swung open and a woman dressed in a stylish black jumpsuit and heels stepped into the room. Her long blonde hair was styled into wavy curls, her makeup looked professionally applied, and her warm smile lit up the room. In one hand she carried a near bourbon in a small glass, and in the other she carefully carried a martini complete with an olive.

"Sorry to interrupt you guys, but I have your drinks right here," she said.

Her voice was lyrical and sweet with the same low country South Carolina drawl as Jimmy and several other South Carolinians that Brian had met over the years. Brian smiled as she gingerly crossed the room and handed him his martini.

"Here's your martini, shug. And here's your bourbon." She handed the bourbon to Jimmy who received it with the warm smile that had been there since Brian got out of the Suburban out front.

"Thank you, darlin'," Jimmy said before he turned his attention back to Brian. "Can we get you anything else, Mr. Sparrow? We could fix you something to eat if you'd like. It wouldn't be any trouble at all, now would it be, Miss Rachel?"

"Oh Lord, no. No trouble at all," Rachel replied and turned her attention to Brian with the same warm smile.

Brian shook his head. "No, thank you. This will be fine for now."

"Okay, well if you change your mind, just let Jimmy or any of our other hosts know, and I'll make sure that you're taken care of. I'm gonna leave you guys to talk," Rachel said before turning and sashaying through the door.

Once the door was closed, Jimmy turned his attention

to Brian who was taking his first sip of his martini. "How's your martini?"

It was a shot of life to his soul, and he told Jimmy as much before Jimmy continued with their previous conversation. "Great. Have we covered all of your needs during your stay with us, Mr. Sparrow?"

"Yeah, you've got it all covered, I think. I do have a question about what to do after I'm done preparing and enjoying dinner, though."

Jimmy had anticipated this question. "You don't have to worry about a thing, Mr. Sparrow. Our team will take care of the utensils, dishes, and any leftovers you may have. We want your experience to be exactly as you desire without any need to fuss over the clean-up."

The anxiety that he had been feeling about what to do once he was done immediately left his mind. "That's great to know. I really appreciate it," Brian said.

"We like to take good care of our people, Mr. Sparrow. Now, on to the matter of payment procedure. Normally, we'd ask for no less than one million dollars." Jimmy replied.

"Wow. That's...significant," Brian responded.

"But because of the work you have done for your mentor over the years and the loyalty you have shown him, he has instructed me to accept $100,000 for the purchase. Did he discuss how payments are to be made?"

"He did. And we also discussed making the payment to Trailhead Consulting," Brian said, draining the last of the martini.

"That's correct, Mr. Sparrow. Trailhead Consulting is listed as a political consulting firm, and any money you pay them from your campaign funds will not violate any campaign finance law. So you see, the hundred grand isn't even coming out of your pocket. It's just another expense that comes with politics. Are you ready to get started?"

The excitement that Brian was feeling could barely be contained. "Oh yeah. Very much so."

"Wonderful. I'm going to put you in the cab of one of our UTVs and we'll head on out to the farm."

Brian's heart skipped a beat as they walked through the back of the mansion, hopped into the UTV, and tore through swampland more dense and remote than he had ever dreamed. After several minutes of travel through bogs, across mudflats, and around massive tree trunks, they finally arrived in front of a large building covered with sheets of brown metal.

His mouth had already begun watering as he followed Jimmy into the building. The interior reminded him of the hunting lodges in Aspen and the fundraisers he often attended there. He followed Jimmy down a long hallway covered floor to ceiling in stained oak, and finally opened the door marked "Pleasure Room."

Brian stepped inside and marveled at the luxurious bed that seemed to be recessed into the floor, the four oak timbers that surrounded the bed, and the young man shivering on the bed. Brian looked at him and felt his excitement kick into high gear. He was slightly built, beautiful, and dressed in the exact yellow briefs that Brian had requested. A sturdy leather collar around his neck connected to a thin chain that was fastened to an I-bolt in the post to the right of the head of the bed.

"How're we doing, so far?" Jimmy asked.

"Oh, wow. So far you guys are doing amazing," Brian replied gleefully.

"Like I said, we aim to please. Follow me," Jimmy said as he closed the door and led Brian to the door marked "Dining Room."

Jimmy invited Brian inside the room, and Brian's astonishment turned into complete awe. The kitchen at the far end of the room had been stocked with all of the potatoes, veggies, and spices Brian had requested, and the luxurious cherry dining room table had been set with all of the requested china, utensils, and wine. Just to the left of the kitchen, with his arms and legs chained between twin oak timbers, stood the most appetizing specimen that Brian had ever seen. The young man seemed to be chiseled out of coffee-colored stone, and Brian felt weak in the knees as he watched the cords of muscle ripple across his perfect body as he struggled against the chains.

"Judging from your lack of speech, I suppose we did well here too," Jimmy said.

"Oh my God, you've completely outdone yourself. Thank you so much. If it's alright with you, I'd like to begin immediately." Brian said, removing his jacket, rolling up his sleeves, and donning a rubberized apron.

"Of course, Mr. Sparrow. If you need anything at all, just hit the intercom button on the wall either here or in the Pleasure Room. Bon appetit," Jimmy said as he closed the door and left Brian and the young Adonis inside the dining room.

Brian retrieved the carving knife and began sharpening it; honing the perfect edge for the exquisite work ahead.

"Please, man. Let me go," The young Adonis pleaded.

"Shhh, it's all going to be fine. You'll see," Brian replied.

The pressure in his nether regions became unbearable as he approached the restrained young Hercules.

"What are you doing, man? Don't you fucking touch me you sick fuck!"

Brian placed his hand on the soft warm skin of this African warrior's rump and felt an electric tingle shoot through every nerve in his body.

"I won't take much to start. Mmmmm," Brian said as he sliced a fist-sized chunk from the man's flesh. The feel of the warm blood oozing down his bare hand and the agonized scream of his own personal Achilles pushed Brian over the edge. The waves of pleasure that came with the climax were more exquisite than anything that he could have dreamed of. He rode wave after wave until at long last, the ecstasy faded and he was able to walk, flesh in hand, to the kitchen. The first of several releases had just been had. Now it was time to prepare the first of many man-meat meals that he and the boy in the Pleasure Room would share over the next couple of days.

CHAPTER 15

Erin McKee's heartbeat picked up the pace with every mile she drove down US Highway 52, across the Craven County line, and on to the small river town of Queen's Bridge. She kept telling herself that this was foolish. She kept telling herself that Ashanti's story was all nonsense. But as she crossed the Black River Bridge, built only 200 yards from the site of the colonial Queen's Bridge, she reminded herself that Ashanti was no fool and that she had been missing for a little over a week now.

She took a left off of 52, which was called the Queen's Highway in Queen's Bridge, and pulled onto Martin Luther King Jr. Street. She still called it Lee Street in her mind every time somebody mentioned it on the local news or in everyday conversation in Florence. It just sounded weird to call it anything other than what the street was called literally her entire life. She didn't have a problem with the name change, though. In fact, she thought that it was probably a good thing the change had happened in the long run.

Ashanti had always told her she didn't care one way or another what streets were named, what statues depicted, or what flags flew. She had always maintained that history needed to be preserved and that heritage needed to be respected. But Ashanti had also said that when "them trashy whites" started revving their engines next to her at stoplights, waved the flag at her when she came out of the Walmart in West Florence, and yelled at her when she crossed the street, that she felt a sudden fear she couldn't explain. She had said that it wasn't necessarily the symbols that those few people flaunted in public so much as it was the way they used them to send a message that had gotten to her. Still, she hadn't thought that removing the monuments or demonizing flags was the appropriate response. Instead, Ashanti thought that changing the name of a street or building statues to celebrate the history of African-Americans, alongside those that were already representing the history of the south, could be something that helped bring the two sides together at last.

Looking at the monument to the Confederate dead that stood outside of the Greek-Revival Craven County Courthouse, and the caution tape that surrounded it, Erin thought it was probably best for it to be removed altogether. After all, hadn't 150 years or so passed since this had all been immediately relevant? Why was it necessary to hold onto the symbols and stories associated with, as far as Erin could see, what was a failed rebellion that defended inhuman practices at its very core? Never mind the shame and the stigma that it had placed upon South Carolina and the rest of the south ever since. Was it really worth celebrating in any way?

That wasn't to say that she wasn't proud to be from the south. Far from it. She just believed it was possible to make the south better. And what could be better than bringing peace to her home and celebrating the contributions of all southerners, regardless of their race or even their sexuality or gender identities? She certainly couldn't think of anything better or more reasonable. Now, it finally looked like many of her fellow South Carolinians felt the same.

Thurmond Spates, the former governor of South Carolina, had really done a lot to get the ball rolling there. A few years ago, there was some serious racial turmoil that rocked the nation as a whole. Police officers had shot young black men in cities like St. Louis, Sacramento, and Boston, and a national conversation had been started about the role of police brutality as it related to black men. Protests devolved into riots in cities across America, and in places like Florence, where the white and black populations made up virtually equal halves of the population, the tension was as thick as a wool blanket. A white nationalist then decided to shoot several black folks at a family picnic in South Carolina.

All eyes were on South Carolina. Most of those eyes then focused on the Confederate symbols there as well. Governor Spates had stepped up and called for the removal of Confederate monuments on state property. Within a week, crews had removed the Confederate monument from the state capitol grounds, along with any references to the state's role in the formation of the Confederate government. Monuments were being removed in cities and towns across South Carolina in the following months. Even Queen's Bridge, the town that Governor Spates was born in, began plans to gradually remove and rename anything in the town that made reference to the Confederacy. According to the local news, the Confederate dead memorial outside of the courthouse was slated to be removed within the month. Erin was really proud of the progress that was being made in her state.

There was opposition, to be sure. Some historians called it a travesty, some due to the removal of the reminders of the terrible cost and legacy of the Civil War and others because of the comparisons to similar campaigns in the former Soviet Union. Many ordinary South Carolinians were not pleased with the campaign and voiced their objections in hushed tones where none could hear them and shame them for their views. Even then, the louder voices of those who championed the removals celebrated it and shouted down the dissenters in the public square while they did the same in the social media sphere.

Erin didn't necessarily agree with the shaming of opposing views, but she did agree that they needed to put those views aside and to get on board with healing the wounds that her beloved South Carolina had carried around for so long. They needed to be re-educated about their views so they could learn how misguided their views were. If only Mississippi, Alabama, and Louisiana saw things that way too.

She pulled her Carolina Blue Mustang GT into the small parking in between the Craven County Sheriff's Department and Lily Belle's Boutique. She checked herself in the car's makeup mirror, touched up her nude lipstick from where it had transferred to the straw of her iced coffee, grabbed her purse and headed into the building. She chose to wear a peach top with white ankle-length skinny jeans and sandals, to eliminate her need to empty any pockets and still look cute enough to meet up with a couple of girlfriends for lunch in Florence afterwards.

To her surprise, there was no metal detector, scanner, or armed sheriff's deputies guarding the front of the small office adjacent to the courthouse. There was just a small waiting room with seven chairs, plus a flatscreen tv mounted to the left wall showing twenty-four-hour news with the subtitles on and the sound down. There was a white wall with a desk that sat behind thick glass with a speaker mounted near the counter that reminded her of the ticket booth at the Swamp Fox movie theater in Florence. Immediately to the right of the window was a reinforced door, and beside that hung a picture of the Craven County sheriff's seal.

She slipped her right arm through the loops on her tan purse, settled it securely in the crook of her bent elbow, and walked up to the counter. A deputy in full olive and black uniform looked up from a smartphone that he clumsily tried to conceal, pushed the intercom button, and spoke into the grainy microphone.

"How may I help you, ma'am?"

"Yes. My name is Erin McKee and I am here to see Sheriff Myers. We were supposed to meet at 10:30, but I'm a couple of minutes early."

"That's alright, ma'am. Let me go and make sure that he's ready for you. Have a seat. It'll only take a second," the deputy replied before he got up and disappeared behind the wall. Erin took a seat in the chair immediately opposite the reinforced door and glanced at the muted news program. A panel was debating a new law passed by the state of Mississippi that would ban abortions after the heartbeat was detected in all instances. No exceptions to the law. Erin read the subtitled words and watched the wild gestures of many of the panel directed towards a calm young black woman who was defending the law.

Erin tried to shy away from this issue whenever it came up, simply because it was too exhausting to discuss, like so many other social issues these days. There was almost never a way to remain civil about it. It was the classic "for us or against us scenario" that Star Wars summed up with Darth Vader's turn to the dark side. It always devolved into yelling and slander. Those who supported the law were called misogynists who wanted to control women, and those who opposed the law were called irresponsible baby-killers. There was simply no reasoning with it at all. That was why Erin tended to keep her opinion to herself.

The door to the office opened and pulled her attention away from the free-for all against the pro-lifer on the news. In the doorway stood a tall man with dark jeans, a gun and badge on his belt, a black dry-fit polo with the seal of the Craven County Sheriff's Department embroidered on the left breast.

"Miss McKee? Hey there, I'm Ray Myers," the man said, extending his hand.

Erin stood and shook his hand. She noticed the cords of muscle that rippled up his arm as he gave her a good handshake. "Erin's fine. It's nice to finally meet you, Sheriff Myers."

"Please, call me Ray. And the pleasure is all mine. Would you like to have a seat in my office, where we could talk privately?" Ray said with a smile.

"Sure, that'd be great," Erin replied.

"Okay, follow me."

He held the door open for Erin, who politely slipped on through the doorway and thanked him as she did.

"I really appreciate you coming down to talk on a Saturday morning. I know being a doctor at McLamb has to keep you pretty busy," Ray said as they walked past several desks on the way to a small office with floor-to-ceiling windows in the back of the room. "Sheriff Raleigh Myers" was written in gold letters on the glass door to the small room.

"It wasn't any trouble at all. I'm not on duty today, so I'm all yours," Erin replied as he held open the glass door to the small office for Erin to enter. The door-holding was making an impression.

"Have a seat; make yourself comfortable. Can I get you something to drink? I've got some K-cups and a Keurig, or I could give you a water. I can get one of the deputies to bring you a Coke from the vending machine in the break room," Ray offered as Erin took a seat in one of the chairs across from his desk.

She set her purse down on the floor beside her chair and demurely crossed her legs at the knee. "I'm fine right now, thank you. But I'll let you know if anything changes," she said with a smile.

Ray gave a nod and took a seat behind the desk, and grabbed a pen and a yellow legal pad as he did so. There was a large wooden American flag mounted on the wall behind him and a rifle mounted on the wall above that. Erin knew, from all of the war movies and documentaries she had watched with her dad growing up, and sometimes every Sunday, that it was a SOCOM M-14 rifle.

There was a shadow box on the left side of the flag interspersed with several unit patches. She recognized the patch of the 82nd Airborne Division, but none of the others rang a bell. On the opposite side of the flag was a picture of several bearded men in combat uniforms with M-4 rifles slung across their chests in what looked like a desert.

She recognized the man standing on the right of the photo to be the sheriff who sat across from her now and flipped pages on his yellow legal pad.

She guessed he was somewhere in his mid- to late thirties. He was handsome. His deep red hair was trimmed close on all sides of his head but left longer at the top. He still wore a beard, though it was meticulously trimmed short and neat. Judging from the picture she saw on the wall, along with the orderly way he kept his desk, she could tell that he was a disciplined person. That was probably why he was in incredible shape as well. He looked at Erin and immediately she was struck by his deep green eyes. Tattoos peeked out from underneath the sleeves of his polo and her heart fluttered in her chest. She tried to discreetly take a breath to settle herself.

What the hell were all of these feelings about? You've seen a hot guy before. Pull yourself together.

For some reason, the look in his eyes, and the fact that they were looking at her, set loose the butterflies in her stomach that had been dormant for over a year. She felt herself flash him a big smile and heard a chuckle escape her mouth. What. Are. You. Doing. Get it together. Think, her inner voice told her. Quickly, she pointed at the shadow box, cleared her throat, and directed his attention away from her.

"You were in the 82nd?" she asked as the butterflies started to settle back to normal flight.

He glanced over his shoulder at the shadow box and back to her. "Yeah, for a few years. I was in a few other units before and after that, though."

"So, what was jump training like? I've always wanted to skydive, but I've never gotten the nerve worked up to go."

Ray cocked his head to the side. "It was kinda terrifying at first. You're loaded down with all of your gear, standing in line at the back of a C-130, with a jumpmaster yelling at you to jump out of a perfectly good airplane. It's different from skydiving, though. Once you clear the ramp, your hook-up pulls the cord on your chute automatically instead of you falling and opening when you want to. Then all you have to worry about is not breaking your ankles when you hit the ground."

"That sounds terrifying," she said.

"I was scared out of my mind the first time. I just had to tell myself that it was important for me to be okay with jumping because the lives of other people may depend on it," Ray replied.

"That's for sure. You guys are required to respond to a crisis anywhere on earth in like eighteen hours, right? And you can bet those jumps aren't anywhere that you aren't going to be protecting people from harm," Erin said.

Ray chuckled and shook his head. "Please don't be insulted or think I'm a sexist or anything, but how do you know so much about the 82nd Airborne Division?"

Erin laughed. A giddy school girl laugh, really?

"My dad is a huge war buff. Ever since I was a little girl, he has been telling me all about different units that are specialized in different things, different wars and how different units performed there, and what the responsibility of those units are today. He's really fond of the 82nd Airborne, the 1st Marine Division, the 75th Ranger Regiment, and the Green Berets."

Ray sat back, his smile widening. "Well, you see that picture on the wall?" He pointed at the picture of him and a few other men in the desert. "That was when I was with the Green Berets in Iraq."

Erin's jaw dropped. "No way. You used to be with the Green Berets?"

Ray nodded. "Yes, ma'am. I was for a little while."

Erin swatted her hand in the air. "And you're still calling me ma'am when I should definitely be calling you sir."

Butterflies were swarming again but she no longer cared. He was hot, he was kind, and he was a hero. It was like he had stepped right out of a dream. She was so wrapped up in what she was feeling that she could hardly believe what came out of her mouth next.

"I'm definitely gonna have to take you home to meet my dad when I go visit him tomorrow. He'd be on cloud nine, picking your brain."

Take him home to meet your dad? What the hell has gotten into you? Slow your roll before you wind up embarrassing yourself even more than you are now. Her inner voice pleaded with her.

Ray flashed a grin and said something that shocked her. "That'd be fine with me. He sounds like a great guy."

CHAPTER 16

Whoa. Did she seriously just get all girly and ask a guy she just met to come and meet her dad? Tomorrow? How had she gone from sitting down to talk about a missing friend to now inviting him to Sunday dinner with her dad? She knew she needed to pull it together and focus on the task at hand. There was something about him, though. Something that interested her like nobody had before.

"But before we get into that any further, would you like to talk about what your friend told you about?" Ray asked, jolting her back to reality.

Erin blinked and nodded. "Yeah, of course. I've never really done this sort of thing before, so I'm not really sure where to start."

"I understand; it can be kind of overwhelming. Why don't you start by giving me a little information about your friend," Ray said as he clicked his pen and scribbled down the date and time of their conversation across the top of the legal pad.

Erin took a deep breath. "Okay. Her name is Ashanti Marie Livingston."

Ray looked up at Erin, "I know Ashanti."

"Really?" Erin asked.

"Sure do. African-American, 34 years old, 5'8", used to have a stylized crown tattooed on the left side of her neck," Ray said.

Erin was stunned. "Yeah, that's her. How do you know her, though?"

"I had detained her under suspicion of prostitution about three years ago. It was Christmas and I'd volunteered to do patrol and give somebody with kids the night off. She had a huge shiner on her eye but she was still trying to work the Pilot parking lot off of I-95. Once I detained her, she started crying, told me how sorry she was, and that she wouldn't do it again. I was mainly just trying to get her to tell me who hit her so that I could make sure that he wouldn't hurt her anymore. She wouldn't give him up, and it was Christmas, so I didn't see any reason to make things worse for her.

"I put her in the back seat of my patrol car and drove her up 95 and dropped her off outside of the ER at McLamb. I told her to go get herself checked out and to leave this life behind. The next day, I got a call from her, thanking me for helping her and telling me the name and address of her boyfriend. She told me that he had a bunch of Fentanyl in the house in addition to him beating her up. We busted him and I didn't hear from her until I was elected sheriff," Ray explained.

Erin shook her head in amazement. "Would you believe that I treated Ashanti that night for her shiner?"

"Wow, that's wild. Who would've thought that we were just a few hundred yards from each other, trying to help the same person, on the same day," Ray said.

"It's a crazy life we live, for sure. I only wish that we could've been introduced through her in a better situation," Erin said.

"I wish that could've happened too. At least we're here now, though. Sorry for the long story. Please continue," Ray said, and picked up his pen again.

"Right, so Ashanti and I have been friends off and on since high school. We kinda drifted apart in college and reconnected on the night that you drove her to the ER. She's been doing so great. She's gotten her life back on track, she's back in school, and she was even working to help get other women out of sex work. She's really incredible. I'm sorry, but did you say she was in contact with you since last fall?" Erin said.

"Yes. She had contacted me when she saw I was elected sheriff to congratulate me and to say that I and another person, who I guess is you, had really inspired her to get her life together again. That was pretty humbling for me. Being in the service for so long, it seemed I was only good at blowing stuff up instead of helping people put it all back together.

"Anyway, she had said she was helping other women get off of the street and had offered to pass along any info she picked up about stuff here in Craven County. Pretty soon she was giving me all kinds of dirt that pointed to Tyrone Weeks and his operation. We never would've been able to put him away without her," Ray said.

Erin was proud of her friend in a whole new way. She was the strongest person she knew for bouncing back from all that she had been through. Learning now that she helped law enforcement take down someone as dangerous as Tyrone Weeks deepened her respect for her significantly. She hoped she could be that strong and brave one day.

"Wow, I had no idea she was helping with that," Erin said.

"Ashanti is an incredible person. So, what's going on with her now, though?" Ray asked.

"So, a couple of weeks ago she came into the ER at night looking for me. I was gone for the day so she had to talk to one of the nurses on duty," Erin said.

"What was this nurse's name?" Ray asked.

"Lacey Robinson. So, Lacey had gone on vacation right afterwards and forgot to tell me about it until yesterday afternoon. She said that Ashanti was acting really erratic, like she was scared or in trouble. Lacey said she kept going on about needing to tell me about this place she calls 'The Woods,'" Erin said.

"Okay. So, she had told you about this place before?"

Ray asked.

"Mmhmm. We had lunch a couple of months back and she told me that she needed to tell me something in case something happened to her."

"What did she tell you?" Ray asked.

"She said that she had been talking to someone who had told her about a place in the woods. A place where...this is gonna sound crazy, but it's what she told me," Erin said.

"I'm not gonna judge you or her. I need all the help I can get with finding Megan Prince's killer," Ray said.

Erin took a deep breath. An icy ball replaced the butterflies in her stomach. "Okay. She said that this person, she didn't tell me any names, said that there was a place somewhere out in the boonies where people are kept kinda like cattle."

She looked at Ray and could find no hint of judgement in his demeanor. Only a strange warmth in his eyes that told her it was safe for her to talk to him about anything. "This person told her that a dangerous group of people like, own it, or maintain it, or something. She said that this dangerous group of people take other people to this place so that they can...fulfill their desires, I guess is a way to put it."

"So, she means like a brothel?" Ray asked

"No, no, not like a cathouse. She was clear about that. I'm gonna be honest with you. She kinda described something out of a horror movie," Erin explained.

"What do you mean out of a horror movie?"

"I mean...so she said..." She let out an awkward chuckle. "This is all gonna sound insane. She said that this place is like a slaughterhouse. That people are raped, tortured, killed. She even said that the person she was talking to said that people had paid this group to allow them to do twisted...like...like...the closest thing I can think of is experiments. She even said that people have paid to experience Roman-style orgies. She also suggested that people may be hunted like animals too."

Erin rested her head on the crook between her thumb and index finger. She avoided Ray's gaze like the plague.

There was no way that he didn't think that she and Ashanti were crazy. At the very least, he had to be thinking about how this discussion was a colossal waste of a Saturday.

"That's quite a story. I'm going to be honest with you. I'm not saying that I don't believe it. But I'd be lying if I didn't say that I had a healthy skepticism, though. So, relax. I don't think you or Ashanti are crazy," Ray said.

Erin fanned her face in an exaggerated gesture. "Whew. That's a relief. I was pretty sure you were gonna tell me to have a good day, send me out, and that'd be the last I heard of you."

"Nah. It'd take a whole lot more than that for me to put you on the road. Besides, I'm looking forward to talking to your dad about the Green Berets." He offered an encouraging smile.

Oh my God. He literally just mentioned meeting your dad. The voice in her head was running a mile a minute. For some reason, she decided to shoot her shot. What the hell, he probably thought she was crazy anyway.

"So does that mean that you're definitely going to come talk to hang out with the old man with me tomorrow after church?"

"Sure. That sounds like fun. It's not too often that I run into folks who know anything about the Green Berets," Ray replied.

Erin was stunned. Seven months of no guys and just like that you're back, baby.

"Okay, I'll tell Daddy we'll have a guest. Say around one or so?" she said with her smile back in full force.

"I'll keep that in mind. I'm really looking forward to it. I do have one more question for you about the story though."

"Fire away," Erin said.

"Why did you think that this story might relate to Megan Prince?"

"Well, there's a couple of reasons. Ashanti told me all of this stuff and freaked me right out with how adamant that she was that I keep it to myself in case anything happened to her. I didn't think too much about it, to be honest, but now she's missing," Erin said.

"Missing? Since when?" Ray asked.

"She hasn't been seen since her outburst at the ER. I tried calling her phone and it says it's disconnected. She had mentioned something about trying to catch a Greyhound to Nashville, but I haven't had a chance to look into that. She didn't leave any forwarding address, so there's no way for me to get in touch with her; nothing. It's like she has dropped off the map. I know that doesn't necessarily mean that she's missing, but I just have a bad feeling that she's in trouble."

"I'll have some deputies make some calls in Nashville and see if she or anyone matching her description has been hanging around up there. When we're done here, I may just ride up to the Greyhound station in Florence and see if she bought a ticket to Nashville or anywhere else. We'll find her, don't worry about that," Ray said.

"Thank you so much. That'll be a lot more than I could do."

"I'm happy to do it. I want her found and safe as much as you do."

Erin was beginning to feel like she could trust him with anything, and that was downright terrifying to her for some weird reason.

"You said there was another reason?" Ray asked.

"Yeah. She had told me that if anything happened to her, that I should contact you directly. That I could trust you. So, when I saw your email and the description of the girl, I knew that it wasn't a coincidence and I texted you right then and there."

"What do you mean that the description of Megan and Ashanti telling you to get in touch with me were not coincidences?" Ray asked.

"Ashanti told me that her contact had seen a girl at The Woods who matched your description of Megan Prince. Down to the tattoo on her inner wrist."

[But Ashanti went missing before they ID'd Megan. Did someone recognize Megan from when she went missing in Myrtle Beach, which I assume would have been on the local news.]

CHAPTER 17

Spending all morning on Lake Murray had been a great idea. Twenty years of being a sheriff's deputy meant that Gary McFadden couldn't sleep past 6 am, and that included on his weekends off. This morning, his eyes shot open at 5:07, he'd only been able to get to sleep sometime around midnight, and he decided there wasn't much point in staying in bed any longer. He got up, made the bed, and shuffled into the kitchen to start a pot of coffee.

After jumping in the shower, he got dressed and grabbed his personal phone before heading back into the kitchen for the coffee that his nostrils told him had finished brewing. He poured himself a cup of black coffee and sat down at the kitchen table and checked the weather app while he sipped the hot liquid. This was his morning ritual for the past four years. When he saw that the weather was going to be clear and 68 until about mid-morning, an incredibly cool temperature for any time of day during a South Carolina summer, an idea popped into his head.

He finished his coffee while he read a news story on one of the three news apps on his phone and headed back into the bedroom to pull on his weekend boots and to grab his fishing cap. It was an old camouflage cap with the logo of the University of South Carolina Gamecocks embroidered on the front. He filled his insulated tumbler with hot coffee and headed out to his truck. He grabbed a couple of poles, his tackle box, and his cooler out of the shed behind the trailer. Ten minutes later, he pulled out of the park with his gear in the bed and his boat trailing behind.

An hour later, after stopping for a bag of ice, a twelve pack of Mountain Dew, and a chicken biscuit, he was on the waters of Lake Murray and headed to his favorite spot on the lake.

The peace of the morning and the calm waters of the lake before the sun came up did a world of good in easing the trouble in his soul. The visions of Megan Prince still haunted him and popped up when he least expected them. Talking with Nora about the case and getting to spend some time with her had gone a long way toward exorcising the particular demon that found him. It wasn't completely gone, though. The recurring dreams about her had been making sure of that.

Still, the morning tranquility of casting a line out on the glassy water had restored his soul. Reeling in a nice largemouth bass on his fourth cast of the day only made it better. Over the course of the next hours, he caught his limit of largemouth bass, crappie, and even a couple of stripers. His mind occasionally wandered into territory that he didn't like, but the sounds of the lake and the earthy aroma quieted all concerns. Now, as he pulled up to his trailer with a stringer filled with fresh, cleaned fish, he liked his prospects for an equally great evening.

As he slowly pulled his truck around the bend in the road that led to his quiet corner of the park, his heart skipped a beat at the sight of a new, black BMW M5 parked on the street in front of his place. That was Nora's car. He slowly pulled past his place and began to carefully back his boat into the space beside the shed as his mind filled with many of the thoughts he puzzled over from time to time out on the lake.

It wasn't that he wasn't happy that she had decided to come see him; far from it. It was just that he had given their relationship a lot of thought over the past few weeks. They had been seeing one another ever since he took that first nervous trip down to Charleston after talking to her for a week or two on a dating app.

She was the most captivating woman that he had ever seen, and the beauty displayed by the pictures on her profile seemed to be enhanced by the information she included about herself. As he scanned a description of her and what she was looking for in a man, he couldn't help but think that he had all of those qualities. When he saw that she was thirty-six, only seven years younger than he was at forty-three, he decided that it was worth it to send her a message.

He was prepared to get no response and move on after a couple of days, which seemed to happen on those sorts of apps more times than not. Surprisingly, she had messaged him back within a couple of hours, and before he knew it, they were texting back and forth and talking on the phone.

They had a great deal in common. They both loved movies, enjoyed the outdoors, and were fans of the Gamecocks. Everything about her seemed too good to be true, but he held onto a little faith that maybe she was the one he had been looking for all of this time.

They met at a quiet lounge in Charleston that he had never heard of, and his nerves only seemed to intensify as he parked his truck and smoothed the fabric of his best sport coat before he entered the place. He nervously told the hostess that he was there to meet someone, and after giving her his name, she led him to a quiet corner booth away from the stage and the smooth jazz band that was playing there.

When he saw her, most of his apprehension melted away. She was even more stunning than the pictures he had seen of her on the app. She was dressed in a deep red cocktail dress that hugged every curve of her body before it closed snugly around her elegant neck. She wore matching high-heeled shoes, lipstick, and nails with dark, sultry eye makeup that lit a fire inside of Gary's belly. Her long blonde hair was immaculately styled as it flowed over her left shoulder to the middle of her chest and highlighted the matching earrings and necklace that she wore.

Gary struggled with a mouth that had just gone dry as he introduced himself. She responded in kind, her breathy voice that was both exciting and interesting him as she spoke. They talked and sipped cocktails for several hours. After they had talked for a while and danced a slow dance or two, she and Gary walked out of the lounge where she surprised him with a kiss on the street. It was unlike anything that he had experienced before, and he could still remember the feeling of her body against his and her breath with his breath.

She had invited him to her home, and he had accepted the invitation whole-heartedly. Before she would get into his truck, she told him that she had a confession to make. Gary had expected that she may have had some reservations about things moving so fast on the first date, but he was more than willing to take it slow. She was unlike any woman that he had ever known, and he already knew that he would go at any speed she wanted so long as he could keep seeing her. The confession she had was not actually anything to do with the speed at which they were moving, but it was about something that could have an effect on how, or if, it progressed from there.

It threw Gary for a loop. There was no way he would have guessed what she told him. But if he stepped back and thought about it, he could see that the signs were there. He was in uncharted territory with this woman, and he had no idea what he should do. In the end, he looked at her and the terrified look on her face, he reminded himself that he really liked this woman and that he could learn to handle the implications of her confession. He wanted to see where this went.

He kissed her again and helped her into his truck. He

drove her to her home close to the battery. Once inside, he began the journey of discovery he had been on ever since. That was just over one year in the past. In the time since, the initial awkwardness and the learning curve that he had been given had given way to closeness and intimacy that he had never known he would enjoy nor that he never knew existed. Where initial attraction, trepidation, and a receptive mindset had been, there now stood a fortress of tenderness, passion, and love within himself.

As he got out of the truck and walked toward the steps, his catch and cooler in hand. He thought back fondly to those times. Those were so much simpler times. Now he wondered what their future might hold.

The Megan Prince case was going to be the last straw for him. He already knew that he was going to see it through to the end and finally take his pension and run. Maybe he would move on up to Rock Hill or somewhere closer to his kids. No, that would be too much for them. They had their life there, and the last thing he wanted to do was go messing up the apple cart there.

Maybe he would move down to Charleston to be closer to Nora. The kids would like coming to see their dad a whole lot more if he were closer to the beach. What would that mean for his relationship with Nora, though? It's not like they could get married or anything. Were they ultimately just wasting their time? It was a conversation that he wasn't sure how to have. It wasn't a conversation that he wanted to have. Things were incredible with her. It was a conversation that he knew he needed to have, whatever consequences that may bring.

He walked up the steps and into the back door of the trailer. "Hey there, pretty lady. I didn't know you were planning on coming up for the day. I hope you ain't been here all by yourself for a while," Gary said as he started to rinse off the freshly caught and fileted fish in the kitchen sink.

"I had nothing to do today, so I thought I would come and surprise my man. I've only been here for about three or four hours. I tried calling you to let you know I was coming. I'll be right there in a second. I'm almost ready," Nora replied.

Nora was in the bedroom and the sound of her breathy voice calling down the hall was music to his ears. He started transferring the filets from the sink to a plate covered with paper towels, patting them dry, as he smiled to himself.

"You mean you didn't get ready before you came this time? Well, that's out of character for you. You ain't scared of me seeing you when you ain't all dressed up?" Gary said as he reached into the cabinet and retrieved a bag of fish fry mix.

"Not exactly. I had thought that you might be out and about. I know you can't sit still for very long. So, I called, and when I didn't get you, I thought it would be safe for me to just bring all my stuff to get ready here for when you came home," Nora replied from the bedroom.

Gary transferred the dried fish filets to a clean freezer bag and double-checked the fridge to make sure there was enough buttermilk to soak them in before frying them up. "You know me so well, girl. I decided to go out and do a little fishing this morning. Ain't too much of a signal out there at my favorite spot on the lake."

"Well, that sounds exciting. Did you get any keepers?" She called down the hall.

"Yes ma'am. Caught my limit in bass and crappie. Got a couple of nice stripers too. Hope you're in the mood for a fish fry for supper," he replied.

"Mmmm. That sounds delicious, lover. Look at you being such a good man and taking care of little ol' me," she said.

He zipped up the freezer bag and gently set it in the fridge. He heard the distinct sound of stilettos clicking across the linoleum floor of the kitchen. "Are hush puppies also on the menu, big guy?"

Gary turned and was stunned to see her standing in the kitchen in a body-conscious dress that hugged her every curve with one dainty hand on her hip and the other touching his shoulder.

"Wow, you look gorgeous. That dress looks great on you, baby."

She pulled him away from the fridge and pushed her body against his. "You like it? Just wait till you see what's underneath, lover," she said as she pulled him into a passionate kiss. Any thoughts of the conversation he knew he needed to have with her melted away in an instant.

CHAPTER 18

Darrin Gaskins wasn't sure what felt better as he laid his head back against the worn-out couch he was sitting on. The meth that he had just smoked or the cranked-out woman that was on her knees doing her best work to pleasure him. She wasn't too bad. Darrin had better head before her, but he also had a lot worse. At least she had lost most of her teeth on the left side of her mouth from her meth habit. Darrin had only felt teeth rub against him once since she had started. That was good enough to earn her bag of crank that she was desperately working on him for.

Darrin moaned in satisfaction, though he still couldn't quite tell if it was the euphoric feeling from the crank or the slowly intensifying sense of pleasure emanating from his lap. If he was honest with himself, it was probably the meth that made him enjoy the head as much as he was already.

He felt another tooth snag him.

"Watch it with them fucking teeth, bitch. Do that shit

again and you ain't getting no candy from me," he said.

The intensity of the mediocre fellatio picked up in earnest, and he could tell that the teeth weren't going to be a problem. He sighed and his limbs felt like they were floating. This was going to be a good trip for him, and he deserved every ounce of peace that it was going to give him.

He closed his eyes to savor the feeling. Immediately, the images he was trying to escape pounced on his mind like a cat on a chipmunk. Images of blood, bone, and body parts. The sounds of screaming, pleading, and praying. The putrid scent of feces, the coppery smell of blood, and the foul odor of rotting flesh. His eyes darted open to banish the horror that hid behind his eyelids.

What more was it going to take for it all to go away? It used to all go away when he spent the money he made taking out the trash. Then it would only go away after good sex. Before long, booze was the only thing that could make it all go away. Finally, meth tended to do the trick. Except that it didn't do the trick; not anymore. He looked down at the girl. Was her name Chelsea or Kelsey? He couldn't remember it for the life of him. She was still going at it like a chicken on a June bug, but any pleasure he had been feeling from it had just drained away.

He glanced at the pipe he had taken the hit out of and thought about sparking it for the fourth time in twenty minutes. He still had enough of his wits left to know that he would be rolling the dice on getting the ride of his life or a trip to the funeral home if he did. Even if it didn't stop his heart cold and he was able to chase the ultimate high, he suspected the ghosts he was running from would still be there. They were waiting for him to close his eyes again.

He needed to get out of there. If he went back to Charlie's house in Queen's Bridge, then Charlie could hook him up with something different than the crank he'd been leaning on for the past few months. He'd take heroin even. All that really mattered was making those ghosts go away.

Darrin pushed what's-her-name back away from his lap and stood up. He wasn't sure if the shakiness of the room was from the head rush of standing too soon or from the three hits of meth he had taken in the last few minutes.

"Quit. That's enough," he said.

What's-her-name looked confused as she wiped the saliva from her lips with her forearm.

"But, but you didn't cum? Don't you wanna cum? I'm real sorry if I was doing it wrong. I'll do it better. I promise. You'll see. Just don't go yet," she said as he buttoned his pants.

"Yeah, I'm sure you would do better. And if cow shit was butter we'd all have a Merry Christmas too." Darrin reached into the front pocket of his jeans and fished out a small plastic bag with three tiny crystals inside. He flicked it onto the carpet in front of what's-her-name.

"Here's your goddamn candy. Next time, you're gonna finish the damn job for it, though. You hear me?" Darrin said.

She instantly began searching the stained shag carpet for the bag, like a rat searches through a fresh can of garbage. Darrin stepped over her and around the piles of dirty laundry scattered all over the small living room of the dilapidated house. Just before the front door shut behind him, he heard what's-her-name, he was about eighty percent sure it was Chelsea, call out behind him. "Thanks, baby. I'll be goo--"

The door shut and cut off the last bit of what she was saying, but Darrin was sure it was something about how good she was gonna do when he came to see her again. He told himself that he wasn't coming back to this shithole. That wasn't true, though. He'd be back in a few days to give her another chance at scoring a little more candy and him another chance at burying the ghosts in his head.

He staggered to his car and flopped down into the driver's seat. The world around him was still shaky and the moss hanging from the tree in what's-her-name's front yard was starting to look eerily similar to an old man with a long beard or a wizard. He couldn't be sure. He shook the fog out of his head as best he could, cranked the car, and pulled out onto the county road. He drove for three miles and only swerved onto the grassy shoulder twice. He turned off of the county road onto 521 and headed back to Queen's Bridge.

All in all, he was doing pretty good. He was staying in his lane for the most part and had only run off the road twice. There were a couple of assholes who had blown their horns at him once he crossed into Craven County. He shot them the finger and kept on moving. He was getting to the edge of the town of Queen's Bridge and swerved through the community of Norwich, which was closer to the county line, when he swerved off of the road and nearly hit an abandoned car on the side of the road.

The near miss gave him a jolt of adrenaline and a brief second of sobriety. He used that second to swear that if he made it to Charlie's place that he wouldn't drive till he knew that he was good and sober. The interior of his car was bathed in flashing blue lights. The light tripped him out for a second, and he thought that maybe it was the light from his phone ringing. His heart sank when he heard the sound of a police siren accompanying the flashing blue lights.

For a split second he thought about running, but he knew he had a better chance of being wrapped around a tree than he had of getting away. If he played it cool, and they were Queen's Bridge police, all he would need to do is mention that he worked for Chief Mungo's boss. Then he'd be on his way to Charlie's. If not, it wasn't the first time that he had faked being sleepy to cover for drugs and alcohol.

He pulled over to the side of the road, put the car in park, and placed his hands on the wheel where they could clearly be seen. In less than a minute, a cop silhouetted by the headlights of his cruiser, shined a flashlight into Darrin's car and appeared at the driver's side window. The cop tapped the window with his light.

"Good evening, sir. I'm with the Craven County sheriff's department. Would you mind rolling your window down, please?" the deputy said.

Damn, he was a sheriff's deputy. The QBPD definitely knew who he was and who he worked for, but it was a lot spottier with the sheriff's department. He might not be completely sunk yet, though. Maybe he was one of the deputies that the people he worked for had in their pocket. He rolled his window down. "Good evening to you, uh, officer, uh?" Darrin said.

"I'm deputy Jerrod Knight, with the sheriff's department, sir. Can I get a look at your license and registration, please. You know why I stopped you tonight?"

Shit. He definitely wasn't one of the guys that he was told would look out for him. He grabbed his license from his wallet and the registration from the glove box along with an insurance card. Time to try the ol' I'm-too-tired-to-drive trick. Darrin did a convincing fake yawn to set the stage for his performance. He handed his identification to Knight.

"No, sir. I have no idea why you stopped me tonight," Darrin said.

"You nearly hit me where I had my car parked on the side of the road back there," Knight explained.

"Really? I'm sorry, uh, deputy. I'm sorry. I must've dozed off back there. This past my bedtime and I'm just looking to get home," Darrin lied.

"I see. Where're you coming from tonight, Mr. Gaskins?"

"Seeing a friend over in Georgetown. We got to talking and time got away from me, so I decided to head home before it got too late."

"Okay. This friend got a name?" Knight asked.

Of course he would ask this question. Now Darrin had no choice but to commit to one of the names he was torn between.

"Chelsea."

"Chelsea got a last name?" Knight asked.

"I, uh, well. To tell you the truth, sir, I don't know her last name. It was sort of a hookup if you know what I mean," Darrin said.

"I know what you mean, sir. You have anything to drink while you were seeing your friend?"

"No, sir. Not a drop," Darrin replied.

"Okay, well just so I can be sure, I'm gonna have you

step out of the car for me, please," Knight said.

"But I ain't had nothing to drink."

"You were swerving an awful lot back there, sir. Could've killed me if you were about half a foot closer to my squad car. Now, step out of the car, please," Knight asked for a second time.

Darrin was screwed. There wasn't anything else he could do but hope that by some miracle he was able to pass the field sobriety tests the deputy was going to throw his way. He opened the door, got out, and hoped that the swaying of the world around him wouldn't translate into the movements of his body.

For the next few minutes, he followed the instructions of the deputy and said the alphabet, stood on one leg, and walked a straight line. Darrin was almost certain that he aced them all. His elation drained out of him like a bathtub when the deputy placed him in handcuffs.

"What are you arresting me for, officer?" Darrin asked.

"Suspicion of driving under the influence of a controlled substance."

"What? I ain't done nothing."

"Your eyes are all over the place and you couldn't even pick one of your feet up off the ground without staggering. You've got all the signs that you're on something," Knight explained.

The deputy began feeling around Darrin's legs and pockets and seemed to stop once his hand passed over his front pants pocket. Darrin began panicking as the deputy reached into his pants pocket and retrieved a small bag with several tiny crystals inside.

"And this here, Mr. Gaskins, means you're now going to jail for possession of methamphetamine."

Darrin rested his head on the cool metal of the hood on the deputy's Charger. He wasn't sure what felt worse. The fact that he was going to jail for a decent chunk of time, or the fact there was no way to get rid of the ghosts in his head once he got there.

CHAPTER 19

SUNDAY, 1:30 PM
127 CHEROKEE ROAD
FLORENCE, SOUTH CAROLINA

It had been a long time since Ray Myers had felt this way. In his line of work, nerves and anticipation were par for the course, but women were altogether different. It had settled into his system the instant he crossed the county line, and it had only grown in intensity as he drove his truck through Coward, Effingham, and South Florence. Now, as he turned left off of South Irby Street and onto Cherokee Road, past the Piggly Wiggly and Timrod Park on his right, and searched for the address that Erin McKee had given him, he thought of how this feeling had been in his life. For most of his life, he had other priorities.

When he was in high school at Craven Academy, he devoted most of his time to perfecting his pitch and practicing his math skills. Morning after morning he was out on the mound relentlessly throwing pitch after pitch into his younger brother's mitt, and night after night he worked problem after problem until he could do calculus in his sleep.

All of his hard work paid off when he took the Craven Academy Crusaders to the South Carolina state baseball championship in Columbia during his senior year. He struck out all-stars from all over the state during the tournament and led his team to victory over the Lancaster High School Bruins to win the first-ever state title for his small school on the coastal plains. His hard work off of the diamond also paid off and helped him maintain a 3.8 GPA throughout his high school career.

Both his GPA and his skills as a pitcher earned him scholarship offers from schools like the University of South Carolina, Clemson University, Louisiana State University, and Mississippi State University. In the end, he didn't choose to play for any of the vaunted baseball schools in college athletics and instead, to the dismay of many, he chose to play for the Citadel, the military college of South Carolina.

He excelled at the Citadel, and the structure of life there gave him the perspective to decide what he wanted to do with his life. He knew that if he wanted to make something of himself and for his life to truly mean something, he needed to proceed from the Citadel to the US Army. His mother cried and his father lectured, but it was something that he had to do. He needed to test and prove to himself that he was worthy of freedom.

Looking back now on the way he thought as a young second lieutenant fresh out of the Citadel, he didn't recognize himself. Thoughts of testing his mettle and proving that he was worthy were naive. He had served with some of the bravest and best people that he had ever had the privilege of knowing. He had seen them die, and he had killed alongside them. He learned that nobody was worthy but that freedom was a gift provided by those who died. He wasn't the same man now as he was then.

His GPS app interrupted his chain of thought and announced that his destination was on the right in 800 feet. Ray turned into the drive of a modern house built in the antebellum style. The two-story home had a porch on the ground level and a porch on the second level, both supported by tapered wooden columns across the front. The house was surrounded by more than an acre of neatly mown grass except for two towering magnolia trees on the left end of the house and an ancient oak in the front that looked as though it was bent under the weight of all of the moss that hung from its branches.

As Ray drove down the short drive, lined by pink flowering crepe myrtles, he took a deep breath. He parked his truck beside Erin's Carolina Blue Mustang, grabbed the pound cake he had baked that morning along with a bouquet of peonies, and got out of the truck. He took one last look in the driver's side-mirror to make sure that he had adequately trimmed his facial hair and combed his hair before he headed toward the steps of the house. He rang the doorbell, did one last check in the window to the left of the door, and hoped he had not put on too much cologne.

Erin opened the door. She was absolutely breathtaking. He could tell from her white sleeveless top, navy ankle-length skirt, dusty booties, jewelry, and perfectly coiffed hair and makeup that she had taken time to look her best after church. He didn't know if that was something that she always did, or if it was something that she did because she would spend the afternoon with him. Ray hoped that it was the latter.

"Hey there, Sheriff. It's good to see you. You have any trouble finding the place?" Erin said.

It was sexy as hell the way that she called him "Sheriff."

"No, no trouble getting here at all. These are for you," Ray said as he handed her the bouquet of flowers.

"Oh my goodness, peonies are my absolute favorite. You didn't have to go and do this." She stood up on her tiptoes and draped her arms around his neck. Ray placed his right arm around the middle of her back and pulled her closer. The firmness of her physique and the warmth of her body felt good against him. The smell of her perfume was intoxicating, and his desire to both get to know her more and to get another chance to touch her again grew.

"It was my pleasure. I just wanted you to know that

I appreciate the invitation to spend some time with you. And–" He released the hug and drew her attention to the fresh pound cake wrapped in cellophane, "this is to say the same thing to your dad."

"Oh my word, is this pound cake?"

"It's my favorite and it's one of the things I know how to make. I figured you could tell me how I did with it," Ray explained as he stepped into the house.

Erin closed the door behind him to trap the cool air inside of the house and banish the hot and sticky air to the outside. "You made that? My, oh my, you're a one-in-a-million kinda man, aren't you? Next thing you're gonna tell me is you cook too," Erin said as she took the cake with her free hand.

"I'm not gonna be on Chopped, but I know my way around the kitchen. Enough to make some halfway decent spaghetti. Anything more complicated than that and you're rolling the dice," Ray said.

Erin laughed at his polite modesty. Though, she suspected that he probably was capable of doing much more than he suggested.

"Well, you need to get yourself a taster, like me for instance," Erin said, exhilarated by her boldness.

"That's a deal. I'll make you anything you want," Ray said, surprised at how comfortable he was talking to her.

Erin grinned. "Okay, Sheriff. You just let me know when you're cooking and I'll be there."

"Who's here, precious?" A voice called from the living room immediately to the right of the foyer.

"It's my friend, Ray. The guy I was telling you about yesterday that had served in the military," Erin responded over her shoulder.

She looked at Ray, her green eyes positively glowing with warmth and adoration.

"Come on, I'll introduce you to Daddy."

She turned and led Ray into the living room. The room was painted a pleasant sky blue and the walls were littered with framed photographs of who Ray assumed were family members and a few that he assumed were of Erin at various stages of her life. Above the brick fireplace, on the far wall, was a portrait of a young woman dressed in white. Ray could see a striking resemblance between the young woman in the portrait and Erin, which led him to conclude that this portrait was probably that of her mother.

Two bookcases were recessed into the wall on either side of the fireplace. The one on the right was filled with mementos from places all over Europe, and the one on the left was stacked with DVDs on the top and on the bottom with a flat screen television mounted in the middle. Across the room from the fireplace and television, three sofas were arranged around a square coffee table with a recliner directly opposite the television.

An older man with a prosthetic leg reclined in the chair and slowly turned his gaze from the Atlanta Braves who were now beating the Washington Nationals by a couple of runs. He glanced up from his baseball game and lowered the recliner. It always amazed Ray to see amputees perform daily tasks that are taken for granted by so many with the same ease as though life had not taken a large part of them. The ease with which Erin's dad snapped up from his recliner and the speed with which he crossed the room to give Ray a firm handshake was no different.

"Good to meet you, son. Ronnie McKee."

The older man vigorously pumped Ray's hand with the warmth that Ray had known from his grandfather's handshakes.

"Pleased to meet you, sir. I appreciate you having me."

"Happy to have you over. My Erin sure seems to think you're something else. She's never really been one to bring a man over to meet the old man until later on down the line."

The old man cracked an impish grin as he cut his eyes towards the reddening face of his daughter. Ray matched the jovial demeanor of the old man as he said, "Really? Hopefully that's good news for me."

Ray stole a glance at Erin who stood with a polite smile and eyes that betrayed her anxiety at her father's casual discussion of how much she liked him. He hoped she knew that the feeling was mutual.

Regaining her composure, Erin placed a hand on her father's forearm before saying, "You'll have to excuse my dad. Discretion was never really his strong suit. You should've seen what he did to my date to the prom. Flat-out told him that I was only going with him to be nice and not to expect any sparks to fly out there on the dance floor. Poor guy didn't know whether Daddy was kidding or whether he was serious."

"What can I say, I just can't help but cut right through all the bullshit," Ronnie explained.

"Watch it, old man. It's Sunday, remember?" Erin remarked.

"You're right, sweet pea. God don't care what you say Monday through Saturday, but on Sunday He starts getting all uptight about it."

Ray couldn't help but laugh along with the older man, and he couldn't help but notice how cute Erin looked as she did her best to stifle her own laughter. She took a sharp breath and changed the subject, "Ray, I hope you like fried chicken and biscuits."

"I love it."

"Well good, because that's what we're having for lunch. I hope you brought an appetite to go with these flowers and this cake too."

CHAPTER 20

The next several hours seemed to pass like minutes. The men were treated to a lunch of fried chicken, biscuits, mashed potatoes and gravy, macaroni and cheese, fried okra, and black-eyed peas. It was some of the most delicious food that Ray had tasted in a long time. The flavors took him back to Sunday suppers at his grandmother's table and the feeling of love and peace he had struggled to rediscover during his military service. The fact that this amazing woman, who he had no idea existed on Friday, had poured her heart and soul into such an incredible meal had only made him appreciate her more.

After lunch, Erin had insisted that Ray and her father retire to the family room while she cleared the dishes. No amount of assuring her that he was old hand at what the army termed "KP" made any difference. With a warm smile and the gentle touch of her hand on his chest, he relented and followed her father into the family room.

He stole a glance at Erin as she tied an apron around her waist. When she turned to grab some of the dishes from the table, she caught him staring. Rather than quickly avert his gaze, he held firm and met her green eyes when they flashed in his direction. For a moment it seemed as if the world had stopped on a dime. They stood and gazed into each other's eyes from across the table, oblivious to the world and only aware of the connection they shared with one another.

The moment was broken by Ronnie telling Ray that if he was a Yankees fan, he had to get out and never come back. Ray joined him in the family room, explained that he too was a lifelong fan of the Atlanta Braves, and dove into a conversation that ranged from baseball stats, college football, religion, politics, and family. He learned that they had many interests and values in common.

Ray learned that the old man had been a lawyer and now he was a judge at the circuit court who eyed retirement with each passing day. He learned that he grew up poor in rural Darlington County and that he had worked and fought for every bit of schooling that he had and for every dollar he had ever made. He learned that Ronnie had always wanted to join the military but an accident while chopping firewood had claimed one of his legs and had shattered his dream of being a soldier. His older brother, however, was able to join the Army in 1966, where he had served in the 82nd Airborne Division. He died during the Tet Offensive in 1968.

Ray discussed some of his own thoughts on his military service. He was honored to have carried on the legacy left by Erin's uncle, and he was humbled by how much less he did in his service to the country than what was done by Ronnie's brother. Ronnie was enraptured by Ray's recollections of training, and he was impressed by how much the army had changed in the ten years prior to Ray's departure from active duty.

He was impressed by Ray's candid first-hand assessment of the situation faced by both the US military and the local civilian populations in nations ranging from Syria to Venezuela. Ray believed that war was the sum of all evils and that it should only be prosecuted when absolutely necessary. He stood firm on his conviction that the US military was a force for good in Iraq and in Afghanistan, and that it was their duty to remain in both nations until freedom could be secured there.

By then, Erin had finished the dishes, swept the kitchen, and joined them in the family room. The conversation quickly turned from the military to countless stories of mishaps or antics that were funny now but were anything but funny at the time they occurred. Ray laughed like he hadn't laughed in ages at many of the stories and couldn't help but feel at home around Erin and her father.

Eventually, as the hours flew by and the sun began to sink, Ray began to think that he had better get on the road back to Queen's Bridge.

As if he could read Ray's mind, Ronnie piped up and suggested that Ray and Erin had had enough of chatting with an old man for one day. He practically ordered Ray to follow Erin to her home off of Third Loop Road and suggested that the two of them spend some time together. Ray wasn't about to argue with the old man on that one, and his heart seemed to flutter when Erin had smiled and said her father had come up with a great idea.

Twenty minutes later, Ray sat on a plush white sofa in the living room of Erin's ranch-style home.

"I've got some pinot grigio and I've got beer, but all I have is this IPA I picked up in Asheville last month," Erin called from the kitchen.

"Beer'll be fine, thanks," Ray replied.

"Coming right up."

Ray heard the closing of a fridge, the popping of a bottle cap, the tinkling of a wine glass, and the clinking sound of glass gently tapping against glass. In a few seconds, Erin emerged from the kitchen carrying two wine glasses, an unopened bottle of pinot grigio, and an opened beer. She handed him the beer, opened the wine, and filled her glass before taking a seat beside him on the couch.

"It's really cool of you to humor my dad as much as you did today," Erin said as she took the first sip of her wine.

"Yeah? Earn me another chance to see you?" he replied after taking his first sip of the citrusy craft beer.

Erin felt heat radiating from her cheeks. "Don't get too confident yet, Sheriff."

Ray chuckled, "Alright, whatever you say, Doc. But I wasn't exactly humoring your old man. He's a pretty cool guy, and it was really fun getting to watch baseball and have a little conversation with him. I'm looking forward to hanging out with him some more."

Erin's heart melted. She had never, never met a man who enjoyed hanging out with her dad. She still wasn't quite sure that he was being one-hundred-percent on the level with her, but she sure did hope he was.

"He didn't pry too much when he asked about you being a cop or a soldier, did he?" she asked.

"Not at all. He just asked me a few broad questions like where I served, what my MOS was, how long I was in, and if I did any time overseas; stuff like that. Then he let me take it from there and just listened. I'll tell ya, your old man really gets it when it comes to talking to vets," Ray explained before he took another sip from the dark brown bottle in his left hand.

"What do you mean by 'he gets it?'"

"Just that he is easy to talk to. He doesn't interject or ask about combat. He just listens and occasionally might ask how I felt about that particular thing. No judgement, no treating you like you're some sort of a hero; he just listens."

Erin took a sip of her wine. "That's really good to hear. I was a little worried he was going to push it too much and that you might be offended by that."

"Luckily, I'm a Green Beret. Offended is not really something that we get."

"Yeah, I guess you have to have some pretty thick skin to make it that far," Erin said.

"That's definitely part of it. The other part of it is just being 'in country' and seeing all that up close and personal."

"What do you mean by that?"

Ray took another sip of beer before answering. "I mean just seeing how bad that life is in combat zones. And then having to keep yourself and your buddies safe while you're operating there as well.

"There was this one time when me and my guys were deployed into Syria. We were out running an operation and gathering some information on ISIS with some of the Kurdish fighters we were supporting in the region. We wound up having to breach and clear this house that was sort of like a compound. I'll never forget blowing this re-inforced door in the basement off of its hinges and seeing these two little girls all tied up and dressed in lingerie. The guy who lived there surrendered to us and told us that the two girls were his nieces and that he had bought their virginity from their father."

The memory sent a meteor of rage to his head.

"We extracted him and took him to a facility to question him further. I just couldn't get that out of my head, though. Dude was just talking about keeping his nieces for his pleasure, like it was as normal as talking about going to the movies."

He stopped talking. He may have said too much. He offered a tight-lipped smile and looked at Erin for any sign that the shocking nature of his story had scared her away from him.

"So yeah, it takes a whole lot to offend me. Sorry. I've never told that story before and I don't know what gave me the idea that it was okay to start talking about it now."

He nervously swigged the last of the beer from the bottle. He felt a small hand come to rest on his forearm. He looked up and felt Erin gently rubbing his skin with her thumb. The look of understanding deep within her green eyes was like slipping into a warm bath. She carefully set her half-empty wine glass on the coffee table before returning her full attention to him.

"It's okay. Please don't feel like you have to apologize for opening up about something that happened while you were in the army. I'm so glad you felt comfortable sharing that with me, and I want you to know that you can trust me." She moved her hand from his forearm to his hand. She gently interlaced her fingers with his. "I want you to feel like you can tell me anything one day. However long that takes."

Ray gently squeezed her hand in his. "You know, if I didn't know any better, I'd say that you might wanna keep seeing me."

Erin carefully slid her body next to his. "I'd say that's for certain."

She slowly moved her free hand towards his face. Her heart was racing as she felt the wiry hairs protruding from the rough skin of his cheek. His heart was also thumping like a kick-drum as he tenderly placed his hand on the back of her neck. His strong hand on the back of her neck felt so good. It felt safe. It felt right.

She was completely at his mercy. She was vulnerable like she hadn't been in years. Yet strangely, she felt entirely secure like she had never felt before. Her heart hung by a thread at that moment. Her mind desperately, pleadingly, hoped he would seize her in a kiss.

His heart was pounding out of his chest. Never had he touched a woman who just seemed to fit in his hands. Never had he opened himself up to harm like he had unwittingly done with her. Yet, never had he instinctively known that he could trust her with the demons that haunted his past. She was comforting and unsettling all at the same time. As he tenderly massaged the back of her neck with his hand, he couldn't help but think that she was both his doom and his salvation.

Her soft skin felt so delicate in his rough hands. The smell of her hair was more intoxicating than the beer he had finished moments earlier. The desire that raged in his chest was set ablaze at the sight of her eyes so delicately closed in the ecstasy of being held fast by a man she desired.

Slowly, he moved his lips closer to hers. He blasted through all the barriers that his mind so desperately tried to construct and tenderly pressed his lips to hers. In an instant, the subtle tingling of electricity raced throughout both of their bodies. The gentle roughness of his lips against hers sent an involuntary moan to escape her throat. She slipped her hand from his cheek to the back of his head. She ran her fingers through his close-cropped hair as she kissed him again and again.

He felt her mouth open wide and the warm wetness of her tongue pressing against his lips. Every cell in his body wanted to thrust his own tongue forward to meet hers, but he desperately kept himself restrained. After one more taste of her strawberry kiss, all of his restraint broke like a dam at a critical flood stage.

He matched her passion. He pulled her tightly against his body and she dug her acrylic nails into the back of his shirt. Time seemed to stand still as they released the passion that had been building since the day before with one another. Each new kiss was somehow more enthralling than the last.

The heat of the moment slowed long enough for both of them to be aware of what had just transpired. Erin gave him one last kiss before she opened her eyes and looked into his. "I know that this all seems kind of fast, but. . . we can take this to the bedroom if you'd like."

She kissed the stubble on his cheek. The prospect of making love to her was easily the most enticing idea that had ever entered his mind. More than anything, he realized, he wanted to give whatever was happening between them the chance to blossom into something incredible. He wanted that more than he wanted to spend the night making love to her.

"Nothing would make me happier than making love to you tonight, Erin. You're the most beautiful, incredible, and amazing woman that I have ever met. I can't even begin to tell you how much I want you at this moment. But I want to give this—you know, us—all the time it needs to work."

Her heart fluttered when he used the word "us," and her body flooded with relief, amazement, and. . . love? Chills crawled up her spine at the thought of that last word. She wanted to feel him loving every inch of her body. She wanted him more than she had ever wanted a man before. But the feeling of amazement, respect, and love that she felt for him in the moment when he told her he was choosing her over a night of sex with her was somehow better.

She smiled and kissed him deeply again. "You're amazing, Raleigh Myers. Do you know that? Absolutely amazing."

CHAPTER 21

Darrin Gaskins lay in a puddle of cold sweat. He stretched out on his back but sleep had evaded him all night. He shook like a leaf and sweat poured from his body. He tried in vain to silence the monster that lurked in his mind and just out of sight in the shadows of his darkened cell.

It had been over twenty-four hours since he had come down from his high and the demons were punishing him for it. He wasn't quite sure if the sweat and the relentless assault by the ghosts were brought on by withdrawals or guilt, but he couldn't stand either for very much longer.

He had made a trip to the infirmary the night before. The possibility of Darrin stroking out from withdrawals was at the forefront of the guard's minds. The doctor on duty had declared that whatever withdrawals he might be going through, there was a ninety-nine-percent chance that Darrin would survive. The brief moment of hope that the knowledge he would survive this forcible detox was drowned out by the images that flashed in his mind every time he blinked.

He could see the face of every piece of trash he had taken out to the hole. He could hear their screams, pleading, and praying as clearly as if they were in the cell with him. The sins that he had worked so hard to bury had come home to visit him. He was exhausted.

He glanced into the darkest corner of the cell and shot straight up in bed. A black woman stood silently and motionless just inside of the darkness. Her long black hair framed a pretty face and nearly concealed the marks left behind by a tattoo-removal laser on her neck. Her lifeless eyes stared at Darrin. He knew who she was.

"You ain't real. I seen you die. You're just in my head."

The woman stood motionless. Her stare fell on Darrin like a ton of steel.

"Naw, you're just a figment of my imagination. That's all you are."

The woman, still staring a hole through Darrin, moved her right hand from her side towards her throat. Her fingernails tore into the soft flesh of her throat, ripping out veins and tendons as she went. She dropped a mass of flesh, arteries, and oozing blood onto the floor in front of her as nonchalantly as a smoker discarding a cigarette.

Darrin tried to scream but no sound left his throat. He cowered in the corner of his bed as his bladder evacuated. She moved both of her hands, one dripping with blood that now flowed from the maw that was once her throat with every beat of her heart, to the middle of her chest. Her fingernails dug into her flesh between her perfect breasts. She pulled her arms in opposite directions, splitting her ribcage in two clear to her back. Organs, blood, and viscera flopped onto the concrete with a sickeningly wet splat.

Darrin found his voice. "What the fuck do you want from me?" he screamed at the woman who was disassembling herself before his eyes. His screams now came through sobs.

"What do you want me to fucking say? I did what I had to do. If I told them no, it'd be me down in that hole instead of you. You can't blame me for that."

"It was my life you took. My body you cut apart. My story that you silenced," the woman said. Her voice was hollow and raspy.

Darrin wept. "I'm so sorry. God, I'm so, so sorry."

He wiped his eyes and looked towards the corner again and found it clean and empty. For a second, he was tempted to chalk the experience up to withdrawals but he knew better. He knew what he needed to do.

He got out of his bed and walked towards the door to his cell. He knew what could happen to him if he went through with it, but he knew it needed to be done. For the sake of the woman and all the others.

"I need to talk to a detective and to the sheriff. They're gonna need to hear what all I've got to say," he shouted.

Chapter 22

It was hard to slide out of bed and leave the warmth of Nora's naked back. Gary did it anyway once he read the text alert that lit up his work phone on the bedside table. Still, the softness of Nora's warm skin made him want to ignore the alert and to stay in bed with her. Gary wasn't the type of man to shirk responsibilities, though.

He sat on the edge of the bed, his muscles groaning from the exertion that she had wrought on them. It must've been twice yesterday afternoon and two more last night. What in the hell brought all that on?

He replayed the events of last night. She had stepped out of the bathroom that adjoined his bedroom in the sexiest lingerie he had ever seen, the sultriest of makeup he had seen her create in a while, and her natural hair that he had never seen. The feel of her skin against his, the expert way in which her hands handled him, and the exhilaratingly new feeling of running his fingers through her actual hair was irresistible.

Once he and she were both spent, he had thought about going one more time. The thought of Nora coping with the soreness that was definitely going to be plaguing her for the next few days stopped him short. Instead, he enveloped her in his arms and breathed her in until sleep took them both.

Now, he rolled over, ran his hand across her chest, and pulled her tightly to him. The cleft in her rump, as it pressed against his groin, sparked the flame inside of him anew. She stirred, covered the hand he had rested on her hip with her own, and spoke to him in a voice made gravelly from a night of slumber.

"G'mornin' lover. You sleep well?"

"I did, darlin'. You kinda wore me out this weekend," Gary said as he kissed the back of her neck.

"Mmmm, glad I could help you rest, lover. I'm a little sore this morning."

"I'm sorry, you just do something to me."

"Oh, I'm not complaining. I feel so much like a. . ." she turned her head and mashed her lips against his. ". . .like a woman."

Gary knew he should've gotten out of bed sooner, but her words and encouragement convinced him to stay in bed just a little longer. A few minutes later, he got out of bed, grabbed a sheriff's department polo, olive utility pants, underwear, and his boots and socks, and headed to the guest bathroom at the far end of the trailer. He showered, shaved, and thought about the incredible weekend he had with Nora.

He had finally seen her as she really was, without all of the help she relied upon. Her beauty had only grown in his estimation. He wanted to be with her more than ever, but he wasn't sure how that could ever happen.

It was a different world now. Unconventional couples like them were being accepted, even celebrated, like never before in society. Even in South Carolina, a state that was known for strict adherence to convention and tradition, there was a tacit acceptance of all of those changes. Still, the thought of openly expressing his affection for Nora was terrifying to Gary. He was terrified, but he was ready to live in the open with her if she was ready to do the same.

Nora lived even more of a double life than Gary. She could only be herself a few evenings a week and on the weekends. The rest of the time she was one of the partners in a respected real estate law firm in Charleston. She couldn't act like herself, dress like herself, or feel like herself. She was extremely careful not to let her professional life intersect with her personal life, and Gary couldn't say that he blamed her. Living in the open would jeopardize everything that she had worked so hard for over the years. Gary wasn't sure that bringing up his desire to be in the open with her would be well received on her part, and he wasn't sure he would blame her if it wasn't.

He pushed the thoughts from his head as he tied his boots, combed his gray hair, and walked out of the guest room. He stepped into the kitchen, filled his insulated cup with the coffee he had set on a timer, and grabbed the keys to his department-issued truck.

"Hey," Nora's muffled voice came from behind the closed door of Gary's bedroom. "I'm gonna have to head out at the same time as you. I had originally planned on leaving here after you had already gone to work, but I just remembered there's a deposition I have to sit in on at 9:30, and if I don't go when you do, I'll be late."

"That's fine with me," Gary replied.

"The thing is," Nora continued, "I'm dressed for work."

Gary could hear the anxiety in her voice. His empty stomach flipped. "That's okay, darlin'. There ain't nothing you should be ashamed of or embarrassed about."

Gary glanced out the window above the sink to see if anyone was out this morning. A quick scan revealed that none of the neighbors had ventured outside. There was just a work truck from the county parked on the corner two trailers down from his and a worker in a neon vest and hard hat examining the light pole on that corner. Gary breathed a sigh of relief when he didn't recognize him and realized the worker likely wouldn't recognize Gary.

"You sure? You're not gonna freak out?" Nora asked

through the thin door.

"I promise, darlin'. I won't freak out. I'll just get to see how amazingly beautiful you are in a different way."

"Okay, I'm coming out then."

The door to the bedroom slowly opened. Gary held his breath as Nora stepped out of the bedroom. Her normal sultry style had been replaced by slacks, a shirt, and a blazer. The luxurious hairstyles she displayed with her wigs had been replaced by her natural, short, and professional haircut. There was not even a trace of the makeup that she expertly used to make her as feminine and glamorous as possible. Even the stiletto-shaped nails she always wore were nowhere to be seen.

Gary took it all in. He couldn't believe it. Other than the multiple pieces of rose gold luggage that she carried and wheeled out of the bedroom, there was absolutely no trace of the Nora that he knew and loved. The person who stood in front of him smiled nervously.

"So, we haven't been officially introduced I guess." They began jokingly, "This is Noah."

CHAPTER 23

It was stressful enough to get the family all loaded up in Gatlinburg, drive all day through western North Carolina and most of South Carolina, and then unpack while feeding the kids, cleaning them up, and getting them ready for bed. The telephone call that came into his private cell phone that morning only heightened his stress-level. They had planned to spend most of the day taking in the majestic beauty that the mountains of east Tennessee had to offer, but that call and the message that their main garbage man in their operation had been picked up for a DUI the night before drastically changed their plans.

Wade felt a storm of emotions in less than a second when he heard the news. Initially, he felt the rage build up in his chest like a volcano ready to explode. It was truly perplexing that Darrin Gaskins could make such a stupid mistake just days after being in the clear from the discovery of Megan Prince's body. The thought of how the fortunes of his family and their enterprise had so drastically shifted in a matter of hours only caused his fury to rage further. He had to vent some of the frustration before he absolutely lost it on his family.

He kept his anger under control during the drive home. His middle daughter, Chandler, chattered on and on about how much fun it was to visit Dollywood for what seemed like hours. Normally, he was good at making conversation with his nine-year old, but the rage kept him limited to short responses. Finally, he suggested that she put her ear pods in and watch a movie on her iPad and that Daddy was trying to focus on driving. His wife was dead to the world in the passenger seat, and the peace and quiet that settled on the car like a blanket gave him time to think.

He had sent a text message that asked that his brothers meet him at Oakmoor Hall that evening, and it pissed him off even more that only Jimmy had acted like it was important. He passed the time and the miles by thinking of all of the shit that had nearly exposed them and how more drastic measures were needed to nip this new fuck-up in the bud. It wasn't that he was averse to taking decisive action, but it was the fact that decisive and bold action would fix their new problem and also risk exposing them further. He glanced in the rear-view mirror and saw the peaceful sleeping faces of his girls and thought about the life they so innocently took for granted.

A chill caressed his skin like the cold hands of a corpse as he thought of how close their tranquil life and promising futures were in danger of being turned to ashes. The thought of them being dragged through the mud because of the business that their forebears had worked to build, and the expansion wrought by Wade, their uncles, and their grandfather was too terrible to bear. Wade knew then what needed to be done. He knew what he would tell his brothers to do. He didn't care what they were going to say. All he cared about was those three sleeping angels in the backseat. He would burn the world down for them. He would sacrifice it all for them.

They arrived at their home, a 3,100-square-foot farm-house-style home on twenty acres of pasture and forest just outside of Manning, and Wade practically raced into the garage. He quickly unloaded the kids, luggage, and all of the trash he could find from the family Tahoe, and then quickly helped get them fed, clean, and ready for naps. His wife knew better than to ask him what was bothering him so much. She learned a long time ago not to push it whenever he said that there was a problem with "work stuff." She just kissed him and tried to figure out if he had a rough idea of when he would be home before he flew back to the garage, fired up his truck, and raced toward Oakmoor Hall.

He arrived at the palatial estate that was nestled into the vast swampland that stretched out for miles. He parked his truck beneath the branches of one of the property's many sprawling oaks, hopped out, and began the fifty-yard walk to the front steps of the house. The heels of his boots sank into the sandy soil with each step, which aggravated him even further, as he approached the portico sheltered by the immense roof and columns of the Greek-revival-style mansion. He stomped his boots on the ancient brick stairs as he ascended the steps to the porch to cast any of the sandy soil that had stuck to his soles back to the ground as he went. By the time he had finally made it to the top, a beautiful woman in a stylish black jumpsuit and matching heels stepped out of the massive front doorway and held the door open for him.

"Welcome home, sir. Your brothers have already arrived and they are waiting in the study. May I get you a drink?" the beautiful blonde asked.

"Thanks a bunch, Macie." Wade began, "Have a bottle of Tito's sent into the study along with some ice and glasses, please. We're gonna need it."

"Of course," Macie answered as Wade stepped through the doorway and into the grand foyer decorated with hunting trophies, rich paintings, and the breathtaking display of two alligators hunting around the base of a massive cypress tree. "If you'd like, I can make one of our assets available for you, should you need to unwind. Or. . ." she stepped toward him, gently placed her hand on his chest, and parted her red lips into a smile, "...I can be available to help you to relax."

The offer stopped Wade in his tracks, and for a brief moment the thought of Darrin Gaskins singing like a bird in his cell was the furthest thing from his mind. Even the offer by this gorgeous creature could only stave off the problem at hand for a short time, though. The aggression that consumed him at the moment would likely only worsen after he had to listen to Hampton droning on and on about how things were going in Georgetown. He could use the distraction and the chance to blow off some steam before heading back to his happy life. Maybe it would do him some good to fuck Rachel again. She liked it a lot rougher and nastier than his wife did anyway.

He smiled at the thought, took Macie's hand, and tenderly held it in his. "That's not a bad idea, Macie. Why don't you go take care of that vodka for me, then go make yourself as sexy as you can. Meet me in the old master's quarters with all of the equipment you know I love so much."

Macie pulled him towards her and kissed him hard. He felt the tips of her fingernails digging into the back of his scalp and he felt the sharp pain of her biting his lower lip. The growing arousal he felt became a forest fire almost instantly. She pulled herself away from him and started past the twin staircases and towards the kitchen. "I'll take care of the drinks, sir. Please hurry with your brothers, though. I've been a bad, bad girl and I need you to punish me."

"Oh, I'll punish you, alright. Don't you worry about that," he said as she disappeared around the corner.

The excitement he was feeling, knowing that he would get to punish her, control her, and fuck her made the next few minutes all the more annoying, though necessary. He stepped into the study, took a moment to admire the alligators before entering the room, and he was greeted with a firm handshake from his brother Jimmy and a nonchalant nod from his brother Hampton. After exchanging pleasantries and pouring each of them a glass of the vodka that Rachel brought in before shuffling off to prepare for her night with Wade, he got right to the point of their meeting.

"Well, boys, I'm afraid we've got us a bit of bad news. Darrin Gaskins got picked up by the Craven County sheriff's department last night and he's been in lock-up ever since," Wade said.

"Who the fuck is Darrin Gaskins?" Hampton asked, nursing his half-drained glass of vodka. His older brother's ignorance only served to incense Wade even further.

"He's one of the garbage men. Takes out what the clients are through playing with," Jimmy explained before Wade could snap at Hampton.

"Jesus. What the hell was he thinking?" Hampton said.

"Got picked up for a DUI, and then they found meth on him. He's cooling his heels till he goes before a judge on Monday. I wouldn't have even known about it had our man at the jail not tipped me off this morning. Needless to say, we need to handle this," Wade said.

"We may not have to do anything," Jimmy said. "Darrin's always been more or less reliable. He probably knows to keep his mouth shut and wait for us to get him out of jail."

"Yeah, we might not have anything to worry about," Hampton added, and relief settled onto him like fog onto the swamp.

Wade shook his head slowly as he took a long sip of the vodka, "Y'all know what happens when you're going through withdrawals?"

His brothers shook their heads. "Well, from what I understand, the person starts by aching and sweating and getting chills. Before long, the aches and pains are more than they can bear; they're so rough. Since he was tweaking when they arrested him, it's a safe bet that he's gonna be feeling it ten times worse than most. He'll probably start hallucinating here and there, and before you know it, he might start spouting off at the mouth to anybody who'll listen."

"Yeah, so what? I don't see how him seeing random shit and going off like a fucking nutbag has anything to do with the operation," Hampton added.

"Did it ever occur to you that this man has been finishing off the leftovers of clients and throwing them to the gators way out at the Yamassee Mounds for nearly five years?" Wade replied. He could feel the veins in his neck bulging with every word Hampton said.

"Yeah, so?"

"So, there's a decent chance he might start seeing all those people he cut up and threw away. There's a decent chance he starts raving about it too," Wade carefully explained. Jimmy sat silently and turned the short glass in his hands as he let Wade and Hampton have at it.

"Big fucking deal. He's coming down from tons of meth. He'd be out of his mind, acting all crazy. You said so yourself. No way that anybody we don't know at the sheriff's department is gonna take him seriously."

"You don't honestly believe that Fucking Captain America Raleigh Myers isn't going to try and run down anything that Gaskins tells him, no matter how crazy it sounds. And with us being a week out from those two boys finding the body of that stupid bitch that got away over at Morgan Swamp? Even you aren't that fucking stupid," Wade said.

Hampton stood up from the leather sofa he was sitting on, balled up his fists, and glared at Wade across the coffee table. He looked like the Michelin man to Wade rather than the UFC heavyweight that Wade was sure he was going for. Wade set his own glass down on the coffee table before he stood up from his own leather chair and prepared to go toe to toe with the fat fuck. He had been pissed all day anyway. Might as well vent a little bit of it by beating the shit out of his shit-for-brains brother.

"Please, sit down you two," Jimmy said before they could come to blows. Each man glared at the other, but they slowly re-took their seats.

"Thank you," Jimmy said. "Unfortunately, Wade is right. The risk that Gaskins might talk to Myers or somebody that's in Myers's inner circle is too great for us to do nothing at all. We need to deal with this as quickly as possible."

"Fuck. This shit never fucking happens in Georgetown.

Only here," Hampton grumbled. Wade wanted to snap back. He wanted to tell him what stupid waste of space he was. He wanted him to know exactly what he thought about him. He couldn't believe that he used to idolize this shithead when he was a kid. He couldn't understand why he wanted to do all the things that Hampton was doing, go where Hampton went, and to be just like Hampton. Now, all he saw was an overweight dumbass who drank too much beer, fucked around too much on his wife, and was more interested in having fun than in keeping the family business safe. He had thought better of Hampton when he was younger, but how could he have known he would grow up to be a loser with no concern for family, their traditions, and their protection. He had the perfect insult queued up in his mind, but his younger brother Jimmy beat him to it before his temper could get the better of him.

"Surely, we can all agree that handling the acquisition, importation, and transportation side of things, like you do for us in Georgetown, has far fewer risks than we do in housing, utilizing, feeding, and disposing of our assets. If something goes wrong when you're trying to grab some kid or girl off the street, or if one of them dies when you bring them in on the hold of a charter boat, or if one of them makes a break for it when you're bringing them here, your next steps are fairly straight forward and low risk. Leave the person on the street, ditch the vehicle in the Waccamaw, and have your man leave town for a couple of months. Throw the corpse of the one you were bringing in off of a fishing boat into the Atlantic. Sharks'll take care of the evidence; same as crabs. You beat and re-tie up the one that tries to escape, or you kill them and bring them to us and we have Gaskins and a couple of others handle the rest.

"See, no matter what goes wrong, you're free and clear to keep running the fishing charters, import company, and real estate office. If something goes wrong here at Oakmoor or at the farm though; well, we have the very real possibility of law enforcement, who are not our friends, following a trail that may lead directly to the farm. The risk is much greater here than it is in Georgetown, so comparing the two isn't really fair or productive."

Hampton snorted, drained his glass, and sat back onto the couch. "Okay then. What do y'all suggest we do?" Hampton asked.

Wade took a deep breath before he spoke. "We need to take him out before he talks or does something stupid."

"Alright. So how do you propose that we take him out, hm? He's in the county jail and we don't have a ton of friends up there," Hampton said. The sarcastic way he said the word "propose" pissed Wade off even more but he bit his tongue and let it roll off of him like water on the back of a duck.

"We've got some friends up there that'll help us. It'll cost us a little bit, but that's not the issue. The issue is that for my plan to work, we're gonna need to pull the trigger within the hour. That's our only shot at getting to him and making it look as minimally suspicious as possible. We also need a contingency plan to fall back on if Darrin Gaskins's untimely demise only gets Raleigh Myers after us," Wade explained.

"I might have something that we can form a back-up plan out of," Jimmy said.

"Go on," Wade said.

"I put a crew on Garrett McFadden a while back. We all know about him, but I just wanted to see if there was any weakness that we could exploit. I've had some people who work for the county in the utilities department doing a little work out in the trailer park where Gary lives. They found something truly incredible, simply by accident."

"What'd they find?" Hampton asked, refilling his empty glass of vodka.

"On Saturday morning, they watched Gary leave with his boat, probably to go fishing out at Lake Marion. A few hours later, a black BMW M4 pulled into the drive of Gary's trailer. A skinny man in khaki shorts and a button-down shirt got out of the car and began removing several pieces of rose gold hard-case luggage from the trunk of the car."

Jimmy reached and grabbed a manila folder from the coffee table, opened it and handed each of the men a photograph of a man, about 5'7", slight build, and neatly trimmed sandy hair removing the pink pieces of luggage from the trunk of the car. "He then used a key on his key-ring to unlock Gary's trailer before he made two trips to bring the luggage inside."

"What does this mean?" Wade asked.

Jimmy handed them each a third and fourth photo. The third picture showed the same man, now in a business suit, and Gary kissing passionately as they leaned against the BMW M4 that the man got out of in the previous pictures.

"This last photo was taken three weeks ago," Jimmy said.

The fourth photo showed a strikingly gorgeous woman in a high-waisted, knee-length, brown leather pencil skirt, white tucked-in tank top, and matching brown high heel pumps. Gary McFadden was kissing her passionately as she was stepping into the passenger seat of McFadden's truck. Wade was starting to put two and two together. Wade looked at Jimmy and thought he could see where his brother was going with this.

"I don't get it. So, Gary McFadden has some hot piece of ass that he's fucking, but here he's swapping spit with some dude. What does this even mean?" Hampton added.

"Gary McFadden is sexually involved with a man behind his girlfriend's back," Jimmy said.

"That's fucking sick," Hampton blurted out.

Wade chose not to comment on the irony of his brother being disgusted by Gary and his lover when he was involved in an illicit enterprise that catered to all manner of bizarre and depraved sexual appetites. It would only piss him off more. Jimmy, on the other hand, chose not to comment.

"This may present us with a unique opportunity," Jimmy said.

For the next few minutes, the brothers went over the details and logistics of their plans and contingency plans.

When Wade finally ascended the staircase and walked into the master's chambers to find Macie, dressed in latex, the whip he liked to use in one of her hands, and a fuzzy set of handcuffs in the other, he was certain of three things: he was going to punish Rachel for all she was worth, their plan to take out Darrin Gaskins was going to work, and that if he kept on pushing it, he was going to remove Sheriff Raleigh Myers from the board forever.

funny, brilliant, and loyal; she was many of the things he had always hoped he would find in a woman. Others had tried, and others had deceived him, but Erin felt different to him, and that scared him.

He had to keep reminding himself to take it easy when it came to thinking of her. Reminding himself about Mallory Burgess and what he experienced with her seemed to do the trick. He had once thought about her non-stop. He was enraptured by her spitfire personality, fiery red hair, and curvaceous body. He had fallen deeply and madly in love with her, but eventually it all came crashing down. He never claimed to be perfect. He knew that he could be critical and judgmental, and he knew his temper was something that could get the better of him if he wasn't careful. What he hadn't known was how a woman that was half of his physical size could completely and thoroughly destroy him.

For months he had endured being whittled down to a stump by her. She demanded everything of him. She had flown off the handle whenever he viewed things differently, and he was ridiculed for his refusal to submit. He had grown accustomed to never discussing anything of more substance than Mallory's opinions of other people and the myriad ways in which she cut them down to size. He learned early on that discussing big questions—whether they were philosophical, spiritual, or moral in nature— were strictly forbidden. The common refrains of "can you not" or "I don't wanna hear this shit anymore" were so constant and predictable that he could practically see them coming in Mallory's facial expressions. Through it all, he had held on and thought that time might change things.

That was the peak of his naivete. He had learned so much about the world and how it worked. He knew the unfathomable depths of depravity to which men could stoop. He knew how common violence was in the world, and he knew how to exercise violence effectively and mercilessly. But he had never learned that people in the country that he so desperately wanted to protect were capable of cruelty both unique and common. In the case of Mallory, he learned the hard way that emotional cruelty, which he now was willing to admit had crossed into abuse, was all too real and shockingly common. He had also learned that this abuse, which he had willingly fallen victim to, would only be tolerated to a point by him.

They had fought the night it all came crashing down. She was angry that he had chosen to work the weekend so he could get a four-day weekend the following week. She had no idea he had bought them tickets to see the Atlanta Braves play the New York Mets at Suntrust Park in Atlanta for that weekend, and the extra day was going to be a romantic night at the Westin in downtown Atlanta. Even now, above the noise of the tree frogs, crickets, and cicadas, he could still hear her: I am so fucking sick of this kind of shit. At that moment, he had perfect clarity. His backbone had reemerged from the dark hole that Mallory had cast it into.

Looking back, he wasn't proud of how he allowed his long-dormant temper to take control. You might've talked to people like that in the past, but I'm gonna be good and goddamned if I'm ever going to listen to you talk to me like that again.

He could still remember how quiet Mallory had gotten. He could still see the wide-eyed look of shock on her porcelain face. She must have been astonished that anyone would question what she felt was perfectly normal and reasonable behavior.

He had gone to his shift without another word, and when he returned the next morning, all of her stuff and some of his was gone from the small house he had asked her to share in town. She left a note that explained how she could see that things were not going to work out, and that it would probably be best if the two of them just parted ways now before they got into something that it was a lot harder to get out of. In a strange way, he had appreciated that she reached the conclusion he had been denying for months. He spoke with her just a few more times, mostly to iron out what to do about the cell phone plan they shared. She had run his name down to a few different people, mostly the closest friends that she kept, but few in town took what she had to say to heart. She was hurt, and Ray didn't fault her for trying to work some of that out at his expense.

Mallory had moved on, moved to Savannah, and married a man that he heard was involved in investments. She sent him a wedding invitation, and he wasn't entirely sure if it was a gesture of goodwill and maturity or a final opportunity to gloat. He chose to believe the former, checked the "celebrating from afar" box, and sent the happy couple a fifty-dollar gift card for one of the department stores where they were registered.

As much as he hated to admit it, Mallory had changed him. She made him more independent. She made him cautious. She made him reluctant when it came to opening himself up to women. She had wounded him.

Before her, the idea of finding the right woman and settling down with her was something that he dreamed about. After her, the thought of becoming physically or emotionally attached to a woman was all at once intriguing, terrifying, and exhausting. A few had come and gone since. None ever made it past the initial dating phase. But Erin was different. She had managed to bring down some of the walls around his heart so naturally and easily that his defenses didn't even register a threat. He could see himself getting to know her more. Maybe he could even see himself being with her.

He forced his mind to bury the thought and focused on the mission as he jogged up the wooden steps to his porch, strode into the house, flew to the bathroom, and hopped into the shower. Once out of the shower and dressed, he checked his watch and felt more than a little triumphant that he was dressed and ready for work with nearly an hour to spare. His mind immediately went to the fridge and the eggs, bacon, and sausage within. It wasn't every day that he was ready in time for a home-cooked breakfast, and the fact he had an entire hour to cook, eat, and relax was all the more satisfying.

He grabbed his department-issued cell phone from the

bedside table and his plans for a home-cooked breakfast evaporated. He was needed at the detention center as soon as possible. A man had been picked up for DUI over the weekend and claimed to have information about some murders that had happened in the county. It was vague, and it may just be the ravings of a junkie coming down from a bender, but at this point, with very little to go on, Ray was willing to entertain just about anything.

The drive from the house to the jail was relatively short but was made slightly longer when Ray stopped to grab a biscuit at Hardee's on the way in. He pulled his sheriff's department truck into the gravel parking lot outside of the jail, which other than the chain-link fencing festooned with razor-wire, could easily be mistaken for a small warehouse covered in rusty green corrugated steel sheeting. He grinned when he saw Gary McFadden's own truck parked in the lot as well. He wolfed down the last bite of his bacon, egg, and cheese biscuit; took a sip of coffee; and started towards the entrance to the old jail.

In less than three minutes, he had been buzzed into the facility, walked through the general population cell block with its ancient iron bars and common seating area, and made his way to one of the jail's two secured interview rooms. He opened the door to the conference room at the end of the interview room hallway and found Gary McFadden leaning against the opposite wall of the room finishing a conversation with Deputy Jarrod Knight, the officer who arrested Darrin Gaskins over the weekend.

"Mornin', buddy," Gary said.

"Mornin', Gary. Jarrod," Ray replied.

"Good morning, sir," Jarrod said, standing up straighter.

"So, what's the story with Mr. Gaskins?" Ray asked.

Jarrod quickly recounted his arrest of the man who now sat in interview room two. Once he had finished explaining why and how the arrest was made, and anything he overheard Gaskins saying, Gary chimed in.

"This morning, I received a text message from Taylor Floyd, the guy on guard duty last night. He said that Gaskins began screaming for a guard at about 5:30 this morning. Once Floyd got there, Gaskins told him he had some information about some murders that had happened in the county. I went and peeked in the window of the interview room about ten minutes ago and the guy looks like hammered dog shit. He's been in that room for about an hour and a half so far, so whenever you're ready, we can go on in there and see what he has to say."

The door to the conference room opened and a stocky man with large forearms and a rotund gut stepped into the room. He was wearing the olive-green utility pants and the black polo shirt of the Craven County Sheriff's Department. His meaty shaved head and red splotchy skin reddened as he pulled up his sagging pants. Lieutenant Kelvin Matthews, his former opponent in the sheriff's race and current commandant of the Craven County detention facility, nodded in Ray's direction.

"Well, Sheriff, how can I be of assistance to you today?" Matthews asked in his smooth low-country drawl.

"Good morning, Kelvin," Ray said to no response.

"I'd appreciate it if you would keep an eye on the cameras for us. He might have nothing of any value to say, but just in case he does, I'd like for the cameras to be rolling," Ray said.

Matthews sounded like an airbrake on an eighteen-wheeler. "I'll do the best I can. We've been having some problems lately with some of the cameras out here. They cut on and off, or just go out without warning. It was one of the things I intended to fix if the good people of Craven County had chosen me as their sheriff last year."

Ray caught the subtle dig at him. He decided to let the explanation go and made a mental note to do what he could to modernize their grossly obsolete county jail.

"I understand. Still, I appreciate you helping us out. I'd like to talk with Mr. Gaskins now," Ray said with a nod.

Matthews returned the nod and turned to lead Gary and Ray down the fluorescent-lit corridor to the interview rooms. Once outside of interview room two, he used his department-issued key card to unlock the door. Once inside, they both heard the heavy door shut with a solid clunk.

Before them, seated at a metal table, sat Darrin Gaskins.

Gary was right. The man looked like death warmed over. His face seemed to hang off of his skull, his arms and fingers were skeletal rather than plump and healthy, and the stench of urine and sweat that wafted off of him burned Ray's nostrils.

"Good morning, Mr. Gaskins. I'm Sheriff Myers, and this is Captain McFadden. I understand that you have some interesting stories to tell us," Ray said.

Gaskins' face twisted into a grin as he let out a cynical snort. "Yeah, that's right. Real fucking interesting to say the least."

"Okay, whenever you're ready," Ray said.

"Can't do that, Sheriff. First I'm gonna need some guarantees from you."

"Why should I give you anything? As far as I know, you just wanted to get off the cell block for a couple of hours," Ray shot back.

Gaskins seemed to consider this for a moment. "You don't understand. What I've got to say is some serious shit, and y'all have got to keep me under wraps. If they find out I'm talking to you, then I'm as good as dead."

"Nobody is going to find out anything. You're here in this room with us and nobody else."

"Bullshit. They can always find out. It don't matter where you are or how safe you think you are. If they really wanna know, they can find out. So, I need some fucking guarantees, or I ain't saying shit and y'all can take me back to my cell." Gaskins sat back in his chair.

For a moment, Ray was concerned that the metal might shatter his skeletal frame. "That's not how this works. You were the one that wanted this talk to happen, not me. As far as I'm concerned, I could be back in my office getting caught up on all of the paperwork on my desk. I couldn't care less about you or whatever story you've decided to use a bargaining chip. I've got no real way of knowing if this is gonna be worth my while or a truckload of bullshit that keeps me from closing other cases I already know I have to solve. Go on back to your cell. Fine by me. But if what you're suggesting is true, and these 'people' really do know every move you're making in here, how long do you figure you'll last once we turn you loose?"

Gaskins began bouncing his knees up and down on his toes. He began working his tightly closed mouth from side to side, chewing on the soft flesh on the inside of his cheeks. Ray could tell that his nerves had just cranked themselves into high gear and he decided to press his luck. "So, either you start talking, and I mean right now, or I'm gonna have a deputy take you back to your cell and you can face whatever you've gotta face on your own. And once I get you in to see Judge Floyd, and I'm gonna see to it personally that you see him before lunch, we'll turn you loose and you can see just how good you are at hide and seek."

Tears began streaming down Gaskins's face and he sniffed back the snot that was starting to drip from his nose. "Look here, I've got plenty of shit to say. You don't even know the half of it. I want to get it off my chest. I need to get it off my chest. But I also need to know that you're gonna do what you can to keep me safe from them once I do."

Ray hated to admit it, but he sort of pitied the broken husk of a man before him. Still, the slight pity he felt did not shake his resolve. "Start talking and then we'll see about what you want," Ray said.

Gaskins sniffed back more snot and gazed at Ray for a moment.

"I have your word on that, Sheriff?"

"You've got my word."

"Okay, fair enough then. Try not to judge me too hard for what I'm about to say. Understand that they would've done the same to me had I not followed their directions, and I mean in a heartbeat."

CHAPTER 25

"I work for an organization of sorts," Gaskins said.

Ray had to concentrate in order to not automatically start rolling his eyes. Grand conspiracies with nefarious organizations were not something that he whole-heartedly believed in. Still, he bit his tongue and tried to force himself to keep an open mind to whatever this man was about to say to him.

"Okay, you mean like the Illuminati or the Masons?" Ray asked.

Gaskins emphatically shook his head. "No, nothing like that. All that stuff is a load of horseshit, if you ask me."

"So, you're saying that you work for the mafia or a cartel or something like that?" Ray asked.

Again, Gaskins shook his head. "No, not in the sense that you're thinking of it. This bunch is local, for the most part. Been around a good little while from what I can gather too."

"This organization got a name?" Gary asked.

Gaskins's eyes darted to Gary, who had been silent as a graveyard up to that point. "Not that I know of. Most of what I know is what they pay me to do."

"And what exactly is it that they pay you to do?" Ray asked.

Gaskins looked at the floor as though it held all of the secrets of the universe, if only he knew how to read the language in which they were written.

"They. . ." Gaskins began. "They paid me to be their clean-up guy. They called it 'taking out the trash.' Only thing is it wasn't trash I had to take out." He took a deep breath and met Ray and Gary's gazes. Tears were flowing in torrents down his sunken cheeks, through the forest of wiry whiskers on his jaw, and onto the khaki jumpsuit the county issued him. "I'm in charge of getting rid of people they were done with."

Gaskins sucked in a breath and quietly began sobbing. Ray and Gary both looked at one another, skepticism coming natural to the two men. Gaskins sucked back snot loudly as he tried to get control of himself. Ray had to think of what to say for a few seconds as he watched the man across the table use the sleeve of his jumpsuit to wipe both his eyes and the snot dribbling from his nose.

"So, you're telling us that you were disposing of people for this organization you work for? You mean dead bodies?" Ray asked, unsure as to whether he should believe the chill that had run up his spine or not.

"Yeah, only sometimes. . ." he stifled another sob and steeled himself before continuing. "Sometimes they weren't all in one piece, or they weren't quite dead yet. So I'd. . . I'd. . . finish 'em off before I started taking them. . . taking them apart." He couldn't hold his emotions in check any longer. He wailed like a wounded calf. Gary and Ray attempted to calm him down. A deputy outside of the room even poked his head in to see if they needed any help getting him under control. Ray sent him out for three cups of coffee and a box of tissues.

Ray wanted to dismiss everything that this guy was telling him as nothing but a pure fantasy cooked up by a mind that had been shattered by years of hard living, hard drinking, and hard drugs. But he couldn't shake the fact that nearly twenty years of experience in the military had sharpened his ability like a scalpel. That experience in combat zones around the globe had shown him time and time again what a lie intended to glorify or manipulate looked like, and it had shown him what the truth looked like. Darrin Gaskins, despite all of the desires that Ray harbored to the contrary, was telling the truth.

By the time the deputy outside had returned with the coffee and the tissues, Gaskins had calmed down enough to continue.

"You've gotta understand that this is quite the story. I'm gonna need to hear more before I know you're not bullshitting me," Ray said as Gaskins sniffed and took a sip of the coffee.

"I ain't bullshitting you, Sheriff. I wish to God that I was, but I'm not."

"You can start by telling us how you got involved in something like this," Gary interjected.

Gaskins, eyes focused on the tabletop, nodded. "It was about, five years ago, I guess. I had just been outta high school about two years, and I had just lost my job when the SapienCorp plant closed down. You don't know what it was like for a twenty-one-year-old kid who had got used to forty-K a year plus benefits to all of the sudden have nothing coming in."

Ray actually did have some idea of what that predicament was like. Every time the government decided to cut the military budget, he had taken a significant pay cut. Whenever the parties decided to play chicken on policy and allow sequestration in a military shutdown, he didn't receive a paycheck at all.

"I was mad as hell. And I was too fucking stupid to see that leaving town was gonna be my best option for finding another job, so I just hung around at my house and hunted while the bills started piling up on me. I went on down to Jo-Jo's one night to have a few drinks and forget about my problems for a while, and when I came back home there was a cardboard box sitting on my doorstep. I was drunk and I must've took it inside because when I got up the next afternoon, it was sitting on my kitchen table.

"I opened it up and inside there was a typed letter and a stack of C-notes. The letter said that there was two grand in cash in the box, and if I wanted to make that every week, then I needed to go to this address out near Manning."

"You remember the address?" Gary asked.

Gaskins sniffed and chuckled bitterly, "Fuck no, I don't remember the address. Hell, this was five damn years ago. All I know was it led me to the side of this ol' dirt road just over the Clarendon County line. I got outta my truck and started walking into the woods and these guys came outta nowhere and grabbed a hold of me. They patted me down and found my pistol in my waistband before they talked to me. Said that they were willing to pay me two grand a week, in cash, plus a little bonus every so often if I'd come work for them. I guess they knew that was in charge of getting rid of the dogs and cats that SapienCorp tested their drugs on, so they figured that I wouldn't mind similar work.

"They said I'd have to agree to the job before they'd tell me what it was, and they were sure to stress that saying anything about it to anybody would be hazardous to my health. Shit, I had pretty much figured out that if I told 'em no that they'd kill me out there in that swamp right there and then and find somebody else to do it, so what was I supposed to do? I told 'em I'd do it and they took me in this four-seater for miles and miles through the marshes.

"Finally come up to this rusty old warehouse-looking place deep in the cypresses. They took me inside and let me just tell you, inside it looked like one of them fancy hunting lodges you see on the Travel Channel. They introduced me to a couple of guys I'd be working with and told me that I'd be responsible for taking out the trash."

He took a sip of his coffee. "I ain't proud of what I did, but you've gotta see that I had no choice."

Gary and Ray took in the tale for a few seconds. Ray wanted to get up and walk out of the room and chalk it up to a wild tale spun by a wild junkie, but as he watched Gaskins' movements, his eyes, and his tone of voice, he knew that he was telling the truth.

"You said they showed you where to dump the bodies?" Ray prodded.

"Yeah, they did. Put back in the four-seater once the sun come up and showed me all the landmarks and markers that they'd left to show me how to get there."

"Where was this place?" Gary asked.

Gaskins took a deep breath after sipping the last bit of his coffee. "Y'all ever hear of a place called the Yamassee Mounds?"

"Bullshit. That's just a story you tell kids at Halloween. There isn't any such place," Gary said.

Gaskins slowly shook his head, his eyes like ice cubes, "It ain't just a story. It's a real place. Most of the stories are true. Holes, mounds, all of it. That's where I took 'em all."

Ray had heard the story of the Yamassee Mounds all of his life. It was a story that was told around campfires, in dark rooms, and in between rounds of spin-the-bottle all across the Pee Dee region of South Carolina. The story was from the last days of the Yamassee War between the Yamassee Indians and their allies against the South Carolina colonial government that nearly resulted in the total destruction of the colony of South Carolina between 1715 and 1717. The Yamassees, along with the Creeks, had gone to war with the South Carolinians over trading disputes. After months of raiding, pillaging, and massacring men, women, and children along the frontier—they even unsuccessfully raided the small settlement of Queen's Bridge at the time—they had managed to push South Carolina to the brink of destruction.

After they surrounded Charles Town and prepared to wipe the city out with the help of their Creek allies, the fortunes of the Yamassees had turned for the worse when the Catawba, who lived in the Piedmont, and the powerful Cherokees of the mountains had come to the aid of the South Carolinians. The following months were filled with more slaughter, only this time it was visited upon the Yamassee by the South Carolinians, Catawba, and Cherokee.

According to the legend, the last Yamassee war band and their families had camped out in ancient Yamassee burial ground deep in the back-swamps of colonial Craven County. A group of British soldiers, Cherokee braves, and militiamen from Queen's Bridge, had set out to exact revenge for the raid on Queen's Bridge the previous year. After two days of marching through the mud, black water, snakes, alligators, mosquitoes, and seemingly endless tracts of massive cypress trees, they discovered the Yamassee Mounds.

Legend says that the Yamassees camped there and hoped that the sacred site would invoke their gods to protect them from the Cherokee and the colonists. They set up camp on ancient burial mounds that rose up out of the dark swamps which, ironically, only made them easier for the Cherokee scouts to spot among the densely packed cypress trees.

The men of Queen's Bridge and their allies had taken their time, and after a short battle, they killed every last Yamassee at the mounds to avenge Captain Archibald Spates and all the other men, women, and children of Queen's Bridge who died in the raid. It was then that the legend took an even more sinister turn as the sodden ground where the bodies of the dead Yamassees had been piled up opened up into a massive sinkhole that swallowed the corpses. At least that's what Archibald Spates's son Marcus had said once he and his men had triumphantly returned to Queen's Bridge two days later.

Ever since then, people claimed that if a person ventured too far into the swamps, especially at night, they would stumble upon the ancient Yamassee Mounds and that the ghost of the last Yamassee chief would grab you by the ankle to drown you in the bottomless pit of the great sinkhole that the Indian gods used to swallow up the corpses of the last Yamassee.

It was a scary legend to hear when you were a kid, even when you were a teenager, but it was just a story that people used to keep their kids from wandering into the swamps and getting lost.

"You're gonna have to show us how to get there on a map then. If you expect me to buy any of the bullshit you've been feeding us, you're gonna have to show me," Gary barked.

"I can't. They didn't show me on no map. They just showed me these different markers on how to get there is all. Showing on a map is a waste of our fucking time, and we ain't got tons of it. They're gonna kill me if we don't hurry and move quick."

Every hair on Ray's body stood on end at once. It could've been a coincidence that the story Gaskins was telling was incredibly similar to the one that Erin had told him about Ashanti. But then again, all of his experience had taught him that there was no such thing as coincidence.

"Then you're gonna have to write down some directions for us," Ray said as he handed Gaskins his legal pad and a pen. For the next ten minutes, Gaskins wrote and Ray and Gary processed the story. Once he had finished, Ray leaned forward and looked hard at Gaskins.

"This so-called organization you mentioned that you cleaned up after their clients. What do you mean by that?"

"They bring in people from all over from what I can tell. Gotta be rich; gotta be powerful too. Wouldn't surprise me at all if there ain't big businessmen or Hollywood types. Hell, they even bring politicians out there to suit their needs or desires.

"There was this one time that Talveaun—he was this fella that kinda worked under me—told me that he had seen this one particular rapper and some NBA star walking out of this room before he went in to remove this black chick they had both been fucking around with. When he brought her out and we got her into the side-by-side, I could see they had tied a dog chain around her neck and arms. Looked like they whipped her bare back and ass with the chain too."

The matter-of-fact tone of his voice chilled both Gary and Ray to the core.

"They had beat the shit out of her face, knocked all of her teeth out. Some of 'em do that so that they can't bite whenever they fuck 'em, you know."

The dazed look on his face reminded Ray of the countless times that traumatized people the world over had recounted the horrors that they had seen, experienced, or participated in to Ray and his guys.

"They had broke her hands and used a coring drill on the back of her head to finish her off. I felt so bad for her, y'know? Like, who was she? She might've been a nice person, or a mom, or y'know, somebody that had people or loved someone. She was pretty; could tell that even though she had been beat to shit. It was a real shame that we had to take her out to the Yamassee Mounds with all the others."

Gaskins went silent and stared into space for nearly a minute. This particular victim had made an impression on him for some reason, and for now, his subconscious had unburdened all that it could of itself.

"Darrin?" Ray said.

Gaskins blinked and shook his head. "Shit, sorry. I don't know what fucking happened. I just drift off from time to time."

"It's fine. You said that you think this has been going on for a long time. Why do you think that?"

"If you'd have seen all the bodies out there at the Yamassee Mounds, you'd know why I said that."

"Okay. So, it's been around for a long, long time. Any idea who is running this organization?" Ray asked

Gaskins got quiet. "Look, I need to know that you're going to keep me safe, okay. I know I've said a whole lot already, but if I tell you any more, I'm gonna need a guarantee. I need to know y'all are gonna hide me somewhere they won't find me and that I can go into, like, witness protection or something once it's all over."

Ray wanted to tell him that the least of his worries was his protection from this cabal he was describing. The Baptist in Ray wanted to tell him that he had better be concerned about the eternal hellfire that he was hurtling towards if all that he was saying turned out to be even partially true. But the cop inside knew that his best course of action was to assure him that he would do all he could to protect him from harm, despite how much he deserved to be punished.

"I'll do everything I can to keep you safe through all this. That's my word," Ray said.

To his credit, Gaskins didn't launch into a diatribe about his word not being good enough. Instead, he just sighed and nodded his head.

"My cousin Nolan works at Pee Dee Powersports in Florence fixing UTVs. I was up there about three months ago looking around, maybe thinking about buying one myself, y'know. I had gone back to the service department to talk to Nolan about what kinda price he could give me, and I saw this four-seater they had been working on. I had seen it before at the farm when I was doing one of my pick-ups. It was wrapped in woodland camouflage, had a lift and swamp tires, and on the grille it had antlers from a big ol' fourteen point buck mounted in place. Real badass looking.

"I asked Talveaun whose it was, and he told me that it belonged to the boss and to shut up about it. And there I was, looking at it in the service center and the guy who owned it was talking to one of the mechanics about what it had been doing when he used it lately."

Gaskins lowered his voice. "That guy was Wade fucking Spates."

Gary was incredulous. "Give me a break. Wade Spates? One of Senator Spates's sons? C'mon man."

"No bullshit. Me telling you this is like signing my own goddamn death warrant."

The fear in Gaskins' eyes was real. Ray had seen it before hundreds of times.

"Now you see why I need protection? I asked Nolan about Wade's rig, and he said that all of the Spates brothers come there to get their UTVs serviced. He even told me what theirs looked like and I had fucking seen them there too."

Ray knew they were in uncharted territory. Launching an investigation into the sons of a sitting United States senator had trouble written all over it. It was the kind of investigation that could end careers if one hiccup were to occur. They would need to have overwhelming evidence before they could even think about making it an official investigation. They were going to need to quietly look into everything that Gaskins had told them.

"Alright. Captain McFadden and I are going to walk out of this room and we will have the guards take you back to your cell. In a couple of hours, we will have some deputies come up here and transport you to a secure location until we've either proven you're a liar or we've made arrests. There will be no deals offered until you agree to testify and unless the attorney general of the state agrees to it. Fair enough?"

Gaskins nodded. "Fair enough. Just keep your eye on Chief Mungo at QBPD. He's a part of it. To tell you the truth, I was hoping that the guy that pulled me over the other night was QBPD because I knew they'd let me go once they figured out who I was."

Ray was no fan of Chris Mungo, but the idea that he and his department were complicit was too much for him to accept at this point. Still, he saw no need to share anything that he had heard from Gaskins with Mungo or with anybody in his department. This needed to stay between him and Gary for now.

"You better be telling the truth. If you're not and I wind up wasting time on this instead of trying to find out who killed a sixteen-year-old girl I've got over at the funeral home, I'm gonna make sure that they throw the book at you," Ray said as he and Gary both stood to leave.

"That's the thing, Sheriff," Darrin said. "Y'all found that girl out in the swamp. That was Talveaun's fuck-up. He was supposed to catch her when she escaped, not kill her. We never even got a chance to get rid of her because the river current took her away. Now Talveaun is in the sinkhole at the Yamassee Mounds."

CHAPTER 26

Darrin Gaskins couldn't quite decide how he felt at the moment. Physically, the shakes, sweats, and all of the other effects of withdrawals were starting to wane. He was even able to keep a Styrofoam cup's worth of bland grits down. He just might be alright after all. As he walked back to his cell, personally escorted by a skinny white deputy named Barfield, he noticed for the first time in a very long time that the monsters who hid just behind his eyelids hadn't been hiding around every corner.

In truth, the feeling was as unsettling as it was exhilarating. How could it be that simply confessing the sins he had committed could bring such an overwhelming sense of peace and serenity?

Bringin' what's been done in the dark out into the light can chase away the devil's army and lift the weight of the world off of a man's shoulders.

The words his long-dead granny had used to say to him resonated with him anew. She said that when he refused to fess up to pinching his cousins or smoking cigarettes he had stolen from his dad while she was alive. Turns out that the proud old lady had been right all along. Darrin just wished he had remembered them long before today and long before he started down the path of death and destruction he had chosen to take.

Maybe, just maybe, there was hope for him yet. Maybe it wasn't too late for him to turn it all around and to do something good with his life. His attorney would work out some kind of deal with the district attorney, but Darrin was smart enough to know that crimes like his would necessitate some hard time at the Lee Correctional Institute up in Bishopville.

Strangely, the knowledge that a significant portion of his life would be spent behind bars didn't scare him or convince him that his life was over. Instead, the peace and the assurance provided by his confession had overrode all of his emotions and it had given him hope for the future. A hope that he had never known himself, but he had certainly heard his old granny tell him about many times when he was younger.

As he waited for Barfield to unlock the door to his cell, he was already certain that he wanted to request that a preacher of some type come and talk to him while he was in the Craven County jail. He had never put too much stock into religion. To tell the truth, he always thought all of those sad morons who talked about being "saved" were just grasping at something to convince them that they weren't entirely powerless in life. Even now he wasn't convinced that he was completely wrong to think that, but the events of the past forty-eight hours had called all that he had assumed into question. He couldn't see the harm in talking to someone who knew about religion and finding out if there was anything to it for himself.

The loud clanking sound of oiled iron bars being slid open snatched his thoughts back to the world around him. He stepped into the eight-by-ten-foot cell and could think of nothing more than taking a nap on that thin mattress.

Darrin lurched forward; it felt like a baseball bat had hit him in the middle of his spine. The air in his lungs shot out of his body like a cannon. He was on all fours, gasping for breath just above the cold concrete floor. He felt a thick bundle of cloth being hastily wrapped around his throat as he struggled for air and his mind struggled to make sense of what was happening to him. The thick bundle of cloth around his throat snapped tight, closed off his airway, and made it feel like his eardrums would burst as his eyes bulged in their sockets. His eyes began burning, pouring torrents of tears down his face as he finally realized that he was being strangled.

His fight or flight instinct kicked into high gear. Adrenaline flooded his brain and he snapped up to his feet. This must have thrown his assailant off balance because the cloth went slack and Darrin was able grab hold of the makeshift garrote. Darrin found his breath but the scream for help that had formed in the back of his throat was silenced by a rapid succession of crippling blows to his back and kidneys. His hand dropped from the ligature around his neck and it snapped tight once again. Darrin tried his hardest to struggle. He fought with all that he had left in his weakened body.

He felt a boot step onto his back as his attacker pulled back on the ligature. Panic gave way to sheer terror. Darrin realized that this was it; he was going to die on the floor of this jail. All of the hope that he had felt only seconds earlier was now gone and a monstrous fear had taken its place. Darrin knew that he was about to find out if there was any truth to what all of those religious whack jobs had been saying to him all of his life. In the instant before his neck snapped, he was petrified that they were right and that he was about to board a one-way train straight to hell.

Once the telltale snap sounded from Gaskins's neck and his writhing body had gone limp, Andrew Barfield relaxed his grip on the rolled up sheet. Deputy Deandre Willis stepped around Barfield and hefted the gaunt corpse upright.

"Get it done quick, man. We need to be outta here in forty-five seconds," Willis said through clenched teeth.

Barfield said nothing and instead focused all of his attention on tying the bedsheet that they had just strangled Gaskins with around the bars at the top of the door to his cell. Barfield had been an Eagle Scout so he had the knot tied and secured in less than ten seconds.

"Good to go," he said to Willis.

Willis nodded and let go of the corpse. Gaskins slumped forward but was stopped short by the makeshift noose that had hastily been tied to the bars of the door. Gaskins toes were touching the concrete floor but the scene told a plausible story of suicide.

Both deputies quickly retreated from Gaskins's cell and made their way to the commandant's office.

"It's done," Barfield said once the door to Matthews's office had been shut.

"It looks like a suicide? Y'all check to make sure you left no evidence behind that said otherwise?" Kelvin asked from behind his oak desk.

"Everything's clean. We wore gloves and made sure the scene told the right story," Willis replied.

"Good work, boys. Y'all go on home. I'll fix the logs to show that y'all weren't here at the time of death. We won't have anybody make any rounds over on that end of the facility for a couple of hours so anyway."

Kelvin reached to a console filled with dozens of buttons and switches and flipped a switch from the down position into the up position.

"Damn shame. Been saying for years that we needed to replace the CCTV cameras in this place. You never can tell when they're gonna go out on you or not."

He entered the passcode into his cell phone and opened the contact for Wade Spates. Hopefully the good news of a successful operation would net him a little bonus. Whether that bonus was in the form of cash or a boy to spend a night with, Kelvin didn't really care.

Chapter 27

Ray was trying his best not to be convinced by the story Gaskins had told them, but with each mile that he and Gary drove into the wilderness, he found it harder and harder to do. Ray had initially been reluctant to run down anything to do with the story.

"C'mon, dude. What else do we have to go on at this point? Worst thing that'll happen is we find nothing but get to go test out the new swampers I got on the Polaris."

Gary McFadden was right, after all. If they were going to pass another day and not find anything new to help in the Megan Prince case, then it might as well be spent out in the woods. Ray changed out of his polo and utility pants and into a t-shirt and a pair of waders before he hopped into Gary's truck and headed to Craven Estates and the new UTV Gary had parked under his car port. Ten minutes of strapping the vehicle in place on a flat trailer, five minutes of hooking the trailer to Gary's truck, five minutes to gas up the UTV and fill a couple of five-gallon gas cans, and they were on their way to the sandy access road at the edge of a vast swamp and the starting point of either a treasure hunt or a wild goose chase.

They pulled off of one of the few backroads that zig-zagged across the national forest and drove the three miles that Gaskins said would get them to the start of one of the two known paths to the fabled Yamassee Mounds.

Grabbing his AR-15, a can of bug spray, and a gallon of water from the truck, Ray was ready to finally see if there was any truth to the story. He climbed into the passenger seat of the open-cab UTV after he helped Gary lug the gas cans into the small bed of the UTV, secured his AR-15 on the vehicle's gun rack, and booted up the GPS that Gary used whenever deer season rolled around. Then they were off, headed due east through a jungle of saw palmetto, tupelo trees, and ancient cypresses.

Ray had to admit, he was impressed with how the vehicle navigated the treacherous terrain with so much ease and relative speed. He was tempted to go and visit Pee Dee Motorsports and to look into getting one himself. It was hard to see how he couldn't use it during deer season or whenever he and Gary decided to go out and bag a couple of hogs. For a few minutes, as the vehicle nimbly glided over gnarled root systems, sliced through feet of pluff mud as it was often called in South Carolina, and whipped back and forth between ancient trees and underbrush, Ray calculated that he could more than afford a $200 a month payment. His savings account would take a hit, but the payoff in thrills and convenience just might make up for it.

"GPS saying how far we are from it?" Gary asked.

Ray's attention leapt from how to finance a brand new UTV to the tracking of markers listed out by Darrin Gaskins. Ray glanced at the screen of the GPS unit and saw they were less than 100 yards from the general area of the first marker. Ray looked to the east and saw a thick tangle of trees that stretched out for miles. A massive cypress, however, had towering knees, the roots that often looked like poles sticking up from the mud all around it.

Ray pointed Gary in the direction of the tree, and in seconds the UTV was close enough to the forest of knees around the base of the ancient sentinel. Ray and Gary both searched each knee they passed, only paying attention to those that were three feet or taller. Finally, Ray spotted one that stood every bit of five feet tall. As the UTV slowly approached, Ray could see the weathered outline of a maltese cross, engraved into the top of the gnarled wood.

"Got it. Maltese cross at the top of this one," Ray announced.

"I'll be damned. At least this part of that lunatic's story is true," Gary said as Ray marked the location on the GPS and plotted out the general area of the next purported marker.

Gary and Ray tore off toward the southeast and the general location of the second marker. The mile and a half zipped by, with Ray observing as the creatures of the swamp—snakes, raccoons, and hogs—gave the UTV a wide berth. It was almost as if they were familiar with the sights and sounds of the vehicle and that they knew to stay away from them whenever they came this way.

As they approached the next marker, sloughing their way through the mud flats of one of the higher areas of this vast marsh, a family of wild hogs darted from the mud flats they had been rooting through in search of food. The group had to have numbered somewhere between fifteen and twenty, and the sight of the massive sow leading the pack was almost enough to make Ray grab his rifle and attempt a shot. But before he could even point her out to Gary, she and her brood had scurried off into the thick palmetto underbrush.

The sight of the sow had momentarily distracted him and the beeping of the GPS that announced they had arrived at their destination refocused him on navigation. Once again, the density of the forest and the abundance of vegetation was daunting, but one ancient tupelo stood out. The mud flats were just beginning to give way to a shallow, slow-moving creek, and the tupelo had taken up residence in the middle of the fifty-yard-wide creek long ago. The shallow water was no challenge for the UTV as it plowed through and sent snakes, turtles, and longnose gar darting off to find shelter.

The tree was an impressive sight. The base had to be six feet across and between twelve and fifteen feet in circumference. It towered into the forest canopy, casting long shadows to the mucky creek below. Ray studied the gnarled tree as the UTV circled. Finally, he found the tell-tale outline of a crown hewn into the bark. The carving had been there for well over a century, as the growth of the bark was close to sealing it up.

Ray marked the spot on the GPS and continued south towards the location of the next marker. They tore through the small brush and plowed through muddy bogs for close to two miles before they found themselves needing to cross a Carolina Bay.

The crater-like depression in the earth, of which there were thousands more stretching from Florida all the way up to Long Island, was filled with dark water, plant matter, and a menagerie of snakes, snapping turtles, and alligators. Rather than plowing ahead, Ray used the GPS to mark the southeastern edge of the Carolina Bay before he guided Gary through the dense jungle of the semi-flooded forest. The detour around the Carolina Bay added fifteen minutes to what had been an hour so far.

Once they had finally reached the southeastern edge, they were in for two more miles of slogging through the mud and dense vegetation. The dense, muddy jungle gave way to a magnificent stand of ancient cypresses and tupelos that towered into the heavens and loaded down with long beards of Spanish moss. The water in which they stood was less than a foot deep, and for the first time in a half hour, the going was easy.

The ancient trees that towered into the heavens reminded Ray of the interiors of the great cathedrals of Europe. The massive trunks of the trees stretched upwards like columns supporting a grand ceiling of branches and leaves. It was a wonder that these trees had been overlooked by the logging companies during the turn of the twentieth century, and Ray couldn't help but fear for their making it another one-hundred years into the future. This old forest, like all things, would pass into the maw of the cosmic thresher of time and of progress.

He pulled his eyes from the colonnade of trees and scanned the horizon. He noticed an area a few hundred yards to the southeast of them. If he didn't know any better, he would've sworn that he was looking at pyramid-like structures that dotted the rainforests of Mexico, Guatemala, Honduras, and Nicaragua, nestled in among the dense trees of the forest. Only these were covered in earth and vegetation. Ray's jaw went slack at the sight as a chill creeped up his spine and down his arms.

"Sonofabitch. Gaskins was telling the truth," he said. Gary said nothing but must have spotted the location as the UTV turned in the direction of the monoliths.

As they approached and pushed through the ever denser and drier forest around them, it became clear there were three of the mysterious earthen structures arranged at the corners of a triangle. As a part of his work with the army, Ray completed several courses in anthropology in order to better understand and work with the various cultures a soldier might come into contact with during their career. It hadn't been all that useful except for the few times in Afghanistan where understanding what tribe lived in any given valley proved useful, and he had forgotten a great deal of what he learned. He did, however, remember learning about how ancient cultures, including Native Americans, constructed monuments to mark places with great significance within their societies. Ray had no way of knowing what that significance was, but he was certain that the builders of this complex had assigned a very deep and important meaning to the place.

Gary pulled the UTV behind one of the mounds, put it into park, and climbed out of the small vehicle. He grabbed his AR-15 rifle and stepped out of the vehicle onto the damp, sandy ground.

"You stack up behind me. We're gonna go around the

eastern edge of this mound. Keep your eyes open for anything out of the ordinary; anything that says we might not be alone out here," Ray said as they both stepped to the front of the vehicle.

"Makes sense to me. Following your lead here, buddy," Gary replied with a nod.

Ray readied his rifle, flipped the fire-selector to single shot, and started towards the edge of the mound. It had been years since he had been in a situation where he needed to be frosty, but his feet and the rest of his body took to it like riding a bicycle. He peered around the edge of the mound and scanned the area. He stepped around the edge of the mound, scanning for threats as he shuffled forward into the clearing between the mounds. The small, sandy area was clear of any threats, but the images his eyes took in turned his stomach.

Bones were scattered everywhere around the small clearing. He gingerly stepped around them to the center of the clearing, and a pit lined with stones dug into the ground. It reminded him of a large well, only the edges of this one was near flush against the ground. He made sure not to kick any of the bones into the pit as he peered inside.

The sight of human skulls, ribcages, viscera, and recently dumped body parts took his mind back to a pit he had seen in Venezuela where the regime had allegedly disposed of their political opponents. That had been the most awful and inhuman thing Ray had ever seen. Now, he was staring deep into the abyss of another pit right here just a few miles from where he had grown up. The smell and the sight made it difficult to keep his breakfast down.

His rage built at thought of all of the lives dumped into this pit, and at the thought of all of the people that had to be responsible for such an atrocity to go unknown for so long. The pit had to be every bit of thirty feet deep and it was at least twelve feet across. For the first time, he noticed the dark silhouettes of turkey vultures dotting the branches of the towering trees around them. The sickening answer for how the random, scattered bones in the clearing had gotten there now all the more apparent.

"Goddamn," Gary whispered in a faraway voice.

"There's gotta be thousands of them here. Or what's left of them, at least," Ray said.

"Have you ever seen anything... I mean. ..." Gary's astonished voice trailed off.

"Once, but it wasn't even like this," Ray said as he slung the AR-15 across his chest.

"We need to get back to the road and call this in. We're gonna need SLED; even the FBI might be a good idea at this point," Ray said as Gary nodded.

He peered into the pit with new resolve to make whoever was responsible pay. He noticed that among the twisted mass of flesh and bone that the head, neck, and left shoulder of a woman was strangely familiar.

Her skin had turned deep red from decomposition, and he was certain that the vultures and other creatures of the swamp had made a meal off of many of her other parts, but he could still tell from the braided weave on her scalp that she was African-American. Her eyes were gone, and most of what had once been her face had been torn away by insects, beaks, and teeth, but the flesh on the right side of her neck was still relatively intact. The outline of a crown was made more visible by decomposition inked into her skin. He wasn't sure what he was going to say to Erin, but in a strange way he felt peace that he had found where Ashanti Livingston had been left to rot.

one of them in the cooler with the beer he had brought. Then, he disappeared below decks to make sure the satellite tv and onboard wi-fi was working properly. This left the lifting of three-day-worth of provisions, clothes, and equipment to Wade and Jimmy.

Wade wanted nothing more than to march down into the hold of the boat and tell Hampton exactly what he thought of him. He was a lazy piece of shit that was so much of a fucking man-child that all he could think of was getting his buzz going and channel surfing while he and Jimmy did the adult tasks. The more he pictured Hampton sitting in the galley lounge, with his feet propped up, guzzling beer, and flipping channels to "make sure this shit ain't crapped out on us yet," the more incensed he had gotten. If he heard him call up from below about somebody walking all the way down there and handing his lazy ass another beer, he was going to come un-fucking-glued.

"I'll go run him one down there, Wade. Just relax. This trip is supposed to help us all come back together," Jimmy said as he grabbed a cold bottle of beer from the cooler and ran it down below decks.

Wade took a couple of deep cleansing breaths to clear his anger about Hampton's uselessness and instead found himself annoyed at Jimmy's diplomacy and his own palpable anger. It had always seemed like Wade had worn his emotions on his sleeve, and Jimmy had always been so good at seeing what was gnawing at Wade and intervening accordingly. Wade knew that it was his way of keeping the peace, however fragile, between he and Hampton, but it still was fucking annoying that Jimmy seemed to cover for that blubbering idiot like he did. He knew that it was because Jimmy loved them. Hell, Wade loved Hampton despite him being a total fuck-up, but deep down he had always wondered if he wasn't keeping the peace to keep the focus on Wade and Hampton rather than on himself.

Wade continued breathing deeply and decided to distract himself with checking to make sure that the boat started, had enough fuel, and all of the necessary navigation and communication equipment were in working order. He climbed up to the bridge and took in the view of Winyah Bay before starting his checks. The view of the salt marshes and widening canals filled his heart with excitement for the next few days.

Fishing was one of his great loves. Every chance he got he was out on the water chasing after whatever was running during that time. On this trip they were going to trawl for sailfish from Georgetown to Cape Hatteras and back. Wade could almost feel the rush of being strapped into the fight chair as he hooked into a monster of a catch. He was miles away from the rage he had felt just seconds earlier and he was fully adrift on the river of freedom that the sea and all of her bounty provided him.

The ringing of his secure cell phone snapped him out of the euphoria he had allowed himself to slip into. He answered the phone without looking at the ID, annoyed at his moment of peace being interrupted. "Yes?" he said.

"We've got a big problem, boss," Kelvin Matthews began. "I looked at the tapes we took of Myers and McFadden questioning Gaskins, and that motherfucker told them all about the Yamassee Mounds. My guy at the office says that he and McFadden have been gone all morning too."

Wade's stomach dropped into his feet like a plane without engine power. "How bad is it?" he asked through a mouth suddenly dry as a Brillo pad.

"Bad. He told them everything. What do you want me to do? I can send some guys out there to clean up."

"No, there's no point. Get Elrod and Manigault on Myers's ass once you hear from me tonight. We've planned for this eventuality. Talk to the others and fill them in. We've gotta be all hands on deck with this. I'll inform the old man so he knows what's going on."

He ended the call and descended back to the main deck of the yacht. Jimmy had taken a seat on one of the long white berths that ran along the edges of the bar area of the boat as Hampton used the remote to find the Braves game on the fifty-two-inch tv mounted above the outdoor bar.

"Hey, dude. We're ready to roll out if you are," Hampton said, never taking his eyes from the television and the players up at bat.

"We're not going," Wade said.

"Why the hell not? We already lugged all this shit on here, and we're just gonna lug it all off again? Fuckin' bullshit if you ask me," Hampton replied through swigs of what Wade figured was beer number four.

"Gaskins told Myers and McFadden about the Ya-massee Mounds. Our guy in the department says they've been gone all morning too." [

Hampton dropped the half-empty beer bottle to the floor with a loud semi-hollow thud.

"We're so fucked. What are we gonna do?" Hampton panicked.

Normally Wade would say something antagonistic to his oafish brother, but for once they had found common ground over the fact that they were indeed fucked. Hell of a note that it took this for them to find it.

"We aren't fucked yet," Jimmy said in a voice as calm as a morning coffee. "We have contingencies in place for this. We need to implement them right now."

Wade nodded. "Go ahead and get your guys to move forward with them. I'm gonna call him and let him know what's going on," Wade said as he dialed the number he had done everything in his power to avoid dialing.

CHAPTER 29

"To be perfectly honest with you, Reanne, I can't think of a situation in which a magazine with a capacity any higher than say, twelve, is necessary," Thurmond Spates said in his polished South Carolina drawl.

"I grew up in South Carolina, and I'm a Carolina boy through and through. I've been hunting the marshes and the pine woodlands back home ever since I was old enough to walk and my daddy did not need to carry me. I'd say that firearms are a part of my life and a part of my culture. Yet, even I will tell you that passing a law that limits the capacity of magazines to twelve does nothing to either keep me from bagging the deer I've been tracking for the past few days nor does it infringe upon my second amendment rights as defined by our Constitution.

"Now, that statement might not win me any friends among the most outspoken of the gun lobby in this country, but I do think that it is a statement that most Americans can see the logic behind and that many would support if given the opportunity."

He smiled his trademark smile as the pretty reporter for one of the major mainstream networks nodded approvingly and looked down at the questions her producer had prepared for her earlier in the day. Thurmond had seen her on the morning shows from time to time, playing the part of objective, or at least quasi-objective, moderator as two pundits with opposing views yammered away about the issues facing Americans every day and their implications for the presidential race next year. He had thought she was gorgeous then, but now that he was sitting across from her, taking in the perfectly provocative yet professional way in which her inky black tresses cascaded over her left breast, appreciating the snug fit of her emerald dress, and breathing deeply the subtle sexiness of her perfume, he was certain that he would have to contact the owner of the network to set up a private, exclusive interview with her at his Federal-style home in DC.

Her boss, a billionaire media-mogul who also styled himself a philanthropist for causes ranging from gun control to reproductive rights, had been one of Thurmond's closest friends for years. The association might seem a little odd to the average spectator. After all, it was no secret that Thurmond Spates and his proposed tax plans were no friend to the wealthy in American society. His friendship with one of the members of what he and his allies had termed the "Haves" in American society would seemingly fly in the face of all that the self-styled country-lawyer stood for. But the fact of the matter was that both men loved an aged scotch with a cigar, enjoyed the company of beautiful people and things, and shared the same views on both the illnesses facing American society as well as what prescriptions would cure those ills.

In fact, many around DC and across America knew of Thurmond's associations, but so few seemed to truly care. Even this doe-eyed creature who sat across from him, scanning the questions for the perfect opportunity to allow Thurmond to shine for the cameras, couldn't care less about his friendships so long as he hammered home his message of equality, justice, and future for Americans. It was because of this that not only was he certain that she would agree to his private interview, but that she would ensure she was wearing the perfect dress and perfect underwear for him. He ran his fingers along his perfectly-trimmed salt and pepper goatee at the thought of it all. Life had been pretty good to the old boy from South Carolina.

"Last question, Senator Spates. The presidential election is looming and there have been many that have speculated that you might be eyeing a run at the White House to succeed President Witherspoon when he leaves office. Either way, the country is going to need someone with a clear vision for the future of America. What do you think that vision should look like, and of course I have to ask if there is any truth to you entering the race?"

Thurmond smiled his charming smile and laughed his charming laugh before answering. "I'm not concerning myself with any plans for the future outside of doing what I believe is best for the people of the great state of South Carolina. And that's gonna have to be my answer for now. Look, I've been at this for a good little while, Reanne, and through it all, from my first election as the mayor of my hometown of Queen's Bridge, South Carolina, I've always seen myself as responsible for the people whom I was elected to represent.

"Now, sometimes that meant rubber-stamping the will of my constituents, and other times it meant making a decision that was right but unpopular among my constituents. I've always been okay with whatever consequences that brought on my career. Fortunately, it had the consequences of being elected to the House of Representatives, being elected governor of the state of South Carolina twice, and now it has privileged me with two terms in the United States Senate. I think that people respect that about me. I think that people count on me to make the right call despite what everybody might think.

"The next president of this country needs to be somebody like that. That person needs to be someone who will make the right call, no matter all the voices screaming and telling them no. They need a person who will have the guts to stand up and say we need some common-sense reforms to our gun laws. Someone who will choose to protect little children in schools, shoppers in stores, and worshippers wherever they choose to worship from a madman armed with a firearm that the government should have had the guts to restrict from circulation.

"They need a person who is willing to face the most fortunate and privileged in our society and demand they pay their fair share whenever tax season rolls around. Someone who will use the vast resources at their disposal to ensure that every American has access to healthcare at little or no cost, who will ensure that every American has access to higher education at little or no cost, and who will ensure that every American has access to a space to feel safe in an increasingly diverse society.

"They need someone who will fight to ensure that every American has the right to love whomever they love, to ensure that every American has the right to be whomever they truly are, and to ensure that every American does not have to be victimized by the bigotry and intolerance of those choose to invalidate them as people. They need someone who is going to protect the rights of people of color and who will finally give them the voice they need to combat the oppression that is so often endemic to many of our law enforcement agencies across this country. They need someone who will do what it takes to protect women and their sovereignty over their future, finances, and bodies.

"I know I'm going on and on here, Reanne, but in short, I think that the country desperately needs a president who has guts to do what is right, no matter the consequence."

Reanne Tyler flashed her best television smile. "Senator Thurmond Spates of South Carolina, thank you so much for talking with us today."

Thurmond gave his own carefully crafted television smile. "The pleasure was all mine."

The cameraman and the producer gave the all-clear sign. Thurmond wasted no time in rising from his chair and shaking the soft hand of the comely reporter.

"It was great fun talking with you Reanne. We must do it again soon; say an exclusive in DC two weeks from now?" Thurmond offered.

Her eyes brightened immediately at the suggestion. Hook, line, and sinker. An exclusive interview after the announcement he was about to make would do wonders for her career, he was certain.

"That would be wonderful, Senator."

"Please, call me Ted. I'll get in touch with Robert when I get back to DC and we'll set something up in a much more intimate setting."

Thurmond squeezed her hand slightly before turning and walking through the door that Johnson, his capitol police security man, had opened into the hallway. Thurmond stepped into the hallway and followed Johnson's lead to the set of the Jerry Jensen Tonight Show to tape his appearance for what was scheduled to run at ten o'clock that evening. Johnson produced a cell phone from a carrying case next to his sidearm and looked at the screen to see who was calling.

"Sir, it's a call from your personal line." Johnson handed the phone to Thurmond who read the name "Prince." Thurmond kept a cool exterior, even though anxiety snatched his gut with the speed of a rattlesnake strike.

"I need to take this in private," Thurmond said.

Johnson ducked into the men's room on the left side of the hallway, announced that the room was clear, and allowed Thurmond to enter. Thurmond knew that Johnson would stand in front of the door and ensure that no one would enter and disturb him during his call. Johnson was a good man, and that was increasingly hard to find these days.

Thurmond answered the call as soon as the door behind him shut.

"Yes?" Thurmond said.

"There's a problem you need to be aware of, but it is being handled as we speak," Wade Spates explained to his father.

"I would certainly hope so. What exactly is the problem?" Thurmond said.

"Raleigh Myers and Garrett McFadden questioned our garbage man this morning. He got picked up on a DUI Saturday night and none of our people found out about it till Myers and McFadden had shown up to interview him. We dealt with the garbage man today, all evidence pointing to self-inflicted," Wade explained.

"I get the feeling that there's more to this story. Otherwise you wouldn't be calling me at all."

There was a hesitation in Wade's response that chilled Thurmond to the bone. "The garbage man revealed all that he knew about the organization to Myers and McFadden."

Thurmond's face burned. He would expect this kind of shitshow from Hampton, maybe even from Jimmy, but never from Wade, his hand-picked protege. Wade continued, "He also wrote them directions to the location of the Yamassee Mounds." [this was never in the phone call from Kelvin to Wade]

The absolute worst-case scenario had been realized. He should never have left the enterprise to his idiot sons. He should've been more involved, just like his daddy had been. Then, maybe they wouldn't be in the world of shit that their incompetence now found them in.

"Son," Thurmond gripped the telephone so hard he was surprised he did not crack the glass of the screen. "I hope that your solution will chop the head off of this snake before it slithers any further into our corn crib."

"It will, sir. Jimmy had already pre-positioned a team in case this was to happen. They're executing the plan tonight. Within eighteen hours, this problem will cease to exist," Wade replied too quickly.

The rage in Thurmond's gut boiled further and he was forced to concentrate on maintaining a measured tone of voice. The last thing he needed was someone in this building saying they heard Senator Thurmond Spates screaming while alone in the restroom with a guard outside.

"We are right at the edge of everything we have been working for. What your grandfather and his father helped us build. We are on the verge of finally being able to bring some justice and sanity to this world. We are finally on the edge of claiming our birthright and building a better world. And here, at the eleventh hour, your incompetence has put this all in jeopardy."

"But I-"

"But nothing, son. You are in charge. You are responsible. I want you to check in with me at every single point of your plan to fix this. I want to be assured that it won't be another colossal fuck-up that puts us even further in danger. I am about to do a taping. I will call you from my car in one hour, and you and your sorry-ass brothers are going to walk me through every step of this solution of yours."

Wade was silent on the other end for a good ten seconds.

"Yes, sir," Wade replied.

"Good. And another thing before I go. If this doesn't work, or if your plan is completely for shit, then you can kiss that seat in the House goodbye next year."

Thurmond let that sink in for a few seconds before continuing. "Your brother Hampton will take your spot. He might not have brains, but he'll fucking do what I want so long as I am alive or Jimmy is there to steer him. You, on the other hand, will have nothing. And as God as my witness, you and your little family might just have an extremely tragic accident. Besides, the American people just love a tragic story. It'll be like the Kennedys all over again. You picking up what I'm putting down, boy?"

Silence.

"Good. Be ready to go in an hour."

Thurmond ended the call. He looked at himself in the mirror above the long row of sinks and saw the unbridled rage that roiled within him. He took a deep breath, closed his eyes, and imagined himself sitting on the patio of his DC home with a Cuban cigar in one hand and a hot little Cuban piece of ass in the other. He imagined taking the threat to himself and his family's legacy, placing it inside of a bookbag, and zipping it shut. He then imagined placing the backpack into a locker, like one would find at a bus station, and closing the door. In seconds, it was as if the problem had been filed away for later and the confident and smooth demeanor that Thurmond was legendary for had returned. He fussed with his professional and stylish cut for a moment, removed his tie, and unbuttoned his collar before heading out of the restroom.

Johnson secured the phone, and Thurmond walked onto the set, shook hands with washed-up comedian Jerry Jensen, and took his place for the taping. Once introduced and after a few moments of witty banter back and forth, a couple of really clever jokes, and a casual discussion of policy, Jensen got to the heart of the matter.

"Senator, you have a reputation as a good guy, and other than a couple of those comments about my mom, I'd tend to agree with that I guess." The audience laughed as cued. "So I'm counting on that honest integrity now. Are you running for president or not?"

Thurmond gave a sly grin. "My daddy always told me to play my cards close to the chest, unless you're for sure and for certain you've got the winning hand. And since I figure all of the cards I've been talking about with setting this country on the right path are winners, I'd have to say yes. I'm running for president, Jerry."

CHAPTER 30

"It is too damn convenient, Gary," Ray said.

"He tells us this wild story in the morning, knowing full well that we would check it out, and then by the time we have verified that it is one-hundred-percent true, he has already offed himself? My bullshit meter is off the fucking charts, man."

Ray sat behind the desk in his small office while Gary lounged, legs extended and feet crossed over top of one another, in the chair opposite the desk. Both men had changed out of their waders and into jeans and boots before returning to the sheriff's office and the unimaginable disaster that waited for them. The mud and the muck were nowhere to be seen on their person, but for some reason Gary couldn't shake the smell of the swamp, gasoline, and rotting human flesh from his nostrils.

They had spent the better part of four hours driving out to the start of Gaskins's map, finding all of the markers, plowing through the swamp, examining the Yamassee

Mounds, estimating the number of corpses dumped, navigating back to the road, loading everything back into the truck and trailer, and then finally getting reliable cellular service, only to learn that Gaskins had been found hanging in cell an hour after they left him fully alive. The discovery they made in the woods immediately took a backseat to the loss of the only witness and any sort of corroboration for what they had found in the woods. Their case was collapsing right before their very eyes.

This was a familiar sight for Ray, unfortunately. While he was in the army, there had been a private contractor who served as a part of the coalition forces in Iraq and decided to take a little R&R. That R&R involved the murder of an Iraqi man and the rape of his widow and thirteen-year-old daughter. One of the guy's men decided to blow the whistle. He led the MPs, to the house, showed them where the body was buried, and had them interview the traumatized woman and her daughter. Everything seemed to be a slam dunk until the guy who had blown the whistle suddenly decided to shoot himself.

His body wasn't even cold before the evidence couldn't be found, the witnesses had vanished, and the contractor was exonerated. In the span of twelve hours, the contractor's fortunes had completely reversed and he was allowed to go home and retire with a full pension alongside his wife, kids, and grandkids back home in Oregon. The whistleblower had been sent home to Oklahoma in a box for his parents to bury. Not even an honor guard there. The fix was in back in Iraq, and Ray instinctively knew that it was in here.

"They're gonna try and make all of this go away, Gary. Just you watch and see. We've gotta do something, and I mean now, before they can get out there and-" Ray's sentence was cut short by the door to his office swinging open.

The closed blinds that hung from the top to the bottom of his office door swung loudly and wildly to the left and right as short and round Elrod Tisdale and lanky and lupine Reginald Manigault stepped into his small office. Elrod closed the door behind them as Manigault flashed a thin smile to Ray.

"Sheriff Myers, it appears that we have a real problem on our hands," Manigault said.

Ray and Gary sat impassive, silent at the man's insistence on stating the obvious. Elrod and Manigault stood silent, gazing at the expressionless face of Raleigh Myers, as if they were searching the faces on Mount Rushmore in the hope they might explain why they were hewn into a South Dakota mountain top.

"Last time Elrod and I stopped by, I believe we discussed why our community did not need any more negative attention drawn to it," Manigault continued.

Ray was pissed that he now had to listen to this weasel of a man and his clown of a sidekick lecture him on how he was both not doing his job and on how they expected him to not do his job. After all, what was a county sheriff if not the arbiter of whether or not tourist dollars get spent on a half-dozen contrived festivals in his county's seat? His eyes moved from the unwanted guests to Gary. In an instant he understood the message behind his friend's eyes. Don't push it. Keep it cool.

"Would you mind explaining to me how the death of a junkie in county lock-up is drawing negative attention to your festival circuit, gentlemen?" Ray asked.

Manigault furrowed his brow. "How about the fact that the sheriff is so poorly running his department that a so-called junkie could manage to kill himself while in his custody. What does that say about your competence with keeping the citizens of this county safe, Sheriff? Not a whole lot, I'm afraid. And that's just part of the negative attention."

Ray let the attack on his job performance and character slide even though he wanted to stand up and list all of the companies that refused to relocate to Craven County as a direct consequence of the mismanagement of County Manager Reginald Manigault IV. The fact that Elrod Tisdale had never done anything with his life other than squabble for the scraps from Manigault's table or successfully fuck a litany of white female aides behind his wife's back for years would've only been icing on top of the massive cake that was the incompetence of these two assholes.

"I'm waiting for you to tell me more ways in which I am single-handedly bringing negative attention to town."

"How about you spreading insane conspiracy theories about the county." Manigault smirked like a fox who had just nipped the heels of a pitbull, knowing full-well that it was just beyond the reach of the dog's chain.

"We heard about your ravings about some sort of a mass grave located at the site of a site from folklore that nobody living has ever found, if it exists at all, and that the people responsible for said mass grave are part of a vast criminal conspiracy involving people throughout our county and city. This is sheer lunacy, Sheriff Myers, and the fact that it is being invented and propagated by you gives us serious doubts about whether or not you are fit to serve as our county sheriff."

"And let's not forget the problems you have with race," Elrod interjected just as Ray was preparing to respond. "Did you know that sixty percent of the arrests that you have made or supervised as sheriff have been against black citizens?"

"I'd say that since about seventy percent of our community is made up of African-Americans and about fifty-five percent of that number is classified as impoverished and at-risk, it probably makes sense that a few more members of that demographic are getting picked up for fighting or petty theft or two," Ray replied.

"Regardless of what you try to say about this injustice, it is clear to everyone with eyes to see that you are targeting black offenders, particularly young black male offenders, at a higher rate than others," Elrod said.

Ray's blood boiled. Being called incompetent he could handle. The way Ray figured, if you haven't ever been told that you don't know what you're doing by someone that clearly had no idea what they were doing, then you weren't doing your job effectively. He could even take being labeled a crazy conspiracist. He'd gotten used to that from pundits, politicians, and personalities over the years with regard to his stance on the second amendment. What he would not take was being called a racist by a man who had demonstrated his own racism every time he decried that there were too many white voices in America.

Ray knew that he should take Gary's advice. He knew that he should remain calm, but as he stood from his chair and witnessed both of the snakes that had entered his office visibly step back, he knew that the calm and collected ship had sailed.

"How dare you. I have done everything that I can to take care of ALL of our community members. You, who actively and openly riffs on the evils of the so-called 'white male' would dare to call me a racist is the most hypocritical thing that I have heard in years. The fact of the matter is that nationally, other agencies arrest black males at a much higher rate than we do here. You know full well that my department and I have partnered with churches and other community organizations in the African-American community, and that we actively promote and focus on ways to keep black males out of the criminal justice system and on paths toward success. So don't you stand here in your Italian suit that you bought by fleecing your own community for what little that they have and lecture me about preying on the black community. You've done that pretty well yourself."

Manigault stood there and looked like a spider that had just snatched a grasshopper that was foolish enough to fall into its web. Elrod, on the other hand, was so angry that Ray was seriously concerned that the blood vessel bulging from the left side of his temple would actually explode. Ray knew that he had played into their devious hands, but he didn't really care. It felt good to finally say what needed to be said.

"Thank you for stopping by, gentlemen. I'd like for you both to leave my office now," Ray said.

Elrod turned and opened the door for Manigault. Manigault smirked one last time. "I hope you remember what we said here today, Sheriff. I certainly know that I will remember everything that you said. In detail and in disturbing implication. Good day to you."

Manigault stepped through the door just before Elrod closed it a little too forcefully. The euphoria of finally getting to tell Elrod exactly what he was had begun to fade as Ray took his seat. He may have just made a grave error.

He looked at Gary and was surprised to see how tranquil his expression was.

"How bad do you think I fucked up?" Ray asked.

"I've seen worse, but not too many. You'd have been better off sitting there and taking it, buddy," Gary said as he laced his fingers together behind his increasingly grizzled hair.

"It's like my girlfriend tells me. The tiger in your mind is as safe as a kitten until you let it loose with your mouth," Gary said.

Ray chuckled. He had certainly turned his tiger loose without a leash, training, or any direction. The first kid it found was getting devoured, and that kid might just be Ray's career as sheriff.

"She sounds like she knows a thing or two about a thing two to me," Ray said.

"Nora? Oh yeah, she knows a whole lot about a whole lot of things. She's a lawyer, though so she kinda has to know the ins and outs of all sorts of things."

"A lawyer?"

"Not like the leeches that we deal with on the criminal side of things, buddy. She's into real estate law. Works for Ravenell and Company drafting and closing deals down in Charleston. She sees it as helping people and companies find their ideal or dream space for a business or home."

"Sounds like she's alright to me. When do I get to meet her?"

Gary stretched and let out a sigh before resting his elbows on his knees. "Sooner than you think, maybe. We've been talking about things getting more serious."

"She isn't already Nora McFadden is she?" Ray asked with a grin.

Gary laughed. "Naw, I learned about moving too fast with Lisa. She's still Nora Thompson for now. We've been dating for a while, though. I figure I'm not rushing into anything at this point."

"Wow, you've managed to keep her all to yourself for this long?"

"I know, sometimes I even surprise myself. That's getting ready to change I think. You ain't moving too fast with the good doctor are you?"

"I don't know. Things just sort of happened and have been going about sixty miles and hour ever since. I can't say that I'm complaining, though. She is pretty amazing," Ray said.

"I'm sure she is. Pretty, personable, successful; what's not to like, right? But if you'll allow an old man to give you some advice, you've gotta learn how to drive a corvette at thirty-five before you can go ninety. Slow it down and enjoy the ride if you can."

Ray nodded as his mind drifted back to the problem that Gaskins's death now presented. He wanted to shake everyone that he came into contact with and scream about the Yamassee Mounds and what they found there. But, as Manigault implied, with Gaskins' death, any mention of the Yamassee Mounds might be seen as the ravings of a lunatic bent on seeing a vast criminal underworld where there appeared to be none.

Any mention that he thought Gaskins was murdered by someone in his own department would only further discredit and alienate him. Dr. Poston had already ruled the death a suicide, but Ray still couldn't accept that the hopeful man they had left in the interview room had so quickly descended into such despair that he would kill himself.

It also had bothered Ray that Gaskins's body was practically standing on the balls of his feet. Ray had seen his share of suicides by hanging, and he had never once seen a successful attempt where the victim stood on the balls of their feet while hanging themselves. It all felt wrong. And saying that it felt wrong publicly would mean publicly calling out his own department. That was a scandal too great to be done publicly.

"You know we need to play our cards close to the chest on this one, right?" Gary asked as if he had read Ray's mind.

"I do," Ray replied.

"Here's what I think we oughta do, and you can take it or leave it."

"Alright, let me hear it."

"I'm with you, buddy. I don't think that Gaskins killed himself. I think that somebody that works at the jail did it. Definitely more than one."

Ray breathed a sigh of relief that Gary saw things like he did.

"I think that Gaskins was telling the whole truth and the people behind this shut him up. We need to be extremely careful moving forward. Let's focus on business as usual outwardly. But secretly, even in our spare time, we need to be working the case. Let it lie today. Take some time off and say that you're gonna take that fishing trip you skipped last week. Then, tomorrow we need to head back out to the Yamassee Mounds to document and catalog that whole scene. Maybe we can ask your lady-friend to help us on that front," Gary explained.

Ray was hesitant to use Erin in such a direct role, but he couldn't deny that her medical knowledge would be a huge help in processing the scene.

"I don't know that we should wait that long. What if they go out there all night and start cleaning it all up?" Ray asked.

"Be realistic, buddy. There had to be more than a thousand skeletons and corpses out there. The only reliably accessible way in or out is with a UTV. Water is too inconsistent to use boats, and the trees are too dense for trucks. Even if they started right now with a dozen UTVs working around the clock, there's no way they would even make a dent in the number until a week or two. Then, where are they gonna take them? You'd be hard-pressed to find another spot as remote as the mounds. A crematorium would raise suspicion with smoke rising in a huge plume from this farm Gaskins told us about. They could throw 'em out offshore, but are they really gonna risk trucking a trailer full of bones all the way to Georgetown, then have to explain how they're gonna put aboard a boat to then dump them?

"There's no way to solve that problem without virtually guaranteeing they get caught somehow. If I can figure that out, I'd bet a buffalo nickel that they've figured that out too."

Ray realized that he was still letting his emotions get the better of him. Had he been thinking logically, then he might've deduced what Gary had sooner. Ray chastised himself for being so emotional at a time when cooler heads desperately were needed.

"You're right, Gary. That grave cannot be moved or covered up."

"Glad you're seeing things in the right light finally. Been trying to tell you for five years that I'm always right."

Ray laughed as Gary continued. "So, we catalog everything in secret. We start looking into the Spates family and their holdings: land, businesses, properties, whatever they have local. Then we keep looking for the farm. Gaskins said that it was about twenty-five minutes south-southeast of the mounds. We go out on joyrides a few times a week and maybe we get lucky. Then, once we have all of that evidence collected, we get a warrant to search this farm and we go public. All in the span of an afternoon."

Ray thought for a moment. Though he wasn't the biggest fan of hoping they got lucky trying to both locate the farm and in examining the Spates brothers, he had to admit, it was the most solid plan of attack they had available.

"Alright, dude. You win. What do we need to do first?" Ray said.

"Go home for the day, or maybe to see your new lady friend. We need her help, after all. Tomorrow you come into work and take a few days off, and we get to work."

Gary stood, sighing as his body creaked and popped along the way. Ray thrust his hand toward Gary, who gave it a firm handshake.

"Guess we're in this together now, dude," Ray said

"To the bitter end, buddy. I'm gonna go ahead and head

on out. Got a big day tomorrow, and an old man like me needs all the rest he can get."

"Say hello to Nora for me."

"You can count on it, buddy."

CHAPTER 31

It was the kind of day that seemed to last a whole week. Everything had started out well enough for Erin. She was up and at it at 4:30 for her morning workout routine; a protein shake in her belly by 5:45; showered, hair done, and makeup perfect by 7:15; and her white blouse, red paper bag pants, navy blazer, and nude heels on and perfect by 7:30. She even had time to splurge and stop for coffee on her way into the hospital to begin her rounds at 8:15. Then, just as she was leaving the drive-through coffee shop with, coffee in hand, the car in front of her slammed on its brakes. Erin had just enough time to stand on her brakes but not enough time to keep her coffee from spilling down the front of her white blouse.

She shoved aside the building frustration by reminding herself that things could have been much worse before she continued on to McLamb Regional Hospital and the spare clothes she kept hanging in a small wardrobe in her office. The white blouse in there was not as cute as the coffee-stained one, but it was going to have to do for the day.

Then, the cases started rolling in. Ten of them were junkies looking to score more opioids, fifteen others were illegals coming to the ER with a runny nose or a headache, two were broken bones, and one was an accidental laceration to the face. Things were hopping so much that Erin didn't have even a second to wolf down the salad she had brought for lunch, nor did she have time to get caught up on the mountain of emails that undoubtedly were weighing down her inbox.

She managed to tear herself away from another man cursing her out because he couldn't understand why she "just won't give him some fucking lortabs" long enough to shoot a text to Ray: Heyyy! Been a crazy day so far here and I can't wait to get home and to enjoy some wine! lol! Just wanted to check in and wish U a happy happy day too!

She pressed send and slid the phone into the back pocket of her pants. She had wanted to tell him that she had really enjoyed the time they shared the night before, but she didn't want to come on too strong. She hadn't heard from him yet, and she was doing all that she could to stifle the annoying anxiety and overthinking that came along with that.

He was a busy guy and he had a very important job too. She was sure he would text her once he got the chance. But that certainty still made her feel like she was about to jump into a pond with no way of knowing if she would hit the water or the rocks on the bottom.

The rest of the day was so busy that she didn't have time to check her phone or even think about whether Ray Myers had texted her back or if he was avoiding her altogether. At 5:34, she finished the few lines of documentation on her last patient's chart, grabbed her purse and her soiled shirt, and trotted out to her Mustang.

She set the brown leather bag in the passenger seat, gracefully swung her legs into the car, and started the rumbling engine before she finally removed her phone from her back pocket. Her heart leapt when she saw the alert that read Ray Myers: New Message. She quickly opened the phone to read his response: Hey back. Thanks for checking in on me, I really appreciate that. Sorry to say that my day has probably been just as crazy as yours. If it's OK with you, I was thinking about grabbing a pizza from Stefano's and maybe stopping by to hear about your day and tell you all about mine?

The excitement built in her chest like water behind an overwhelmed dam as she read those words. She looked quickly to see when he had sent her the message and panicked that he had sent the response only thirty minutes before. If she hurried home, then she might have just enough time to give herself a rag bath, change into something sexier, and fix her hair and makeup before he arrived. Her fingers were blur as she typed into the phone: Sounds like a date to me! Lemme know when UR on UR way, kk?

She sent the message, threw her car into gear, and drove as fast as she legally could back home. She flew in the door, stripped off her clothing and underwear, and began quickly washing her body with a warm washcloth. She pulled her hair out of the messy bun she had put it into, teased the gentle curls out of her dark brown tresses, and set everything in place with a generous helping of hairspray. Her makeup took a few minutes, but in the end she was confident she had created a bright, sultry look that exuded subtle pink hues and sex appeal. She sprayed her naked skin with her favorite perfume and paid particular attention to her wrists, cleavage, and her inner thighs before stepping into a cute navy wrap dress that was classy from the pink floral designs and sexy from the mid-thigh length.

She had just stepped into a pair of four-inch brown leather heels and checked herself one last time in the mirror before she heard the knock on the door. She took a deep breath and did her best to settle the flock of butterflies in her stomach before she sashayed to the front door of her home.

In one fluid motion and without any thought at all, she

opened the door, draped her arms around his tree-trunk of a neck, and kissed him. The passion of the kiss was a surprise to them both as she slid her tongue past his lips as if it were as natural as saying hello. She could tell that Ray was taken a little off guard. To be honest, so was she, but for some reason she just didn't care. She kissed him with passion that was burning as hot as a lava flow. For the first time, she could feel Ray starting to give in to his overwhelming desire.

Suddenly, he broke the kiss. "I've got something that I need to tell you. Before we get any further," he said.

Her excitement deflated like a balloon and scenarios began running in her head as he closed the door behind him and set the pizza on the coffee table of her living room. Had she been too forceful? Was she moving too fast with this? All of the scenarios were running through her head a million miles a minute.

"You need to hear about my day, and you might wanna sit down for this," Ray said.

Erin said nothing and crossed her arms securely across her body in an unconscious attempt at comforting herself before she took a seat on her sofa. She had expected him to tell her why he didn't want to see her anymore, and she was doing everything that she could to mentally and emotionally prepare herself. In the span of a few seconds, she had determined that she was not going to be a passive party in this conversation and summoned all of the courage to speak.

"I hope that it's nothing too serious, like to do with you and me."

Ray looked confused. "No, nothing like that at all. I think you're amazing. It's really just about what all happened today. I don't want you to think that what I'm about to say has anything to do with how I feel about you. Far from it. Okay?"

Erin nodded her head, suddenly feeling incredibly foolish for working herself up into a tizzy. "Yeah, of course. Please, go ahead and tell me what happened."

Ray started by telling her about the interview that

they had with Gaskins and the insane story he told them that lined up perfectly with the rumor that Erin had shared with him on Saturday. He filled her in on the rest and ended with Gaskins's suicide and the conversation he had with Elrod and Manigault in his office.

When he finished, Erin's eyes had widened and her gaze was distant. She sat there in silence for a moment, astonished that Ashanti had been right all along. It felt strange. One minute, everything was fine; she was sure of herself and the world she lived in. A minute later, everything suddenly felt upside down. Could she ever trust that most people were genuinely good again? She had the sinking feeling that some vestige of her innocence had just been put to death.

"There's one more thing," Ray said.

She looked at him quizzically. What else could he possibly say that would add to the nightmare that he had just told her existed out in the woods?

"When I was examining the pit, not everything was uh...skeletal. Some of the victims still had...flesh on their bones," he explained.

Her curiosity heightened. "So they're still actively dumping bodies out there?"

Ray nodded. "Yeah, that's pretty clear. But the thing is, while I was looking into the pit, I saw this woman."

Erin made eye contact with him and hoped he wasn't about to say what she so desperately feared he was about to reveal.

"I'm not gonna go into detail about how she looked. I just wanted you to know that. . . I found Ashanti Livingston's remains in that pit."

It felt like someone had hit her in the stomach with a wrecking ball. The whole room started spinning and she could feel the scream of emotion building in her chest as her eyes started to sting. She willed herself to stay composed.

"Are you sure that it was Ashanti?"

"I'm certain." He looked at her. In the shadow of that look, she nearly buckled into a heap of emotion.

"I'm sorry that I couldn't save her, Erin. With all of my heart, I'm so sorry."

The tears that stung her eyes rolled out of them like bowling balls, and the scream of emotion left her lips as a pained sob. Before she knew what was happening, Ray had wrapped his arms around her and held her tight as she gently sobbed into his chest.

Ashanti had been her best friend. She had helped her find her confidence. She had helped her find her voice. She had taught her how to have fun under pressure. And she had taught her how to pursue her goals with a dogged tenacity. Now, she would never see her, feel her touch, or hear her laugh ever again. Her friend was gone, and Erin was left to carry on without her.

Her grief became anger. Not anger at Ray; he had truly done all that he could to find out what had happened to Ashanti and bring her home. She was angry with herself. If only she had taken Ashanti to the authorities the day she had confided in her. If only she had taken her seriously. If only she had believed her, then she might still be alive today. It was a terrible realization to come to; that you bore some share of the responsibility for the murder of your best friend. It was a fact she would have to learn to live with for the rest of her life.

She clung to Ray, who held her tightly. The security and comfort that she felt in his arms was unlike anything she had felt before and she couldn't bear the thought of ever leaving them. For several minutes, they sat in relative silence as she clung to the small handfuls of his shirt and he held her fast and firm. Eventually, she managed to pull herself together, carefully wipe her eyes on his damp shirt, and lock the sobs back within her wounded soul.

"Thank you, Ray, for finding Ashanti for me." She looked deep into his eyes and saw the tender compassion and the terrible resolve in them.

"I'm going to help you catch the people who did this to her and all those other people. Whatever it takes. I'm with you no matter what."

She could see that Ray was about to reply, but her emotions and the connection she felt with him took control of her. She kissed him tenderly at first. Her tongue gently found its way past his lips to dance with his own. The grief she felt began to turn to raw desire for the man who had found her friend and so tenderly held her through the pain.

She continued the volcanic kisses and felt the last vestiges of Ray's ironclad self-control fall away like leaves in November as he slid his right hand underneath her barely covered derriere and lifted her into the air. She knew what to do next, and in an instant she wrapped her toned legs around his waist as his powerful arms crushed her against his hard body. She was in absolute ecstasy; her body quivering with anticipation at what would await her if he took her to her bedroom.

She broke the passionate kisses, and driven by her base instincts, she began showering his neck with kisses and nibbling on his ears as if her survival depended upon it.

"Bedroom is at the end of the hall," she little more than breathed as she kissed him passionately again, running her fingers through his short hair.

Ray said nothing but must've gotten the message as she felt his iron legs pumping as he carried her down the hallway and into her bedroom. They fell onto the plush queen-sized mattress. Her desire became a supernova when his rock-hard body pinned her to the bed and she felt the unmistakable prodding that his body involuntarily gave to her inner thigh.

She gently pushed him back and melted as he immediately complied with her gentle direction. This man could not ever hurt her or take advantage of her. She was certain of that fact. Erin stood, glided to him, and began gently kissing him as she helped him slip his polo shirt over his head. A shiver shot through her as she saw his chiseled chest and the tattoos and scars that marked it for the first time. With her left hand, she gently ran her fingers across his chest, delicately outlining his tattoos and the raised edges of the scars left behind by the wounds he suffered for his country. A gentle groan escaped his throat and she caressed his chest and unfastened his belt.

She gently ran her fingers along the edge of him before she took hold of him. She could feel the animal inside of this man desperately trying to break free from his chest like a lion inside of a cage as she moved her hands in rhythm around him. He was barely in control when his powerful hands slipped her dress off of her shoulders, around her hips, and onto the floor.

The control was slipping further as his powerful fingers unclasped the bra and removed the last bit of modesty from her body. The instant her underwear hit the floor, the lion within him broke free of its cage.

Erin wasn't sure how long it had lasted. The only thing she was sure of was the exquisite marriage of dull, delicious pain and unimaginable, delectable pleasure that crashed into her body with every thrust of his. Her fingernails dug into the hard flesh of his back, her legs locked around his body like a vise, and her throat let loose the cries of ravishment that she had never known she was capable of producing.

He held her arms firmly above her head with one strong hand, while he held himself aloft with the other. Erin groaned as she felt the hard hand holding her arms firmly in place. Time and space seemed to disappear altogether for her. For what could've been seconds, or what could've been hours, he drove wave after drowning wave of pleasure into her body and soul.

She felt the waves of overwhelming pleasure beginning to build in intensity in her body. She could feel it breaking through the dam of her self-control with every push he provided. The volcano of ecstasy had just reached the point of no return and she could feel in every fiber of her quaking body that the eruption was imminent. A grunt from him and the volcano within her exploded.

It was too much to bear and for a moment she lost herself. The sounds of whimpering and pleasured screams filled the room. Ray too roared as he fired his love into her in wave after delicious wave.

Ray was desperately trying to catch his breath as he pulled her naked body against his in a tender embrace that seemed to go on for forever.

"Wow, that was... that was... insane," Erin said breathlessly.

"I'm sorry, I don't know what came over me," Ray replied in between breaths.

Erin lovingly placed her small hand against his cheek. "Don't be sorry. I wanted this. I needed this. And it was beautiful. It was beautiful beyond any words I could use to describe it," she replied.

This feeling that she felt for him was deadly. More deadly than any disease or lifestyle known to man. It scared her more than spiders or the thought of being underdressed at an event. Still, she couldn't shake the feeling, and now, more than ever, she felt like she could give into it like just had done with him.

He was amazing. He was everything she had always wanted in a man. He was sweet, strong, honorable, and respectful. All of those were traits that she was convinced were found in her dad and in him alone until the day that she was led into his tiny little office to talk about a friend that was missing. Now, she was lying in bed, her naked skin against his naked skin, marveling at the fact that God had seen fit to create such an amazing man as he, and marveling at the fact that He had seen fit to put Ray in the middle of her own path.

She wasn't sure she should say it, but at this moment she knew it to be true. Her heart hadn't loved in a long time, but she knew for certain that she loved Raleigh Myers.

CHAPTER 32

Regardless of all of the crazy things that had been happening within the last twenty-four hours, the tower of paperwork on Gary McFadden's desk was not getting any shorter. Once Ray had left the office, Gary decided that he couldn't go home yet like he had told Ray that he would. The world didn't stop spinning just because it had suddenly started raining shit down on top of you and your best buddy. He walked into his cubicle that was decorated with pictures of his kids, the fish he'd landed, and deer he'd killed, and got to work. The monotonous tasks seemed to take his mind off of the Yamassee Mounds, the bones in the clearing, and the rotting dismembered corpses they had found in the central pit.

It was easily the most horrific sight that he had seen in all of his forty-three years on the earth. It was like something you could see being included in the plot of a horror movie; an atrocity so horrible that the only place it could exist was in the frames of fiction. It was all too frighteningly real, though. The sights, sounds, smells; they all conjured up images from his youth that he had been hopelessly unsettled by and desperate to pretend were never discussed with him.

When he was twenty and just starting out as a deputy on the road, his dad had seen fit to take his son on a fishing trip to Indian River in Florida along with Uncle Lenny. Lenny wasn't really his uncle—he and his dad had served together in Vietnam—but he had grown up loving whenever his Uncle Lenny would come all the way up from Daytona Beach for a visit. During this trip, however, Lenny and Gary's dad both hit the beer and the whiskey a little too hard. Before long, they were both telling, reliving was more accurate, stories about their time in Southeast Asia that Gary had never heard.

Up to that point, Gary had known that his dad was a Vietnam veteran, and he had found out that his dad had seen a considerable amount of combat from talking to his mother, but he had never ever seen his dad talk about what had happened there, nor had he never learned firsthand what his dad experienced. That night, twenty-three years ago, the alcohol had done the trick.

Sitting at his desk now, filling out reports, and filing other monotonous paperwork, he could still hear the haunting words of his father saying, "I couldn't tell man from woman or child from elderly. They all seemed to have fused into this one mass of flesh, bones, and teeth once we had found them. I know our boys did some sick shit out at My Lai in '68, but ain't nobody ever talked about the sick shit that the 'Cong or the NVA did to them poor people if they ever helped us GIs out."

"What'd y'all do about it?" Gary asked.

"Lenny and I tracked them with the rest of our SOG team." He took another pull of whiskey. "Tracked them right out of Kontum and across the border into Laos. We caught up to 'em two days later. They thought they was safe in Laos on account of American troops being forbidden from crossing the border, so we surrounded their platoon while they'd made camp. We killed every last one of them sons-of-bitches and high-tailed it back to Kontum."

The story had shaken young Garrett McFadden to the core. He couldn't recall if they had caught any fish or not during that trip, but he was certain he had learned more about his father than ever before, and he wasn't sure whether or not he regretted that. His father had witnessed the cruel depravity of man with his own eyes and it had changed him forever. He had never understood what his mother had meant when she told him "Horace was different before the war."

Now that he had seen the Yamassee Mounds, he finally understood what his mother had meant. Gary had now, like his father before him, stared into the darkness that is made possible by the evil in a man's soul. He just hoped that he, unlike his father, wouldn't learn that the darkness of man's evil stares back at you.

Gary had worked for another two hours, completed his paperwork, and struggled with the darkness he had encountered in the woods before he decided that it was time to call it quits and to head to the house.

He logged off of his computer, grabbed his insulated coffee mug, and walked out to his truck without saying a word to anyone else. Ray was right after all. There were almost certainly multiple persons within the department who were involved with this somehow, and that knowledge had changed his entire demeanor and perspective on the whole place. He wasn't so sure he could keep coming into work after this like nothing had ever happened. This place seemed tainted to him, and he wanted nothing more than to divorce himself from it.

He had been with the department for twenty-three years, and in that time he had managed to work his way up to captain in charge of the criminal investigation division, though that wasn't saying a whole lot in a department of twenty-three people. Ray had been talking about promoting him to the position of chief deputy, work right underneath Ray, and receive a nice little pay bump in the process.

Gary was always interested in better pay; not that

he was hurting with his captain's salary, but he had ultimately told Ray that it was a bad idea. Everybody knew that the two of them had been close friends for years, and the last thing that Ray or the department needed was the appearance of favoritism in the command structure. Besides, once he reminded Ray that he was an involved and hands-on sheriff, it became clearer and clearer that creating the rank of chief deputy was completely unnecessary. So, Gary kept his role and he was happy and content. The day he had just gone through unfortunately had vaporized any contentment or peace of mind he had worked so hard to cultivate.

He thought about how he felt about his future as he walked out the front door of the office. The thoughts continued their race through his soul as he got into his truck. When he started the engine and the radio began blaring a country classic from the 1990s, he knew he had made his decision. He was going to see this through to the end. He was going to see the people responsible brought to justice. Then, he was going to take his early retirement from the department.

Financially, he would definitely take a hit, but he knew that Ray would do what he had to do to make sure he received his full pension and benefits. In truth, he wasn't all that worried about how he was going to make ends meet. He now knew what the next step was in his life, and he was ready to embrace that no matter what the consequences might be.

He and Nora had discussed their future while she was visiting him over the weekend. She still didn't want to live out in the open; too many risks came with that, but she had told him that she wanted them to be together while she either worked towards living in the open or while she continued putting on her so-called mask when she was in the professional world.

One day they might get married, or they may never. Gary didn't care just as long as he got to be with her, without her mask, every day for the rest of his life. With his pension and her salary, they would be set. All he would have to worry about would be her and getting to see his kids more often than now.

He pulled his phone out of his pocket and opened his texting app. He sent the same text to both of his kids: Hey, this is your dear old dad. I was thinking about you and just wanted you to know that I love you and I am so proud of you. I hope that maybe one day you can both be proud of me too. I'll see you soon. Also, you want to hear a joke about construction? I'm still working on it.

He smiled and snorted a laugh as he hit send. He knew they would read the last part and roll their eyes, but they'd still smile and have a little laugh at their old man's corny sense of humor.

He tapped on the conversation he had been having with Nora next and began typing: Hey you. I'm gonna video call you in an hour, so go start getting yourself together haha. Been a particularly rough day, but I wanna talk about something else with you more. Nothing bad, I promise. See you in a few, beautiful. Love you.

He hit send, set the phone on the console of his truck, and pulled out of the parking lot.

His stomach grumbled and he decided that Kung Pao chicken and fried rice sounded like heaven on a plate. He pulled into Peking Restaurant's drive-through and slowly ordered his food while listening intently to Jian's broken English to make sure that he had the correct change for him. Once he pulled up to the window, chatted with Jian, and paid for his food, he pulled out his phone to see if he had gotten any responses.

Both of his kids had sent an emoji rolling its eyes, followed by Love you too, Dad. He smiled knowing that his corny joke had done its job. Nora had also sent him a response: I'll be ready with bells on when you call, lover. Can't wait to see you. Love you too.

He broke into a grin as he read her words. The whole world might be going crazy and crumbling around him, but at least he could count on her to be there for him. In a few more minutes, he had his food sitting securely in his passenger seat as he headed home. The drive was quiet, and the twenty minutes of fields, swamps, and woods helped to soothe his battered soul as he drove. He would certainly miss this place once he moved to Charleston.

The swamplands, cotton fields, and pine woodlands had been his home ever since his parents had taken him home from McLamb Regional Hospital in Florence. Now, for the first time in his life, he was preparing to leave the home that he loved so dearly for a woman that he had grown to love even more. He had gone from being uncomfortable about her unique situation, to not noticing it, and finally seeing her as the woman that he knew she so desperately tried not to be but was incapable of not being.

He no longer worried what might be said about him in Craven County once he was finally gone. He couldn't say that he would blame some of the people in the county for their disapproval of his choice. Truthfully he didn't necessarily approve of it himself. But for some reason, she was different to him. She had tried not to act on the preferences and compulsions she had felt her entire life. Still, she couldn't escape them despite all of her efforts to the contrary. He felt for her there. He respected her for trying so hard to resist. He had fallen for her for those reasons, and now he couldn't care less what anyone had to say about it. All he worried about was being the best that he could be for her.

He pulled into the trailer park and parked his truck in the gravel drive beside his trailer. He grabbed the bag of Chinese take-out and trotted up the redwood steps to the trailer's porch. Once inside of the trailer, he set his food on the counter beside the microwave, walked into his bedroom, stripped his clothes off, and hopped into the shower. The shower lasted less than five minutes, and two minutes after that he walked back into the kitchen wearing his gym shorts and tank top.

He grabbed his phone from the table and tapped the icon to video call Nora. The phone trilled, letting him know that it was attempting to connect the call, and ten seconds later the trilling stopped and connected. Nora looked stunning with her long, honey-blonde hair in wavy curls.

Her darker eye-makeup made her green eyes shine, and her shimmery nude lips made her lips appear fuller and more sultry than they normally would. Her small golden hoop earrings and matching necklace helped to pull the whole look together with her low-cut white top in a way that Gary found absolutely irresistible.

"My, my, my, don't we sure look pretty today. You got some fella coming over tonight that I don't know about?" Gary asked with a grin.

Nora smiled and revealed her perfectly straight teeth as white as the snow that dusted the ground once every third January.

"Yeah, don't you know that I've got all the boys just lining up to come and take a look at little ol' me," she said.

Her breathy voice still captivated Gary, even after nearly two years of seeing one another. "Well, I don't blame 'em with you lookin' as pretty as you do."

"Easy there, cowboy. Flattery'll get you nowhere. How was your day? Catch any bad guys?"

"On the trail of some real bad ones, I'm afraid," he said.

"Tyrone Weeks bad?" she asked.

"Worse," he replied.

Gary filled her in on all of it, from the interrogation to the dumping ground, "suicide," and the strongarming of Ray. Her perfectly manicured appearance twisted into faces of pain, disgust, and outrage as he detailed every bit of the story in all of its gruesome detail. When he finished, he looked at her and smiled sheepishly through the screen.

"Sorry, I just had to get that off my chest."

"Don't be sorry. I'm glad that you told me what is going on. You know, what they're doing with Ray is wrong and really makes you wonder how high this thing might go. If they could get to a witness in secured custody, and you have to worry about who in the department is on your side or not, this could get incredibly dangerous for you. Please be extra careful. Keep Ray safe too, but you need to be looking out for yourself. I don't even wanna think about anything happening to you," Nora said.

"You know me; Mr. Careful is my name. Don't worry

about me, girl. We've got us a good plan, like I was telling you about, and I'm pretty sure we can see it through to the end. Ray's a good guy, you know, and together we're gonna get these people brought to justice. Then, it'll be all over and you won't have to worry your pretty little self over it anymore. And that's kinda what I wanted to talk to you about, anyway," Gary replied.

Nora furrowed her thin eyebrows. "What do you mean? Like after the case is over and I'm not worrying myself like I'm going to now?"

"Yeah, but without the worrying part," Gary said with a grin.

A smile cracked her stoic face. Yep, can't help but fall victim to my country charm, Gary thought.

"Once this is all over and done with, I'm gonna take my early retirement and get out of this business altogether. I thought I had seen it all, but I now know that after today I've seen too much."

Her eyes went wide. "Whoa, retirement? Are you sure you'd be able to swing that financially or that Ray would even sign off on that?"

"Ray'll definitely sign off on it. He'll do right by me and turn me loose with the most I can get outta my pension. I've figured a way to make the finances work out a whole lot better, but it's gonna take you signing off on it too."

"Well, that's good to know that Ray will do whatever he has to do to set you up right, but why do you need me to sign off on anything? If you needed money or anything, you know I'd give you whatever you need," Nora said.

"I wasn't figuring that exactly. I was just thinking that things might go a whole lot better if we took things to the next level," Gary explained.

"Like how?"

"You know that I love you, right? That I'd do anything in the world for up to and including keeping you and me private from now on or stepping out into the spotlight with you and all that that would entail, right?" Gary asked.

"Yeah, of course I know that, lover. What are you trying to say?"

"I'm saying that I want to be with you, Nora. I want to wake up with you, to eat dinner with you, and to go to bed with you. And I don't just want to do it a couple of weekends a month or the odd week or two. I wanna do that with you all the time, and I don't care if that means you step out of the shadows and throw your mask away for good, or if that means that you only take your mask off when you're at home with me. I just wanna be with you, that's all. You and only you. What do ya think?" Gary said.

The look of surprise was evident on her face. His heart raced as she seemed to sit in silence for an eternity that he was certain was less than a second or two. Her look of surprise transformed into the widest and happiest smile he had seen on her face since he first told her how he felt about her. Tears welled up in her eyes and started running down her face in silvery streams over her highlighter and foundation.

"Really?" she said. "You're ready to do that for me? Even if I need to keep my personal and professional life separate?"

"I'd do just about anything for you. Would you have me down there with you?"

"Of course, lover. Of course I want us to be together like that. More than anything."

Gary felt the most profound feeling of relief since finding out that his children and ex-wife were all okay on the days of their births. It was really happening. Finally, he had his fresh start with a woman he had grown to adore. How could a country boy like him get so lucky?

"Alright, then. Let's do it. I love you, darlin'," Gary said.

"I love you too," Nora replied as she gently dabbed her eyes with a tissue. "Ugh, if I don't stop all of this cryin' my hour's worth of getting cute for you is gonna run off of my face and into my lap," she said with a chuckle.

"You'd still be as pretty as ever, darlin'. I'll start packing stuff up and maybe moving a thing or two whenever I get a chance-" The sound of his hose pipe turning on at the far side of his trailer interrupted him. He groaned in dramatic frustration.

"Those damn kids three trailers down are out there running my hose again. Lemme call you back once I go run 'em off. Then we can talk about moving some stuff in here and there," Gary said as he stood up from his chair and kicked on his Crocs by the back door.

"Okay, I'll be here. Don't shoot those kids, Gary."

"Ah, I'll just wing 'em a little bit. Builds character."

Nora laughed. "I love you, you fool."

"I love you too, beautiful. Be right back."

Gary ended the call and slipped his phone into the pocket of his shorts. He stormed out the back door, down the redwood steps, and around his trailer; the gravel crunching underneath his soft rubber soles as he went. Those Kilmer boys had a bad habit of coming around and using people's hoses to squirt one another on hot days. Gary didn't necessarily mind that sort of mischief; it beat the hell out of the other kinds that they could get into, but he did mind how Craven Utilities really stuck it to him on his summer water usage. That meant that the light-hearted mischief needed to stop.

He rounded the front of the trailer with a command telling the kids to cut the water off and go home ready to fire in his chest. But nobody was there, and to his surprise, the hose was still neatly rolled up around the spigot. He looked around for a minute or two, just to check and see whether or not the kids were hiding behind his azaleas or hydrangeas, but found nothing and headed back into the trailer.

Maybe those kids had finally learned to listen for movement inside so they could run off undetected. Crafty and clever if you asked Gary, but he'd still go and have a chat with their father Billy. Nothing would put a stop to it quite like a good ol' fashioned whipping.

He closed the door behind him and stepped through the kitchen and into the living room. He reached into his pocket to call Nora back when he felt something strong and immovable loop itself around his throat. Immediately his fight or flight response was activated but to no avail as he felt his arms and legs being seized by equally strong and firm grips. He fought with all his might but only managed to shake his torso very little. He tried to scream for help but what he now knew was an arm around his throat prevented anything but labored gurgles from escaping his lips.

The men who had seized hold of his body lifted him into the air and plopped him down in his recliner. A man wearing what looked like a cross between hospital scrubs and a jumpsuit stepped into his view. The man wore a surgical hair net and a surgical mask, as well as latex gloves and sterile covers over his shoes. Gary saw that in his right hand he held a syringe and he instantly knew what these men were here to do.

He fought with all of his might. The man holding his right hand briefly lost his grip and Gary landed a hard blow to the man's solar plexus. Anticipating the opening, Gary thrashed with his left arm only to feel the grip around his neck tighten and feel the man he had just managed to hit regain a tight grip on his right arm.

"Lift up his fucking leg," the surgeon at his feet commanded to the man holding his left leg.

Gary fought but the added pressure of an elbow pressing into his flesh just above the kneecap made his leg give way despite his best effort to keep it taught. Tears were streaming down his face from the pressure around his neck, and Gary began to genuinely fear that the man was going to choke him to death. He watched as the surgeon, with the strangest Southern accent he had heard in a while, deftly clicked open the syringe and stabbed the needle between toes number two and three.

The sharp pain shot through him like a bullet and confusion quickly gave way to horror as he felt his mind clouding. The horror that he felt now, strangely, gave way to peace as the terrible realization that this was to be his end settled on his mind like a warm blanket. He could feel his consciousness slipping away as the black abyss at the corner of his eyes began to creep closer to the center of his vision.

As the blackness closed in around him, he found himself at peace with the death that he was sure would follow. He thought of his ex-wife. They hadn't worked out, but he respected the hell out of her and still cared deeply for her, if he was honest with himself. He hoped she knew that he tried his best to make it work and that through it all he had always hoped that she got the best out of life, whether that was him or not.

He thought of his kids. It wouldn't be easy on them losing their old man like this and at their age. He felt a twinge of regret that he'd never get to see them make something of their lives; that he wouldn't get the chance to witness them struggle and succeed. He regretted that he wouldn't be there to give all the talks and advice that only dads seemed to know how to give. He wished that he would've had the opportunity to see them fall in love and maybe make him a PaPaw one day. Man, that sure would've been something. He hoped they knew it wasn't their fault that he and their mom didn't work out. He hoped they knew how much he loved them both and how proud he was to be their dad. He hoped they'd think of him and laugh whenever they heard a corny dad-joke.

Finally, as the last of the world slipped away into cold blackness, he thought of Nora. He hoped she knew that he thought the world of her. That he admired her struggle against herself and the courage that some might call hypocrisy of disapproving of your own predilections while being unable to escape them in her life. He hoped she knew that he had loved her with all that he was and that he would've endured secrecy or public scorn in the name of being with her as they both tried to figure out how to make life work. He hoped she would move on from him and find another rock, find strength to keep being who she was in spite of her compulsion to become someone new, and that she would finally have the courage to step out of the shadows and accept the light and whatever consequences that might mean.

A few moments later, a single gunshot echoed its muffled report outside of the trailer, and the six men in surgical gear streamed from the trailer and melted into the

woods and the car they had parked on a dirt road a quar-
ter-mile through the dense forest.

CHAPTER 33

The morning was one of the most hectic that Ray Myers had experienced in years. The night before had been a
major contributor to the breakneck pace his morning had
held so far. He had originally gone to see Erin for innocent
reasons. It was part of his job to inform the party who had
reported a loved one missing, as Erin had basically done
regarding Ashanti the previous Saturday, and it was only
right that she got the news in person. The pizza, which
eventually was half-eaten, had been both his way of bringing sustenance to the bereaved and his way of being there
for her as her. . . what was he to her now anyway?

He hadn't expected the night to become what it had
become. Passion and grief both in ample supply and in
maximum intensity were their companions through the
night. Ray hadn't planned on succumbing to his natural
desires, but the way she kissed him, touched him, and the
way that she seemed to need him were too much for his
self-discipline to bear. He was lost in the maze of her beau-

ty, touch, and sexuality before his conscience even had a chance to say no.

He had worried once both he and Erin had reached the culmination of their carnal dance that she would suddenly regret the decision to share her body with him, like a client who suddenly realized that the seance they had just attended had given them no new insights into their future. To his surprise and delight, she had kissed him intimately and began to initiate a second experience of sexual ecstasy that somehow seemed to surpass the bliss of their initial encounter. They had fully explored the act of love with their bodies that second time, and after munching on cold slices of pizza with lukewarm glasses of wine, they had fallen asleep in each other's arms.

Ray's internal clock, rather than his phone, woke him in the morning. The sight of Erin's head resting on his firm chest, her dark brown curls cascading down his side and covering her left shoulder from shoulder blade to delicate collar bone, and the feeling of her warm, gentle breaths against his skin, had been the most magnificent morning greeting that he had received in his entire life. It may have even topped Christmas morning when he was nine.

He was careful not to stir and worried that even the slightest move would wake her and end the saccharine sight of an angel sleeping soundly. For what seemed like half an hour, he tenderly watched as she slept until she drew in a sharp breath, tickled his chest with the eyelashes on her right eye blinking rapidly against his skin, and turned her head to get a good look at his face.

"Good morning," she said in a sleepy voice.

"Good morning to you," he replied.

She stretched and rose onto one elbow. The sight of her perfect body and her ample bust caused both a spark in Ray's mind and in another part of his body. For a few seconds, she just lay there gazing into his eyes, saying nothing at all. Ray worried that the regret he feared she would be feeling was now bubbling to the surface of a mind made clear by the catharsis of intercourse.

His fears were allayed when she leaned forward and

pressed her lips to his; the kind of kiss Ray had felt before. The kind that a lover gave to her man to thank him both for the intimacy that they had shared and for still being there when she woke up in the morning. The kind that yearned to be returned with the intimate message that her man was not going anywhere.

Before he knew it, he was ready for her again and she incredibly slipped her soft lithe body onto his and looked deep into his eyes as she guided him with her hand. The good morning greeting extended itself into a slow and sweet time of gentle intimacy. The slow build of their inevitable release gently increased with each fluid roll of her hips. The intensity of Ray's building release was almost too much for his mind to handle. He knew the same was true for Erin as she gnawed her bottom lip, the force of the bite increasing with every roll of her hips, as Ray curled his toes beneath his soles to keep withstanding the onslaught of pleasure.

Finally, the wall could withstand no more strain and he broke into her with a cascade of love and pleasure. The guttural groan that escaped his throat was matched by her own feline purring.

The sweet intimacy was unlike anything that he had experienced in his life, and for a brief moment he thought that he heard Erin, who had nuzzled into his neck as she panted from the experience, whisper the word love. He couldn't be sure, though.

"That was incredible," he said as he pulled her closer to him.

He could feel the smile curling across her face as she pressed her lips against the soft skin of his neck.

"Yes, it was," she said.

They lay quietly for a moment. Ray could tell that the silence was not from the exertion of their morning lovemaking. He could tell that the atmosphere of her bedroom was leavened with apprehension. He also knew that it was likely due to her uncertainty about his feelings for her and his intentions moving forward. How could it not be?

Erin wasn't the type of woman to recklessly invite a

man into her life; that much he had learned by spending the afternoon and evening with her the previous Sunday. She definitely wasn't the type of woman to engage in such a precious and intimate act as sharing her body with a man for the sheer pleasure of it before moving on with her life as usual, either. She needed to know there was something more between them. She needed to know there was a future for them together. Otherwise, she had wasted sharing the gift of her body with a man who would only throw it aside and search for the next bauble.

"I want you to know," Ray began, "this wasn't just a fun fling for me. I think that it meant more to you too."

"It did. So much more," she replied as she nodded into the nape of his neck.

"I want you, Erin. I want to be with you and to be yours. The way that I have felt around you is incredible. I'm falling for you," Ray said.

"I guess it's okay to say you're my boyfriend now, right?" Erin asked.

"Only if I can say you're my girlfriend," Ray replied.

Erin quickly slid on top of him again. "That's fine with me, boyfriend."

Ray kissed her again. Erin's eye darted open and she cut the kiss short. "Oh shit, what time is it?" she said.

Ray hadn't been thinking about the time either and now shared in her mild panic. Erin rolled off of him and towards the table on the opposite side of the bed. He heard her pick up her cell phone and then heard it thud back to the wood.

"Shit, it's 6:37. I have a shift starting in one hour!"

Erin threw the light pink and white comforter off of her, slid her naked body out of bed, and darted into the closet. Ray also swung his legs out of bed and began the less than savory task of turning the underwear and socks that he had worn yesterday inside out to wear today. Erin emerged from the closet, her body wrapped in a satin robe, and saw Ray performing this uncomfortable necessity. She laughed and kissed him on his scruffy cheek, "Don't worry there, Sheriff. You're gonna be keeping a few spare sets of clothes over here in no time."

Ray smiled as she sauntered into the master bathroom. If there were any doubts about her being just as crazy about him as he was about her, they had just been put to bed.

He pulled his Sheriff's Department polo over his head, stepped into his jeans, and fastened his belt. As he was pulling on his brown cowboy boots, the phone that was still clipped to his belt, rattled a silent alert. He removed the phone and was alarmed to see that he had seventeen missed calls and thirteen unread texts from both the department and Deputy Jerrod Knight. The texts all read the same.

You are needed at the department as soon as possible, Sheriff.

Ray grabbed his wallet from the floor and entered the master bathroom where Erin had just finished spraying her hair with dry shampoo and was now quickly applying her makeup.

"I'm sorry to rush, babe. But there must be something big happening at the sheriff's office. I've got a bunch of missed calls. I've gotta run."

Erin stopped applying makeup and looked at him. "If it's big then you need to get there quick. Just be careful, okay? And did you just call me babe?"

Ray hadn't been thinking when he said it. It just came out as naturally as asking for strawberry jelly when he ordered a sausage biscuit at the Hardee's in Queen's Bridge.

"Yeah, I guess I did."

She smiled, stood on her tiptoes, and kissed him deeply. "Well, that's pretty cool to hear, babe. Be safe headed to work, and if it's okay, would you mind letting me know that you made it okay?"

He returned the kiss, "Bet on it. Gotta run. Want me to call you tonight?"

"That'd be great, unless you wanted to swing by again."

"We'll see. Gotta run."

Ray rushed out the door, hopped into his truck, and tore down Highway 52 and to the town of Queen's Bridge.

He got to the sheriff's office in thirty-eight minutes and practically sprinted through the front door of the office.

Knight glanced through the window and saw Ray bounding up the stairs and met him as he came through the front door.

"Heads up, Sheriff. There's some of the county higher-ups that're going to pull you into the conference room. Looks like they're all pissed about something, I don't know what, though."

Ray's defenses went up. "Who's in there, Jerrod?"

"Seen Trent Burgess, Preston Brown, Chief Mungo, Elrod Tisdale, and Mr. Manigault head in there about ten minutes ago. Watch your six, Sheriff."

"I will,and thanks for the heads-up," Ray said as he walked through the buzzer door and onto the office floor. The door to the conference room, to the left of Ray's small office, swung open to reveal the trademark tailored grey suit and toothy smile of Reginald Manigault.

"Sheriff Myers, we'd like to speak to you, please." Manigault stepped to the side and motioned with his hand for Ray to enter the conference room.

Ray was already wary, but seeing the false front of affability put up by Manigault was like watching a wolf trying to slip on the costume of a sheep. Ray wasn't fooled for a second. He didn't know what they had planned for him behind that conference room door, but he knew that it was nothing good. Manigault was a wolf-in-sheep's-clothing to be sure, and Ray knew he had walked right into his trap.

Ray stopped in his tracks and started walking towards the open conference room door and past the still-smiling Reginald Manigault who stood beside the door.

"Good morning to you too. What's on your mind?" Ray said as he stepped through the door to the conference room.

The other members of the cadre were seated around the conference table in the plush, high-backed chairs that the county was bizarrely willing to splurge on rather than replace mattresses at the county jail. Ray could tell right away from the expressions on the faces of scions of the county that this impromptu meeting was nothing but trouble.

"Please, take a seat," Manigault more instructed rather than offered as he shut the door behind him.

Ray silently complied. Sitting across from the gaggle of county officials at the far end of the long oak table, Ray saw a mixture of emotions ranging from anger, sadness, and disbelief, except for Chief Mungo's perfectly proportioned features and Elrod's porcine face. Both of the bastards looked to be bursting at the seams with smug glee. Ray's eyes drifted to the large manila envelope stacked on top of a manila folder that Chief Mungo casually rested his chiseled forearms on. Ray didn't know what they contained, but he knew they were the reason for this meeting.

"We have had some. . . interesting material turn up, Sheriff. Material that, unfortunately, does not seem to bode very well for you," Manigault said as he stepped to the left side of the long conference table.

So that's the game we're playing. Make me go crazy trying to speculate what's in the folder and envelope before you drop the hammer on me.

"Get to the point. I've got a ton of paperwork to get to," Ray said.

Manigault's eyes flashed with anger. Good. Ray's refusal to play his game had struck a nerve. Manigault, never breaking eye contact with Ray, extended an open hand to Chief Mungo, who handed him the folder.

Well, that tells me which hand feeds Chris Mungo.

Manigault opened the folder with a flourish that Ray guessed was supposed to scare him. It didn't.

Manigault removed a stack of between three and six five-by-seven–inch photographs. For a moment, Ray was puzzled by the presence of photographs like those. Who still had five-by-seven photos produced these days? It seemed like most people were too busy posting them all over social media or having them printed onto large canvases like they were priceless works of art. Why did Manigault have photos like that in a folder?

His question was answered as Manigault slid them

across the glossy surface of the conference table to Ray. Ray decided to play along out of sheer curiosity and picked the photos up before he flipped through them. All were pictures that had been taken from a distance; likely taken from a zoom lens as they had clearly been zoomed into the subjects. Ray was confused even more than he had been before once he had flipped through them all. Manigault must have seen a look of confusion across Ray's face.

"Come now, Sheriff Myers. There's no need to act surprised by these photos," Manigault said.

Ray was surprised nonetheless. In one of the pictures, he saw Gary dressed in one of his good button-down shirts tucked into a pair of his good jeans. He was standing out in front of his trailer with a striking woman with honey-blonde hair that cascaded down the middle of her back in long waves.

She was dressed to the nines in a sheer white blouse, jeans that fit her curves like a glove, and nude high heels that would make her irresistible to any man. The next photo showed her perfectly applied makeup and her gorgeous smile as she looked at Gary opening the door to his truck for her. The next photo showed her pulling him into a sultry kiss as she stepped one stiletto onto his running boards. The fourth showed the kiss growing in passion as her arms were now draped around Gary's neck and he had pulled her gorgeous body against his.

So, this must be Gary's girlfriend from Charleston. He was right, she is beautiful. Good for him. He deserves to be happy. Why're they showing this to me though? Why do they care if Gary is seeing a hot younger woman?

The final photo showed a man in khaki shorts and pink pastel polo, leaning his slight body against a black BMW while Gary was leaning in and kissing him.

What the fuck?

Ray was shocked. He was far more confused than he was shocked to find out that his best friend and colleague was romantically involved with both a stunning woman and what appeared to be a clean-cut man.

It wasn't unheard of, Ray knew. Many people that Ray

had known through his years had surprised him with their sexuality, including people he had known at the Citadel and served with in the army. There was even Deputy Inman who had worked for him when he was in charge of the tactical unit. It wasn't common knowledge that he was gay, but Ray had found out when his boyfriend, a senior at Francis Marion University in Florence, had been assaulted by a group of women who "didn't want no fags stealing their man."

Inman told him about the situation in confidence and asked if he knew anybody at the Florence County sheriff's office that could help. Ray contacted an old buddy that played baseball with him in high school, a Florence County detective named Jake Gribben, and filled him in on the situation. Inman's boyfriend provided a description of the women, in addition to their given names and street names. Within twenty-four hours, all six women had been picked up, and within seventy-two more, they had all been charged with first degree aggravated assault.

Inman had been appreciative but Ray felt it was what anyone would've done in that situation. A year later, Inman's boyfriend had graduated and Inman accepted a job with the Fulton County Sheriff's Department in Fulton County, Georgia. As far as Ray knew, he was still living in the Atlanta area, and Ray had no doubt that he was just as good of a cop as he ever was in Craven County.

Gary, though, just seemed so out of left field that Ray had a hard time wrapping his head around it.

"I'm serious, Manigault. What am I looking at here?"

"I've already said, there's no need to act like you haven't seen these before. We know the truth."

"Then why am I here? Just so you can tell me that my friend is seeing an attractive woman and he is also seeing another man? This seems like an incredibly elaborate way to pass along some juicy gossip, even for you." He jutted his chin towards Elrod. "And for him."

Ray could see the muscles on Manigault's jaw rippling as he clenched his teeth and he could see the jiggling of Elrod's jowls as he did the same.

Struck another nerve.

"Don't play dumb with us, Myers. We have all of the evidence that you not only were aware of Captain McFadden's relationship, but that you did not approve and that you were not willing to tolerate him in your department. In fact, we know that you have been abusing Captain McFadden for quite some time, even going so far as to harass him, threaten him, and make his life a living hell," Manigault said.

Manigault snatched the envelope from underneath Mungo's powerful forearms and tossed it at Ray. Ray picked it up and saw a label stuck to the front. The word "faggot" printed in capital letters on the label. Manigault then reached into the manila folder and handed Ray a printed note that read: I will not have any fags or any other freaks working in my department. Not now and not ever. I may have to accept niggers as deputies by law, but I don't have to accept faggots at all. You have got two choices. You can resign and get the fuck out of my county and never come back. Go live with your little butt-buddy if you want. If you don't resign, I'll send these pictures to your ex-wife, to your kids, and to your pretty little girlfriend. Then you can explain to them why you just can't say no to a little faggot's ass. Give me your answer by tomorrow or suffer the consequences.

Ray was disgusted and furious by what he had just read. He was disgusted that anyone would ever concoct something so vile and bloodthirsty towards his friend. He was furious that Manigault and his gang insinuated that Ray was the author. He could feel his blood boiling.

He wanted to jump out of his chair, grab the telescoping baton that he knew Mungo carried, and beat Manigault to death with it. He wanted to see what that conniving brain looked like once you cracked the skull that encased it and pulled it out onto the table. Then he wanted to see just how deep he'd have to stab Elrod to get past his layer of blubber and puncture anything vital. It had been a long time since he had seen the gritty bright yellow fat from inside of a man's body being cut out and tossed onto the floor to mingle with the purple intestines and deep red muscle that was hidden underneath it all. But he was ready to see it all again today, just for the hell of it.

Ray gripped his chair, ready to pounce.

Let it go, man. It's bullshit and you know it. Don't play into their hands. Beat them at their own game, Gary said in Ray's mind.

He loosened his grip and relaxed into the chair. It would be nice if Gary were there to calm him down, though. He'd clear this shit up for sure.

"It's a shame to finally have proof of what I have been saying all along, Sheriff Myers." Elrod began. "It's shameful enough to learn of your out and out hostility to LGBTQ persons, but hearing of your utter disdain for black people only confirms that I have been correct about your priorities as sheriff. Even your zeal against someone like Tyrone Weeks is now something I can't help but question. Was it due to your following the law or your hatred of black people? Either way, you're not fit to be the sheriff of our community."

Ray rose from his chair and stabbed his finger in the direction of Elrod Tisdale.

"You wanna talk unfit? Let's talk unfit. How about being useless your entire life until your first wife dies mysteriously and leaves you some insurance money? How about using that money to open a juke joint on the county line where a ton of drugs get dealt, heads get smashed, and tricks get turned?

"How about using the ill-gotten gains that were hidden away in shell companies to become a phony philanthropist out to buy votes? How about promising the people of this town, the black people of this town in particular, that you were going to clean up the south side of the tracks only to let it fall deeper into squalor? How about then using all of that money that was mysteriously made to buy your way into the good graces of him," his finger pointed at Manigault, "and then to lick his boots to guarantee you can be mayor until you die? How about that Elrod?

"And I didn't even mention the fact that you keep going down there to the Huddle House at 2 am to get a blow job from Karlie behind your wife's back. Yeah, I know all about that. I know because I have done my job when it comes to making sure that the Huddle House has a deputy posted within sight every night in case it gets robbed. I've done everything I can to get people like Tyrone Weeks off the streets because his crack was being smoked by black kids and his bullets were killing black people on the south side of the tracks.

"Never mind the fact that I've also been the most pro-active sheriff this county has ever seen about working with the black community to prevent crime before it even happens. Oh yeah, and one more thing, I've hired six new deputies since I've been here and they've all been black. So Elrod, it's safe to say that I have done more for the black community in a year than you have in your entire life.

"But the worst way of all that you have failed, betrayed, and preyed upon the people of this county, Elrod, is that you have race-hustled your entire life in this town to get ahead and to do his bidding by keeping black folks in line and compliant. You're no champion for racial justice; you're a pimp and the overseer for people like him that run the plantation."

Ray turned his attention to the stunned man in the gray suit.

"And before you keep trying to slander my character with trumped up charges, Mr. Manigault, I have never said anything derogatory or defamatory towards anyone that I have known or worked with who happened to be gay. Turns out, I don't much care who you sleep with so long as you're nice and you do your job well. I may not personally agree with everything that the LGBTQ lobby is saying or doing, but I have always and will always treat people in their community as human beings. I didn't take those pictures, I didn't put them in that envelope, and I certainly didn't write that letter. This slanderous meeting is over. Get out of my station. I'm usually one to let stuff go, but you can expect an answer for this in court."

Ray was still furious but he could see that Elrod Tisdale was positively nuclear with anger. His breathing was so labored and the veins in his temple were bulging so rapidly that Ray thought he might need to get the EMTs in here if he has a coronary. But Manigault was altogether different. He looked at Ray and smiled like a fox that just heard a rabbit scream. The look curdled Ray's blood and he feared that he may have just made a grave mistake.

Manigault handed Ray one last sheet of paper: For months now, my supervisor and former friend, Sheriff Raleigh Myers, has been relentless in his campaign to intimidate me and to threaten me for my sexual orientation. I wanted nothing more than to live my life in private and to keep my work life separate. But after receiving the pictures and the letter demanding that I resign or be exposed to my family and girlfriend, I have seen that there is no way for this to end. Tell my kids I'm sorry and that I love them very much. I only hope that they can forgive me for what I have to do.

It felt as if a cannonball had settled into his gut and that no amount of controlled breathing could make it shrink. He looked at Manigault who still wore the smile of a predator who had just cornered its prey.

"What the Hell is this, Manigault?" Ray asked.

"That is a note that Garrett McFadden wrote yesterday. It was found when one of your deputies, a good man, unlike his boss I'm afraid, went to check on Garrett last night. Right after he put a gun in his mouth and shot himself," Manigault said.

Ray was stunned and slumped into the chair. They were lying. They had to be lying. Then he thought like Gary had always pushed him to think. Literally all of this evidence could be countered by Gary walking into this conference room and saying, "I'm seeing another man in addition to my girlfriend, and all that stuff you're trying to pin on Ray is utter bullshit."

But that didn't happen, and judging from the look on Manigault's face, it would never happen. Gary was dead.

Ray was numb. He sat in his chair staring at nothing in particular. His closest friend was dead and they were saying it was because of knowledge that Ray never had and threats that he never made. This, Ray knew, was the work of the Spates brothers and their organization. Gaskins's staged suicide was step one in the cover up, then Gary's staged suicide was step two in the chain of silencing all who had seen the Yamassee Mounds.

By building a plausible story, with fabricated evidence to back it up, that Ray was threatening his friend over supposed bigotry, step three. This discredited Ray to the point that people wouldn't believe him if he said that the sky was blue. Clever bastards.

Ray wiped the tears that had welled up from his eyes.

"That's not all, Sheriff, or should I say Mr. Myers. We are demanding that you go on indefinite leave. We can't force you to by law, but we can have Chief Mungo arrest you on suspicion of harassment if you don't comply. We have also lodged a formal complaint with the office of Governor Adams. You're to appear at a hearing in Columbia next Thursday. Then, in light of the evidence that we now have, the governor will remove you as sheriff of Craven County."

CHAPTER 34

The two-story home was one of the countless that had been reconstructed and refurbished during the renaissance Charleston experienced in the 1990s. The brilliant white home was built in the Imperial style that was popular throughout Europe and the Americas during the mid- to late nineteenth century, featuring upper and lower galleries, a garden enclosed by brick and wrought iron fencing, and a brick and mortar driveway. The distinctively Charleston style of the home was solidified by the tall palmetto tree rising from the inner garden and the wreath of magnolia leaves hanging from the black door of the ancient home.

Ray and Erin put his Silverado in park in a narrow space along the already narrow King Street. It had been a whirlwind of emotions that had led him to this point. The news of Gary's death had devastated him in a way that he hadn't known possible. He was no stranger to death; he had seen more than his share across the globe. But the death of a man whom he had admired, respected, and cared for as deeply as he had Gary was something he had been fortunate to not experience despite all that he had encountered along the way.

The knowledge that his time as sheriff was about to come to a premature and abrupt end almost seemed trivial when compared to the pain of losing a friend that was more like a brother than a colleague. He just wanted the pain to stop, and he knew only one way to make that happen quickly.

He went into his office and retrieved his personal weaponry: a SigSauer P365 pistol and an M1A SOCOM 16 rifle, and walked out of the sheriff's office without a word to anyone. He climbed into his truck, drove to the package store on the edge of town, and bought himself an old enemy: whiskey.

He drove the fourteen minutes to his secluded home past the rural community of Hebron, tucked the pistol behind the small of his back, set the rifle on his desk in the front room study, and poured himself two neat fingers of the amber liquid.

He stared at the glass for a long while, torn between an uncontrollable urge to down it and fill the glass again, and an unshakeable conviction that to imbibe even a drop was an existential threat to his life and general sobriety.

It had been years since he last partook of this Tennessee siren, and he had vowed he would never fall victim to her siren's song again. Daily, then weekly, then monthly, he had reminded himself of what would happen if he gave into her again, and for years he had stayed away from her. The unimaginable pain wrought by Gary's death, however, had made her distant, whispering song as loud as if she were singing directly into his ear alone. This time, he knew, he wouldn't turn away from her. This time he would listen to her.

He picked up the glass and knocked the whiskey back into his waiting gullet. The smoky flavor and the burn in his throat greeted him like the devil had once greeted Faust, and in an instant liquid euphoria crashed into his brain. The feeling of pain was dulled, but Ray now felt an irresistible craving for more as he refilled the glass and gulped it down as well. The feeling of relaxation was beginning to bring on the familiar tingle throughout his body that signaled the impending buzz.

The thoughts of Gary were still there, but they were becoming fuzzier and fuzzier. Suddenly, he remembered that he had promised to let Erin know what he was so urgently needed for and he fumbled in his pockets and retrieved his phone.

He clumsily entered the wrong passcode twice before successfully opening it on the third try. His fingers suddenly began to feel as thick and dexterous as sausages as he tapped the texting app and his conversation with Erin.

Hey. so the meetung wass a bug problem. Im gonna be removedd as sherriff next weeek becuse of somethnig i didnt do. Found outhat Gary is deaad too, so im home now.

He fumbled around and hit send. His mind was working well enough to know that his message was horribly misspelled, but the whiskey had dulled his will to correct it. Immediately bubbles popped up as Erin typed out a response.

What!? Your friend Gary is dead RU OK???

He wished that he had the wherewithal to type in a lie, but the alcohol had already removed his ability to deceive.

Nope im drinkkning.

The bubbles popped up again.

What's UR address, babe?

Ray took his time, trying his best to get the address as close to correctly spelled as possible before sending it to Erin. Once he had typed it out and sent it to her she replied almost immediately.

Slow down on the drinks. I'm on my way.

Ray smiled through the tears that had begun to run in rivulets down his face as he saw the kissy face emoji she sent at the end. He poured himself another drink and took a seat on the couch in his small living room. He wasn't sure how much time had passed. He was pretty sure that the whiskey had put him to sleep, but before he knew it, he heard a knock on his front door. He staggered to the door and felt more alert and less drunk than he did however long it had been since he sat down on his couch, and opened the door to find Erin standing there, her arm looped through two grocery bags.

She steadied him with her hand and helped him into the kitchen.

"Easy, babe. Let's get you a seat, okay?" she said in a voice that was strangely sweet and reassuring.

Ray complied and took a seat at his small kitchen table. He watched as Erin produced two bottles of yellow sports drinks from the grocery bags and a bag of coffee. She searched and found where he kept the glasses, poured him a tall glass of the sports drink, and set it on the table in front of him.

"M'kay, I need you to drink this for me, okay? Don't chug it, but drink it as quickly as you can so I can fix you another glass," she said as she started measuring out scoops of the ground coffee into his coffee maker.

Ray downed the glass in two great gulps. Erin gilled the glass again, and again he drained it. His mind began to clear further, and within a minute or two, he needed to visit the bathroom. Once he reemerged, under Erin's watchful eye, she asked him sweetly to drink even more sports drink. Within ten more minutes he had finished off one 128-ounce bottle of sports drink and was working on his second bottle. After another trip to the restroom and a cup of the strong coffee that Erin brewed, he felt lucidity return to his consciousness along with remorse and embarrassment.

"I'm sorry about this. It's been years since anything like this has happened," Ray said.

Erin lightly stroked his hair and smiled compassionately. "You've got nothing to be sorry about. You had trouble with liquor in the past, though?"

"Yeah, went through a bad patch about eight years ago. Right at the tail-end of my active military career. I went through the program and did all the steps and stayed sober ever since, minus the odd beer or glass of wine. It's something about whiskey that gets me like this."

"That's nothing uncommon. It's quite an accomplishment that you said no all this time. It's also good that you understand that a little tumble off the wagon doesn't mean that all that work was for nothing and that you aren't gonna start down that road you left behind," Erin said, gently kissing his cheek as he sipped the piping hot coffee.

Ray nodded his head. "The whiskey?"

"I already poured it down the drain."

Ray wrapped a strong arm around her small waist and pulled her into a desperate, grateful embrace. "Thank you for getting rid of that for me."

She returned the embrace fiercely. "Anything for you, babe."

She pulled herself away from him and looked deep into his eyes. "You feeling up to telling me about everything?"

Ray nodded and told her everything that had happened: Knight tipping him off, the trumped up evidence, Gary's sordid affair, his temper getting the better of him, Gary's apparent suicide, and Ray's imminent removal as Craven County sheriff. The pain came flooding back, but it was cathartic to talk about it as Erin listened without comment or interruption. Once it was clear that his account had come to an end, Erin asked a question.

"What do you need to do as your next step?"

"I don't know that there is a next step to be honest. They've got me over a barrel here, and I can't see any way out. My best bet might just be to go ahead and resign before any of this can be put on record," Ray said.

Erin's gentle demeanor hardened in less than a second.

"That's not an option," she said.

Ray was slightly startled by the seriousness in her voice and the look of gravity in her eyes.

"You're the sheriff of this county. More than that, you're a veteran of the 82nd and a Green Beret. You don't just throw in the towel when things go bad. You formulate a plan, execute it, and win. That's who you are and that's what you're gonna do. So don't sit here and dishonor Gary by giving up and letting them win. Meet them head on and beat them."

Ray was pleasantly shocked at her boldness. She was right. It was not who Ray was to give up without a fight. Fighting with all of your might until you either won the day or died in the attempt; now that was who Ray was. That was who he was raised to be. That was who he had been trained to be during his knob year at the Citadel. That was who he had relied on during his years in the military. That was who he was today. Ray was just surprised that this amazing woman had seen so clearly who he was and that she had been brave enough to remind him of it in his darkest hour.

"You're right. That's not who I am," he said.

"I knew you'd remember it. Now, what is your next move?"

Ray hadn't been thinking of next moves at all up to that point. All that he had been capable of was thinking about the pain he was feeling over Gary. Now he was aware that Gary would've busted his balls for being so damn emotional at a time when a level-head was needed. Ray paused and thought for a moment. His brain was moving so fast that it seemed like his skull would overheat. Finally, two moves presented themselves. They were both long shots, but they were all that he had at the time.

"I saw the tag number of Gary's... I guess boyfriend in one of the pictures. Would you hand me a piece of paper and a pen from the grocery pad on the fridge?"

Erin tore off a leaf of paper and grabbed the pen magnetically stuck to the fridge and handed it to Ray. Ray closed his eyes and pictured the scene in his mind. He had learned how to relax and to search his memory for specific information when he was in the army. More than once it had helped him remember a face that was out of place in a crowd or a line of code in a coded message. He wrote the license plate number CPF-892 onto the paper.

"This is his tag number. I can run it and find his address on the laptop in my study. Then, maybe we could pay him a visit and ask him to come forward to refute all of the claims they made. Maybe Gary mentioned me, or maybe he can say that Gary never told him he was being black-mailed. It might not be a huge help, but it would sow some doubt in their case," Ray said.

"Okay, run it, get the address, and let's go talk to him. I'm driving though. It'll be a few hours until your blood alcohol level evens out," Erin said as she grabbed Ray's keys from the counter.

The tag had been issued to a Noah Thompson who lived at 20 King Street in Charleston, South Carolina. Erin keyed the address into the GPS app on her phone and they were off towards Charleston.

The two-hour ride was peppered with small talk that all new couples share about subjects ranging from best childhood memories to dreams for the future. The pain of Gary's loss was still heavy on his heart, but the light-hearted conversation was a welcome distraction that Ray appreciated.

Now, as he and Erin crossed the ancient brick sidewalk and began to ascend the stairs to Noah Thompson's door, Ray was suddenly apprehensive. Would Gary want him to contact this man, especially since Gary had obviously kept him a secret? Ray wasn't sure about the answer to that, but he was certain he had to talk to him at the very least, or he was almost certainly going to be subjected to public humiliation and removal as sheriff. As he knocked on the black door, he felt Erin's small hand slip into his, interlacing her fingers in his as she squeezed reassuringly.

Ray could hear the sound of footsteps growing closer and closer to the door. His stomach somersaulted as he heard the latch clicking into the unlocked position and as he saw the door swing inward. In the doorway stood Noah Thompson in much the same way as he appeared in the pictures. He wore a pair of fitted skinny jeans, a powder-blue t-shirt that read "North Carolina School of Law," and his bare feet were ensconced in a pair of loafers. His body and facial features seemed to be more androgynous than in the picture he had seen. His blonde hair was cut into a fashionable quiff style that only made his general androgyny appear to be slightly more feminine than masculine. Ray could see by the pleasant look in Noah's green eyes that he had absolutely no idea who these people on his doorstep were but that he intended to be friendly all the same.

"May I help you, folks?" Noah asked in a breathy voice that featured the lilt of a low country accent.

"My name is Raleigh Myers and this is Erin McKee. If it's alright with you, we'd like to talk with you, privately."

Ray could tell from the flash in Noah's eyes that he recognized the name Raleigh Myers, even though his face remained pleasant and friendly. Ray hoped that was a good thing for him as Noah's friendly expression stretched into a polite smile. This was the moment of truth. Either Noah would hear them out, or he wouldn't and Ray's fate hung in the balance.

"Sheriff Myers. I've, uh, heard a lot about you. Please, come on inside." Noah stepped aside and gestured for both of them to enter his home.

Ray breathed an internal sigh of relief. The fact that he had not shut the door in their face was the first bit of luck that had gone Ray's way since Darrin Gaskins's death in the jail. Ray hoped that this man who had some affection for Gary held him in high enough regard to publicly vouch for Ray. That happening, however, was entirely different than being invited into his home to chat.

The inside of the home was tastefully and elegantly decorated. The walls were painted a dusty blue and festooned with black and white photos of Charleston, Savannah, and Charlotte, set into tasteful silver frames. Butternut wooden tables and accent pieces gave the space an earthy, simplistic feel that Ray was certain was not present in the hundreds of other historic homes in Charleston.

The parlor immediately off to the left of the foyer had been converted into an office decorated tastefully with a butternut desk and bookcases, an elegant gray cloth office chair, silver laptop, and a small vase filled with an arrangement of fresh white and blue hydrangeas. The more of the house he was seeing, the more Ray was certain that Noah was also in a relationship with a woman. After all, the place seemed to have all of the evidence of a woman's presence in the home.

Ray glanced quickly around the walls of the study. Behind the desk, which sat at the opposite end of the room, was a large black and white photo of the instantly recognizable Angel Oak of Charleston. The sprawling live oak tree was truly an impressive sight to behold. It had stood the test of time through it all from the British Army, Union Army, and Hurricane Hugo, to name a few tests of the ancient tree's might. Now, the greatest test to the tree was the encroachment of development originating from the very city that had sought to save the iconic plant.

It was hard for Ray to imagine that this great tree had originated from a tiny acorn during the reign of King Henry VIII of England, and it was hard for him to imagine it persevering despite the inevitable march of development and progress. It, like all things, would be consumed by the relentless march of time.

Ray was about to turn and follow Noah into his living room and hoped that his more than conspicuous look into the parlor/office hadn't seemed odd to their host, when he noticed three more frames on the wall opposite the angel oak picture. Ray scanned the one furthest to his left and was unsurprised when he read "the University of North Carolina at Chapel Hill," and the words "Juris Doctorate." The remaining frames surprised him. The frame in the middle housed two papers for display one above the other. The one on the upper part of the frame was an artist's depiction of the battlements and gates to white castle. The lower part housed another certificate which read "Bachelor of Arts in Political Science" across the middle and "the Citadel" across the top.

"Citadel, huh?" Ray couldn't help but say as he nonchalantly pointed in the direction of the frames.

Noah had noticed that Ray was showing a keen interest in the study and now he understood just what had caught the eye of the Craven County lawman.

"That's right. Did my undergrad work there," Noah said as he glided towards where Ray stood.

"I'm a Citadel guy too; 2nd Battalion, Echo Company, but I'm pretty sure that I came through a few years before you did," Ray said.

"Really? That's great. I was in the 3rd Battalion, India Company," Noah explained with a bright smile. "I don't know how I survived my knob year, but I'm certain that the guys in my squad got me through. The rest of it was amazing, though. I even had the honor of being a Summerall guard and commanding the cadets before I graduated. That place is special to me in ways that I can't quite explain."

"You were a Summerall guard and you were the regimental commander of the corps of cadets? I didn't know that I was standing in the home of a legend. I only made it up to sergeant major," Ray said as he extended his hand to shake Noah's.

Noah's gentle but firm grip on Ray's hand was reassuring of the man's character, and Ray found himself hoping that his suspicion that Noah had a wife or girlfriend in addition to Gary was not true.

"You're too kind, really. It was just how things worked out for me, that's all," Noah said.

"Nah, you're being modest. That's an achievement that I would've done anything to reach, other than give it my all in chemistry," Ray said.

Ray and Noah both shared a laugh while Erin struggled to understand the humor in the remark.

"Well, I might not understand why all that stuff is a big deal, but at least I can say 'Go Heels' to a fellow Tar Heel grad," Erin said.

"That's right. Go Heels," Noah replied as he now shook Erin's hand.

The third frame held an honorable discharge certificate with the distinctive anchor and globe of the Marine Corps printed across the middle and the name "First Lieutenant Noah L. Thompson."

"Marine too?" Ray asked.

Noah gave a polite nod, "I served after the Citadel. I was in for six, but most of it was spent as an adjutant. I wanted to make a bigger difference after Marjah, but all I found was more bullshit, so I got out."

"A lot of blood spilled in Marjah. I was out toward Kandahar around that time. Y'all survived a hornet's nest," Ray said.

"Most of us did, anyway," Noah said.

The Battle of Marjah, Afghanistan, is not as well-known as the Battle of Fallujah, Iraq, but the size, intensity, and casualties are comparable to one of the defining engagements of the Iraq War. The battle had taken months and forces from the US, UK, France, Canada, and the Afghan Army to finally secure what General McChrystal had described as a bleeding ulcer in Afghanistan.

"But enough of walking down memory lane. I believe that you needed to talk with me, Sheriff Myers. If you wouldn't mind following me into the living room," Noah said as he led them to the living room.

It, like Ray assumed the rest of the house was, was also painted dusty blue with brilliant white trim and molding on the ceiling. The room was dominated by an ancient fireplace and weathered brick hearth. The room was arranged with elegant furniture that coordinated perfectly with the walls and the decorative throw pillows that adorned the seats. Above the fireplace was a flat screen television mounted to the wall, but the mantle was tastefully decorated with magnolia branches and blooms. The butternut coffee table in the center of the two opposing couches and the dual flanking chairs was adorned with a tall vase filled with an arrangement of magnolias and peonies that seemed to pull the entire space together.

Noah invited them to take a seat on one of the couches. "You'll have to excuse this mess," Noah said as he cleared away a small white coffee cup and saucer from the corner of the table. "I wasn't expecting any company this evening so I decided to enjoy a cup of tea in here while I caught up on Netflix."

Noah gracefully picked up the cup and saucer with his right hand, and nimbly grasped the throat of the vase in the middle of the coffee table with the other. "I'm just gonna go and set this in the kitchen so that we can chat more comfortably. Now, I don't have a wide selection, and I'm not sure if y'all are going on back to Queen's Bridge tonight, but I would be more than happy to get y'all a glass of wine," Noah explained as he daintily clutched the vase and the cup and saucer.

Ray was surprised at the warmth and hospitality of their host. He had visited with many men unannounced many times in both a professional and personal capacity, and not once had he ever been offered a drink, much less what he was going to guess was a glass of fine wine. Noah Thompson was a genuinely nice guy. He thought back to the efforts that Erin made to sober him up after he had decided to fall off of the whiskey wagon earlier and decided that he would politely decline the offer.

"None for me, thanks. My conversation isn't exactly of the entirely social nature, I'm afraid," Ray said.

Noah nodded to Ray. "I understand completely. Would a glass of sweet tea do instead? I make it myself and I must admit that I am desperate to have someone try it and tell me what I could improve."

Actual wine was one thing, but the table wine of the south was another thing entirely. The mere mention of the words "sweet tea" set his mind to recalling hot summer days of his youth and the sweet relief that his grandmother's tea provided. He wouldn't say no to that offer. What's more, how could he say no to an offer made so graciously? It was strange, but Noah's movements, his way with words, and his strict attention to Southern etiquette with regard to guests struck Ray as incredibly feminine in nature.

"Sweet tea sounds good to me. Thank you for the offer," Ray said.

Noah motioned with his vase of flowers as if he were delicately swatting a fly with the back of his hand, "Ach, it's my pleasure, Sheriff. For you as well, Erin?"

"I'll take a glass of wine, actually," Erin replied.

"Thank you, I was afraid that I was going to be drinking alone. Excuse me for a moment; back in a flash." Noah explained as he disappeared through an ornately furnished dining room and around the corner to what must have been the kitchen.

"Think he's gonna talk to us?" Erin asked Ray once Noah was out of sight.

"I think he'll talk, at least. He wouldn't have invited us inside if he wasn't prepared to do that. He seems like a pretty decent guy, so maybe he'll help us. You've got to be a very honorable and dependable person to become a Summerall guard, and to become regimental commander you've got to have about the most rock solid reputation for honor and dependability of any cadet who has ever been a part of the Citadel's history. Serving in the corps takes the same qualities too. I just hope that he hasn't forgotten those over the years, and this house makes me worry that he has forgotten it." Ray said.

"The house? Like, the fact that he lives in an historic home? What's dishonorable about that? Looks to me like he's preserving it," Erin asked.

"Not that he lives in this house; I'm talking about the interior. Look around, tell me what you see," Ray said.

Erin complied and surveyed the living room. "Well, the walls are a very pretty color, and the way that it complements the white accents on the trim and molding is super gorgeous. The furniture is all perfectly coordinating with the greys, blues, and whites of the fabrics. The butternut color of the woods kinda sets it all off really cute in how it kinda brings it all together. And I absolutely love that fireplace. The exposed brick and the magnolias on the mantle are so beautiful that I might try and copy it whenever we get back to Florence. And. . . I guess that's what I see. Did you mean something specific?"

"All of those things you listed off: the color scheme, furniture, wood color, flowers, fireplace. Looking at all of that and not knowing that this is his house, who would you assume lived here?" Ray asked.

Erin furrowed her brows and thought about the question. In less than a second her eyebrows rose sharply, "A woman. I'd assume that a woman lives here. Wow, that's incredibly sexist of me, geez," Erin replied.

Ray smiled at her pronouncing herself a sexist. "Nah, you just recognize a woman's touch is all. It might be a tad on the sexist side, but I've not seen it to be untrue yet. I hope that I am wrong, and I very well could be, but I hope that we don't find out that he is sharing this house with a wife or girlfriend. It was bad enough to find out that Gary was cheating on his girlfriend with Thompson, but to find out that Thompson is doing the same thing? That'd wreck everything that I thought I could count on about life," Ray said.

They both quieted as they heard Noah's voice growing louder and clearer as he moved from the kitchen, through the dining room and back into the living room.

"Sorry it took a minute or two. Like I said, I wasn't expecting company but I am not going to treat you like anything less. What kind of a host would I be then?"

Noah floated into the living room carrying a long tray made from rustic butternut wood. He set the tray down on the coffee table and lightly took a seat on the couch opposite Ray and Erin. The tray held two wine glasses, both half full of chardonnay along with the opened bottle ready for refills. The other end of the tray held a tall glass filled with dark brown liquid and perfectly square ice cubes. A large glass pitcher, likewise filled with the dark liquid and ice cubes, set beside a small saucer of sliced lemons. In the middle of the tray was a wooden charcuterie board filled with neat patterns of various smoked meats, cheeses, and crackers. The small stack of cocktail napkins only helped to solidify the southern etiquette bonafides of their gracious host.

"I hope that there is something here to each of your likings. I know that the first time I ever tried prosciutto and havarti, I couldn't sip my wine fast enough to remove the taste. Please, y'all help yourselves and let me know whenever you need a top-off to your glasses." Noah said as he delicately picked up his wineglass, sat back on the plush couch, and crossed his legs at the ankle.

"This is extremely hospitable of you, Mr. Thompson,"

Ray said as he placed a lemon slice into his glass and took the first sip.

"This here is all my mama's raising, but please, call me Noah. How'd I do with the tea?"

"It's as close to perfect as I've ever tasted, but I'd be lying if I said I didn't still prefer my Mamaw's," Ray replied as he took another long sip.

Noah smiled and nodded knowingly. "That's a standard I'm afraid nobody has a prayer of holding up to."

"Mmmm, this gouda and salami is delicious with this wine," Erin said.

"I'm just glad that I had the right cheeses and meats to complement this Chardonnay. I was a bit worried I was going to have to serve y'all cheddar and honey ham with it."

Noah took a long sip of his wine. There it was, the final bit of courage before the inevitable question came.

"I hope that I'm not being too rude by being so direct, but may I ask what exactly you would like to discuss, Sheriff?" Noah asked.

Ray fumbled with the words, "It's, uh, it's hard to say."

"I suppose that Gary has told you about us; his and my relationship. I've got to be honest with you, Sheriff Myers. I'm wondering why my Gary didn't come with you to drop in for a visit. Not that I'm not enjoying the company of Erin, you're lovely in every way by the way, but I think that this first meeting would've been much easier had he come along with you. At least I could have gotten dressed properly so that our first meeting would not be so awkward. Just so you know, I didn't put Gary up to this. He came to that decision on his own," Noah said as he sipped a long sip of wine.

Ray was confused. "What do you mean that you didn't put him up to this?"

Now it was Noah's turn to be confused. "His plans for once you wrapped up the case about Megan Prince and the awful things y'all found out at the Yamassee Mounds. He said that he didn't want to see that sort of thing anymore and that he was going to tell you he was taking early retirement. Please don't try to talk me into convincing him to stay, either. I may have a certain power over him, but not so much as to change his mind once it's made up. Besides, having him here to come home to sounds like heaven on earth to me, and don't you go messing up my heaven on earth," Noah admonished with a friendly smile.

"Is Gary on the way? Do I have enough time to run upstairs and get changed for him before we all go out?" Noah asked.

Ray hung his head; the weight of the news he was about to share with someone who had loved Gary was momentarily unbearable. How do you say such a thing? How do you approach the unapproachable? Ray took a deep breath and steeled himself for what he had to do next.

"Noah, I'm sorry that nobody has told you yet, and I'm sorry that I have to tell you. Gary is dead and I'm here trying to figure out why."

CHAPTER 35

Noah had wept bitterly into Erin's shoulder for nearly an hour. He had initially thought that Ray was joking with him. An unfunny and slightly sick joke, but a joke nonetheless. Once he saw the terrible seriousness in Ray's eyes and the tears that were beginning to form in them that he knew the horrifying truth. The man that he had loved and who he had planned to spend his life with was dead.

So he wept; uncontrollably at times, softly at others, but all the while the wails of a heart thoroughly broken filled the space in which they sat. Erin had gone to him, to hold him and give him something to hold onto as the first wave of grief wracked him. Ray sat there, his own tears leaving warm wet spots on his pants as he watched the expression of sheer anguish sitting across from him.

Noah had slowly regained some of his composure and had asked Ray to tell him everything and to leave nothing out. Ray obliged. He told him of the ambush Manigault had set for Ray once he entered the sheriff's office, he told him of the pictures, threats, and the supposed suicide note left by Gary. Noah looked at Ray, his face a mixture of confusion and grim amusement as he completed the story.

"So, they don't really know about us. They do but they

don't; not really. I can't believe that we were able to keep it hidden so well or that I am so convincing. Gary always told me how beautiful I was. I never believed him, though. But I guess he was right, in a way," Noah said as he wiped his eyes then nose with a tissue.

"What do you mean they don't know? Do you mean Gary's, uh, girlfriend doesn't know?" Ray asked as delicately as he could.

Noah laughed a bitter laugh, the sudden sound startled Erin.

"You don't know either, then." Noah stood up. "If y'all'll excuse me for a second or two, I'm gonna go change into something a little more comfortable and grab something that might help me explain things a little better."

Noah ascended the steps and once again Ray and Erin discussed what had happened so far.

"This is awful, babe. He really loved Gary. This wasn't just some fling for him; not even close. You don't cry over a guy you're just using like that. That's the kind of crying you do when you lose a guy that you are in love with. Trust me," Erin said.

"I think we both agree on that, but that's gotta mean that Gary was just using his girlfriend or something like that. Oh, shit. You don't think that me mentioning a girlfriend might've sent him over the edge, like Gary was seeing someone other than him do you?" Ray asked.

"He didn't seem surprised about the girlfriend stuff. I think he knew and we just confirmed it. In a weird way, maybe it helps us out. Maybe he's willing to come forward and say you didn't send that envelope."

Their conversation was interrupted by the sound of light footsteps on the stairs. Noah had changed clothes and was clutching a photo album and two framed pictures across his chest. Ray and Erin were both puzzled by his new attire. He now wore a fitted low cut Citadel t-shirt; a design that Ray had seen women wearing exclusively. His jeans had been traded for black athletic leggings with a strip of black mesh that ran from Noah's hip down to his ankle. Again, this was a fashion he had seen exclusively worn by women. Finally, he had left his shoes upstairs and was padding down the plush carpet in his bare feet. The toenails of his feet were painted with nail polish in the gray-purple shade of mauve.

He crossed the living room and sat beside Erin once more, only this time he tucked both of his legs beneath him as he sat. He held up the framed picture so that both of them could see it clearly. The picture was of Gary's girl-friend standing in front of a bare wall, wearing a champagne dress that hugged every curve and plunged half-way down her chest. She smiled happily through ruby red lips as she held onto a matching clutch purse with one hand and ran her fingers through her honey-blonde hair with the other.

He then showed the second framed photo to them. Once again, they saw Gary's girlfriend dressed the same, but this time she was posing with her right hand on Gary's chest, and her right foot raised behind her, stabbing the air with her stiletto heel. Ray and Erin were more puzzled than ever.

"Gary's girlfriend knows all about lil' ol' me, Ray Myers. She knows because she is me."

The revelation that Noah and Nora were both one and the same hit Ray like a thunderbolt. It all made sense now. Gary wasn't cruising for guys to hook up with. Hell, in Gary's mind he probably wasn't even in love with a guy to begin with. He probably thought of it as falling in love with a woman who happened to have something more when it came to secrets.

The question of how something like Gary and Noah could have happened all made sense now. And the fact that Gary supposedly wrote a suicide note apologizing to his girlfriend for Noah absolutely obliterated the case that Gary committed suicide. In light of this new evidence, Gary's death was a murder.

"My whole life, I've had this strange compulsion. When I was little, I used to think I could magically change into a girl, but as I got older I learned that what I was struggling with was just my cross to bear. We all struggle with different things, some bigger than others, and this one was mine. I did everything I could to avoid acting on it. I controlled my thinking, what I watched, I went to the Citadel and joined the Marines to keep myself from acting on it. Then one day, one of my friends at Carolina asked if they could dress me up like a girl for a Halloween party. I couldn't see the harm, so I let her do my makeup and dress me up. I was hooked.

"I dressed in secret for a while. Told myself it was okay so long as I didn't act on the urge I had towards other men. I tried and tried to say no, but curiosity got the better of me. I decided to make an online dating profile. I was having so much fun fixing it up, loading all of my best selfies on there; it just felt so liberating. A few hours later I knew I had gone too far so I decided to delete my profile. When I opened it, I saw I had a message and I was just.. curious. It was Gary and he used some line comparing me to the prettiest puppy he had ever seen. It was stupid and funny all at the same time, and before I knew it, I was texting him into the night. I liked him and I was too curious to turn him down when he asked me out, so I went.

"I almost went back home when I got to the lounge, but I told myself that I didn't spend three hours fixing my makeup, hair, and picking the perfect dress just to go home. So, I went in, had a few drinks, and fell for him right then and there. I knew I needed to tell him the truth, and when I did, he didn't get upset. He just said he wanted to get to see me more often and that he wanted to ignore my extra stuff if that was fine. I fell in love with him then and there and I have loved him ever since.

"He didn't kill himself, Ray. We had made plans to be together. We were going to make it work. He wanted to introduce me to you; that's why I assumed we were getting acquainted earlier. He said that you might not approve of what we were doing but that you were a good guy who would be good to us both. I respected that because even I don't approve of what I'm doing here. But I know you didn't send that envelope, and I know you would've done anything you could've to help us both. You're a good man,

Ray Myers. I know because Gary said so."

Noah stopped talking and sat there motionless. Ray was about to ask the question they had come to ask when Erin chimed in. "You don't have anything to be ashamed of Noah. Don't you see? You're a woman. You always have been; just accept that."

"I'm not, though. I'm a man who has a compulsion to behave, dress, and live as a woman. No matter what I do, even if I were to go through a full transition, I'm still not really a woman. I'd be a man with female features, hormones, and no properly functional penis. I'd just look the part," Noah said plainly.

"That's a very narrow and transphobic way to look at it though, " Erin said.

"It might be, but it's the true way to look at it. And the truth is what matters most. Don't misunderstand me. I'm still going to dress like a woman. I'm still gonna call myself Nora. I might even look into that being more permanent one of these days, but I'm not gonna say that I'm a woman just because I feel like one and am driven to be like one. I'm many things, but a liar isn't one of them," Noah explained.

The room fell silent for a moment and Ray decided to break the silence.

"I know that you've been through a lot. I know this is the last thing that you need right now and that I'm asking a lot. But they're gonna remove me as sheriff next week if the truth doesn't see the light of day. Would you be willing to come forward? Would you tell them that Gary was murdered and they're trying to discredit me using a fake suicide?"

Noah furrowed his brow and stared hard at Ray. "I would love to help, Ray. I would. But the company I work for might decide they want to find another real estate broker afterward. The awkwardness of having an employee who may or may not be intending to chemically and surgically start appearing more and more womanly aside, the media circus that would surround me and the firm would be too much for them. They'd have to let me go just to stay out of the news, and I wouldn't blame them. That's my livelihood. My whole life. I want more than anything to help you, but I know in my heart that Gary would want me to say no and to keep myself out of the spotlight as much as possible.

"This is all nonsense they came up with anyway. You don't need me. All you need to do is keep pursuing the truth. The truth is always brought to light."

Ray was prepared to argue. He was prepared to bring up honor, justice, and truth. He was prepared to use their bond over the Citadel to compel him to help, the kinship they shared from both going downrange in combat, but in the end, he knew that Noah was right. Enough lives had been wasted and destroyed in the course of this case, and Ray couldn't bring himself to see another be tarnished just to save his own skin. Gary wouldn't want that; but most of all, Ray didn't want that either. The truth might find a way out into the open, but not until after Raleigh Myers had long been removed as sheriff and those who murdered Gary and so many others had long gotten away clean.

Chapter 36

The sight of the winding gravel road that led to a modest white house back in the pines was strangely comforting to Ray Myers's soul. It was his oasis, fortress, and sanctuary. The home and nine acres were his first big purchase once he returned home from a decade and a half of military service. For the past few years, the place harbored him from the troubles of the world. It was more than a home. It was more of an old friend to him.

It could be worse. I could be stuck with a place in town. At least here I can be at peace once it's all said and done.

The disappointing news that Noah Thompson, despite being sympathetic and willing, would not be able to help Ray prove his innocence and, more importantly, the existence of a plot that likely involved Gary's murder, was likely the final nail in Ray's coffin. He grasped at one last straw and placed a call to an old friend who might be able to help. He heard the phone ring five times and then connect to a generic voicemail. Ray sighed and explained briefly what was going on and asked humbly for any help that his friend may be able to provide before ending the call and staring blankly out of the window of the Silverado as Erin zig-zagged through the streets of Charleston.

It was after dark when he and Erin finally left Noah's home. Noah had graciously insisted that they stay the night in his spare bedroom.

"I may not be able to help directly, but y'all could at least do me the honor of having y'all get a restful night's sleep in the spare room. I keep it ready and clean just in case such an occasion arises. My friends from Raleigh all assure me that the mattress is soft and the comforter is warm. Won't y'all please stay and head on back once the sun has come up?" Noah asked as they headed towards the door.

Ray offered a polite and sheepish smile. "You're really too kind, but we need to be headed back. Maybe some other time."

Ray offered Noah a handshake and he grasped Ray's hand before covering it with his free hand.

"I am so sorry that I can't be of more help to you. I loved my Gary deeply, and I want so badly to help you find out who killed him. If I didn't keep hearing his voice telling me not to get involved, just to stay safe for him, then I would. That being said, I would ask that you grant me a small request. Really, three small requests if you would permit me?" Noah asked.

"Absolutely, anything I can do to help," Ray replied.

Noah's feminine face reddened. "As you can imagine, I haven't yet had the opportunity to become acquainted with any of Gary's family or friends. We were planning on making the introductions gradually, sort of easing them into the idea of us being a couple. So, I have absolutely no way of contacting anyone about Gary's arrangements or anything of the sort. I was hoping, if you don't mind, that you would let me know when visitation and the graveside services are being held so that I can say goodbye."

"Of course. I'll let you know as soon as I know."

Tears welled up in Noah's eyes again. "I appreciate

that. Seeing as I don't have a great deal of experience with this sort of thing, nor do I know anything about anyone who might attend, I was hoping that you and Erin might accompany me to the visitation and graveside service. I know it's a lot to ask of you, and it's very unladylike as well, but it would mean a great deal to me."

It was a request that caught Ray off guard, but he understood the underlying reasoning behind it. He couldn't imagine how difficult it was going to be for Noah to attend the funeral services of someone that he loved alongside people who knew nothing of him or who may not approve of his choices in life and with regard to Gary. Before he could answer, Erin jumped in and answered for both of them.

"Of course we will. If you'd like, you can come up the day before and stay with me in Florence. We can go and find you a couple of new dresses for the funeral, and I can help you with your makeup. It might be a nice little distraction."

Noah smiled as the tears rolled down his face. "That would be lovely, Erin. I'd like the distraction very much."

Noah's face darkened suddenly, and Ray saw the familiar fire of vengeance burning behind Noah's green eyes. "And lastly, I would ask that you catch whomever killed my sweet Gary and that you make them pay. Make them regret ever having touched Gary. Promise me that you'll do that for me. Promise me that you'll do that for Gary."

Ray nodded grimly and squeezed Noah's hand reassuringly. "Rest assured, they'll pay. If not by me as sheriff, then by me as a private citizen. They'll be cursing their mothers for bringing them into this world once I am done with them. You can take that to the bank."

With that, they left the home of Noah Thompson, leaving only Ray's business card behind and Noah's contact information in both of their phones. Ray was silent after the failed phone call, and Erin desperately tried to fill the air by skipping songs on her phone until she found just the right one. Ray hadn't been paying too much attention to where she was going. He was too consumed by the dark tentacles of melancholy to be aware of much other than his crushing failures and impending doom.

When she put the truck into park outside of the Francis Marion Hotel, he finally was aware of the world around him. She stubbornly resisted his protests to the gesture; simply casting it off as, "I believe in taking good care of my man. What kind of a feminist would I be if I didn't?" when she rented them a room and led him by the hand to the gourmet restaurant inside of the hotel's lobby.

She had further doted on him by ordering a sampler of signature southern fare including pimento cheese, pickled okra, smoked pork belly, and a grilled baguette. She had followed up this sumptuous appetizer by ordering him the ribeye, she successfully deduced that he preferred his medium rare, served with homemade potato salad, grilled asparagus, and sauteed Vidalia onions.

The meal was delicious and Ray was moved by such a selfless act of love on the part of this amazing woman he had started falling hard and fast for. The room likewise did nothing but impress him further with her generosity. They soaked in the tub before they wrapped themselves in robes and climbed into the plush bed. There, he thanked her for the incredible gesture. The emotions of the day, the richness of the food, and the exquisiteness of the sex all conspired to put him fast asleep before he knew what was going on.

The next day he checked to see if his friend had at least returned his call and was disappointed to see no new alerts other than his daily reminder that it was time for a run. Erin awoke and pulled him in for what she erotically called "breakfast." Once he was relaxed and she was satiated, she sensually wiped her lips with the corner of the sheet, slid her naked body out of the bed, and steamily shrugged on her robe. She then ordered breakfast to the room and insisted on showering Ray with even more love and affection.

By the time breakfast arrived at their door, Ray wondered just how many more times he could perform should the need arise. They ate and talked, mostly about their dreams and visions for the future before dressing, checking out, and heading back to Queen's Bridge. Once again, Ray was quiet and contemplative for most of the ride back but Erin didn't seem to mind all that much as she played her favorite country and pop hits from the 1990s and sang along.

Now, as they rolled down the gravel lane shaded by a tunnel of green leaves and brown branches, Ray thought of what life would be like as a disgraced former-sheriff. He contemplated the possibility of leaving this place behind altogether and starting over in Florence or wherever Erin wanted to go. A change of scenery and a new start away from where it had all come crashing down might be good for him. Ray knew this idea would never materialize, though. He wasn't made for backing down from a fight; even when it came to a fight that he couldn't win.

Erin pulled the Silverado behind her Carolina Blue Mustang and they both exited the vehicle, walking hand in hand into the rustic farmhouse that matched Ray's rustic and renovated soul. Once inside of the house, they both walked back to the kitchen.

"Y'know, I think I should make you my famous baked ziti for dinner? Whatcha think, Sheriff? A little ziti and a sip or two of wine before you try to get lucky with me sound good?"

Ray smiled at the way she called him sheriff. He'd never admit it to her, but he liked the way she said it all the time. It was cute and sexy as hell. "Sounds like a plan to me. Whatever your advice is, Dr. McKee, I intend to abide by it."

Erin giggled at his acquiescence to her prescription as she draped her arms around his neck and pulled him into a slow, passionate kiss. He could spend forever in this kitchen with this woman. Ray knew that whatever happened, he was going to be okay so long as Erin McKee was in his life. Everything about her amazed him, and he was increasingly more certain about what his true feelings for her were with each passing second.

His attention was diverted by the sound of gravel beneath rapidly rolling tires. Ray's antennae immediately went up. Nobody came down his drive unless they were invited or had told him ahead of time that they were coming. The sound of speeding engines only added to his alertness. The sound of vehicles skidding to a stop on the gravel outside his house caused his level of readiness to turn up to eleven.

Erin must have been startled by the sudden change in Ray's demeanor. "Ray, what's wrong? Is everything okay?"

The sound of doors opening and closing and the sound of feet running across the gravel finally activated the part of his brain that always lay dormant until the specter of danger made an appearance.

"Get down, put your back against the inner wall," Ray said.

Erin didn't question him. She quickly obeyed his instructions just as the chopping sound of automatic gunfire piercing the wooden walls of the house began. Ray crouched beside Erin, his eyes fixed on the back door that gave access to the kitchen. He pulled his SigSauer P-365 from the small of his back and pointed it in the direction of the back door.

The bullets from the automatic gunfire raking the front of the house began zipping and cracking their way through drywall and wood paneling before slamming into the opposite walls of the kitchen. Erin was terrified.

Why in the hell isn't he shooting his pistol at them?

Her question was answered when the back door splintered and swung open. Two men stepped into the room dressed in acid washed jeans and colorful hooded sweatshirts. They swung their AK-47 rifles up and prepared to aim them at Ray and Erin, but Ray had already fired his pistol.

Erin covered her ears instinctively as she heard the pop-pop-pop of Ray's pistol. Two rounds struck the man who was farthest into the kitchen in the center of his chest. Two more struck the man just outside of the kitchen door center mass before a third struck him in the bridge of his nose and exploded the back of his skull like a watermelon.

The man just inside of the kitchen crumpled into the kitchen floor before Ray delivered a coup des gras to his forehead and a splattering of blood, bone, and brain matter to his kitchen cabinet. Ray moved quickly, dropped the half-shot magazine and retrieved a fresh magazine from the holster at the small of his back. He inserted the fresh magazine and racked the slide to ensure the weapon was charged and ready to fire.

Erin was still in shock and held her hands tightly against her ears as she drew her knees as close to her chin as she could possibly get them. Ray needed her to be alert and to listen, and he didn't have time to wait for her to calm down. He grabbed a hold of her arm and shook her hard to get her attention back on the situation and away from the safe place that he knew she had gone to in her mind. She snapped back to reality and looked desperately at Ray; her green eyes filled with terror.

"Take this. It's ready to shoot. I left my rifle on the desk in the front room. Once they reload, I'm gonna make a run for the rifle. Our only chance is if I take the fight to them. I need you to watch this back door. If anyone comes through there, I'm gonna need you to shoot them in the chest until they're on the ground. Then put one in the head, even if they're already down. Can you do that for me?"

Erin nodded her head rapidly as the men out front continued their assault on the house. "Shoot until they fall, then shoot the head. Okay. Don't leave me, Ray. Ray, I need you. I'm so scared."

She began to cry and Ray cupped her cheek. "You can do this. I'll be right back."

The men out front stopped firing and Ray knew they were dropping dry mags and grabbing fresh ones. Now was his chance. He shot up from his crouched position and ran as fast as he could down the hall and towards the front room. The walls looked like they had been hit with a hurricane of lead and he had some serious concerns that the old house might fall in if it took much more of a beating. He had just reached his study when the indiscriminate spraying of his home with bullets resumed.

A barrage of lead flew through the shredded walls around his study and he suddenly felt like a white hot hammer had nailed him just above his right hip. The pain was excruciating and immediate, but with the help of his adrenaline, Ray was able to ignore the pain of the gunshot that he knew he had just absorbed as he grabbed the M1A SOCOM 16 from his desk. He always kept a full twenty-round magazine in the weapon and he charged the weapon before opening the bottom drawer of his desk to grab two more twenty-round magazines. He stuffed the mags into the back pockets of his jeans, duck walked to the window that faced the side of the house, and rolled out of it and onto the ground covered by the trunk of an oak tree.

The remaining shooters had stopped shooting again, Ray assumed to reload, and he peered around the tree with his rifle at the ready. Ray saw a black Tahoe, meaning as many as five showed up to kill him, and deduced there were only three left to worry about. Not the worst odds he'd ever had, but this time he had no support and a gunshot wound that he could feel leak rivulets of blood with every step he took.

A black male, dressed in a red hoodie and black jeans, took cover behind the engine block of the Tahoe. Ray could also see a red bandana tied around his head as he swiveled his head from left to right.

Tyrone Weeks's crew?

Just as he looked at the other shooter, he darted out of cover and ran around the opposite side of the house. A chill shot up Ray's spine. The shooter was going around the back to check on the others and to finish the job if necessary. Erin was all alone in the kitchen and she might not stand much of a chance if they had any sort of military background. Ray had to act fast.

Ray bolted from the cover of the oak tree and sprinted towards the Tahoe. He fired three rounds in quick succession at the hood of the Tahoe, which caused the shooter to duck for cover. Ray dropped to the gravel, ignored the pain of hundreds of jagged rocks slamming into the flesh of his forearms and the lightning bolt of pain that shot from his wound to his brain. He saw the man's lower legs exposed beneath the vehicle.

He fired the rifle twice. One round slammed into the front of the man's left shin, snapping the bone like a twig, and the other tore through his right ankle which nearly severed a foot that was now dangling by jagged flesh and sinew as the man collapsed and screamed in unbearable pain. He wasn't dead but he was definitely neutralized.

Ray hopped up from his prone position and sprinted through the front door of the house. He bounded over fallen and shattered boards and posts as he heard the distinctive pop-pop-pop of his SigSauer sound off within the house. He ran with all he had in him to get to the kitchen. The excruciating agony that each step brought from his wound only served as fuel to push him harder and faster.

He made it to the kitchen to find the shooter laying on his back, two wounds in the center of his chest and one on the left side of his neck coughing up geysers of blood as he gasped for air. Ray didn't hesitate or think twice before he shot him through the head streaking red and pink tendrils across the tile floor.

Ray then desperately looked for Erin and found her in the same spot where he had left her. She held the gun out in front of her, staring off into space as her arm trembled. Ray set his rifle on the ground and gently helped her to lower the gun before enveloping her in his arms.

"You okay, babe? Talk to me, let me know that you're okay," Ray nearly pleaded.

"I-I-I killed him."

"You did what you had to do, babe. I'm so sorry. I'm so sorry."

Ray hugged her tightly as tears of joy and of pain from his wound streamed down his face. She hugged him back, hard, before planting kisses of joy all over the left side of his face.

"You're alive. Oh, thank God you're alive, love," Erin said.

She placed her hand on his side and she saw him wince.

"Are you hurt?" Erin asked as she looked at her hand and the blood that covered it.

"Oh my God, Ray. Where'd you get hit?"

"In the fatty tissue just above the hip I think."

She immediately went into doctor mode, tearing his t-shirt to get a good look at the wound; a black hole in his white skin.

"Looks like it went through and through. I need to stitch you up, and then we need to get you to the hospital."

"Heads up, Hootie. I'm coming in and I'm friendly," yelled a voice from outside of the house. Ray immediately recognized the cadence and the thick North Alabama drawl. Ray looked at the back door and was filled with hope as Joseph "Bloodhound" Wilcox sauntered into the room.

"I got your phone call, and shit, you weren't kiddin'. You're seriously fucked."

CHAPTER 37

Joseph "Bloodhound" Wilcox was out in the field running through tactical drills with Lamar "Mountain" Clarke and Alex "Cub" Martinez when Ray called him. The voicemail Ray had left wasn't noticed until Bloodhound grabbed the phone from the counter before sitting down to watch a little Netflix six hours later. He flew into action once he listened to Ray's call for help, grabbed his guys and his gear, and left the compound of Yellowhammer, Bloodhound's private security firm, outside of Hartselle, Alabama, in just under two hours. It had taken them eight hours to make it to Queen's Bridge, and another fifteen minutes to make it to the sandy road that was also Ray's driveway. They had kept driving when they saw a black male, his red hoodie and matching bandana not nearly as eye-catching as the AK-47 casually held at the hip, was doing his best to stay behind a small thicket of pines at the edge of the road.

They stopped their truck just around the bend, let Cub out into the woods, and drove a quarter mile up to the next turn off. They headed back in the direction of Ray's road and slowed to a crawl once they made it back to the sandy drive. As expected, the man walked out from behind the thicket and brandished the Ukrainian knock-off rifle that was already a quasi-knock-off of a German design while encouraging Bloodhound to keep his Ford Excursion moving past the road and the green tunnel towards Ray's house. Bloodhound and Mountain raised their hands into the air and began to frantically plead with the man not to hurt them as Cub emerged from the jungle of pines, oaks, and palmetto scrub that lined either side of the two roadways.

Cub pressed the cold steel of a suppressed Walther PPQ pistol into the base of the man's skull and explained to him that he had three seconds to either lose the gun or to lose his brains. The man dropped the Ukrainian AK-47 as Bloodhound and Mountain exited the vehicle, bound and gagged the young man, and stashed him in the back of the large SUV.

As they completed their task, the sound of automatic gunfire echoed in the distance and the three men were back inside of the vehicle and tore down the dirt road to Ray's home in the woods. Just under five minutes and two and a half miles later, the Excursion skidded to a halt outside of an old farmhouse that looked like it belonged somewhere in Iraq rather than in South Carolina.

The men had readied themselves for battle as they flew down the road by strapping on olive ballistics vests, stuffing full magazines into the front of the vests, and locking and loading their M-4 rifles before they scrambled from the large vehicle, scanned the trees, the vehicles in front of the house, and the house itself for targets.

They found the corpse of one assailant lying half on the grass and half on the pea gravel driveway, flies already swarming the corpse that had been lying there for less than two minutes, and they found the writhing figure of another man desperately trying to cope with the pain of right leg nearly severed mid-shin and the opposite foot practically severed at the ankle. The blood was now flowing from his wounds in a steady trickle with each heartbeat, rather than the jarring spurts that would have come immediately after his injury.

Bloodhound took one look at him and he could tell that shock was already setting in. Hell, the four or five seconds he took to look at the poor bastard seemed to show him weakening in real time. He signaled his guys to take up flanking positions on either side of the house. No point in even bothering with the guy on the ground. He'd be dead in the next five minutes either way.

A gunshot cracked from inside of the house. Bloodhound knew from the report that it had come from a rifle, probably a 7.62 or a 30-06, and it didn't have the telltale chopping sound of an AK.

"Erin? Are you okay?" came the muffled words through the shattered house. Bloodhound breathed a sigh of relief. He couldn't see why any of the shooters would be worried if someone was okay or not, and he started walking around the house towards where the back door was likely to be.

Bloodhound called out as he rounded the house and stepped over the corpses of three shooters clogging up the doorway. He explained to Ray that he had gotten his message and that he and two of their old buddies had immediately loaded up and came running to help. Ray stood up and shook Bloodhound's hand as Erin chased after him and tried to treat his wound as she did so.

"Might wanna sit down and let the lady handle that," Bloodhound said, noting the blood that had soaked through the makeshift bandage Erin made out of a dishrag.

"Hey, Cub. Hootie took one close to the hip. It ain't too serious, but bring us the kit anyhow. Mount, go retrieve our buddy from the truck. He's got some 'splainin to do."

"On it," Cub answered.

Bloodhound slung his rifle across his chest, cleared off the table in the dining room, which had surprisingly not taken a bit of damage in the onslaught, and helped Ray onto it while Erin ran upstairs to grab a pillow and some towels from the master suite. By the time she returned, Ray was lying on the table, Cub had opened up and spread out the various items they had kept inside of their kit, and Mountain had just clomped into the house carrying a bound man with a dark hood over his head over one shoulder like he was a log.

"Kitchen?" Mountain stopped to ask Bloodhound at the entryway to the small dining room.

"Good a place as any. Keep an eye on him, and don't worry about being gentle. Reckon we're past that," Bloodhound replied.

"Aight," Mountain replied as he strode into the kitchen and shook the now rickety house as he dropped the man onto the floor like a bag of dog food.

Erin, who took the time to scrub her hands in the upstairs bathroom, got right to work packing Ray's wound with clean gauze and dressed each end with clean bandages. The suture kit that came standard in the medical kit Cub had brought in would be used once they had slowed the bleeding down. While she worked, and in between gasps and curses, Ray filled Bloodhound and his guys in on all that had happened over the course of the past few days. When he finished bringing him up to speed, Bloodhound shook his head.

"I figured you were in deep shit, but damn. They've got your balls in a vise for sure. How do you want me and the boys to help?"

"I need people I can trust. I'm pretty sure there's at least one guy in my department that I can, but I can't afford to risk his life over this. Not after what happened to Gary. To tell you the truth, I'm not so sure that I shouldn't tell you and the boys to pack up and head on back. This is too big of a favor to ask of y'all too."

"Fuck that. I spent about a hundred and fifty dollars after diesel fuel, snacks, and chew just getting here. I'm gonna be good and damned 'fore I see my investment pissed away. Besides, been a couple years since Mountain's got a chance to put the hurtin' on somebody and if you wanna tell him 'naw bro, I was just bullshitting you,' and that he can't scratch that itch, be my guest, dude. So, the way I figure it, you're stuck with us and I don't wanna hear no more shit about you risking our lives for nothing. Keep your deputy as safe from this as possible. I'm all for it. Now, where do we come in?"

"I know that Thurmond Spates and his boys are ultimately behind all of this, but I ain't got anything I can prove just yet. All I've got is the word of a now-dead junkie. Nobody is gonna take that seriously. Even the location of the Yamassee Mounds is nothing. All I have is my word, and that ain't exactly perceived to be what it used to be," Ray replied as Erin began to wrap a bandage around his waist.

"So, what do you need to be able to prove that these guys are guilty and that you've been subjected to a frame-up job?" Bloodhound asked.

"I need some compelling evidence. Not just a witness, but something concrete, beyond reproach. I need something that's gonna tie the Spates family to this thing. Something that can't be explained away. Finding out the location of the woods or the farm or whatever they call it would be good, and finding some evidence there would be a home run."

"Okay, so I'm guessing you're gonna need to deputize us or something like that," Bloodhound said.

"Yeah, something like that."

"Hold your horses for a bit on that. Reckon we should get you out of here before we do anything else. Hey, Cub?"

Cub Martinez stepped the ten feet from the kitchen to the dining room. "Yeah, boss?"

"I want you to take Hootie and his lady out to the truck, make sure they're squared away, and then come on back inside. We've gotta ask this fella we found hanging out by the county road a question or two," Bloodhound explained as Cub and Erin began packing up the different tools and meds inside of the medical kit.

"Why do we need to be at the truck for that?" Erin asked.

"Just so that the county sheriff can neither confirm, nor deny what I'm about to do to get some answers," Bloodhound replied.

"You're going to torture him? Are you hearing this, Ray?"

Ray nodded. "Help me to the truck, would you?" he said.

"So, you're just gonna let this happen? Just gonna let them go wild?"

The look in Ray's eyes was colder than the ski trip she and a college friend took to Vail.

"Yes. I don't much care if he comes to kill me; he's gotta do what he's gotta do on that one. But coming up here to kill you as well? Fuck him. Will you help me to the truck or not?"

Erin clenched her jaw and slipped her arm around Ray's back. Ray winced as he sat up and took his first two steps. Shit, ten years ago he could've taken a hit like this, packed the wound, and kept going for another six to eight hours or more. Now, it seemed like every step launched a new avalanche of pain. The old man was right after all; getting old sucked.

As they hobbled down the hall and navigated the brick-and-mortar steps to front of the house, Ray couldn't help but cringe at the sight of a man lying in the summer sun, his body being ravaged by a swarm of flies so loud you would have thought a hornet's nest had been kicked up. It was bad enough that Erin had to witness him putting down two in the kitchen, then finishing off the last one as he lay bleeding from the hole Erin had blasted into him. Coldly acquiescing to what was about to happen to the last one couldn't have helped his standing in her eyes either. He was almost certain that she was turned on by the excitement of dating a cop, but he had serious doubts that she had expected the excitement to be as intense as this.

Cub trotted ahead of them, opened the back door of the Excursion, and busied himself with moving packs, firearms, and other essential gear into the third row seats.

"How come your buddy keeps calling you Hootie?" Erin finally asked, breaking the tension.

"Callsigns when we all served in the same operation detachment. Mountain got his 'cause, well you saw him. He can bench 300 like it's nothing. Cub was the youngest guy on the team for a while. And Bloodhound has left a trail of broken hearts in most cities and towns that he's been to, but he was always hunting for another one to break.

"When I came aboard as Bloodhound's first lieutenant, it got around pretty quick that I was from South Carolina. Bloodhound got a real kick out of playing a song from that band from down in Charleston every time I walked into the barracks, mess hall, command center, you name it. So, he assigned Hootie as my callsign on the radio and the name stuck."

He climbed up into the vehicle and took a seat as Erin checked his bandages. "That's kinda stupid," she remarked as she unzipped the medkit and fished out two prescription bottles.

"Yeah, but there's gotta be something stupid to take your mind off of everything in that situation. Laugh at something or go nuts, I guess."

Erin snorted a cynical laugh—she still hadn't gotten over her indignation—as she opened the bottles and fished out a pill from each before placing them into Ray's hand.

"One of these is a round of cefoxitin, an antibiotic. The other is a Vicodin for the pain."

"If it's all the same to you, I'll take the antibiotic and two ibuprofens instead."

Meanwhile...

"Go ahead and get the hood off of our friend here. He's got a few things he needs to clear up," Bloodhound said as Mountain removed the black hood from the man's head.

Bloodhound figured that this guy was somewhere in his mid-thirties, and judging from the way this whole operation had gone down, he figured that he had probably cut his teeth in the military just like Bloodhound and Ray had. That presented something of a problem moving forward.

Not that he had any qualms about hurting a fellow veteran, but rather his concerns were related to the kind of training this guy had been given with regard to resisting interrogation techniques. There was at least a better than average chance that whatever pressure he applied, this guy would have a tried-and-true strategy to fall back on to resist and prolong the process.

That wasn't to say that there was no way to break him and get all the information he wanted, up to and including the address of his mother and his girlfriend's bra size. Everybody had a breaking point, and Bloodhound was confident that if he broke enough of his fingers, removed enough teeth or fingernails, that this guy would reach his. The problem lay in the amount of time it would take for him to reach that point. Time that Ray didn't have to waste.

Bloodhound drew a 9mm Walther PPQ pistol from a holster tucked into the back of his pants and carefully began threading a nine-inch suppressor onto the barrel of the weapon.

"The thing is," he said, addressing the black man glaring at him from the floor of Ray's destroyed kitchen, "you've got some information locked away in that head of yours, and you're gonna give it all to me."

The man smirked and Mountain answered it with a savage kick to the man's solar plexus. Immediately he began gasping for air as Mountain stepped forward, grabbed a hold of the man's bright red hoodie, and yanked him up into the seated position against the wall. Cords of muscle rippled up Mountain's coffee-colored arms as he tightened his grip on the man's hoodie.

"Now if I were you, I don't believe I'd be getting smart with me again, or my friend here is gonna have to hurt you again until I have your full attention. You picking up what I'm putting down?" Bloodhound said.

The man nodded through a clenched jaw.

"Glad we finally have gotten to a place of mutual seriousness."

Bloodhound casually crossed his arms at the wrist and pointed the barrel of the newly suppressed PPQ towards the floor as he continued.

"Let me explain how this is gonna go so we're both on the same page. I'm gonna give you one chance, just one, to answer all of my questions fully and truthfully. If you start spitting a line of bullshit, or you tell me to go fuck myself or anything like that, then I'm gonna make you tell me everything I want to know. And believe you me, you're gonna be desperate to tell me everything if we get to that point. The ball is firmly in your court.

"We'll start with something simple. What's your name?" Bloodhound asked.

The smirk reappeared on the man's face. "Man, I ain't gonna tell you a godda-"

The snap-snap of two suppressed 9mm hollow points being fired from Bloodhound's PPQ into the abdomen of the man now seated against the shredded wall of Ray's kitchen stopped that sentence in its tracks. Dark blood oozed from the wounds in a rapid cascade down the fabric of the hoodie and into a pool forming on the floor. The man released a sound that was part shirek and part moan as he rolled onto his side.

"Whoowee!" Bloodhound shouted. "Damn, that right there will ruin your weekend. What do you think, Mountain?"

"His schedule just opened up if he had any plans."

"I mean, I kinda knew you were probably gonna choose this route, but shit. I bet you wish you had chosen to go with door number one right about now. Whoo!"

He looked at Mountain again as the man moaned on the floor. "Gotta hand it to him, man. Dude likes to party."

Bloodhound stooped down, grabbed a handful of the red hoodie just above the wounds, and pulled him back up into the seated position, ignoring the guttural moans and the half-moon of darkening blood smeared on the wall behind him.

"Lemme explain the current situation to you now, wild man. You just took two hollow points to the gut."

Bloodhound sniffed conspicuously. "You smell that, Mountain?"

"Smells like shit, boss," Mountain replied in his deep baritone.

"Sure as hell does. Know what that means, wild man?"

Bloodhound asked.

"Don't strain yourself. I'll let you know. That means that them two hollow points just tore the hell out of your small and large intestines as they ripped right on through to your back. Now, I figure you mighta spent some time over there in the sandbox, and there mighta been a time or two you woulda seen wounds like this, but just in case you didn't, lemme break it down. If you ain't in an ER in say, oooh, 'nother thirty-five minutes or so, then you're gonna be seeing all of your buddies that come up here with you, today, in hell by 3:30."

The look of pain, panic, and terror that flooded in the man's eyes told Bloodhound that he had him right where he wanted him.

"Remember what I said just a second ago? I'm willing to bet you a buffalo nickel that you're plum desperate to tell me anything I want to know. So, I'm gonna do like I did before and give you two choices again. Choice number one: you tell me everything I want to know whenever I ask it. Then, I might be inclined to make sure that the para-medics know about you being out here and in need. Choice number two: you keep on with the silent treatment, and I leave you here and don't tell a soul. Now, what'll it be? Door number one or door number two?"

CHAPTER 38

"It's done, where are we meeting?" read the text message that was sent to Jimmy Spates's secure phone. The day had been stressful for many reasons, and Jimmy was relieved that this particular albatross of anxiety had just fallen off of his neck.

"Same place as before, park at the Bean Market and walk up to the back entrance. Knock twice and I'll come to the door," he replied.

The sense of relief slipped over him like a warm blanket once he hit send. All day, he had been pulled in a thousand different directions. No less than three national news organizations, two newspapers out of New York City, two out of Washington DC, one from Chicago, one from Los Angeles, and at least a dozen online news organizations had contacted him through phone and email to request a time to set up an interview with him and his brothers.

Turns out the American people wanted to know what it was like growing up the sons of the man that many had called the "Conscience of the Senate" over the many long years of their father's political career. And each of the media organizations that had contacted him was chomping at the bit to be the first one to interview the "brothers of the new Camelot." All the comparisons between them and the Kennedys was amusing and unsettling.

His father had already instructed him before his announcement that he was to go with the news organization out of Atlanta for television, the older newspaper out of New York City, and the podcasters out of Los Angeles. So,

Jimmy had spent a sizable portion of his afternoon jug-
gling portfolios for the family real estate firm, purchas-
ing local advertising for their new offices in Nashville and
in Orlando, and responding to emails from the dozens of
news outlets that clogged his inbox.

The fact that he was also required to answer his cell
phone at least once every two hours to either talk Hampton down from the ledge or answer a question that he had
about how to do something at the farm in the swamp only
seemed to make the day seem like a week.

Wade, for his part, was nowhere to be seen or heard
from since they had all left the Miss Vickie and scattered
to attend to the various needs of the family enterprise.
Not that Jimmy blamed him for going dark for a while.
He didn't need to hear what their father had said to him
on the call that Wade was forced to make to know that it
wasn't anything good to hear from one's father.

Jimmy had been in this game his entire life and knew
exactly how each of his family members thought, operat-
ed, and executed. His father probably placed sole responsibility for Gaskins on Wade's shoulders and probably
threatened Wade with grave consequences should things
go awry. Again, nothing that one wanted to hear from
one's father, but on a base-level, Jimmy understood where
both of them were coming from in the present situation;
his father's threat to Wade and Wade's need to clear his
head.

Thurmond and Wade were both so ambitious, so emotionally attuned with one another and with people in general. Jimmy had always heard people say that fathers and
sons were "just alike" in many ways, but he had never really seen it to be as true in others as it was between Wade
and their father. Hampton was the simpleton who was the
apple of their father's eye, Jimmy was the stoic who flew
under the radar of his brothers and of his father, and Wade
was the charismatic heir to the family throne who couldn't
help but lock horns with the current occupant over nearly everything. And more often than not, Wade was left
storming out into the wilderness to blow off steam before

he exploded onto everyone around him.

Jimmy understood it, but it still would have been nice if he had instead sought to oversee the operations at the farm for the next few days so they could park Hampton at the Georgetown offices where he could distract himself with all the fishing, drinking, and lounging he could handle. It would have cut down on the constant interruptions that Hampton couldn't help but cause, but it would also have made things much safer to handle during this time.

The text message he had received and replied to earlier in the day, however, had melted a great deal of his worries away like the snow that fell once every three years and only lasted for three hours in the early morning. He busied himself with replying to the news outlets once more. He had cleared through all of the emails, graciously demurred the requests of their respective outlets, and finished replying with dates and times to the television network in Atlanta and the newspaper in New York City when he heard a solid thunk-thunk emanating from the back door of the office space.

He got up from his chair, reached into his satchel case for a fat envelope of cash, and strode to the door. He opened the door wide and heard a muffled pop, felt every muscle in his body simultaneously tense as hard as a rock, and fell onto the cheap carpet. The click-click-click sound that had followed the initial assault to his senses ceased and his rigid body relaxed. His mind was clouded from the shock and the pain of the onslaught that he could neither make sense of what was happening nor could he seem to move his body effectively.

He felt strong hands grab him, heard the zip-zip of flex cuffs being secured around his wrists and ankles, and he saw blackness fill his field of vision as what he assumed was a dark cloth bag was draped over his head. Another set of hands joined those, and he felt himself be lifted up and carried out to a running vehicle of some type. He was tossed into the floorboard, the doors were shut, and the vehicle darted off to an unknown location.

The fog was slowly clearing from Jimmy's mind as

the vehicle raced into the twilight. He felt unbridled fear clawing up his chest and through his throat, but he willed himself to think about the situation logically. There wasn't a scenario that ran through his mind that could explain who had abducted him or why.

There were no criminal organizations that were aware of their enterprise, at least not beyond the knowledge of the services that they provided, and even then, none would dare to make a move against them. At least not so long as Thurmond Spates could direct the awesome power at his disposal to influence the attorney general and the Department of Justice to systematically dismantle their operation practically overnight. If they thought that what Pablo Escobar and the Cali Cartel got was bad, they hadn't seen anything like what Senator Thurmond Spates would rain down upon them.

This had to be a group who had very little to lose and everything to gain. Somebody like al-Qaeda or ISIS, maybe. And that thought terrified Jimmy in a way he had not previously known he could be terrified.

The vehicle slowed to a stop and doors opened, men moved, and doors shut. Sweat started to soak through the hood draped over his head as his mind filled with images of him being paraded in front of a camera and his head being lopped off with a machete or a scimitar. His bound arms and legs began to tremble involuntarily, and he felt warm urine soaking through the front of his canvas pants as fear took hold of him.

The door behind him opened and he was dragged out onto the grassy ground before he was dragged into what he assumed was a small wooden building judging from the distinctive sound of boots against an old wooden floor. His limbs felt like they were made of strawberry jelly as the two men who were carrying him in between them lifted him up by his arms and set him down onto a metal folding chair. He felt his legs and wrists being taken hold of and heard a much longer zip tie being threaded through both his wrist and ankle restraints and then being zipped together.

The heavy boots that clomped here and there through-out the room suddenly filed out of the small building, slammed a metal door shut, and left him in dark silence. He was still frozen, petrified to move even an inch. He sat rigidly still for he didn't know how long until he could no longer take the uncomfortable feeling of his back being held at such a bizarre angle. He shrugged his shoulders forward and his growing terror was somehow made bi-zarrely more intense as he discovered that whenever he hunched his shoulders forward his legs were pulled up un-derneath the chair. What the hell was going on?

The wild scenarios returned, and for a time he allowed himself to be swept along the current of the irrational side of his brain. He didn't know how long he had indulged into every theory that his emotions could muster, but he man-aged to wrestle control back from his panic-stricken emo-tional brain. If it was al-Qaeda or ISIS or some group that had snatched him and brought him here, then surely they would've removed his hood by now.

He didn't claim to know a great deal about the mo-dus operandi of Islamic terrorists, but he knew enough to know that removing his head and posting the video to the internet would've already happened by now. Beside that fact, there was the issue of why they would feel the need to target his father by killing him in the first place.

His father had been fairly consistent in his calls to end what he termed "Islamophobic Neo-Crusades" in the Middle East and to instead extend the hand of friendship. Killing the son of one of the most Islamophilic members of the United States senate, even if he were running for the presidency of "the Great Satan," as the Iranian regime was fond of calling the United States, just defied all logic.

The panic was starting to well up inside of him again with each breath he took. The now sweat-soaked hood seemed to deprive him of the ability to get a good breath of air. His reptile brain seized control, and in an instant he was desperately gasping for any air that would stave off the suffocation that he felt was imminent.

His panicked gasping was interrupted by the sound of

the door opening, boots stomping against ancient wood, and the blinding sensation of his hood being yanked from his head. The white light that stabbed his eyes blinded him and forced him to squint them tightly shut as he took what felt like his first full breath in hours. He drank in the precious, cool air in great gulps as he slowly cracked his eyes and allowed them to adjust somewhat to the seemingly blinding lights inside of the room.

A cloth was securely pulled over his face and the chair tilted back. He struggled, shook his head back and forth, and screamed into the cloth but to no avail. He heard the unmistakable thoonk of a five-gallon water jug being set down on the wooden floor close to him. His blood curdled as he felt the cold liquid being poured onto the cloth in a steady stream.

The water ran down his nostrils and down his throat. He gurgled, tried to shake his head away from the stream but was held in place as the water relentlessly kept pouring across his covered face. He couldn't breathe, and the feeling of drowning was more terrifying than anything he could have conjured in his wildest dreams.

The steady flow of water stopped and the cloth was removed from his face. For a brief second, he struggled to breathe and was horrified when his body didn't respond. His body reacted, the muscles in his stomach and throat tightened and expelled what felt like gallons of water from his throat onto the wooden floor. He coughed and gasped for breath, thankful for the sweet blessing of air in his lungs.

"The time has come, Mr. Spates," a distorted voice said from the darkness beyond the lights.

Jimmy was too scared to speak. The voice seemed to know this and continued. "The day of reckoning that you have feared for so long has finally arrived."

"W-w-who are you?" Jimmy asked.

"I am a harbinger. I speak for the innocent souls that you and your family have taken. They cry out for you. They cry out for you to take your place among them along with your brothers, your father, your mother, your nieces, and anyone else that you hold dear."

Jimmy's lips quivered, panic setting in deep now, as tears streamed down his cheeks. "Please, I-"

"Please? How many times did the people you sent into the swamp beg you? How many times did they ask you, please?" the voice said.

"I-I don't know. I just handle the-the operations side of things mostly."

"And you think that this. . . absolves you or shields you in some way?"

"No, it doesn't," Jimmy replied in little more than a whisper. "But it doesn't change the fact that I don't want to die. Tell me what you want. I'll do anything that you want; just don't kill me."

Silence fell over the room. Jimmy's heart pounded in his chest like an engine hitting fifth gear. The sharp click of the light directly in front of him being switched off caused him to jump and nearly tip his chair over. A tall man dressed in black stepped from behind the now switched-off light and into Jimmy's field of view. He wore black leather gloves, black slacks, a black suit coat, black vest, black shirt, and black tie. The helmet/mask that covered his entire head was also black with slits for eyes and nothing else. The shiver that shot down his spine became a steady quiver the instant that he saw the menacing mask. The man casually lifted the water jug by its neck and strolled closer to Jimmy.

"I will offer you one chance and one chance only. You will tell me the exact location of the farm that your family has in the swamp. You will tell me exactly what type of security you have there. You will tell me any passwords that I need to know. You will tell me the locations of any records that your family have squared away. You will tell me who you have working with your family, and you will sign a sworn statement to that fact."

The man let the water jug fall to the wooden floor with a loud clunk. The sound once again startled him out of his seat.

"If you do not do exactly as I have told you, then I will

pour the entire contents of this jug down your throat until you drown in the very chair that you are sitting in. This is my only offer. What is your decision?"

Jimmy was nearly paralyzed with terror, but the most reasonable course of action was obvious.

"May I have the use of my hands so that I can write all of this down for you?" Jimmy asked.

Chapter 39

The 4 am runs that had been a part of Ray's morning ritual since his active-duty days had paid off in more ways than he could've ever dreamed. Not only did it give him the physique and fitness that he relentlessly sought to maintain, but it allowed him to sustain the endurance of a man in his prime. That endurance had proven invaluable as he, Bloodhound, Mountain, and Cub had all been forced to hike a grueling two and a quarter miles from the indistinguishable banks of one of the hundreds of unknown back-creek tributaries of the Black River through some of the most unforgiving swampland that he could remember ever setting foot in.

While the first leg of the trip, an eight-mile trip down the Black River by boat, was as simple as steering the engine in the right direction, it had only gotten tougher since the mile trip up the unknown back-creek by paddle. The walk through the semi-stagnant water and hip-deep mud, and around the massive root systems of the sweet-gums and cypresses that filled the land for miles around would've been challenging with only waders and a walking stick, but several pounds of gear, weaponry, and ammunition made it especially punishing.

The nearly two-hour slough through the dark swamp at long last led them to the outline of a long building covered in dark brown sheet metal. He couldn't tell too much about the structure in great detail, but it reminded him of the old rundown warehouses that dotted the docksides in Georgetown. Every now and then, you'd see something like them out in the country, only they were auto shops, boat repairmen, or the occasional tobacco barn. He squinted his eyes, looked past the towering trees that surrounded it, and saw that the roof was covered in thick camouflage netting and that a small section closest to him was torn open by what he assumed must have been a tree. The breeze singing through the trees peeled back the edges of the brown tarps that covered the section to reveal the white tile walls of what looked like a bathroom or shower.

Erin had been pissed that he was going into the woods with Bloodhound. She had been pissed ever since Bloodhound and the guys came back to the truck without the guy they were supposed to question.

"Where is the guy y'all snatched by the road?" she asked.

"Turns out he had a pretty nasty couple of gut shots. Poor bastard bled out right there. Craziest shit I've ever seen. But before he bled out, he told me that Jimmy Spates hired him to kill you both and to make it look like some fella named Tyrone Weeks had ordered it," Bloodhound replied.

If looks could kill, then Erin's face would have ended every life in Craven County at that moment. Ray had reached out to touch her on the shoulder, only for her to shrug his hand off and gaze out of the window as the Excursion rocketed to her home in Florence. She hadn't said a word as she properly dressed his wound, and she said even less whenever they planned the interdiction of Jimmy Spates.

When they returned after they questioned him and left him secured inside of a shack in the woods close to the Georgetown County line, Ray was worried that she may not let them into her house, much less help with the next phase of their plan. Surprisingly, she welcomed them inside, directed Bloodhound and the guys to a stack of pizza boxes, and pulled Ray into her bedroom.

"I don't approve of what y'all have done, or what your buddy did, but I want you to know that I understand what y'all are doing. I'm sorry I was such a bitch earlier. You've been through hell, and I didn't make that any easier. You were just trying to keep me safe, and I wanted to thank you for that," she said.

She embraced him, despite the sweat and smells that he was certain permeated every inch of his body, and pulled him close.

"I don't blame you for being angry, Erin. You've been a trooper, and I've put you in a situation that has demanded a lot from you. I'm just grateful that you haven't thrown us out or told me to lose your number yet."

She kissed him. "Don't lose my number just yet, Sheriff. Is there anything that I can do to help?"

"Actually, we are going to need you to do something for us, and you might not like it."

She hadn't liked it. She insisted on going along with them into the swamp, if for no other reason than to serve as a medic of sorts, but all of her attempts were quashed. She begrudgingly agreed to her part but still maintained that she could contribute in greater ways. Ray was certain that she had the heart for it, but he knew that she didn't need to bear witness to what they were about to do.

He looked at Bloodhound, who nodded in unspoken agreement as to the plan of attack. Mountain and Cub started the painstaking process of silently navigating roots, quietly sloughing through mud, and calmly wading through black water. Mountain moved to the far side of the compound, and Cub moved through the thick jungle along the nearside of the nondescript building. So far, they had been able to confirm that Jimmy Spates was telling them the truth on at least two accounts, and it was not long before they were to discover if the rest of his story was true as well.

Ray rechecked his weapon and his gear. Satisfied that the weapon was indeed primed for action and there was not so much as a string hanging from his gear that could make a sound, Ray refocused his mind on the task at hand. He had reverted back to his training and was surprised at how easy it was to view the mission before them as he had viewed others in foreign lands. Even the actions that they were about to take would be questionable in the legal sense here in the United States, they didn't give him an ounce of apprehension. It needed to be done whether the law approved or not.

A loud clap of thunder rang out across the darkness and lightning flashed white in the night vision goggles, or NVGs as he had learned to call them, Ray was wearing and gave him a slight start. The forecast was right within five minutes. The steady roar of heavy rain, combined with the sound of it battering the ancient metal sheets on the compound, drowned out everything else. The chances of success just went up substantially.

"Cub in position. Two tangoes in view; one high and one low," came the whisper in the radio earpiece.

Three things had been true so far. Ray hoped that they could keep batting 1,000.

"Mountain in position. Got the same on my side too." That made four.

Ray and Bloodhound watched as a man dressed in woodland camouflage and toted an AR-15 hanging from a strap across his chest casually strolled underneath the eaves of the compound nearest to them. They watched as the man casually puffed on a cigarette and ambled forward without a care in the world. On the far side of the compound, they observed another man, similarly dressed and armed, round the corner of the compound. He was more purposeful in his movements, scanned the wood line every few seconds, and rested his hands atop his own AR-15.

The smoker rounded the corner and called out to his

companion just above the steady roar of the wind and the rain.

"Need a pick-me-up?" the smoker hollered.

"Naw, I can make it through the last hour," the non-smoker shouted.

"Good for you. I'm fucking exhausted. Smokes are all that's keeping me going," the smoker shouted back as he approached the non-smoker.

"Ready to fire on your go," Mountain whispered over the radio.

"Kick it off whenever you're ready," Cub added.

Ray glanced at Bloodhound who gave a slight nod before resting the barrel of his suppressed M-4 on the moss-covered log that he and Ray were taking cover behind. Ray watched as his old friend took careful aim at his target.

Ray took a deep breath and performed the ritual he had performed before every single engagement he had been involved in. He spit out the chewing tobacco he had put in when they arrived at the compound a half-hour earlier, took five consecutive deep breaths, and silently prayed for protection for both he and his guys. This was going to be like when they were boots on the ground back in the day. They would either succeed, or they would all die.

Ray finished his prayer, set his suppressed M1 SOCOM rifle on the log, and took aim at the two conversing guards.

"Left or right?" Bloodhound whispered.

"Take left after my go," Ray replied.

He switched on his infrared laser mounted on top of his rifle and looked for the star-pattern that his laser painted onto his target. He watched as the star settled center-mass on the back of the smoker. He flipped the safety switch to the off position and took one last deep breath. He held the breath in, looped his finger around the trigger, finalized the position of the target laser, and squeezed the trigger.

The muffled SNAP of his suppressed rifle registered but was dulled by the cacophony of the rain storm around him. The 7.62mm round left his rifle and streaked towards its mark at 2,800 feet per second. The bullet smacked into the smoker in the center of his back and ballooned out a massive cavity within his chest before it shattered against the backside of his sternum and exited his chest in hundreds of fragments of lead, bone, and blood. He was dead before his legs crumpled underneath him.

The SNAP-SNAP-SNAP of Bloodhound's rifle followed near instantly, and he and Ray watched as three 5.56 rounds tore their way into the chest of the other man and ripped new cavities and passageways through his body as they exited into the swamp behind him. The grin on his face from reacting to something that the smoker had said was now permanently affixed to his lifeless corpse that lie crumpled next to his friend.

The faint SNAP-SNAP-SNAP-SNAP from Mountain and Cub's position told Ray that they had heard his commencement announcement. For an agonizingly long two seconds, Ray waited to hear the chop of returning fire from the shooters that his two guys had been sent to eliminate.

"Tangoes are down. Two in the trees and two on the ground," Mountain announced over their communications network.

Ray breathed a sigh of relief. So far, so good. He relaxed but was still on his guard for the specter of Mr. Mayhem to show up and to thoroughly fuck up all of their carefully laid plans. He waited a few more seconds, heard no return fire from any shooters that they may have missed, and proceeded with the plan.

"Move up. Cameras should be facing the trail, so stay out of their field of view. Prepare to breach. Wait for our command. Preparing to infiltrate the compound. Make sure that the patches are visible," Ray said as he and Bloodhound grabbed their weapons, vaulted over the log, and made their way to the breach in the back of the building.

They removed the NVGs once they were through the breach to the shower room, placed olive drab Craven County Sheriff's Department caps on, and uncovered the olive drab patches attached to their ballistics vest that read "SHERIFF" in muted green letters.

Ray took point and gingerly stepped into the neatly tiled room. It was roughly the size of an average high school classroom and lined with shower nozzles at even intervals all around. The center of the room was gently slanted towards a metal drain. It immediately brought back memories of showering off after a game and the long bus ride home, except that half of this room was filled with stacks of construction supplies for the impending repair project.

The two men crossed the room as silent as a midnight graveyard and stacked up, one behind the other, to the right of the closed door to the interior of the compound.

"Breaching set. Waiting on your go," Cub breathed into the comms system.

Ray glanced over his shoulder at Bloodhound. His friend gave him a nod and Ray gently and slowly turned the handle of the door. Ray felt the subtle click from the door's opening mechanism. He methodically began pulling the door inward. The hinge of the door let out a quiet squeak and Ray froze in place. Beads of sweat instantly formed on his temples, suddenly aware of the oppressive heat caused by his ballistics vest. Bloodhound patted him reassuringly on the side and Ray watched as his friend slipped from behind him and across to the other side of the doorway. Bloodhound reached into the cargo pocket on his right leg and produced a compact can of WD-40. Ray watched as he attached a thin plastic straw to the nozzle before he gave each of the door's three hinges a liberal spray of the industrial lubricant. He replaced the can inside of his cargo pants and shot Ray a grin before stacking back up behind his friend.

Ray waited a few seconds before slowly pulling the door open, step by agonizing step. He peered through the crack made between the door and the door jamb and saw a long hallway stretching out before them. There was rich oak flooring, paneling, and ceilings with eight matching doors on the right and eight doors on the left. He didn't see any guards or cameras in the hallway as he opened the door fully.

He stepped out of the shower room and onto the wooden floor and checked the corners with his rifle as Bloodhound popped out on the left side and began to scan the corners as well. They were alone in this part of the compound. They moved like ghosts down the hallway, and Ray took notes of signs posted on the doors that read Paradise Room, Punishment Room, Fantasy Room, and Dining Room, among others. With each step they took, the louder the sound of a television grew.

At the door to the shower room the sound was unintelligible, but as they grew closer the familiar sounds of one of Ray's favorite comedies grew clearer. The sounds of laughter also grew louder as they approached the end of the hallway. Ray stopped just short of the corner that opened up into a common area decorated with taxidermy heads of whitetail deer, African gazelle, zebra, and a variety of other common and exotic animals. A full bar ran alongside the wall to his right, stocked with some of the finest liquors and some of Ray's old favorites, with a mirrored backdrop behind the bar. In the mirror he could see a plush leather couch flanked by matching high-backed chairs arranged around the slate hearth and chimney of a sprawling fireplace. Above the fireplace was a mantle constructed out of rough-hewn oak timbers upon which rested the lifelike preservation of a red fox that looked as if it were perking up to listen for the sounds of a rabbit screaming in the distance. Above that was a seventy-two-inch television mounted onto the slate chimney that climbed up into the ceiling above.

In the chair on the left sat a man in woodland camouflage; his AR-15 leaned against the arm of the chair as he laughed at the antics on screen. Another sat on the couch in the middle with rifle resting across his lap, and one more sat in the chair on the right where his rifle also leaned against the arm of the chair.

"I love this part. Y'all shut up!" came the unmistakable voice of Hampton Spates, who stood behind the couch, a bottle of beer in his hand, and his attention solely focused on the movie playing on the tv.

There would never be a better time than now, Ray reasoned. He reached for the radio attached to his hip and keyed the microphone button twice.

CHAPTER 40

The blast nearly caused Hampton Spates to fall to the floor as he whirled around in the direction of the main door to the compound. He saw it swing open and two men in camouflage and tactical gear rushed into the room with rifles at the ready. His eyes went wide with terror.

The men who only seconds earlier were sitting around enjoying the comedy on the massive television scrambled to their feet, wrestled with their weapons as they stepped towards the threat at the entrance.

"Sheriff's Department!" came shouts from behind Hampton.

He turned and saw two more men in tactical gear step out of the long hallway that led to the shower room. Leon, the man who was sitting on the couch, raised his rifle in the direction of the two men in the hallway. The man closest to Hampton fired his weapon twice and punctured two holes into Leon's chest and turned the crown of his head into a canyon. Leon fell back onto the couch; blood and brain matter sloshed from the valley atop his head like a recklessly held bowl of soup.

Hampton turned and ran with all that he had for the door to the office behind him. He saw Troy Neal, a man he had hung out with many times at numerous bars over the years, cut down by the men who had blown the door to the compound open. The thud and the spatter that accompanied his drinking buddy's death drove his panic into overdrive.

He reached the door to the office and fumbled with the handle to the door. His breath was coming in short gasps, his stomach had tied itself into knots, and his hands had become slick with sweat as he attempted to turn the handle only to fail for a second time. Behind him came the sound of more suppressed shots and the sickening sound of rounds hitting flesh and bone.

He managed to grip the handle with his soaked hand, turn it into the open position, and slam the door shut behind him as the voices behind him began to yell for him to show them his hands. He flipped the tab into the locked position behind him and caught his breath for a moment as he leaned against the cold metal door.

"This is the Craven County Sheriff's Department. Open the door, Mr. Spates," came the muffled voice on the other side of the door.

What was he going to do? The security team had been taken out, and he had seen men that he had known for years die right in front of his eyes. His mind raced thinking of ways he could survive this ordeal.

You are going to die just like they did.

He was just supposed to watch the place and make sure that the guys were doing their job and that the clients were happy. That was all. He wasn't cut out to handle this. He didn't know where to even start. He needed help, and he needed it now. But there was no help to be found here, and the panic that had ruled him since the blasting of the door further sank its claws into his soul.

His eyes darted to the desk and cell phone that he had left to charge sitting atop it. His heart leapt at the sight of the lifeline he had left himself atop the desk. He knew what to do then. He shot up from the floor, grabbed the phone, and dialed the number of the person who was best suited to snatch him from the jaws of death.

Meanwhile...

Wade was sitting on the porch of his home high in the Tennessee Smokies. He sipped his bourbon as he watched the breathtaking sunset over the mountains and heard the sounds of his little girls playing hide-and-go-seek in the meadow just beneath the porch. The smell of woodsmoke and slowly roasting meat filled his nostrils. His mouth watered at the thought of the delicious supper of porterhouses, mashed potatoes, and braised broccoli that he would enjoy in just under ten minutes. He should really get up and go help Annalee set the table, but the view of the last rays of sunlight slipping behind the ridgeline was too good to miss.

He felt the soft touch of a hand caress his stubbled cheek. He turned his gaze and saw Annalee, a vision in her white minidress with the pink peony print that drove him wild.

"Dinner's almost ready, hun," she said in a voice as decadent as dark chocolate.

"Can I have my dessert early?" Wade asked as he caressed her perfect rump with his free hand.

Annalee sashayed her way around him, the heels of her pink stilettos thumping along the wooden deck in perfect time with the beat of Wade's heart. Her auburn hair was down and cascaded over her shoulders in long wavy curves, and her makeup was done in that bold and sexy look that he adored. He marveled at her as she made her way in front of his field of vision, bent over at the waist, and delicately pushed his legs apart with her hands.

He felt himself stiffen as she worked her talented, nimble fingers up to his belt, unbuckle the belt, unbutton his khaki shorts, and unfasten his zipper. She shimmied his shorts down expertly and placed her hand upon his growing member, being careful to maintain eye contact as she fished him out of his Jockeys.

"You'll get your dessert later, Cowboy. But I'm gonna have a taste of mine now," she said as she slipped him into her mouth.

Wade closed his eyes tightly and rode the waves of

pleasure that her soft tongue and warm mouth provided. He slipped into the reverie of the experience and was confused when he heard the sound of a cell phone ringing. He ignored it and chose instead to enjoy the pleasure he was receiving from his wife, but the sound only grew louder. He focused all of his energy on his wife and the job she was doing for him, but the now deafening sound of the cell phone was practically unbearable.

Wade's eyes opened with a start and to his disappointment, he wasn't sitting on the porch of their Tennessee mountain home, nor was he receiving some absolutely first-class head from his wife. He was instead lying on his plush California King-Sized bed and his wife, her auburn hair pulled into a messy bun and an old Clemson t-shirt of his covering her body, was gently snoring on her side of the bed. The ringing of the cell phone, however, was still present.

His wife gave a gentle snort. "Ugh, answer the phone, babe. Sleepy," she murmured in a half-conscious state.

The dream had been a magnificent one, but waking up next to her was just as good.

He reached to the bedside table and grabbed his phone off the charger. He glanced at the screen with one eye, kept the other eye firmly closed, and saw the name "Hampton" flash across the screen.

Goddamn it. If that dumbass is calling me at 6:30 in the fucking morning just to ask how to work the tv or some shit, I'm gonna fucking kill him.

He tapped the answer button, put the phone to his ear, and closed his eyes. "What do you want, Hampton?"

"Wade, they're here attacking the farm."

Wade's eyes opened; an icy ball formed in the pit of his stomach. "What do you mean they're attacking?" he muttered into the phone.

"Them, the-the-the sheriff's department. They killed all our guys and they're trying to kill me now. Help me, Wade. Please, I don't wanna die," Hampton sobbed.

Wade threw back the covers and swung himself onto the floor of their bedroom. "Get your shit together, Hampton," he said.

Annalee stirred and sat up onto one elbow and looked at Wade as he started to walk towards the door of their bedroom.

"What's wrong, babe? Everything okay?" she asked, her mind still foggy.

"Hang on," he told Hampton before he lowered the phone to his chest and walked to her side of the bed.

"Everything's fine, Peaches. Hampton just needs help figuring out how to check Miss Vickie's engine before he takes her out fishing today. I'm gonna go talk to him in my study so I don't wake you."

"Okay, but come back to bed quick. It's awful cold in here without you," she replied with a sleepy smile and a kiss.

"You can count on it."

He kissed his wife once more before he headed to his study. Once he was inside of the room, filled with mementos from his trips to Bolivia, Romania, and Bangladesh, he brought the phone back to his ear.

"Have you got your shit together yet?" he asked.

"I'm trying to Wade. I really am. They're all dead," Hampton replied.

"Where are you now, Hampton?"

"I'm in the office. I got in here and locked the door before they could kill me too. I watched them kill Leon Ross, Wade. Blew the top of his head off right there next to the sofa."

"I know you're scared, but I need you to get a fucking grip." The icy ball had grown from the size of a marble to that of a softball. He glanced at the clock on the wall of his study. 6:27.

"Alright, you're in the office. That door is made of steel, and there ain't no way that they can kick that shit in. How many did you see?"

"It all happened so fast, I just don't know I-"

"Think. How many did you see?"

There was a pause on Hampton's end of the line. Wade couldn't help but picture the dumbass counting on his fingers.

"Four."

"Four? You're sure?"

"Yeah, I only saw four."

The icy ball was growing in size again as the fire began to burn in Wade's chest. For once, Hampton hadn't been the one to completely fuck everything up, and it pissed him off that Jimmy had.

"Okay, Hampton. Sit tight in there. They can't break that door down. Shift change is coming up in forty-five minutes. You'll be fine. I'm gonna make some calls. Just relax. I'll call you right back, okay?"

"Don't leave me here to die, Wade. Please. I know that we don't see eye-to-eye, but I'm your fucking brother. Please," Hampton said.

"I'm not going to leave you there, you dumb fuck. I'm gonna make some calls to get you some help. Now let me go and make them, okay?"

"Okay, Wade. Please call me right back."

Wade ended the call without another word. A forest fire of rage had built up in his chest as he made his first call. His instructions were short and understood immediately. He ended that call and scrolled through his contacts to find Jimmy's number.

I'm gonna rip him a new asshole for this. Last time I trust him to do a goddamn thing, that's for sure.

With each passing ring, his rage grew closer to being unleashed.

"You've reached the voicemail of Jimmy Spates. I am unable to get to the phone at this time, but if you would leave your name, number, and a brief message after the tone, I will get back to you as soon as possible. BEEP!" said Jimmy's voice on the mailbox.

Wade exploded.

"Answer your goddamn phone, Jimmy! Your little plan to kill Myers didn't fucking work because he is up at the farm right now. You better pray to God that he doesn't survive this, and even if he does, there's no telling whether or not Dad will cut your fucking throat and sink you thirty miles out. You fucking get what I'm saying, you asshole? You fucked us all over." He ended the call and immediately redialed the number.

The phone went to voicemail again. He dialed a third time and once again he got the voicemail. Each time he tried to call Jimmy, the heat of his fury subsided and the icy ball of anxiety grew within his gut. By the eighth time he was directed to Jimmy's voicemail, the icy softball had grown to the size of a beach ball. There were only a couple of reasons that his brother wasn't answering his phone, and neither were good for him.

He looked around the room. The picture he had taken of his family at Disney World last year sat in a frame on his desk. He could recall how happy that day had been. He looked at a picture of him and his wife dressed to the nines at a fundraiser for his dad's reelection campaign five years ago. That was the night that Caroline had been conceived. All around him memories and reminders of all that he held dear called out to him. They reminded him of what had been and what, as of a few moments ago, was his perfect life. The clarity of what he needed to do chilled him to the bone. His eyes filled with tears as he tapped away on the keyboard of his desktop.

In ten minutes, he reentered his bedroom to find his wife still sleeping. He dressed quickly, punched in the code on a wall safe inside of their walk-in closet, and grabbed what he needed before he walked to his wife's side of the bed. He gently caressed her cheek and, memorized the contours of it; the smoothness and warmth. Her eyes opened and a smile crossed her face.

"You get Hampton all figured out?" she asked through a stretch.

"Sort of. Got another call while I was in there. Gotta go to work, Peaches."

She kissed him and he savored every second of it.

"Don't work too hard, Cowboy."

"Never do," he replied as he walked out of the bedroom.

CHAPTER 41

"That door ain't moving, so you might as well put aside any notion that you're gonna kick that shit in. Sumbitch is steel," Bloodhound said as he examined the door closely.

"I've got some det cord left," Cub said.

He unslung his pack and began to rummage through it and eventually produced a segment of explosive detonation cord two yards long.

"Blow that shit down," Ray replied.

Cub measured out a couple of feet and began to arrange a short coil around the door handle while Mountain began to stick the cord along the top and bottom edges of the doorway. In less than a minute, both men had their sections of det cord primed for demolition, and all four of them stacked up around the corner of the office, careful not to step in the lake of blood that had spread out across the wooden floor. Ray closed his eyes, covered his ears, and opened his mouth wide to stop the pressure of the blast from rupturing his eardrums.

"Fire in the hole," Cub nonchalantly announced before pressing the trigger on the detonator.

The wooden floor vibrated and the air filled with a resounding THUNK. The four men moved forward, passed the door that swung, smoking on its hinges, and filed into the office.

"Get down, get on the fucking floor. Hands where we can see them," instructed Mountain, going back to his days of kicking doors in Kandahar.

Hampton Spates lay on the floor, dazed from the concussion of the blast in such a confined space. He clutched his ears with both of his hands as he slowly rolled from side to side, moaning intermittently as he did so. Mountain placed one tree stump of a knee on Hampton's back and pulled his arms away from his ears with the ease of extending the wing of a chicken before zip-cuffing his hands securely behind his back. He stood up when finished and looked at Ray as he retrieved a notecard from a pouch on his ballistics vest.

"Wait till he's a little more on the lucid-side. Then you can mirandize him, Deputy Clarke," Ray said.

Mountain beamed at the prospect of doing the work of a law enforcement officer. "Badass," he replied.

Ray and the others searched the office. It was furnished with similar leather chairs as those outside, including a luxurious high-backed office chair behind a solid oak desk. Trophy mounts of ducks, geese, and a red-tailed hawk adorned the walls and the desk. Other than a few papers on the desk, a collection of invoices for construction supplies, the office was clean.

"Me and Mountain'll go clear the rooms on the hallway if that's good with you, Hootie," Cub asked.

"Fine with me. Let us know if you find anything, though," Ray replied as the two men bounded out of the office and disappeared around the corner.

"Got something here, Hootie," Bloodhound said.

Ray looked at the door to a large walk-in safe that was concealed behind a walnut bookcase, mounted conveniently on a concealed sliding rail, that Bloodhound rolled to the side. The door was painted dark black to conceal the silvery steel that it was constructed from, and rather than the cliche combination lock knob that appeared so often in movies, this one had a digital keypad mounted above the latch handle.

Ray removed a scrap of paper from a pouch on the chest of his ballistics vest and stepped towards the safe. All that Jimmy Spates had told them had been true up to this critical point, and Ray silently prayed for a continued run of success. He reached out and pressed the numbers 9-5-3-4-7-1 into the keypad.

The safe whirred to life with a satisfying CLUNK. Ray reached for the latch and turned it into the open position. The latch gave a metallic CLINK and the massive door swung open.

Ray and Bloodhound stepped into the safe, which was as large as a bank vault, and noticed that the walls were lined floor to ceiling with leather-bound ledgers. Ray started on the right and Bloodhound on the left, and pulled ledgers down and flipped through the pages. Ray pulled the one closest to the doorway and opened it to the page with the most recent entries. The entries were organized by date, name of client, service provided, and the signature of the proprietor and their representatives.

The entry at the top of the page was from over the weekend. Congressman Brian Sparrow of Colorado had purchased two young men, one for the purposes of sex and the other for the purpose of butchering and eating. In the next section were two pictures, clearly taken from a small hidden camera, that showed Sparrow in the act of raping a young man tied to a post, and the other showed him in the process of butchering another young man like the pigs Ray helped his dad butcher his whole life.

Ray had to concentrate on preventing his protein bar breakfast from coming back up as he kept reading. He scanned to the section furthest to the margin, the signature line, and read the words "Wade L. Spates on behalf of Thurmond J. Spates."

"Dude, this one I've got is hard to read. The cursive is

faded, but it says March 12, 1729. A guy named Percival Burgess bought fifteen male Angolan slaves, three female Yoruba house slaves, and two Yoruba female comfort slaves. Signed, Captain Marcus O. Spates, Royal African Company. These people have been doing shit like this since way back when," Bloodhound said.

Ray looked around the vault at the hundreds of leather-bound ledgers. "Looks to me like they never skipped a beat. Mine's about a congressman from Colorado buying two young men to rape one and to eat one."

"You're fucking kidding me."

"No, wish I was. It's written here along with this one-"

Ray stopped in the middle of his sentence as he read the most recent entry in the ledger he held. The next name shook him deeper than it probably should have. It had to be a mistake. He had known the man all his life. He used to hang out with Ray's dad for God's sake.

"Hey, Hootie," Cub called out from the office. "Got some stuff you probably oughta know about."

He replaced the ledger, walked out of the vault and into the office. Hampton Spates was seated in a leather chair opposite the desk, his face downcast as he gently sobbed. Sitting beside him was the shirtless avian form of Dr. Leonard Poston.

"We found the old man in the one marked 'Punishment Room,'" Cub explained. "He was in the middle of- Well, he was....." Cub stammered.

Ray's eyes blazed at the man that he had known his entire life. Dr. Poston couldn't bring himself to look past the floor.

"He was in there with a teenage boy," Ray finished what Cub was trying to say.

Cub nodded. "Yeah, how'd you know?"

"'Cause it was recorded in a ledger from that vault."

Ray's eyes smoldered with hate. "Where is the boy now? Is he okay?"

Cub nodded again. "Mountain helped him down the hall to the shower room. He's in there with him now. Kid's hurt pretty bad. And there are others."

"How many?" Ray asked, his fury growing by the minute as he looked at the two zip-cuffed men seated before them.

"We found seventeen. There is another wing to this place with little holding rooms, kinda like bedrooms for them to sleep. It's bad, Hootie."

It took everything in him to subdue the animalistic desire to kill. He wanted to snatch up Dr. Poston and beat him to death on the floor of this office. He wanted to literally nail him to the wall and make Hampton Spates watch as he slowly cut him apart. The urge to kill was momentarily insatiable, and he lunged towards the old man.

Bloodhound reached out and grabbed hold of him and held him back long enough for Cub to pull the now terrified old man out of Ray's reach.

"It ain't worth it, dude. You know it, and I know it. Put him away and let him be somebody else's bitch and see how he likes it. That'd be a whole lot worse than anything you've got in your head to do right now. Guarantee it," Bloodhound said as Ray forced himself to settle down.

"We got a bigger problem than that, Hootie. This other guy said he managed to call his other brother and they're gonna be sending all that they got at us in twenty minutes."

CHAPTER 42

Noah had walked down King Street so many times he could practically do it in his sleep. The stores, restaurants, bars, and even the tables where the Gullah women wove baskets from sweetgrass and the Gullah boys twisted palmetto fronds into roses; all were so familiar to him that he could draw an accurate map of their placement along the busy thoroughfare. The walks, to be honest, had become rather mundane to him after a few years of living along the busy street. This time was different. This time he was walking hand in hand with Gary, strolling without a care in the world.

"I'm just saying that I'm proud of you, sugar," Gary said to him as they walked past people that Noah knew and worked with along the road.

"For what, Gary? I'm still living in the shadows, you're no longer here, and to top it all off, I just told one of my Citadel brothers, a brother veteran, AND your closest friend that I wouldn't stand up and defend him because it would mean stepping into the light. What could you ever be proud of me for?" Noah replied.

Gary stopped abruptly. The shade of a palmetto tree gave Noah some relief from the sun. Gary gently pulled his hand so that Noah faced him.

"But you didn't do any of that, Nora. You stood up and did what was right. That took guts, sugar, and I couldn't be prouder of you for it."

"What are you talking about, Gary?"

Gary pointed at the store window behind Noah. "Just look."

Noah allowed Gary to turn him around. What he saw in the reflection confused him. Looking back at him in the Nieman-Marcus window was Nora's reflection; her honey-blonde hair cascading in waves over a black and white snakeskin bodysuit and matching high-waisted black denim pants. She looked down at her hands to see perfectly manicured white stiletto nails that matched her white pumps. She looked back at the reflection then back to Gary.

"I did?"

"You did, sugar. I always knew you were tough enough to do what was right."

Noah woke from a fitful night's sleep in a cold sweat. For a moment he thought that what he had seen was real and that Gary and he were spending a lovely day together walking down King Street, window shopping as they went. Now, in a dark bedroom, alone, he realized that it was just a dream. He tried not to, but he cried once the reality of Gary's death settled in anew. He managed to pull himself together. Gary wouldn't have wanted him to cry a single tear more than the million he had cried for him over the past thirty-six hours. He checked his phone to see what time it was. The phone read 3:23 am.

Noah gave himself a little more time to settle down before he pulled the covers up and tried to sneak in a couple more hours of sleep before his morning workout routine and then work. He tossed and turned for what felt like hours.

I always knew you were tough enough to do what was right echoed in his mind every time he closed his eyes. His frustration and heartbreak combined into an emotional fury that Noah had never experienced as the words incessantly pummeled him.

He sat up in bed and cried out to the ceiling. "What am I supposed to do? I don't know what to do."

The sobs and the tears came back anew as he clutched his knees to his chest and fell onto his side as he wept. How was he supposed to carry on? How would he have the strength? How would he stop the fear that kept him prisoner?

The answer to all of his questions glided into his mind, and in an instant his heart felt as tranquil as the surface of a pond. He wiped his eyes, got out of bed, and walked into the bathroom. He started the shower as he washed his face with cold water until he thought he looked somewhat human. He stepped into the shower, took care to wash himself with all of the fragrant soaps and shampoos that he only used on occasion, and painstakingly shaved every inch of his body.

Once toweled off and moisturized, he pulled on a soft robe and padded down the hallway to what he called "Nora's room." He stepped onto the tastefully elegant rug in the center of the room and felt a new determination burn in his belly. He opened up Nora's closet and took care to select the perfect ensemble for what he was about to do.

After all, first impressions were most important of all when it came to introducing yourself. He emerged from the walk-in closet with the perfect combination and laid them out on the elegant four-poster bed before he turned his attention to the matching vanity across the room.

He took his seat and once again took care to select the perfect shades and construct the perfect look. Satisfied with the look that had been created, he set the makeup before he slipped into the outfit he had painstakingly chosen. He took care when placing the wig on his head to avoid any smudges as he styled the hair until it fit his vision. He selected his pearl earrings and a matching necklace before completing the look by slipping on a pair of blood-red four-inch stiletto pumps.

He took a deep breath before he stepped in front of the floor mirror in between the vanity and the closet. Nora stood in a high-waisted grey and black plaid pencil skirt that hugged her curves and stretched just below her knees. Her black bodysuit with plunging neckline enhanced her womanly attributes well, and the red shoes provided the perfect pop of color that brought the whole outfit together. She grabbed the purse she had picked out and gave herself one last look before grabbing her wallet and keys and drove her BMW M4 coupe north towards I-95.

CHAPTER 43

Caleb Sweeney had been up for an hour, exercised, and fed himself when the call from Wade Spates came in. It had taken him a good fifteen minutes to get all of his guys awake and outfitted with gear before they were anywhere close to being ready to roll. Nevertheless, he had assembled and armed a group of twenty-three men at Oakmoor Hall by 6:50 am. That was a feat he hadn't seen since his days in the army. Despite the frustration of the early call and the inconvenience of it all, he was damn proud of what he had managed to accomplish.

Twenty minutes later, he was riding shotgun in a four-seater UTV headed towards the farm compound at breakneck speed. The situation was a little dicey for Caleb's taste, they only were sure that four men from the Craven County Sheriff's Department had raided the compound and that urgent help was needed in order to eliminate the threat posed by the deputies. It all made Caleb uneasy to be headed into the fray against, as far he was concerned, an unknown number of sheriff's deputies with no idea about their support.

Killing cops didn't bother Caleb. He had killed more than his share over the years. It was just unheard of that he would be called on to kill multiple cops in less than a week that bothered him. Killing Gary McFadden two days prior was easy and quick. This stood to be much more complicated if things went south on them. The extra firepower the extra guys would provide should ensure that Murphy's Law was not proven true that day.

The scenery was becoming familiar and Caleb knew they were less than a minute out from the compound. With any luck, they'd catch the deputies with their pants down, hopefully while they were combing the place for evidence, and they'd all be dead before Caleb and the others had a chance to fully exit the UTVs. The sheer amount of men and firepower was overkill, but Caleb learned in Afghanistan that overkill is a lot better than the alternative.

He chambered a round into his M-4 and prepared himself for battle as the UTV started to round the familiar final curve before the small clearing in front of the farm revealed itself. He heard a metallic snik coming from the front of the UTV and ducked just before a thin metal wire snaked its way up the grille and across the passenger seat of the UTV.

BANG-BANG-BANG-BANG rang out through the pouring rain behind them as the UTV skidded to a halt in the pea gravel in front of the farm. The sounds of falling trees, crashing vehicles, and the screams of the men behind him sent a chill up his spine. He bounded out of the stopped vehicle and sprinted for cover.

Whatever can go wrong will go wrong.

He made it to the tree line just as the chainsaw-like sound of a squad assault weapon, or SAW as he called them in the military, opened up on the swamp where he and the three other men in the UTV with him were taking cover. The swamp behind him came alive with the sounds of three explosions in rapid succession and the sounds of the dying that came afterward.

Caleb was pissed more than he was scared. He should've known that the sheriff would've had a surprise or two in store for him. He should have been more cautious in his approach rather than rolling in hot with guns blazing. Now he was neck deep in a river of shit and under fire with an unknown number of dead or wounded behind him. He needed to get a handle on this situation.

"Somebody bring up the tube," he shouted behind him.

Meanwhile....

The small armory that the farm's security team kept on site proved invaluable. Jimmy had told them the exact location, and he had even given them an accurate account of what sort of equipment was housed within. The assortment of M-4 battle rifles, AK-47s, and one squad assault light machine gun went a long way to evening the odds. The four claymore anti-personnel mines that Jimmy said his brother Hampton insisted on having because they "were useful as hell on Call of Duty" had also been put to good use in the woods surrounding the compound. Mountain's discovery of a chainsaw in one of the pleasure rooms, and Cub's remaining det cord made for a simple but effective tripwire mechanism to wreak a little havoc on the approaching vehicles.

So far, much like with taking down the first security team, everything was going according to plan. Ray remained in cover, behind what had been a towering Tupelo tree before Mountain and Bloodhound brought it down across the narrow clearing in front of the compound. The relentless ripping of the belt-fed SAW light machine gun that Cub was using to spray the tree line filled the damp air and drowned out the sounds of the rainstorm in a storm of metal.

Bloodhound and Mountain, along with Ray, popped up from behind the massive felled tree at various intervals, firing short bursts into the trees from captured M-4s. The men in the UTV that had made it past the tree tripwires scrambled out like the vehicle was filled with hornets and darted into the woods. All except for one guy who was just a step slower than the rest. The SAW had stitched crimson across his chest and damn near cut him in half before he ever got clear of the now smoldering UTV.

They had the attackers on their heels, but the fight was far from over. Ray pressed the call button on his radio. "Cub, time to reposition. Don't need those boys getting a fix on your-"

Just then the treeline emanated the whoosh of a shoulder-fired missile and Ray watched as a streak of white light screeched across the clearing and exploded just below where Cub was tied into a repositioned treestand. The force of the explosion turned the ancient pine and Cub into a hurricane of splinters in less than a second. Ray glanced at the tree, anger boiling inside his chest, and returned to the mission; his friend's death put out of his mind like seeing a car accident during a drive to work.

A fusillade of small arms fire erupted from the tree line. Ray and his friends took cover behind the hulking log. The smack-smack-smack of rounds slamming into the wood and into the front of the compound encouraged him to get as close to the soaked pea gravel as possible. The withering onslaught lasted for a mere ten or fifteen seconds but felt like minutes. Once the sound of small arms fire slackened, Ray and his friends shot up into a kneeling firing stance to return fire. He needed to improve his fighting position if he wanted to make it out of this alive.

It felt like he was hit with three different baseball bats in rapid succession in the middle of his chest and along the right edge of his ballistics vest. The force of the shots robbed his lungs of air and made his right side feel as though he had just tumbled down the rocky side of a mountain. He fought to keep his mind focused on fighting for his life as his lungs made him instinctively fight for air.

Ray aimed his rifle, his chest and right side now completely numb, and dropped the man closest to him in midstride. He gasped and forced himself to snap his vision to a man in hunter's camouflage, bolting to Ray's right in an obvious move to flank the now dazed sheriff. The man fired his weapon blindly at Ray just as he had lined up his shot. Ray took cover behind the log and snapped back into firing position. He found his target for a second time and sent two rounds into the man's chest. One round bored a dark red hole into the man's cheek and a fourth round tore a ragged chunk out of the right side of the man's neck. The wound showered blood like a sprinkler system onto the ground as the attacker collapsed into a heap onto the far end of the log.

Ray turned his attention to Mountain and Bloodhound. He swung his rifle in their direction in time to see Bloodhound take a direct hit from an M-4 rifle, just beyond the edge of his vest, below his right collarbone. Ray dropped the shooter before he could finish the job and rushed to tend to his wounded friend.

Bloodhound was pulling himself back to his knees with his left hand when Ray got to him. The bullet, luckily, missed his clavicle before exiting just beneath his shoulder blade. Bloodhound was still in the fight, but using his right arm in any meaningful way wasn't going to happen.

"You're good," Ray said to his friend.

That's when he noticed it. The pain inside his chest was excruciating. He thought that the shots to the vest had only bruised him, but now as he attempted to lift his right arm, the brilliant shots of pain along his right side confirmed his fear. One or more of his ribs were broken and the agonizing pain inside his chest likely meant that his right lung had been punctured. With each breath, the agony reached new heights, and with each breath, he knew his time was running out.

CHAPTER 44

Jarrod Knight had just gotten to the department, did roll call, and was headed out to his car for another day on patrol. He had received a text message from Sheriff Myers the night before that told him how to get to a location way out in the sticks, close to the Georgetown County line, to pick-up what he described as a "material witness" and take him into custody. He had explained that Jarrod was to write in his report that he had been contacted by the witness, and after hearing his story, decided to take him into custody so that he wouldn't skip town and that he could be protected from any bodily harm. The sheriff had assured him that despite the situation the witness found himself in, he would corroborate that particular chain of events.

Knight wondered what exactly the sheriff meant by describing a material witness as being in a "situation." Whatever it meant, and whatever his boss had done, he was certain that Sheriff Myers had done it for a good reason and that he needed to back him up on it.

Myers was an honorable guy; the kind of leader that Knight had always respected and would have followed into the mouth of hell itself. The kind of leader that always had the best interests of his people and of the public at heart, whatever decision or actions that needed to be taken. He was the kind of leader that Knight knew that the department and the county needed.

Sheriff Killen had been a great man too, but years of maintaining his integrity and being worn down by the likes of Manigault, Elrod, or Chris Mungo had taken a toll on the man. Killen had taken a hard stand against the county machine when he hired James Peay, the first black sheriff's deputy in the history of Craven County. Nowadays, that wasn't particularly courageous; a full third of the department was black. But in 1975, with Robert Magruder being the mayor and Edmund Manigault as the county manager, that was as brave as attacking Omaha Beach alone with nothing but a BB gun.

Knight's dad had told him about how everybody on the southside of the tracks finally felt like they had a say in how the county was run, and he also learned how it had taken a toll on ol' Sheriff Killen. The pressure he must have been under had to have been nearly too much to handle. His brother died in a car accident soon after, and he never seemed to have fully recovered from it. He more or less stayed out of the way of the county government and the city police and kept his head down.

Knight wasn't sure what had happened, but something had broken the man, and he never was quite the same. That's probably why he had pushed Sheriff Myers to run when he retired. He knew he would have the guts to stand up to the machine and that he had the backbone to weather the storm. He was who Sheriff Killen should have been after his stand.

Knight headed out to his cruiser, got himself situated inside the car and pulled out onto Martin Luther King Jr. Boulevard, though he still called it Lee Avenue, and followed his GPS to the location Sheriff Myers had sent him. The drive took him through a half hour of back roads, pine bottomlands, and swamps before it finally led him to a red dirt road back into a thick pine forest. The trees had grown together so thick and tall that they seemed to block out the early morning sun entirely and plunged him back into the darkness of the night.

He followed the dirt road as it snaked back deeper into the forest. At last, the road opened up onto an old shack that was close to being consumed by the jungle surrounding it. Knight got out of the cruiser and took a good look at the dilapidated structure before entering. It was constructed out of rough-hewn clapboards, probably pine if Knight had to guess, a roof covered with rusty sheet metal, and a wooden foundation that rested on ancient timbers that were driven into the ground beneath it. From the looks of the place, Knight guessed that it had probably been there for over a hundred years.

Why the hell would Sheriff Myers have a witness all the way out here?

He ascended the ancient wooden stairs and examined the antique windows with his flashlight. The windows had been painted with what looked like matte-black paint on the inside. The ominous vibe of the place just increased by a factor of ten.

"Sheriff's Department. Anybody in there?" Knight asked through the rickety window.

"I'm in here, deputy," a voice answered from within the building.

Knight removed his sidearm and held it at the ready before he tried the rusty doorknob. He opened the door, shined his light, and pointed his weapon as it swung open. He checked the corners and found nothing. He shined his light into the middle of the single room of the shack and onto the figure seated in a folding chair.

"Lemme see your hands," Knight commanded.

"I would, but I can't. I'm sort of tied up," the smooth voice of the man said.

Knight lowered his light to the restraints and saw that his legs were flex-cuffed and a long zip tie was looped through them and likely connected to the flex cuffs that

CHAPTER 45

Nora pulled her black BMW M4 into a parking space along the street in front of the courthouse. She flipped down the visor and reapplied her dark red lipstick that had smudged on the coffee cup she had gotten from a McDonald's drive-through in Manning. She checked her teeth for any coffee stains, crunched a mint, replaced the tin in her purse, and got out of the car. She looped her right arm through the purse, carried the bag in the crook of her elbow, and checked her outfit one last time to carefully smooth out any wrinkles that had formed during the drive up, checked her wig, and headed towards the steps.

The satisfying click of her heels as she gracefully ascended the time-worn whitewashed steps gave her a boost to her shaky confidence.

Whatever happens, at least I look fierce doing it.

As she stepped onto the top step, the door to the building swung open and was held in place by a pleasantly smiling sheriff's deputy.

"Good morning, ma'am," he said in a thick drawl that reminded her of Gary.

Her heart was racing. What if he was able to clock her by her voice? It was more feminine than most, but it still would be lower than most women's voices. What would he do if he figured out that she wasn't all that she seemed?

Maybe this was all a bad idea.

"I always knew that you were tough enough to do what's right," echoed in her head.

The confidence that pushed her to get out of bed, put herself together, and drive all the way up here surged anew. She stood straighter and offered a polite smile.

"Good morning to you too," she replied.

"I'm trying my best to make it good, that's for sure," he replied.

Her confidence boosted even further. Her breathy voice had checked out.

"Well, I hope it works out for you," she replied.

"I appreciate that, ma'am. Would you mind setting your purse on the conveyor and stepping through the metal detector for me?"

"No problem, deputy," she replied as she set her bag down and stepped through the scanner. The deputy looked at the screen showing an x-ray of her purse as it passed through a large machine.

"You don't have anything I should know about in here, do you? Knives, grenades, your phone number or Insta page? Anything like that?" he asked with an impish grin.

This guy is flirting with me like it's nothing. Her confidence got another huge boost.

"I'm afraid not," she said as she picked up her bag and replaced the handles in the crook of her elbow.

"My boyfriend might not like it if some other guy started blowing up my phone with texts and likes. Have a great day," she replied with a pleasant smile.

The deputy, clearly dejected but still held out hope, smiled wider. "You too, ma'am."

Nora turned and sashayed across the old wooden floor of the courthouse foyer and to a door on the left with the words "County Council" stenciled across the frosted glass. She opened the door and continued walking down a narrow hallway lined with doors with names stenciled on the frosted glass. She sauntered on until she found the door that read "Councilwoman Liv Kirby."

With another breath to settle the butterflies in her stomach, she opened the door to a small waiting area. There was a leather sofa and two leather chairs arranged around a coffee table stacked with everything from Vogue to Field and Stream. A few feet in front of the small waiting area was a wooden desk topped with a computer monitor and two stacks of neatly organized papers. An older woman with a bottle blonde pixie cut, kind eyes, and a love of beaded necklaces with a tassel on the end, looked up at Nora and smiled.

"Good morning and welcome to Councilwoman Kirby's office. How can I help you today, young lady?"

Nora felt a flutter of endorphins at being referred to as a lady. "Good morning to you too. I'm here to speak with the councilwoman, please."

"Do you have an appointment, dear?"

"No ma'am, but it's very important that I speak to her," Nora paused. "It's about Gary McFadden."

The secretary's eyes got serious in the blink of an eye. "I'll let her know that you're here, Miss?"

"Thompson. Thank you."

Nora continued standing as the secretary stood up, softly knocked on the door behind her, and entered the office. Nora could hear the hushed tones of the women speaking but couldn't quite make out the words. A few seconds later, the secretary popped out of the office and smiled pleasantly. "Go on in, dear."

"Thank you so much."

Nora stepped into a small office decorated with family pictures and two framed degrees from the University of South Carolina. The office had a window with a view of the small garden beside the courthouse, and Nora could see the purple irises in full bloom beneath the live oak. A middle-aged woman with a smart business suit, a figure that she was working hard to maintain, and a classy asymmetrical bob stood and offered Nora a hand. "I'm Liv Kirby. Nice to meet you, Miss?"

"Thompson, for now. I appreciate you seeing me on such short notice."

"It's no problem at all. Please, have a seat."

Nora sat down in the leather chair opposite the desk and crossed her legs at the knee. Liv took her seat. "So, what can I do for you, Miss Thompson?"

"Well, to tell you the truth, it's kinda hard to say. Um..." Nora trailed off for a moment.

"If I may," Liv began with a thin empathetic smile. "Why don't I start by asking you a question or two and then we can see where it goes from there? That be okay?"

Nora nodded. "That'd be just fine, Councilwoman Kirby."

"Please, call me Liv. I love your shoes, by the way."

"Oh, thanks. You're sweet, got 'em from a little boutique in Savanna,." Nora replied, giving her blood-red pumps a glance.

"They're four-inch stilettos?" Liv asked.

"Mmhm. I can't say no to a cute high heel."

"I'm the same way. But these days I only wear them when it's date night. Too much walking around here for anything that high."

Nora chuckled at Liv. Strangely, the small talk about shoes was reassuring for Nora. It was nice she had something in common with this woman. It almost made telling her about herself easier. Almost.

"What about you? Do you wear those on date nights too?" Liv asked.

"I did a couple of times, whenever Gary and I would go-" Nora stopped short, fighting to keep the tears from ruining her makeup; fighting to be strong.

Liv grabbed a few tissues from a box on her desk and handed them to Nora.

"Thank you," Nora said as she dabbed her tear ducts before her mascara could be ruined.

"I'm so sorry about Gary. He was a fine deputy. I know

that it has to be terrible for you."

"Thank you. It's been hard."

"I know it has, honey. I wish that I could say something that would make it easier, but I'm afraid that all I can do is make it worse," Liv said.

"I already know about what happened to him, and what people are thinking about him," Nora replied.

Liv looked both confused and flustered for a moment. "I'm sorry that you had to find out about Gary's. . .. activities. Believe me, I don't understand what would make him be uh. . . unfaithful to such a beautiful woman as you like he was with a. . . um."

"With a man," Nora replied; the strength in her voice rising.

Liv now looked uncomfortable. "Yes, uh, with a man."

The moment she had been dreading for as long as she could remember was now here. She didn't know if she could go through with it.

"Gary wasn't cheating on me. He would never have done that."

"I know that it's hard to believe, honey, but we have irrefutable evidence that he was."

Nora grabbed her wallet from her purse. She smiled because she hadn't taken the time to transfer her credit cards and driver's license from her "Noah" bifold wallet and into one of "Nora's" wallets. She had just grabbed it and went out the door. She pulled out her driver's license and held it to where only she could see the picture and the information.

"I'm proof that he never cheated on me," Nora said before handing the driver's license to Liv.

Liv took the card and studied it closely. Her eyebrows pinched together in confusion. She looked up at Nora with new eyes. The confusion had given way to new understanding.

"So, this is your driver's license, correct?"

"Mmhm."

"I'm so sorry. I had no idea that you and he were. . . well I mean that you were, uh. . .."

"Feminine. To be honest, I am still figuring that out for myself."

Liv nodded her head before the look of confusion returned. "Why did you come to me with this, though? You probably know about our history."

Nora dabbed her eyes again, careful not to smudge her mascara. "Do I look like a racoon from these tears right now?" she asked Liv.

Liv laughed at the question. "No, you look just as fabulous as you did when you walked in here."

"Thanks. The reason I came to you is because Gary always spoke highly of you. He said that of all the elected officials in this county, you were the only one that he could trust and who he knew to be honest."

Nora smiled a compassionate smile. "It didn't matter to him that his marriage to your sister didn't work out. He always thought you were great, so who else could I come to?"

Tears began running down Liv's face and it was Nora's turn to give her some tissues.

"Don't worry, you don't look like a racoon either," Nora said.

Liv laughed, and the ice was momentarily shattered. "He really said that I was the only elected official in the county that he trusted? That he knew was honest?"

"Mmhm. You and Raleigh Myers. That was it. And he had no idea about me until the day before yesterday," Nora replied.

Liv's eyes widened and her jaw went slack for a moment.

"Oh my God. This changes everything. You change everything. The suicide note; he couldn't have written it. That means that somebody killed him, and it also means that Sheriff Myers is innocent."

CHAPTER 46

"What's wrong, Hootie?" Bloodhound asked as bullets whizzed past them on all sides.

"My... chest. Every time I. ... breathe it. ... Oh God!" Ray replied.

He screamed as the pain in his chest became unbearable. He tried desperately not to breathe but the pain was so great that delirium was beginning to set in. Bloodhound knelt, rested his rifle on the log, and sent four rounds through the chest cavity of the last shooter that was sent to rush them.

"Mountain! Look in Cub's pack. Hootie needs the med-kit now or he ain't gonna make it," Bloodhound shouted.

Ray gasped for air and moaned as the waves of agony drowned him. He could feel himself becoming light-headed and see the blackness at the edge of his vision as he watched Mountain grab hold of him and drag him into the compound, which was their Alamo if things went south. The blackness kept moving closer to the center of his vision.

Scenes from his life began flashing in his mind. He

hoped that he wasn't all bad in life. He hoped that the people that he loved knew that he loved them. He hoped they knew that he didn't do what he was being accused of doing, and hoped they knew that he was better than that at least. Most of all, though, he wished that he could've seen what would become of him and Erin. They could've been something great.

Now, all he could think about was how the pain wasn't as excruciating as before. All he could think about was letting go and slipping into that cold black lake that he felt like he was floating in. All he had to do was just let go. Everything would be over, and he'd get to see what happens after death. He was ready to meet his maker. He was ready for a little rest.

CHAPTER 47

The flight from Florence regional airport to Char-
lotte-Douglas International was just over an hour in
length. Plenty of time for Wade to arrange all of the necessary wire transfers to his own private Swiss bank account
and mask the crippling shame of cutting his tail and running. By the time he made it to Charlotte, he was good and
buzzed.

He hadn't abandoned Hampton. Not technically, anyway. He did call Caleb Sweeney, the one guy that Jimmy
employed who always seemed to come through, and tell
him to gather as many men as he could and to hit the farm
with all that he had. He had even called Hampton back,
after his failed calls to Jimmy, to tell him that everything
was going to be okay, and he had almost believed it himself. Then, he heard the explosion on the other end of the
line.

Even then, he had a sliver of hope that things might
work out. Then he remembered how angry he had been at

Jimmy for being so fucking stupid in hiring Lamar Williams and his group of gangbangers to take out Ray Myers.

Wade had recommended they use someone that they could trust; someone that they knew wouldn't get sloppy. But Jimmy assured him that his sources said those guys were good. That they were professionals. Then they botched the job and Wade decided to take his rage out on Jimmy. In detail, from his phone, mentioning his father's name, violent tendencies, and involvement in the enterprise, all on a wireless carrier's voicemail box.

Now he had no choice. He had to run, and he had to run now. If his family's enterprise was going down, he wasn't going to go down with them. He was going to make sure that he got away clean. He was going to make sure that he went somewhere they couldn't find him; somewhere they would never expect him to flee. He hoped against hope that his plan would come off without a hitch because the grim reality was unthinkable if it didn't. Life inside a federal prison was bad enough, but if his father managed to make all of this go away, like he had done with so many things in the past, he would certainly make sure that Wade died in a tragic accident. That scared him the most.

He made it to the ticket counter, picked up his tickets, and showed them his passport to verify that everything was in order. He didn't particularly like the name Greg Vincent, but the passport and other IDs he paid for under that name were the closest to legit that a fake set of documentation could get. The best part was that nobody but him knew that Greg Vincent existed, nor did they know that Mr. Vincent had squared away north of $350 million into an account only he could access. All he had to do now was get where he was going and lay low for a few weeks in the best hotel that money could buy.

He passed through security without a problem, boarded the flight, and took his seat in first class with nothing but the clothes on his back. He ordered four fingers of Maker's Mark neat and sat in the seat. He sipped on the amber liquid and willed himself to relax as the plane pushed back from the gate and began its taxi to the runway. He tried his hardest not to, but he couldn't stop images of his little girls from flashing in his mind.

They'd be alright. He'd wait for a couple of months and then he'd get word to them that he found a way for them to be together. That was just a lie, however, that he had told himself to keep from losing his nerve.

The feds and his father would be watching his family like hawks to see what moves that they made. If they just up and went to the airport to fly off for an international vacation, the US government and possibly his father would escort him back to the states in leg irons, or they would toss him out the door of a perfectly good airplane somewhere over the Gulf of Mexico.

He would never see his family again and that, to tell the truth, was the most awful part of it all. He sipped the whiskey and began to sob in his cubicle as the plane began to accelerate for takeoff.

His mind drifted to the last moments he spent with his wife, lounging in bed, before his world forever changed. The last thing that he had said to Annalee was "Never do." He didn't even tell his wife that he loved her more than anything before he left her forever.

Wade downed the whiskey and ordered another. He wanted to get drunk and forget all that had happened. He wanted to forget all the pain. Lucky for him, it was a long flight to Mexico City, and an even longer flight from there to his final destination.

CHAPTER 48

Bloodhound returned fire with his good arm and kicked the door to the compound shut behind him. He hobbled over to where Mountain had laid Ray on the floor. He had taken some shrapnel in his left leg from a bullet that shattered against the log rather than embedded itself inside, and the pain was just now starting to register in his mind.

"Where's the kit?" he asked Mountain.

The colossus of a man handed him a plastic box before he rested on his own haunches. Bloodhound looked him over and saw multiple grazes on his arms, plus what looked like a direct hit in his left forearm.

"You good, Mount? Can't have you falling out on me. No way I'd be able to pick your big ass up," Bloodhound said as he searched through the plastic box.

"I'm fine. Just help Hootie, then look after yourself, man," Mountain said. He sounded like he had just run a marathon, and Bloodhound was more than a little concerned that blood loss was going to take him out of the fight.

He looked down at Ray and saw that he had stopped writhing and moving all that much. He could see his eyes fluttering and knew he had seconds to find what he needed and to act. He frantically searched the kit while he held the box with his near-disabled right hand and fumbled with his left hand.

"Where is it, goddamn it? I know I put that shit in here. Hell, Cub made sure I did 'fore we left," Bloodhound said.

A jolt of pain shot down his right arm and the box tumbled to the wooden floor below. "Shit! No-no-no!" he screamed.

He ran his good hand through the pile and discarded unneeded items left and right as he went. Ray was nearly still. Time was almost up. He looked through the pile, tossed aside a stack of gauze, and there it was. A metal tube, about the width of a drinking straw, with a release valve on one end and the other end sharpened to a point with laser precision.

"Yes, I got it! Mount, I need you to lift his right arm up, like he's resting his forearm on top of his head. Quick, time's-a-wastin'," Bloodhound instructed.

Mountain pulled himself out of his groggy stupor and did as instructed. Bloodhound felt along Ray's right side for the correct spot.

"Shit, he's got about three of these sumbitches broke. I'm gonna have to guesstimate it."

He grabbed the metal tube with his left hand, felt for where the rib in the center of his underarm should be, and stabbed the metal tube into his chest with a sickening crunch. He pushed the tube in further, careful not to push it too deep, and then turned the valve into the release position. A jet of air shot out of the tube with a high-pitched whistle.

Ray's eyes bolted open and he screamed in pain. He drew in a breath and was back in the land of the living once more.

"What the fuck was that?" Ray shouted.

"That was me turning you into a human Capri Sun. And you're welcome, asshole." Bloodhound smiled widely.

Ray returned the smile as shots rang out from behind them. Mountain's right shoulder took a direct hit, snapped his collarbone, and blew out a wound the size of a golf ball on the way through. Bloodhound slipped his Walther from his leg holster and fired five 9mm rounds into a man coming from the left side of the hallway. They each streaked through the man's chest and sprayed the floor, now sticky with old blood, with a fresh coat before Bloodhound too took a round to the left hip and toppled backward.

Adrenaline flooded Ray's battered brain and he rolled onto his side; the chemicals dulled the pain that hit his cortex like a bolt of lightning. He struggled to his knees, pulled his own sidearm, and aimed it at the lone attacker rushing his direction. The attacker, his weapon pointed at the center of Ray's bare chest, squeezed the trigger on his rifle. Ray braced for what was sure to be the last thing he ever felt: a bullet tearing through his heart, only to hear the sweet click of an empty magazine.

Ray raised his pistol and aimed for the kill shot, only for the man to close the distance, put his shoulder into Ray's chest, and drive him into the floor. The wind that was in Ray's good lung was forced out all at once, and he gasped for life-giving air as the attacker held the wrist of his gun hand in an iron grip and pummelled his left side with punch after punishing punch.

Ray launched a barrage of strikes to the man's solar plexus with his left arm and struck him hard in the groin with his right knee. The man wailed in a pain-crazed rage and slammed Ray's gun hand so hard against the floor that he lost his grip and the weapon skittered across the floor.

Ray fought for his life. His ribs screeched pain as he slapped the attacker's ears with both hands. He repeated the attack twice to no avail. The man simply grabbed hold of the pressure valve protruding from Ray's chest and stabbed it further into his chest.

Ray howled as the sharpened metal tube slid deeper and deeper into his flesh. The man capitalized on the opening and wrapped both of his hands securely around Ray's throat. He squeezed with all his might. Ray felt the pressure building in his skull and his eyes beginning to bulge. He struggled for breath but his airway was firmly choked off. Desperation set in and miraculously he remembered where it was. He reached his right hand to his leg and felt for it. His fingertips touched the handle but they couldn't reach the grip.

"How's that feel motherfucker?" the man taunted.

Ray reached again, no grip, world going darker.

"I'm gonna kill you, just like your friend McFadden. I want you to know that before the lights go out."

The rage that Ray had worked so hard to control exploded from within. He reached with all of his might and gripped the handle. He pulled the knife free of its scabbard, and with the last of his strength, he plunged it between Sweeney's ribs. Ray grunted as he thrusted the six-inch blade to the hilt, angling it up as it sliced through veins, arteries, and the heart itself. With a last gasp of strength, he gripped the handle under-handedly, and pulled the blade downward and sliced the flesh and tissue in between the man's ribs and opened a horrific gash from his back around to his side.

A look of pain crossed the man's snarling face, then a look of desperate confusion. Warm blood cascaded onto Ray's side and filled the room with the scent of cordite and copper. His grip on Ray's throat softened and he collapsed, slipped off of his chest, and onto the floor beside Ray. Ray stared into Sweeney's eyes, drinking in every ounce of terror held in them, until the lights went out completely.

Ray rolled onto his back and stared, exhausted at the ceiling. The farm was oddly peaceful. No sounds except for the spinning of the ceiling fan. For once, Ray felt at peace. He gasped for air, and coughed up something wet and warm. He wiped his mouth with his left hand and saw it had been smeared red.

It was a hell of a note. After all that he had been through, all that had been sacrificed, he was going to die right here on the floor of this butcher's shop. If that's what it took for the people here to go free, then he would gladly take it. At least his death would mean something.

The whirring of the ceiling fan seemed to get even louder, buffeting in a loud CHOP-CHOP-CHOP noise that seemed odd to Ray's tired mind. He was just so tired. As the fan got even louder, he decided it was his cue to finally get some rest. He took a gasping breath, closed his eyes, and let the eternal sleep embrace him.

Chapter 49

The call came in just after 6:45 that morning that deputies from the Craven County Sheriff's Department had uncovered a major center for human trafficking that involved severe local governmental corruption. The additional information that the deputies were going to be under imminent attack from multiple armed individuals by 7:20 meant that the combined forces of the South Carolina Law Enforcement Department, or SLED as it was commonly called, and the South Carolina Highway Patrol, had less than an hour to be suited up and in the air to provide support.

Major Kent Strom of the highway patrol, and Chief Ron Hastings of SLED had also been deployed to Queen's Bridge and the joint command post of the two state law enforcement agencies at the county courthouse.

The reports that kept pouring in from the site, an area referred to as "the farm," deep within the vast swamps of the Francis Marion National Forest, were an ever increasing nightmare of human depravity. Chief Hastings had been in law enforcement for over twenty-five years, and the images and information that was relayed back to him by agents and troopers of both agencies' tactical units on the ground were enough to shake his own calloused perception of what human beings were capable of to the core.

So far, seventeen individuals, ranging in age from nine to sixty-eight, male and female, had been rescued from the compound, and mountains of evidence of rape, torture, and murder had been recovered. The ledgers, found inside of what could only be described as a vault, provided exhaustive documentary evidence of crimes that implicated a shocking number of people of varying fame and power. This was certain to be the case of his career, if not the defining case of South Carolina law enforcement.

After the first wave of reports started trickling in over an hour ago, Hastings looked at Major Strom and said, "We better get comfortable here. We're gonna be here for a few months at least."

Chief Hastings, Major Strom, Councilwoman Liv Kirby, and acting sheriff/coroner Lavion McCutcheon had just ended a video conference with Governor Michelle Adams, who they kept abreast of the situation, when the doors to the small conference room flew open. Reginald Manigault, the county manager, strode into the room, followed closely by Mayor Elrod Tisdale, and police Chief Chris Mungo.

Manigault, dressed smartly in a tailored navy and white plaid suit, seethed with a fury that neither Liv nor Lavion had ever seen in all of their dealings with them.

"Pardon the interruption, but I'd like very much for somebody to explain to me and my colleagues why our county has been invaded by militarized forces of the state," Manigault said.

"I'm Chief Ron Hastings of SLED, and this is my colleague Major Kent Strom of the state troopers. Who might you gentlemen be?"

"I'm the county manager. The mayor and the chief of police and I demand some answers as to why law enforcement officers, armed to the teeth, are bushwhacking our woods and commandeering our courthouse. Are you fellas all that's coming, or should we expect the national guard to be called into this outrage next?"

Hastings offered a polite smile. "Don't be silly, Mister?"

"Manigault."

"Mr. Manigault. The national guard has not been activated as of yet, but I just spoke to Governor Adams, and she has assured me that should we require them, they'll be at my disposal within the hour. You've got some serious problems in this county."

"You have no right nor any real authority to do any of this. I demand to speak to the governor myself. Or better yet, I'll go directly to Senator Spates."

"That's certainly your right, Mr. Manigault. But you see, I do have very real authority. I am here at the request of your sheriff, Raleigh Myers."

Manigault scoffed at the name. "A common criminal responsible for the intimidation of one of his own deputies to the point of the poor man committing suicide no more than two days ago. Were you not told that Myers is set to appear at a hearing next week in Columbia, where I am confident that the governor will have him removed from office before he faces charges with regard to the death of Deputy McFadden?

"Or didn't you check into that before you rushed off from Columbia, all gung-ho like some cowboy to come the aid of a man who now will have to answer to the charges of extra-judicial killings to satisfy a personal vendetta, if I'm to understand what your office is reporting occurred at a facility in the woods. I also demand that this man be removed from the premises posthaste."

Manigault pointed at Lavion McCutcheon. "He is little more than a lackey for Myers, and he will do nothing but further the crimes already committed by his master."

Manigault's face twisted into a smirk. Hastings's expression, however, remained unchanged. The confidence in the demeanor of this asshole from Columbia shook Manigault to his core, though he would never show it.

"That's quite an accusation, Mr. Manigault. I'd like to

take the time to address them all, just so we're both on the same page as to how things are going to go from here on in. Mr. McCutcheon, per the laws of our great state, is acting sheriff of the county since Sheriff Myers is fighting for his life at McLamb Regional. He's not going anywhere.

"As for the charge that you just made about so-called extra-judicial action. Sheriff Myers had a search warrant for the property in the swamp, signed and filed by Judge Ronald McKee of the district court in Florence last night. He was well within his rights to legally search the grounds for incriminating evidence. The fact that he met heavy resistance on the part of the suspects, and his subsequent use of lethal force, makes no difference in the eyes of the law. As for the supposed suicide brought on by his actions, I'm gonna let Councilwoman Kirby speak to that."

Manigault cut his eyes at Liv like a knife as she began to speak. "Two days ago, you convened the county council to review evidence that you purported to have been gathered by Chief Mungo of Sheriff Myers's wrongdoing. If you'll recall, the suicide note left by Garrett McFadden contained apologies to his girlfriend for cheating on her with another man, and that this was the main target of the alleged abuse by Raleigh Myers, correct?"

Manigault was uneasy. "That's correct."

"This morning I received a visit from Garrett McFadden's girlfriend." Manigault's stomach twisted into a knot as she continued.

"Lovely young woman. We talked at length for over an hour, until all of this started happening, and she revealed some truly amazing information."

Manigault began to panic. He scrambled mentally for a plausible response that could undermine whatever information that the girl shared with Liv, but he kept coming up blank at every turn.

"It turns out," Liv said, "that she and Gary's supposed 'boyfriend' are one and the same."

Manigault's heart dropped into his shoes, and suddenly he felt weak in the knees.

"She's transgender and has issued a sworn affidavit

outlining not only that Sheriff Myers had no idea of her existence before Monday, but also that she and Gary were in love and had planned to start a life together once the Megan Prince case was resolved. So, you see, Gary McFadden would have never written that note. It simply was not based in reality."

Manigault turned towards the exit. He needed to get as far away from this place as possible. Three state troopers emerged from the hallway and blocked the exit. Manigault felt like he might vomit as he turned back to the people in the room.

"That means," Hastings began, "that not only is Sheriff Myers completely innocent of any alleged wrongdoing, but that you conspired to fabricate evidence that would frame him for a murder of which you are now the prime suspect."

"Mungo gave it to me. I had nothing to do with any of this," Manigault blurted out in desperation.

"That's bullshit. You came to me and told me that Mr. Spates and his sons wanted us to present this to the council so that Myers was out of the way. You're not gonna throw me under the fucking bus here, Reggie," Mungo replied.

"I'd like to make a deal. I'll tell you everything so long as I have immunity. It was all them two and the Spates family who did all this," Elrod pleaded.

"Shut your goddamn nigger mouth, you fat fuck," Manigault screamed as state troopers placed him and his minions in handcuffs before they were hauled off to join Kelvin Matthews in the very jail he so recently oversaw.

CHAPTER 50

Ray's eyes fluttered open, then immediately squinted closed from the trauma of the fluorescent lights. The beep-beep-beep of a heart monitor machine grabbed his attention, followed quickly by the tangles of wires and tubes connected to and injected into his body. He cracked his eyes open and tried to sit up in bed, only for the pain receptors along his torso to light up like a Christmas tree.

A moan escaped his lips, and in seconds he felt the gentle touch of soft hands on his face. He opened his eyes to see Erin's gorgeous face in front of his, her dark hair pulled back into a ponytail, and her emerald eyes glistening with tears.

"Hey there, Sheriff. I've been waiting on you to wake up," Erin said before she planted a series of kisses, pregnant with passion, onto his parched lips.

"How long have I been laying here?" he asked, trying to clear the cobwebs in his mind. "Last thing I remember is laying on the floor of that compound and watching the ceiling fan spin, waiting to die."

"You nearly did," Erin said, as she wiped a tear from her eye with a tissue.

"SLED and the troopers got there a couple of minutes after you had lost consciousness and they evaced you to us."

She pulled her chair closer to his bedside and took his hand in hers. "You got here with four broken ribs on your left side and three on your right. Your left lung was punctured and had collapsed, plus your spleen had ruptured from all the trauma your left side had been through. Dr. Mitra was in surgery with you yesterday from morning until the afternoon. It was pretty touch and go for a while, but Dr. Mitra was pretty confident that you were gonna make it. I was scared out of my mind the whole time."

Ray grinned, and even that seemed to hurt. "If I didn't know any better, Dr. McKee, I'd say that you're kinda fond of me."

"Yeah, I kinda love you, dude." she said and kissed his hand.

For a moment, Ray thought he had imagined her saying that. "Really? Even after all that's happened, all that I... you know, did?"

"Of course. Of course, I feel that way about you, Ray. I'm not gonna lie. I haven't been able to sleep well since, and my heart races whenever it crosses my mind, but it doesn't change anything about the way that I feel about you. Not one bit, babe," Erin said.

"Good, 'cause I'm pretty sure I love you too," Ray said.

"For real? You're not just messing?"

"I'm serious as a heart attack."

Erin leaned in, kissed him, and held tight to his hand as if life itself depended upon it. Ray returned the kiss, as best as his battered body could, and savored every second of the gesture like a fine wine. Some of the last thoughts he had before blacking out had been of her, and he intended to savor every second with her.

The sound of the door to his room opening broke the kiss.

STEPHEN HARRIS

"There he is. Tell ya what, Hootie. I was fixing to get good and pissed if you went on and died on me after all that shit I done to save your ass," Bloodhound said.

Ray glanced in the direction of the door and saw his friend struggling to wheel his wheelchair into the room with his left arm while his right was immobilized in a cast and sling. Erin got up from her chair and helped push him next to Ray's bed.

"I tell ya what, Hootie. This here doctor friend of yours is a keeper. Helping an old hound dog on the mend out. I'd say that's right Christian of you, Doc."

Erin chuckled. "Well, I appreciate such high praise coming from someone as esteemed as you, Bloodhound."

"Well, you ought to, cause I'll have you know that the people of Latin America call me El Perro Loco. That's a pretty high honor; just ask anybody from around those parts and they'll tell ya. But enough of that, it ain't why I come all the way down here from the next room over. I came down here to tell you that I think I'm in love."

Ray laughed. It hurt to laugh too. "You've been in love with every skirt you've come across from Kansas City to Kandahar, dude."

"Now that is a helluva thing for you to say, Hootie. Just 'cause I've loved many women in my time don't mean I can't be in love for real this time, you judgmental sack of shit."

"There's somebody else who might like to see you," Erin said, "so I'll let you boys have a visit while I go get them from the cafeteria."

She walked to the door, and Ray just now saw how beautiful she looked in her leopard print A-line skirt, black top, and matching black heels, white coat draped over the whole ensemble.

She stopped in the doorway and looked over her shoulder at Ray; an impish grin spread across her face.

"Love ya, Sheriff," she said before she walked out of the room and down the hallway.

"Looks like I ain't the only one that's been bitten by the ol' love bug. Keep this shit up and we're gonna have to start calling you Hounddog instead of Hootie," Blood-hound said.

"Whatever you say, dude. Who're you all in love with now?" Ray asked through a painful chuckle.

"Oh yeah, well you see there's this nurse named Rachel; comes in and sees me every night. Always makes sure I've got enough pain meds and gives me that look when she calls me darlin'. You know the one I'm talking about. Well, she ain't exactly said nothing to me more than that, but I can tell man, she's crazy about me. Just a matter of time before I get to introduce her to my little buddy I got down there," Bloodhound said, pointing at his lap with his good hand.

Ray laughed another painful laugh at his friend; the good of seeing him alive outweighing the desire to avoid more pain. "You'll have to let me know how it works out. You making it okay?"

"I ain't never been better, Hootie. Turns out I took one just beneath my collarbone and the sumbitch popped right out my back without hitting anything vital, took a little shrapnel to my right knee, and managed to get another round put through me above my right hip by that asshole you apparently knifed to death while I was on the floor. Ain't nothing worse than I got in the sandbox, that's for damn sure. All-in-all, pretty badass vacation if you ask me," Bloodhound replied.

"Glad you're gonna be fine, dude." Ray hesitated. "What about Mountain and Cub?"

"Well, Mountain took one right in the middle of his left forearm and a couple slipped on past the vest. Damn near got his shoulder blown off too. He'll be alright but he ain't gonna be raising that right arm any higher than his shoulder from now on. Reckon I'm gonna put him in charge of training new hires at the company. That big ol' bastard always did love getting to tell a recruit, in detail, all the ways they were fucking up."

Bloodhound took a deep breath and let it out as a sigh. "Cub, on the other hand, didn't make it."

Ray's heart sank as Bloodhound continued. "One of

the fuckers hit him with an AT-4 anti-tank missile. That's why it blew up so damn big. Troopers said they found him, as much as they could, and your buddy Lavion said he was gonna have him placed in the nicest casket he has before sending him back to his sister in Navisota. Don't reckon ol' Cub woulda give a shit about whether he went home in a casket or a Ziploc bag so long as we put him to rest in Texas dirt, but I sure did appreciate it all the same. And I'm sure his sister will too."

Ray shook his head. Tears welled up from the pain of moving and the pain of losing an old friend like Cub Martinez.

"It's my fault. I shouldn't have-"

"Shut your goddamn mouth before you piss on his sacrifice. He went to meet his maker with a smile on his face knowing that he gave it all to help out a friend he loved. A friend who woulda traded places with him if your roles were reversed. Don't take that away from him, Hootie. Honor him by letting him own it and by remembering him for it."

Ray sniffed back the tears. "You're right, dude. Thanks for keeping my shit straight. Thanks for everything you did for me. I'll never be able to repay you for it."

"Considering all the times you pulled my ass outta the fire overseas, I'd say I'm still behind you in the count twelve to seven."

He smiled and clutched Ray's hand. "It was my honor to fight beside you again, brother. Just like it was for Mountain and Cub."

A knock on the door to the room interrupted the two old friends. The door opened and Erin stepped inside of the room again.

"Reckon I better get on back to my room before Rachel starts to missing me. Tonight's the night I talk her into giving me a sponge bath. Then she ain't gonna be able to say no to my charm. Be good and rest up, Hootie. I'll come and holler at you tomorrow."

Erin walked over to Bloodhound and pushed him towards the door. "I'll make sure Bloodhound gets back to his room while you visit a little while."

As Erin pushed Bloodhound and his wheelchair out into the hallway, he could hear her asking about the nurse named Rachel and telling him that she didn't, as far she knew, have a boyfriend.

Once they were out of the door, a tall woman with honey blonde hair, perfect makeup, white tank top, snakeskin pencil skirt, and matching white stilettos sauntered into the room. For a moment, Ray was confused as to who she was, but the look in her eyes was instantly recognizable.

"Good to see you N-, I mean, Nora," Ray said, stopping himself before saying Noah. She smiled at him politely and timidly stepped to his bedside.

"I know that you've been through a lot, so I won't take up too much of your time."

"And thank you for not taking up my time. As you can see, I've got places to go and people to see," he said in an attempt to comfort her nerves.

"Yeah, I guess you aren't gonna be going anywhere for a bit," she replied with a nervous laugh.

She took the seat that Erin had been sitting in next to Ray's bedside, crossed her legs at the knees, and continued. "I just wanted to let you know that I didn't leave you hanging. I did what I should have done from the start for one of my Citadel brothers. I got dressed and told Liv Kirby my story. She made sure that your name was cleared and that you wouldn't be railroaded for what happened to Gary."

"That must have been pretty tough for you, and I appreciate it more than you know." He paused. "Does that mean that you're…."

"Yeah, it means that I am officially 'out'. It's part of the court record that I'm…well…feminine, I guess," she explained.

"Has it affected your work or anything like that?"

She flashed a thin smile. "Well, I'm told that reporters are camped outside my house in Charleston. Erin's been super sweet and has let me stay with her for a few days. It's been really great having some girl time, go shopping, have a little wine, and figure out what to do next.

"All the networks are talking about the trans woman who helped to blow the lid on what may be the biggest scandal in American history. It's irritating that they say that; they never even asked me about the trans woman stuff. And I don't like it being suggested that I was somehow instrumental in all this. All I did was tell the truth."

"That's more than most people are willing to do."

Nora smiled. "Thanks for saying that. So, yeah, my firm called me and said the media circus surrounding this is publicity they aren't sure that they want. They think that it's best that I move onto better things."

"I'm sorry, Nora. Really. If there's anything I can do, I'll do it."

"You're sweet for offering, but I'm gonna be fine. I've got some money saved up, and who knows. Maybe it's time they get some competition from a new firm, and maybe it's time the state hears a new voice," Nora said.

"So, start a new firm. I think that you'd be awesome. You've got the heart to help people, you've got the know-how, the smarts, and the look. Can't miss," Ray said.

"You think so?"

"I know so. You can do your own thing, Nora. Forge a new path forward."

"Maybe I'll do that. But right now, other than a little retail therapy, all I can think about is going out on the water and chasing some snapper," Nora said.

Ray perked up. "You like deep sea fishing?"

Nora laughed. "I'm a lady that loves all of the more delicate pursuits in life, but I'm also a lady that loves spending a day on the water."

Ray smiled and the two of them talked for so long as they swapped fishing stories and discussed guns and sports until he forgot the pain he was in.

CHAPTER 51

"What do you have to say about your son Hampton be-ing indicted on federal charges for human and child traf-ficking?" shouted the reporter from the newspaper in New York City.

"How involved were in you in the selling of human be-ings?" asked the reporter from the television network in Atlanta.

"Do you have a response to people calling you the 'Butcher of the Senate' rather than the 'Conscience of the Senate?'" hollered the reporter for the podcast and website in Los Angeles.

Thurmond Spates and his security team shoved their way through the throng of reporters who screamed ques-tions on the sidewalk outside of his Federal-style home. Once inside the door, the screams dulled into a low hum of discontent that rumbled like the sea of anxiety deep in the belly of the embattled senator from South Carolina.

Three days after Myers and his men raided the farm,

Thurmond was forced to suspend his nascent campaign for the presidency. He stated that it was time for "fresh faces and fresh ideas to take on the mantle of the presidency," which is the typical bullshit response expected of an old politician about to be put out to pasture. Now, he worried that he wouldn't simply be put out to pasture. He was worried that he was about to be put into the prison system.

His security detail retired to the kitchen as Brynna, his most loyal staffer and most loyal lover, popped out of the parlor to the right of the foyer. The grim expression on her pretty young face a harbinger of yet more bad news to come.

"Hampton is being indicted today in the federal court in Columbia, and Jimmy is said to be one of their star witnesses. They now have video evidence that shows Wade boarding a flight to Mexico City at the Charlotte airport the morning of the raid on the farm. People, both Republicans and Democrats, are calling for you to be expelled from the senate. And now every favor I called in for you hasn't returned my calls, except this one." She handed Thurmond a sticky note with a phone number and the name Frank Trent written above it.

"What do we do now, Ted? I'm freaking out and I'm running out of excuses to give the press," Brynna said.

"Now, now, darlin'. Everything's gonna be right as rain. My boys have gotten themselves mixed up in some bad business. The Mexican cartels are trying to frame me as some kind of a monster; the thanks I got for voting to help immigrants come to America easier. I promise you. Just keep the vultures off of me until things settle down a little more and the truth has a chance to come out and have its day. You trust me don't you, sugar?" Thurmond asked.

Brynna looked at him over the top of her large, stylish tortoiseshell glasses, her blue eyes filled with concern. "I trust you, Ted. I'll do my best."

"Thank you, darlin'." He kissed her. "I'm gonna go into my study and start drafting my statement for the floor of the senate on Friday."

He turned and walked through the sliding oak doors into his oak-paneled office festooned with hunting trophies, awards, and accolades. He took a seat on his plush leather sofa and turned on the television above the fireplace. He paid close attention to the broadcast.

"Federal agents," narrated the voice of the pretty Asian anchor, "raided the home of Colorado Representative Brian Sparrow in Boulder this morning. The embattled congressman has been connected, along with more than two dozen other members of congress, to the 'Black River Butcher Shop' in South Carolina. Sparrow was not in the home, but federal agents were seen leaving with several plastic tubs of evidence including pornographic material depicting deviant and illegal acts, according to an anonymous source close to the investigation. Federal officials now believe that Sparrow has fled the country in much the same way as Wade Spates, one of the sons of alleged 'Black River Butcher,' Senator Thurmond Spates of South Carolina."

Thurmond turned the television off. The roiling sea of anxiety in his belly began to boil. If they had already come for Sparrow, then how much time did he have left? Was it just a matter of time before armed FBI agents broke down his door and carted him off to an inevitable life inside of a federal prison? The very thought frightened him beyond words. He couldn't, no, wouldn't allow that to happen.

He got up and strode to his desk, took a seat in his office chair, and retrieved his secure cell phone from the top drawer of his desk. He tapped in Frank Trent's number and hit send. The ring tone droned twice before the gruff New Yorker answered.

"Did you call from a secure line?" Trent asked.

"Of course I did, Frank. What can you tell me is happening?" Thurmond asked.

Many years prior, he had helped Frank Trent, then just a desk jockey working out of one the NYPD's Bronx precincts, land a job with the FBI that had now blossomed into an important position within the bureau. Now, with all of his other favors refusing to be called in, Frank was his one and only lifeline.

"It's bad news, sir." Trent said. "The DOJ has all the evidence they need to charge you as the criminal mastermind of the 'Black River Butcher Shop.' The FBI is going to serve the arrest and the search warrants at 6:30 tomorrow morning. I'm sorry, sir. There's nothing more I can do."

Thurmond's heart turned to jelly that ran down his spine and onto the floor. "Thank you, Frank."

"Good luck, sir," Frank said before he ended the call.

The realization that in less than twenty-four hours he would be in federal custody, never to set foot outside of a federal correctional facility for the rest of his life, settled onto his heart like a one-hundred-pound bag of concrete.

He sat in his chair, numb to the world around him, lost in the thought of how close they had been to making a better, just world for all. A world where like a benevolent father, he could bestow the bountiful gifts of the federal government onto his American children; ensure that all had access to basic human needs, economic justice, and sexual and racial equality; and more concern for their planet rather than just for their country. The beautiful land to which all that he had done, that his sons had done, and to which the work and sacrifice of their forebears, all the way back Marcus Spates, was leading to was now gone as quickly as it had appeared. A grey prison cell replaced the promise of a better world.

Spates took a blank sheet of paper, complete with his own personal letterhead across the top, and spent the better part of an hour writing it all down with his fountain pen. Once it was done, he signed the bottom of the page with a flourish and replaced the pen inside the leather case on his desk. He reached into the bottom drawer and retrieved the M1917 revolver that his father had been issued during World War II.

Without saying a word, he put the barrel of the .45 caliber pistol in his mouth and splattered the rich oak-paneled walls with blood and pulverized bits of his skull and brain.

The security duo had gone out into the backyard for a smoke and never heard the gunshot, but Brynna heard it and came running into the room. She found her mentor, idol, and lover sitting in his office chair, staring blankly into space, and a sunburst of crimson fanned across the wall behind him.

She was too shocked to cry but not too shocked to walk to where Thurmond Spates's lifeless body sat in his office chair. She wiped the sweat from her palms on her navy skirt, and with a trembling hand, picked up the last thing he had written, being careful not to touch the small flecks of blood that dotted the page.

She read his confession. She read how he had used the farm, as he called it, as a tool to gain leverage and clout. She read in his own words about the despicable things that took place there, but she also read the incredible vision for the future that the sacrifices made at the farm would usher in. She read of how the evil done there was necessary for the land of milk and honey that he was going to create for them to flourish. She swelled with pride as she read how those who disagreed would be cast down and a new generation would be educated in the ways of the utopia to come. A land where there was no need for strife, no need for possessions, no need for money, no need for the shackles of old morality, and no need for any God other than this man who had just taken his own life.

She wept as she placed the paper back onto his desk, but not for the action that Ted had just taken. Instead, she wept for the beauty that he and his family had created in that dark swamp in South Carolina, and how she wished more than anything that it would have been so. She wiped the tears from her eyes and fell to her knees before this man, this revolutionary, this Messiah, and she wanted nothing more than to join him. She gently climbed into his lap and intimately nuzzled her nose into the nape of his neck before she placed the gun in her mouth and blasted her brain onto the wall with his.

EPILOGUE

TWO YEARS LATER...

Gustavo Uribe Navarro-Perez lounged on the veranda of his palatial estate. The mansion, a square building that surrounded a central courtyard, was nestled into a hillside outside of Sucre in Bolivia's southern highlands region. To many of the American, Canadian, or Australian backpackers who passed within sight of the mansion on their way to Sucre, it bore a striking resemblance to the Alhambra. The Alhambra, the famous Moorish palace that dominated the mountain overlooking the city of Granada, Spain, had existed in some form or another since AD 889, whereas this vaguely similar mansion, had only been standing for the past 136 years. It mattered little to Señor Navarro when the place was built. It only mattered that it was beautiful and secure.

The warm night air felt good against his skin as he sipped a deep red wine produced in the vineyard he owned in Argentina. The peace of the night made him feel like all was right with the world. His beautiful wife Paola, a former Miss Bolivia, slept peacefully in the luxurious bedroom behind him. A day spent playing with their seven-month-old daughter, Noelia, wore her out. Navarro didn't mind. He was more than content to enjoy the peace and quiet all on his own while his little family slept peacefully under a blanket of stars.

The security team that patrolled the grounds were so skilled that he rarely saw them unless he left the villa, as he liked to refer to the mansion, and he never heard them patrolling the grounds.

We are here to keep you safe, Señor. Not to be seen or heard.

Those words had impressed him, and for the past two years they had proven true. It had taken him a month or two to fully settle into the new place, become used to being accompanied by the team, and embrace that he needn't ever worry about anyone threatening him, his family, or his money. He had once thought that he would never again know peace and happiness, but now he couldn't see why he was so concerned in the first place.

"Are you coming to bed soon, mi corazon?" Paola asked from within the palatial bedroom.

The sound of her silky voice never ceased to excite him.

"In a second or two, darlin'. Just wanna soak up the last little bit of starlight before I join you," Navarro replied, his eyes never leaving the twinkling brilliance above the mountains.

"Take your time. We ain't got to be anywhere for a while."

The blood drained from Navarro's face and pooled in his feet. He had heard that voice before. It was weaker whenever he heard that voice being used in high school, and it was less clear when it was amplified at the owner of the voice's campaign rally, but it was never as terrifying as it was to hear it just over his right shoulder.

Where the fuck was his security team?

"That team that you hired was pretty good. Clever, even. Would you believe that they had a fella with a high-powered rifle stationed up in the bell tower at the northeast corner of your little hacienda? Not a bad idea if you're defending against people that don't really know what the hell they're doing. He died first, before all the rest of them."

Tears welled in Navarro's eyes. The man behind the voice was many things, but a liar he was not. There was no escape from him now. The only thing he could do was face him and pray that he didn't hurt his young family.

Navarro set his wine glass down, an inch of wine still pooled in the bottom of the glass, and rose to his bare feet. He turned around and saw a man dressed in multi-cam fatigues, a matching ballistics vest, and a matching neck gator, a cloth used by military forces to cover the nose and mouth, pulled just beneath his eyes. His suppressed M-4 was at the ready as he pulled the neck gator down to reveal the horrible truth behind his voice. Raleigh Myers was standing on his balcony, and he had finally tracked down Gustavo Uribe Navarro-Perez aka Wade Leonard Spates.

Wade glanced past Ray to see a frightened Paola, clutching a comforter over her naked breasts as another man, whom Wade assumed was Ray's friend, Joseph "Bloodhound" Wilcox, aimed a suppressed M-4 in her direction. Wade's throat went dry.

"Please, don't hurt them," Wade said.

"He's just keeping you and her honest. We ain't checked that bed super well. Maybe she has a pistol stashed away in there somewhere," Ray replied.

"There's no fucking gun in bed with her. Jesus Christ."

"You expect me to believe you? After all the shit you pulled back home? I'm gonna play it safe if it's all the same to you."

Ray looked around. "Sure done well for yourself here, Wade. New life, fancy house, new family. I would ask you how you sleep at night, but I figure if you didn't have trouble after all that you done to them people at the farm, then you wouldn't have any trouble after ripping off your own family and living large. Hampton's doing life at the federal prison in Atlanta, Jimmy is in witness protection somewhere, and your dear old dad is taking a dirt nap after blowing his own brains out, while you're living in a mansion. They wouldn't even bury that sorry sack of shit in a cemetery because your family is so hated. They had to cremate him and scatter his ashes. Nobody wanted anything to do with him. Annalee and the girls send their regards, by the way." Ray said.

The mention of Annalee's name, the woman he had loved more than anything in the world, only to leave without so much as an "I love you," struck a nerve.

"They didn't have anything to do with it. Leave them the fuck out of this," Wade screamed.

"I know that they didn't. Still don't change the fact that you left them high and dry. Ruined their lives and forced them to change their names and move away. I helped them get the name change and get settled down in Oviedo," Ray said.

Wade felt a grin forming at the corner of his mouth. Of course Annalee would want to move them to Oviedo. It was just outside of Orlando, and the girls had always loved Disney World. They might have a shot at being happy there. Maybe they'd be okay.

"Man, you weren't the easiest bastard to find," Ray said as he stepped out onto the balcony. Wade took an involuntary step back as his nemesis casually picked up his near-empty wine glass.

"I mean, we had people looking for you everywhere. After Mexico City, you just seemed to vanish. The FBI were looking all over Europe. They even thought that they had you found in this little cottage outside Krakow once. But Bloodhound and I figured they were looking in the wrong place. Besides, as far as we could tell, you had never been to Poland before, so we started our own little search.

"Your little safe of aliases ran dry after six months, but something kept nagging at me. I kept going back to that tape of you at the counter, checking your ticket at the Charlotte airport. Would you believe it, but nobody at the FBI had thought to track down the woman that helped you get squared away? Shit, those guys get a lot of credit for the work that they do but, I mean, you can't think to track the last person to have seen you down? That's just unreal."

Ray took a step toward Wade. "So I rode up to Charlotte, asked some people, and finally tracked her down. Real nice lady. Finally moved out of her apartment and got her own place off Shopton Road. American dream stuff. Well, she said that she remembered you checking in as Greg Vincent. She remembered it because, well, you made a big deal about there being whiskey in first class, you didn't have any luggage, and when she asked you about your cell phone, you told her to keep it. I mean, who does that? Definitely not the sort of thing you forget.

"So we tracked Greg Vincent to La Paz, Bolivia, but we ran cold. Didn't give up, though. We knew you were in Bolivia; just didn't know where exactly and we figured you changed your legend. Took us another year of monitoring any big deals going down or purchases happening in Bolivia, but still nothing. We even looked into this house getting bought outta the blue by some unknown buyer, but it wasn't enough to go on. Then you fucked up six months ago."

Wade wracked his brain.

What happened six months ago?

"It just so happened that my buddy back in there," Ray motioned to Bloodhound who still kept his rifle trained on Paola, "was sitting around watching Netflix with his girlfriend. She is always on her damn phone, just scrolling through her Instagram feed looking at all of her favorite things. She loves all these accounts about puppies, interior decorating, and style tips, like most women, but do you know what her most favorite accounts deal with?"

Wade said nothing.

"What's Rachel's favorite accounts all talk about, dude?" Ray asked.

"Wine, dude. She can't get enough of that shit," Bloodhound replied.

"Yep. She just happened to be scrolling through and came across this picture of six people casually sipping wine in front of an absolutely beautiful view just outside of Mendoza, Argentina. Apparently, she loves the Malbec produced by Viña Montaña, and she just couldn't help but tell my buddy all about how it had been bought by this un-known Bolivian guy named Gustavo Uribe Navarro-Perez. This Canadian wine-blogger she follows snapped a picture and wrote all about it on her Instagram page. Natural-ly, she shows my buddy and he sees you standing there laughing at something while everybody takes a drink. The blogger even pointed out that you were the guy in the mid-dle of the shot. I'll be damned."

Fucking social media.

"So, we tracked you here, learned your habits, your security, and about your new smoking hot wife and new baby. We even knew that most nights, especially when it's warm, that you like to sit out here and watch the stars. For the last week, we've watched your every move. Got-ta hand it to you, you run a tight little ship. Too bad you can't control which random Canadian woman was gon-na snap a picture and plaster you all over Instagram. We might've never found you otherwise. Which brings us to what comes next."

Wade's chest tightened. "What do you want from me?" Wade asked, suddenly feeling like his bowels and his blad-der would release at any moment.

"I just want one thing from you. Annalee told me what you said to her before you left, and I want to give you an-other chance with Paola over here. I want you to tell her that you love her."

The tears flowed along with his bladder. He felt like ev-ery inch of his body was shaking all at once.

"Why? What are you going to do to me?"

"Tell her that you love her. That's all that I want from you."

Wade looked at the rifle across Ray's chest. He ran the scenarios in his head. There was very little he could do now. He looked at Paola, her eyes red and swollen, and marveled at how beautiful she looked, even now.

"Paola, my darlin', I luh-"

It felt like Ray had punched him in the left side of his neck. He tried to say the last words but only gurgles escaped his lips. A sharp pain tore through his throat as his mouth filled with warm, coppery liquid. To his horror he watched as Ray Myers took a step back with a bloody knife in his right hand.

He collapsed onto the white tile floor, an arterial spray from his carotid artery spurting Jackson Pollack-like patterns of reds, pinks, and oranges across the shimmery floor. Ray watched as Wade Spates convulsed, shuddered, and then went still. The light in his eyes went out with his last breath.

He turned and looked at Paola, traumatized by the violent death of her husband, who lay dead on the floor. Ray got her attention and spoke in his carefully crafted Peruvian Spanish.

"We will call the police in one hour. You tell them that your husband was involved in drug smuggling and that a team of Jalisco Cartel assassins came down from Mexico to kill him. If you tell them anything different, my friend and I will come back here and you will join him. Nod if you understand?"

Paola nodded emphatically. "I understand. I will tell them what you want."

Ray and Bloodhound were out of the mansion in under a minute and jogged three miles down the hill and to the small Toyota Hilux they had left beside the small dirt road to Sucre in less than an hour. They drove four hours and ditched their weapons, fatigues, and other military-gear inside a three-foot hole they dug and covered, before they continued another three hours and crossed into Argentina and La Qiaca. Within twenty-four hours, they had flown out of Buenos Aires and landed in Miami.

"I'm telling you, man. I've gotta keep taking vacations with you," Bloodhound said as they parted ways. Bloodhound drove back to Hartselle, Alabama, and Rachel, the nurse that he not only had managed to land a date with, but with whom he had actually fallen in love with. She moved out of her two bedroom apartment in Florence and into Bloodhound's house outside of Hartselle. Ray still couldn't believe that it had worked out for him, but he couldn't be happier that he had found love at last.

After Ray had gotten settled into his rental car, a Dodge Journey that the nicest Enterprise rent-a-car agent he had ever met hooked him up with, he removed his cell phone from the metal box he had stored it inside. The box blocked the signal from being tracked while it was locked in an airport locker in Miami for the last two weeks.

He plugged the phone in and allowed the battery to charge as he navigated the streets of Miami in the pre-dawn hours and merged onto I-95 north. He stopped to fill up the SUV outside of Fort Lauderdale, turned the phone on, and opened the secure text app. He typed in the username they had agreed upon and typed out his message.

DONE

He hit send, hopped back into the SUV, and rocketed north toward Georgia and South Carolina. If he made it home in under twelve hours, he had about eighteen hours to sleep and recover before he needed to be back in the office. The people of Craven County were fine folks and they deserved to have their sheriff well-rested and sharp before he went back on duty, no matter how far he had to travel to collect justice's debt.

Acknowledgements

Ever since my childhood I wanted to be a writer. For years I filled the pages of notebooks with story fragments, lines of dialogue and descriptions of observations that I had made. I started the story that would become Black River in the summer of 2017. After years of writing, re-writing, and completely trashing the first ten chapters to start fresh, this work has finally become a reality. I could not have brought this to you, dear reader, without the help of many people along the way.

First, this novel would still be a file on my drive if not for the tenacious encouragement of my Wife, Melissa. Through countless edits, writes, and brainstorm sessions she has been ready to give her thoughts and to record my ideas as dictated to her. When I wanted to take a break, she would encourage me to write just a little more. When I was unsure and frustrated by the publishing process, she would push me to keep going. Without her love and without her support this novel would have never made it to print. I could thank you for the next one hundred years and it would never be close to adequate. I love you with all of my heart.

To my Mother, Christi Widener, for her encouragement of my creativity from my earliest days. Her taking a little boy to the Gardendale Public Library in Gardendale, Alabama, introduced me to the magic of books. Her encouraging me to read the Hobbit sparked a life-long love affair with the written word and it sparked the dream of becoming an author one day myself. Thank you for your love and for planting the seed. I hope that you are happy with the fruit that it has borne.

To William Hunter, for his kindness and encouragement as I began this journey. His works Sanction and Fallout are masterful thrillers that I am privileged to have read. Without his candid advice and gracious reading of my first draft this novel would not be published nor would it have ever been seen by more than my wife and I. Go Gamecocks, buddy!

To Jack Carr, for his masterful work and incredible contribution to our country. The James Reece novels were the first time that I thought that becoming a published author was a true possibility for me. I hope to one day shake your hand and to thank you for your incredible stories and for your amazing service to our country overseas.

To Greg Iles, for his incredible Penn Cage novels. The story and the world that he crafted in his hometown of Natchez, Mississippi, first inspired me to discover the stories in rural South Carolina. If you have not had the chance to read his Penn Cage novels then do yourself a favor and go read them. One day I hope to chat with you about the South that I believe we both love dearly and how we can work to build a better South for the future.

To Stephen King, for the amazing worlds that he has shared through the page for the past half century. The unforgettable characters, the tantalizing dialogue, and the terrifying monsters that he has discovered over the years have inspired me and fascinated me since my teenage years. Thank you for showing us how chilling the world around us can be and for growing the next generation of writers. I have to see Maine and the world that inspired you.

To Andrew Young, for being the first to read the first draft and to offer his thoughts. We became friends in 2007, standing outside of the Arts and Sciences building at Haywood Community College in Clyde, North Carolina, while I talked and he smoked. Thank you for being a true friend through college, young adulthood, and now into "real" adulthood. Thank you for being my friend through it all and now across the country.

To Hannah Merrill, for being an honest reader who was not afraid to give me honest feedback on my characters and on the plot. Thank you for teaching me to be a teacher, for pushing me to be myself, and for being like a sister to me. I cannot wait to start a "Front Porch Bickering" podcast with you someday. Thank you, friend. Spurs up!

To Sharla Lincoln, for being an enthusiastic reader and for giving such detailed feedback on what worked and what did not for the plot and the characters. I can say, honestly, that I hit the lottery when you became my mother-in-law. Thank you for constantly putting up with me picking at you and for raising such an amazing woman who I am proud to call my wife.

To John Davis, for having such an honest assessment of the initial draft of the novel and for asking me tough questions to ensure that I had thought this through. I look fondly onto those days at Western Carolina University, where we first built our friendship, and I am proud to have you as a friend today. Keep living the dream in "Ruffton" and know that I am always down to grab dinner in Shelby. Go Cocks and No Vols!

To Chris Robinson, for providing so much information about how law enforcement agencies and officials go about their duties in the state of South Carolina. I appreciate all that you do around the school house and how you're always ready to lend a helping hand whenever it is needed. You're one of three decent Tennessee fans. Listening to Rocky Top isn't nearly as aggravating to me now because of you.

To Stephanie Wilkerson, for graciously giving me a glimpse into the day-to-day life of a South Carolina law enforcement officer. I could have never captured the political, administrative, and professional nature of law enforcement without your insights. Thank you for all that you do daily and for setting the standard of what a strong woman is like for all of our students. You are an inspiration and I am proud to count you as a friend.

To Brandon Davis, for allowing me to peer into your experiences in Iraq as a member of the United States Marine Corps. Your honest, and emotional, conversations about training, life, and combat as a Marine are treasures that I hide in my heart. Your viewpoint and your experiences shaped so many aspects of some of the characters and I hope that they, in turn, reflect your dedication and honor. Thank you for nearly a decade of friendship and I am so overjoyed that your and Kendra have found happiness with one another.

To Sam Traywick, for being a friend and a confidant. Words could never express how much you are appreciated.

To Daniel Covin, for enduring my incessant talking about my manuscript and for helping me determine the personality types of my characters. you truly helped me bring them to life and you encouraged me to keep pushing even when I wanted to throw in the towel.

To Ashley Williams, for befriending a rookie teacher without a friend in Lake City, South Carolina. Your insights into the African-American experience in the Pee Dee region were essential for this novel. Thank you for your friendship and for your wisdom.

To the faculty and staff at Ronald E. McNair, for taking me in and for showing me the beauty of the Pee Dee and her people.

To the faculty and staff at South, for providing me with a home and a family for the past five years. Y'all really are wonderful and y'all represent the best that the Palmetto State has to offer. I am honored to be a Mustang.

To Kyle James, whose insights into the Citadel and the storied traditions still practiced by the Military College of South Carolina were invaluable. Thank you, sir.

To my dad David, for putting up with my crazy dreams as a kid. I hope that this novel is a point of pride for you.

To my brother Nick and his wife Kelsie, for putting up with me as roommate for a few years and for being there through all of these years.